# The Moon Over Kilmore Quay

Carmel Harrington is from Co. Wexford, where she lives with her husband, her children and their rescue dog, George Bailey. A *USA Today* and *Irish Times* bestseller and regular panellist on radio and TV, her warm and emotional storytelling has captured the hearts of readers worldwide.

Carmel's novels have been shortlisted for an Irish Book Award in 2016 & 2017 and her debut won Kindle Book of the Year and Romantic eBook of the Year in 2013. Her recent books include *My Pear-Shaped Life*, *A Thousand Roads Home*, and the official ITV novel *Cold Feet: The Lost Years*.

To keep in touch with Carmel, follow her on social media or visit her website.

Twitter | Facebook | Instagram @HappyMrsH
www.carmelharrington.com

Also by Carmel Harrington

Readers love to

# *Curl up with Carmel*

'I was caught completely off-guard by this lovely book. It's a story of family and friendship, love and loss, and just when I thought I'd made it through without crying: boom – the ending got me'                    *Maïa Dunphy*

'This is a book about family and friendship, about love and about knowing where you come from, about forgiveness and about holding on tightly to the people you cherish most'                    *Amazon reviewer* *****

'A love letter to New York, to Ireland, to family and friendship, and above all, to love [. . .] It will make you smile. It will definitely make you cry. But ultimately it will lift you up and make you want to live and love that little bit harder'                    *Goodreads reviewer* *****

'An emotional read that had me hooked from the very beginning. I loved everything about this book and I can't recommend it highly enough'
                    *Goodreads reviewer* *****

'A beautifully written story of friendship, family love and loss [. . .] a heartwarming and emotional story'
                    *Goodreads reviewer* *****

'A totally marvellous story of love, loss, betrayal and friendsh                    *****

# Carmel Harrington

# The Moon Over Kilmore Quay

HarperCollins*Publishers*

HarperCollins*Publishers* Ltd
1 London Bridge Street,
London SE1 9GF

www.harpercollins.co.uk

HarperCollins*Publishers*
1st Floor, Watermarque Building, Ringsend Road
Dublin 4, Ireland

First published by HarperCollins*Publishers* 2021
This edition published by HarperCollins*Publishers* 2022
1

A catalogue record for this book is available from the British Library

ISBN: 9780008415860

Set in Sabon LT Std by Palimpsest Book Production Ltd,
Falkirk, Stirlingshire

Printed and bound in the UK using 100% Renewable Electricity
by CPI Group (UK) Ltd

All
repr
in
pho

This boo

For n

*For Catherine Ryan Howard and Hazel Gaynor*

We started out as book friends, but
I'm so happy that somewhere along
the way we've become best friends too.

# PROLOGUE

## *Bea*

### 31 March 2020

### *Innisfree, Prospect Avenue, Brooklyn*

I thought I had life all figured out. Yet it only took one letter and a devastating secret to turn my world upside down. But I've also learned that sometimes change can bring you to where you need to be.

If you'd asked me who I was before recent events, I'd have replied that I was Bea O'Connor. A proud daughter and granddaughter of Irish immigrants. (Yes, both!) Brooklyn-born and reared in a house called Innisfree – a three-storey brownstone that my Great-Great-Uncle Richard bought and planned to fill with a family of his own. But destiny had another purpose for him, one that didn't include a wife and children, which in turn changed my grandfather's life, because Innisfree became his home and he filled it with all of us instead.

Great-Great-Uncle Richard, my grandparents and my mom are all gone now. Grandad always said that when you leave a place that you love, you never really go. Your echo can still be heard if you listen closely enough.

*Oh God, I hope so.* There's something so comforting in knowing that the people I love, both those here and those that are gone, are around me still. Loving me. Catching me when I fall.

My Irish heritage is a big part of who I am. I grew up listening to my grandparents speak of their birth country in revered tones. Ireland was a greener, friendlier, funnier, happier place than New York was. Every anecdotal tale they shared was cushioned in a cloud of nostalgia. It was the same for Dad and Uncle Mike too. As first-generation immigrant kids, most conversations at their dinner table included a trip down memory lane to our beloved Ireland. And then there were the ballads. I learned pretty quickly that these songs of Ireland went hand in hand with being a member of the Irish-American diaspora. And as we Irish tend to love a good sing-song, most of us have one special song where every lyric and note is a reminder of Ireland, family and home. A what might have been. 'Danny Boy', 'The Streets of New York', 'The Mountains of Mourne', 'Spancil Hill'. For the O'Connor family, it has always been 'The Isle of Innisfree', the song that inspired the name of our home. At the many gatherings that were held in our large family room over the years, we'd sing about folks who were dreamers. Folks who were just like me.

I've dreamed of Ireland, the birthplace of my mother and grandparents, my entire life. And every time I sang 'The Isle of Innisfree' I felt, deep down inside of me, the siren call of home. But there's the rub. How can I call myself a New Yorker if I'm not sure where my heart belongs? They say home is where the heart is, yet somehow my heart is split in two. The city I live in and love, and the home of my ancestors – somewhere I lived only in my dreams.

This is why I had no choice but to go looking . . . looking for the truth of who I really am, where I came from and where I belong.

It's quite a story as it goes and, as I've got time on my hands for a while, I've decided to write it down. You see, I've had to hit the pause button on my life for a bit and there's nothing like time on your hands to make you reflect on the events of the past couple of months. My story belongs to my parents too, because the ripples of their life pooled out wide to touch the lives of so many other people too.

It all begins with a letter I wrote to my future self, when I was ten years old . . .

# 1

Dear future me

Hello from the past! This is Bea. You. Me!

If you are reading this, then it means that my teacher Ms. Dryden <u>did</u> post our letters as she promised she would! We've been working on a project in school on how we think the world will look in the year 2020. That gave Ms. Dryden the genius idea that her students would all write letters to our future selves. She will hold them in a time capsule until New Year's Day 2020. She also made us spend hours practicing our handwriting. Not so fun. Jimmy Del Torio, <u>my least favorite person in school</u>, reckons there will be flying cars in 2020. While I'd love to own a car that could fly me over the Statue of Liberty, I hope he's wrong. I sometimes daydream that Jimmy trips up and falls down a manhole. I don't want him to die or anything, but a few months without him in school would be nice. He is "so good" all the time—or at least that's what he wants everyone to think. When we were in first grade I saw him kick a tiny baby bird who'd fallen from its nest. He only stopped when I launched myself at him, knocking him to the ground.

I ran home and told Grandad what he'd done and Grandad said, 'His halo is held up by the devil's horns. Watch out for boyos like that Bea.'

I told my family that I never want to leave Innisfree. Grandad says why would I? The park and subway are a minute's walk away, the church and school up the road. He says when he lived in Ireland he lived in the arsehole of nowhere, which makes Gran laugh and give out, because it's not nice to say. He says he had to cycle his bike for hours to get anywhere. I told him that I want to go to Innisfree in Ireland one day, but Gran says that Innisfree is actually anywhere in Ireland that your heart desires it to be, because it represents home. I love them both so much. They say that I am the light of their lives. And they are my favorite people too, except for when they make me do a jig or sing because they want some entertainment and there's nothing on the T.V. I mean, come on, we have seventy-five channels! And when I do give in and sing for them, Gran always cries. But Grandad says they are happy tears.

We did a project last week about the dangers of cigarettes. I gave my project to Uncle Mike to read, because he is always sneaking out the back of our house to have a smoke. But I don't think he appreciated my efforts. I worry about Uncle Mike. We all do, because he nearly died two years ago during the 9/11 terrorist attacks. Uncle Mike is an NYPD police officer. He says that it's his job to help people, but I still get nightmares thinking about that time. We didn't know where he was for hours and all we could do was pray and wait. Uncle Mike doesn't like to talk about it much, but sometimes he gets this look on his face and I know he's remembering all his cop friends who died. Grandad used to smoke but he stopped because of a wheeze. I told Uncle Mike that people can die from a wheeze. And lots of other horrible diseases like pneumonia, ~~emfisina~~ emphysema and lung cancer. <u>I will never smoke</u>. Because I plan on living till I'm one hundred years old so that means I have to be careful what I put into my body. If I do have to die young, I want it to be from a parachute jump that goes wrong. Or in the line of duty when I save the president from the clutches of a dastardly villain. I'm very concerned about President Bush's safety. I told

Uncle Mike about my concerns and he said he would talk to the president personally to make sure he takes extra precautions. Because of Uncle Mike's job, he knows everyone. Grandad says it is very handy having a police officer in the family.

Oh, and I have most definitely decided that in 2020 I will never, ever, cross my heart and hope to die, eat Brussels sprouts. <u>So gross</u>. While I don't hate school, I'm not overly fond of it either. My favorite subject is recess, when I get to play with my best friend forever Stephanie. I'm not too keen on math, English or geography. And judging by my test results, they are not too keen on me either. When <u>I'm older I'm going to be a world-famous detective</u>. I will solve all the unsolvable crimes. People will pay me huge sums of money to find the president when he is kidnapped by the Russians or the Chinese. I will speak at least four languages, to help solve all the crimes. I have a brand-new friend who is Serbian – Katrina Petrovic. I think I will be fluent in Serbian pretty soon. She starts school tomorrow and will be in my class. <u>She is very cool</u>. Gran said she's a little too cool for her liking. Her family moved into the house next door to us yesterday. Katrina was wearing a cropped top over a pair of leopard-print skin-tight leggings, listening to music on her headphones. I've never seen a cooler person in my life.

'That young wan will catch her death,' Gran said, tutting and sighing as her eyes moved up and down Katrina's scantily clad body. I half expected her to run out and put a coat over her. I would have literally died if she had.

'I think she looks cool,' I said quickly, and moved my body closer to the door in case Gran did decide to do anything mortifying. Dad and Uncle Mike both spluttered that over either of their dead bodies would I ever wear a cropped top like the one the girl had on. Good job they don't know that I spent last night cutting up my new green T-shirt.

Is Dad still a famous author? He won't let me read his books yet. There's probably bad words in them. Like the F word. When I am twelve, Dad said he will think about letting me read them. Yesterday Dad collected me from school and we spent the afternoon at the American Museum of Natural History. He is researching a new storyline for his next novel. I helped him find the right trees and plants that would be found in the forests in the 1890s when his book is set. Dad says I'm really good at finding things. It's my number one favorite thing to do. I just wish there was a way to find my mom.

I have so many questions about her and her life in Ireland. Like, did Mom have Spock ears same as I do? I can't tell from the photographs because her hair is covering them. All of the O'Connors have perfect round ears. So I think it must be a thing from her side of the family. I haven't told Dad this, but I sent my aunt, my mom's sister, a card today to wish her Happy Holidays. Maybe she has the same ears as me too.

Sometimes I pretend Mom didn't die. I ask her to help me choose my clothes when Gran tells me to wear something "nice" for Mass. I can never work out what "nice" is, because my jeans and T-shirts are all lovely as far as I'm concerned. I know Mom can't hear me in heaven. I'm not crazy. But I can hear her voice in my head when I need her.

I wonder if Mom is annoyed that Dad has a new girlfriend? If he's still with her now, as you read this, it means my plan to split them up has failed. Gran says it's time that Dad met someone new and that I should be a big girl about it. It's been seven years since Mom died. But why did he have to choose my teacher out of all the people who live in New York? I mean, it's mortifying because he's making a spectacle of himself, as Gran would say. When he came to the school gate yesterday to pick me up, he was all over Ms. Dryden. Everyone was watching. I put salt in her coffee last week, but she just took a sip, made a face, then put the cup down and never said a word. I mean, what kind of a person doesn't try to find out who put the salt in? I was all ready to declare my innocence

and make Dad take my side. But <u>Ms. Dryden
is very very tricky.</u>

I thought I'd put Uncle Mike's police officer
handiness to the test. So I told him to run
a full background check on her. See if Ms.
Dryden has any hidden husbands. Uncle Mike
wasn't too keen, he said Corinne was a fine-
looking woman and to leave them be. But
what would he know? He's single and always
ready to mingle as he forever tells everyone.
Gran says Uncle Mike has the worst taste in
women. If she's a bad 'un, he'll pick her, she
says. He doesn't seem to mind. He told me he's
having the time of his life picking up the
bad and the good 'uns, saying the women love
the uniform. Maybe it's the shiny buttons.

Stephanie and I love to watch Full House.
Sometimes I daydream that I'm married to
someone who is as handsome and nice as
Jesse is. But NO children, thank you very
much. They seem like a lot of work. Stephanie
is the prettiest girl in our class. But she reckons
that title belongs to Tiffany. I am not a fan
of Tiffany. She cries too much. Yesterday she
cried because she spilled her milk at lunchtime — literally cried over spilt milk.
Stephanie on the other hand is made of
sturdier stuff and rarely indulges in any
boohooing. We met on our first day in St.
Joseph's School. She didn't want to go inside
the classroom and begged her mom to take
her home again. So I opened my new pencil

case and found my new unicorn eraser that Dad bought me. And I gave it to her. Her mom said, no, you can't give away your new eraser, but I didn't mind. I had a rainbow one too. Dad often buys stationery. He says it's the curse of all writers. Anyhow, on that first day, Stephanie linked arms with me as we walked into the class. I hope we link arms with each other for the rest of our lives.

When I go to Irish dancing classes, Stephanie comes with me. To be fair, because as Gran says, it's not always all about me, when Stephanie goes to her piano classes, I sit outside on the wall waiting for her to come out. She's getting really good and yesterday she played LeAnn Rimes's 'How Do I Live' from start to finish, without a single note wrong. I was so proud of her. When I get sad about Mom, Stephanie always listens to me. Like last year, on Mother's Day, she knew I wasn't really sick when I cancelled going to the Kings Plaza mall for a class outing. I couldn't face all of the banners that hung from every shop window talking about a mother's love. The problem is, I don't know what a mother's love is. I'm not sad about that all the time or anything. But sometimes I wonder what life would have been like if she was still here. At holidays, it feels like I have a hole in my heart. Dad tries to fill the hole, and most days he does a really good job. He tells me how much she loved me, how she used to sing to me every day and loved to brush my hair and put it into pigtails. I feel so bad that I don't remember any of that. She loved me and even though I don't remember her, I love her too. Stephanie knew the real reason I didn't go to the mall that day. And she wanted to make me feel better. So she collected photographs of Mom from Dad. Then she made a scrapbook for me. She glued pictures of me in Mom's arms in all sorts of places. The mall, the park, the movies, the school gates. Stephanie said that way I could pretend they were real memories. That's why she's my BFF. She always always ALWAYS thinks of me first. And we'll never stop being BFFs. Not till the day we die.

I have written nearly eight pages now, which I think is enough. Ms. Dryden said she wanted at least four. Stephanie has only written half a page and I bet most of that was about Full House.

I hope that you are living your best life. And that <u>every day is full of fun and love for you, for us.</u>

I can't wait to meet/<u>be you</u> . . .

With love from Bea, You, Me! x

# 2

## *Bea*

### New Year's Eve 2019

*Innisfree, Prospect Avenue, Brooklyn*

'Ten, nine, eight . . .'

I wasn't sure I could bear to hear one more number being called out. I reached over to the remote control and considered switching the television off. The temptation to curl up into a ball on my sofa and pretend that time was not ticking on was strong. The ball glowed, purple, gold then pink into the dark sky.

'Seven, six, five . . .'

I've never been any good at pretending.

'You wear your heart on your sleeve,' Grandad always said. Only because I learnt that from him. My kind grandad, who was always the first to suggest we help neighbours, friends and strangers alike. His heart was so big we were forever doing good deeds for all and sundry.

One weekend when I was eleven or twelve, we were on our way back from this French guy, Christophe's, apartment, where we'd just dropped off cups and plates, a saucepan and a blow-up mattress. My grandad didn't really know him – he'd only met him in Sidetracks restaurant earlier that day. They got chatting and he learned that Christophe had nothing in his apartment but a blanket for the floor. Then when we were on our way back from his apartment, we passed a dumpster on Windsor Place. Grandad stopped and made us all rummage through it on the hunt for more gems we could give to our new French friend. 'One man's trash is another man's treasure,' he loved to say. But I'd had enough of being a Samaritan, so I refused to get out of the car.

'I hope you never need a help-out from your neighbours, Bea.' He looked so disappointed in me, it broke my heart into tiny pieces.

'People are looking at us. Don't you care what they think?' Shame made me belligerent.

'I couldn't care less what people think. But I do care about that poor wee lad Christophe. He doesn't know anyone. He's in a strange country, away from family and friends.' Grandad pulled out a mirror, the frame a little battered, but otherwise perfect. 'This will look grand over that mantelpiece for him. Care more about what you think about yourself Bea, less about what others think. Remember that.'

I've never forgotten that lesson.

On the TV screen in front of me, the countdown continued. Every second marched me closer to a new year and an uncertain future. A pain sharpened inside my head.

'Four, three, two, one . . . Happy New Year!'

Fireworks exploded into the sky on either side of the tower. Confetti streamed over the revellers who cheered and screamed with joy in Times Square. I smiled, despite my dark mood, as the camera zoomed in on a couple who were dressed in matching plastic see-through anoraks. They wore funny hats with the year 2020 emblazoned across them. And then they snogged, as if it were their last kiss. Good for them.

Journalists and TV presenters, dressed in their best overcoats and scarves, smiled for the camera as they danced awkwardly with each other. Mayor Bill de Blasio waltzed with a brightly dressed pretty blonde. Without warning another pain pierced me, so sharp this time it made me jump up and cry out.

I should have been out there, dancing with Dan.

Cheek to cheek, slow, slow, quick, quick, slow.

Instead I shouted 'Happy New Year' to my empty studio apartment. The haunting melody of 'Auld Lang Syne' echoed around the room.

'We'll take a cup of kindness yet . . .' I sang in a whisper. I couldn't finish the line. It would be the end of me.

The ghost of my mom seemed to be everywhere. She was never far from my head and heart, even though she'd been gone for twenty-three years. Holidays made me feel her loss more acutely, although I missed her every day in some way. Only yesterday I had seen a mom wipe a child's face with a handkerchief, and the gesture, the caress, had been a déjà vu moment for me. A forgotten memory, buried deep, of my mom doing the same for me – or was it just me wishing for a memory like that? Either way, it hurt.

My phone had been going non-stop. When I looked at the screen, it was Dan again. I opened his text.

Happy New Year. I can't stop thinking about this time last year. Do you remember? Please, Bea – don't keep shutting me out. We can talk it through. I know you are upset and scared. But we have something special. I can't believe I imagined all of that. I'd give anything to see those blue eyes of yours right now. Please call me. Or text. Just don't ignore me.

With tears blurring my vision, I typed a response.

Dan, I can't stop thinking about you either. I remember everything and I love you . . .

I paused. Then deleted the message word by word. If only I could erase my feelings with a tap of a button too. There were good reasons why I had to stay away from Dan. Nothing changed just because 'Auld Lang Syne' had made me sentimental. I felt another wave of tiredness hit me. Before Grandad died, he used to say his bones ached. I understood that sentiment tonight. I looked at my bed and contemplated falling into it. Why not give in to the tiredness? But I was too stubborn for that. I caught a glimpse of my face in the long, tall mirror that was propped up against the wall. I looked miserable, not a good look for me. Gran's voice rang in my head. Her childhood warning to me, often given, whenever I made a face. 'Take that look off your face, Bea O'Connor! You need to buck up, young lady. Because, mark my words, however you feel at midnight on New Year's Eve is how you'll be feeling for the rest of the year. That's a fact known to all.'

I'm not sure what scientific evidence backed up Gran's old wives' tale, but when I was a kid I believed everything she told me. Mind you, I often used her advice to my own advantage too. I made it my business to kiss the best-looking fella I could find at midnight every New Year's Eve. Hoping to ensure that the rest of my year would be spent making out with a good-looking man.

No good-looking man for me this year. No Gran and Grandad.

I raised my bottle of Corona and toasted my image in the mirror. While my reflection looked like a right old killjoy, she was all I had for company. 'Looks like we're in for a pretty shit year, Bea.'

The thing is, I chose to be here on my own, so if I was grumpy, sad, morose and talking to myself in a mirror, it was my own fault. Dad practically got down on his knees begging me to go out with him and Uncle Mike. They'd be milling out of Farrell's about now, onto Prospect Park, with paper cups of beer in hand. Uncle Mike would be leading the conga. In another hour he'd be singing old Irish ballads. I hoped he was having fun tonight. Uncle Mike had worked throughout Christmas, pulling the short straw, holiday shift-wise. The NYPD had unsocial hours. He'd paid a hefty price for that. About six months after he married a woman called Eugenie, she'd found solace from her loneliness with a guy she met at the gym. They divorced before their first anniversary. She got their house and Uncle Mike moved home again. I'm glad he did. It's good to have him here with Dad and me. I thought about moving out a few years back. The need for privacy was strong. But rent is high in New York, which put paid to my need to be alone. Compromise was reached, and Dad converted the basement into a self-contained studio for me. They had planned on doing the same for him and Mom, one day. But before they got the chance, she died. It had a bathroom, a small kitchenette (that I rarely used), and a sitting room with a Murphy bed you pull out of a wall. It also had its own entrance, albeit one that most ignored. Somehow, it worked.

Katrina was pissed with me too, because I hadn't gone out with her – the first time in over ten years of New Year's Eve shenanigans that we were not together. We didn't always come home together, but that was another story. She'd even promised that we would steer clear of Saints and Sinners bar, so there would be no chance of bumping into Dan.

Bloody Dan Heffernan. It always came back to him. Why couldn't I forget him? It had been a few weeks now. Surely that was enough time? Adulting was so hard. The irony wasn't lost on me that when I was a child all I wanted was to be old enough to go out partying instead of staying at home. And now that the world was my oyster, or at least New York was, I chose to stay in my little studio apartment, in the basement of Innisfree.

The house might have been empty apart from me, but it was full to the brim with memories. The small kitchen at the back of the main house had served hundreds of meals, all from a small stove. A fridge covered in magnets that clung to photographs of three generations of O'Connors, celebrating seven decades. Our living room was spacious – two rooms knocked into one by Grandad when Uncle Mike was born. The O'Connors were a social lot. Neighbours and friends were always welcome. As Grandad said, we'd made our own little village in Brooklyn over the years, with songs and tall tales spun in our living room. Grandad with his bodhran on his knee. Chairs pushed back against the wall so that I had room to perform an Irish jig.

I was the only grandchild and youngest in the house. The adults were all at my beck and call. As Katrina often remarked, I had it sweet.

Now though, I returned my attention to the television. The camera paused on the face of a woman. She was in her sixties, I guessed, standing on her own and crying. She dabbed her tears with a handkerchief. Her face, like something out of an Edvard Munch painting, was twisted and pierced with pain. I felt angry at the camera for zooming in on her personal grief.

'Move on!' I shouted at the TV screen. And as if the camera person heard me through the airwaves, it did. I hoped this year would be kinder to that woman. For many, this time of year came with the black dog nipping at their heels, their hearts and their heads. People often did crazy things over the holidays. I never understood what that was like until recently. But when the black dog came by to visit, it was hard to shake him off. Persistent bugger. I'd never suffered with depression before. In fact I'd always been one of those irritating people that were happy and optimistic. Dan used to say that's why I was forever ten minutes late: I assumed I'd have time to get from A to B in less time than it took. He was right too. Since he told me this, I'd noticed that the majority of optimists were the worst timekeepers.

And there I was again, bringing it back to Dan. No

matter how hard I tried not to think about him, he was there. And no matter how many times I told myself that no good comes from looking back, it seemed impossible to stop my mind drifting to the same time last year.

It took me twenty-six years to find Dan.

That night one year ago was the happiest I'd ever been in my life.

But a lot can happen in a year.

I decided to go upstairs to the main house, hoping a change of scenery would knock this mood I was in. I picked up a bundle of post that sat on the hall table. Rifling through the bills, late Christmas cards and junk mail, I was surprised to see a letter addressed to me. A pretty pink envelope with neat handwriting. It was thick too. A memory nipped at me but then it went, before I had time to grasp it. I brought the letter with me into the kitchen.

# 3

## *Lucy*

### April 1992

*The Three Amigos apartment, Maynooth, Dublin*

Three letters sat on the small square pine table in our kitchenette, my eyes focused on the one addressed to me, *Ms Lucy Mernagh*.

I looked at my sister Maeve and best friend Michelle. Their faces mirrored mine. We knew that the contents of these letters could be life-changing.

Only a couple of months ago Maeve had told us about Bruce Morrison, an American congressman, who'd allotted 48,000 American visas to the Irish.

'Visas for America! Imagine,' Maeve had screamed. She bounced around our flat in excitement at the mere possibility. 'All we have to do is apply and, if we're chosen, we get a green card. We can follow our dreams! We can go live in the States, like we used to talk about when we were kids.'

I looked at her eyes, bright with excitement and enthusiasm, and couldn't help but get carried away with her. In her mind's eye, her bags were already packed and the flight booked. She was always the same when she got an idea in her head.

'We've as much chance of winning one of those as getting into the audience of *The Late Late Toy Show,*' Michelle said, topping up each of our glasses with Blue Nun wine, our drink of choice. It was cheap and gave us a decent buzz. Michelle was our neighbour from home in Wexford. We'd shared this same flat in Dublin for the past three years while we went to college. We called ourselves the Three Amigos, a nickname we gave ourselves one night when we were kids and Michelle came for a sleepover. We'd rented the Steve Martin, Chevy Chase and Martin Short movie from Blockbuster's and we laughed so much as we watched it that we missed half of the one-liners. So we immediately watched it a second time and that still didn't feel enough. I think we ended up owing about twenty pounds in overdue fines for that movie. When Mam and Dad went to Blockbusters to rent *My Left Foot*, they had to settle our fine before they got out of the store and there was hell to pay! But Mam calmed down eventually and even bought us a copy of *The Three Amigos* for Christmas that year. Since then it's been our go-to feel-good movie to watch. We knew all the catchphrases and thought we were hilarious when we quoted them in random situations. I dated a guy a few months back who 'forgot' to disclose that he was also dating another girl from college. When Maeve found out, she walked up to him and shouted, 'You dirt-eating piece of slime. You scum-sucking pig. You son of a motherless goat.' He had no clue that she was doing her best Lucky Day line. And instead of feeling upset that I'd been dumped, I laughed for hours, picturing his face as Maeve shouted at him.

'Right, let's open them,' Michelle said.

'Wait. I'll get us a drink first,' I replied. I grabbed a bottle of Blue Nun and poured three glasses. I grabbed the ice tray from our small freezer. I tapped it upside down until the dozen cubes fell onto the table, then I added a couple into each glass.

'Just think,' Maeve said, holding her glass up, 'this time next year, we could be drinking wine in a New York loft apartment. It will overlook Central Park, naturally, where we'll go jogging every day. 'Cos over there, we'll have to be more mindful of our bodies.'

I grabbed a cheese Dorito and dipped it into the tomato salsa. 'Er, you're not selling New York to me, Sis.'

'OK, we don't have to jog. But think of all the cute guys we'll meet in Cheers Bar.'

'That's not a real place, you know. It's just on the TV show. Tadgh told me so,' Michelle said. She'd started to date him a few weeks previously and was at the stage where she was so loved up, she had to mention his name in every single sentence she uttered. I giggled as Maeve threw her eyes up to the heavens.

'But there will be places just like it. Full of cool people like Sam, Woody and Fraiser,' Maeve insisted.

'What about Diane, Carla and Rebecca?' I asked.

Maeve ignored that. She wasn't a girls' girl, preferring the company of boys always. She reckoned they were less bitchy. 'Do you remember Karen?'

Michelle and I shook our heads.

'Karen with all the spots. You do know her. She went to Maynooth with me.'

We continued shaking our heads.

'She got so pissed at the Christmas party in Flynn's that she started to strip as she sang "Patricia the Stripper",' Maeve said.

'That Karen!' I said, laughing at the memory.

'I was mortified for her,' Michelle said.

'She's some set of lungs,' I agreed. 'What about her?'

'Well, Karen's first cousin went to New York last summer. On a student visa. And she was mobbed by the men. Mobbed! The American men love Irish women. It's the accent. It drives them wild.'

The idea of being mobbed by men did have an attraction, but I still wasn't convinced.

'Don't you think it's a bit drastic to move to the other side of the world, just to get more dates?' I asked. 'Besides, you get loads of attention over here anyhow.'

This was true. While the two of us were almost identical, often mistaken for twins, Maeve had one thing that I didn't have. Sex appeal. I don't know what it was, but men would walk by me and head for her every single time.

'Boys. That's what I get over here. I want a man. A New York man. Someone like . . . Kevin Costner.'

'I always preferred Tom Cruise. Do you think Tadgh has a look of Brad about him? I do. Around the mouth,' Michelle said, topping our glasses up again. 'Actually, your Karen story just reminded me. I was sitting beside this young wan on the bus going home the other week. And she was telling me about her sister who went to America. She met this couple on the flight who were second-generation Irish. They had been home to find their ancestors.'

'Wearing Foster and Allen knitted jumpers, I bet,' Maeve said, making me laugh. Our dad loved the Irish singing duo, who were partial to an Aran knitted sweater.

'Yes. The very ones,' Michelle agreed. 'Anyhow, they were mad rich. And they took a shine to this girl. And invited her and her friends to move in with them.'

'That's a bit odd. And potentially dangerous,' I said. 'Were they ever heard of again?'

'The couple were lovely. Loaded, by all accounts. The girls had their own suite in the house. And all they had to do was a few jobs to pay for their keep. They got jobs in the local golf club. They had the best summer ever.'

'I don't like golf,' I said, knowing that I sounded like a misery guts.

'Me either,' Michelle agreed. 'Too much walking. And the clothes are awful. Nobody can pull off those plaid trousers. You'd have to be a size six or something.'

'You are missing the point!' Maeve said, standing up to illustrate how frustrated she was with the pair of us.

We both looked at her expectantly. 'Come on then. Enlighten us.'

'The point is that America is so full of opportunity that even when you are on an aeroplane minding your own business, trying to drink your vodka coke in peace, people are doing stuff for you! Can you imagine the craic the three of us would have living over there? Dating all the hot men. Working in fashion or advertising.'

'But we're doing an arts degree. We're going to be teachers,' I said.

'Well, you can be a teacher over there. But I want to work in Bloomingdale's or Saks.'

'I'm not sure what I want to do when we finish our degrees,' I said.

Maeve sighed and I knew she was getting annoyed with me. 'Don't tell me you want to work in the pub?' She threw her eyes to the heavens in case I missed the tone of annoyance.

Our family had owned Nellie's pub in Kilmore Quay for generations. We'd grown up in that pub. And it was in my blood. Maeve hated being there, but it was different for me.

Michelle, the mediator for us two when we began to bicker, as only sisters can bicker, quickly said, 'Right, what did we say when we applied? If we're not in, we can't win. Let's see if any of us got lucky . . .'

# 4

## Lucy

### May 1992

*The American Embassy, Dublin*

A few years back, one of our neighbours from home was holding a charity night, to raise money for their little cousin who had cancer. It was incredibly sad and the family were broke from all of the time they had to spend in hotels in Dublin while their boy had treatment. I went along to the fundraiser, but Maeve, Michelle and most of our friends couldn't make it. Instead they each gave me £10 to spend on raffle tickets. In all, I bought £110 worth of tickets for us. I had hundreds of numbers in front of me. And as every business in County Wexford had donated something, there were prizes for practically everyone in the room.

But even so, I didn't win a single thing for me, or for any of the tickets I was caretaker of. You see, I am the unluckiest person alive and it's a truth known to everyone that I wouldn't win an argument with a baby. But despite this, the one raffle I wasn't even sure I wanted to win . . . you guessed it, I came up trumps.

Both Maeve and I opened our letters to find out that we were picked in the draw and now, one month later, I'm sitting in a long corridor waiting my turn to be interviewed by the American Embassy. Maeve said that the fact we both were chosen was further proof that the finger of fate wanted us to go. Michelle was relieved when she opened her letter and it was no. Tadgh worked for the council and had ambitions to be a TD one day. Since he'd confided this to Michelle, it was clear she had ambitions to be his First Lady. I should have known that both Maeve and I would have come up though. She had this will that was impossible to say no to. Even the American Embassy couldn't resist her.

We had yet to share the news of our possible emigration with our parents. They would be devastated. We figured we'd see if we passed the interview before we mentioned it. They relied on us both to work in their pub, Nellie's, at the weekends and throughout the holidays. We'd been doing that since we were kids. At first, we collected and washed glasses. Maeve and I would sit on the end of the bar, dangling our legs in front of us and polish the glasses with a tea towel. Mam and Dad would then check our handiwork to make sure there were no smears before they placed them on the racks above the bar. The regulars often gave us their small change too, which we placed in a silver tankard beside the till. When it filled up, which it did most Christmases when people were full of the festive spirit, literally, Dad would swap the change for notes.

By the time we reached the double digits of ten, we could both pull a pint and reach the optics to pour a vodka or gin. We didn't work in the pub officially back then, but on a Saturday night if there was a lock-in – there usually was – we'd sneak in and help out. If anyone got too drunk, Mam would usher us out the door down the corridor towards our house that was next door to the pub. But rows were infrequent and either ways we thought they were great craic. We were placed on the payroll on our eighteenth birthdays and had worked in the bar every weekend since then.

Mam and Dad assumed that, once we'd finished our finals, we would go home to Wexford for the summer. Then we would get jobs in a local school. That way we could still both work in the pub with them as we've always done in our spare time. It had never crossed their minds that we might leave Ireland. To be fair, it hadn't crossed mine until Maeve suggested it. The whole thing felt surreal to me. I couldn't really see us ever leaving Ireland.

One of the criteria for the application was having an American sponsor on board. Someone who guaranteed us a job when we arrived over there. While half of Ireland had family in New York, we'd nobody. Our family didn't have the imagination or bravery to emigrate either in the famine, or the Fifties, Sixties and Eighties when thousands bailed. The Mernagh tribe stuck it out. But the little detail of having no sponsor did not deter Maeve. With the help of Michelle, who knew someone who had a cousin who worked for a catering company, we were sorted. Two pages of headed paper were posted to Michelle, who passed them on to us. Maeve wrote the letters, offering each of us a full-time position with a decent salary. It was some of the best fiction I'd ever read. We'd practised our cover story over and over, so much so that I almost believed it.

I checked my Swatch. Maeve was late. But then again, she was always late. And as if the mere thought conjured her up, she came running in through the double glass doors, her long brown hair flying out behind her.

'Jesus, the traffic was horrendous. I swear the bus driver fell asleep at one point, he was stationary for so long! Have they called you yet?'

'No. I'm next, I think. Shut up for a minute, I'm trying to hear what's going on with the guy who's in there now. The window is open, look.'

A low murmur came out through the open window and we strained to hear the conversation.

'Uncle . . . job . . . pub . . .'

'He's got a job in his uncle's pub,' Maeve translated.

I gave her a dig. 'Shh . . . have they started to whisper? I can't hear a word now . . .'

We gave up eavesdropping when it became apparent there was nothing to be learned. 'Do you have all your documents?' I pointed to her folder.

Maeve opened it up and held up her letter from the Guards, her job offer and her chest X-ray and blood test results. 'Check, check and check.'

I looked through my own folder for the tenth time to make sure I had all of mine.

Maeve said, 'I was sweating buckets waiting for the blood tests to come back. Remember that young fella from Bridgetown, the Clancy boy? Did you hear that he got chlamydia? The shame! And I thought, imagine my luck if I had it too.'

'Someone in the pub was talking about that last week. Poor fella. But when did you sleep with him?' I thought I was privy to every dalliance Maeve had had.

'I didn't sleep with him. As if! He's not my type.'

'I heard he got it from a wan he met when he was in the Canaries after he got his Leaving Cert results.'

'Yeah, that's what I heard too. Anyhow, all that talk got me thinking. What if that guy I rode from Australia last summer had something.'

'But you used a condom that night!' That was one of our Three Amigos rules, a non-negotiable one at that.

'I know the rule. Ride who you like, but only if you have a saddle on,' Maeve said, and we both giggled. We'd made that up one night when we were fifteen and wanted to be twenty-five. None of us had gone further than a quick grope from a boyfriend then. But sex was on our minds a lot and we talked about all possibilities. It was good to be prepared.

'As it happens the saddle was on for all three rides that night!' Maeve squealed, and that was it, we were gone. Tears from trying not to laugh leaked from the corners of our eyes.

'Stop!' I begged, to which Maeve answered by saying 'Giddy up, Cowboy!' That made me worse, I had to double over, to stop myself from howling.

It was only when we heard two chairs scrape against the floor that we stopped. We watched the door to the interview room open and a small guy who looked like he was wearing his communion suit came out.

'Ladies.' He nodded at us both, then shook his head with a sorrowful look on his face. 'They put you through your paces in there. Watch yourself.'

'Lucy Mernagh.' A voice called out. Stern. Like the kind of person who would trip you up. Especially if you had fake documents.

'Oh shit, Maeve, I don't know if I can do this. I'm a crap liar. You know I am.'

'You'll be grand. Just tell them what we rehearsed. That fake job is rock solid. Go on.' She shoved me through the door and I took a deep breath.

# 5

## *Bea*

### New Year's Eve 2019

*Innisfree, Prospect Avenue, Brooklyn*

The beer wasn't enough for me. I decided to go upstairs to raid Grandad's whiskey stash. As I walked up the stairs into the hall, the house echoed with the emptiness I felt inside.

Over the last five years, life at home in Innisfree had changed so much. It started when Gran and Grandad, the King and Queen of the Irish social scene in Brooklyn, both began to fade. They preferred to stay at home to watch their favourite shows on TV, rather than go out to socialize. Normally one of them would talk the other into going out for a drink, using some cheery line like, 'we could be dead next year.' None of us could ignore the fact they'd lost a little of their colour over the past year. But between Dad, Uncle Mike and me, we figured we could take over some of their workload without them realizing what we were up to. I took kitchen duty. Tricky, because it was Gran's territory and she hated anyone interfering. But I knew the dishwasher was difficult for her; bending down made her back ache. Even though I rarely ate with them, I started to call up to visit after mealtimes, so I could load and unload for them. They knew what I was up to, Grandad said as much, but they didn't stop me all the same. Never mind water-cooler moments. We had dishwasher moments. Oh how I treasure those conversations with them now.

Gran went first. We didn't have time to grieve her because two weeks later we found Grandad dead too. And while everyone agreed that it was for the best, because neither of them wanted to be here without the other, the pain was unbearable. I still feel winded by it now, when I think about the hole they left in my life.

They were our anchors in this house. And since then, we've all been adrift. Sometimes a wave sends us towards each other, but weeks and months can go by without Dad, Uncle Mike or me sitting down to eat together.

I threw the bundle of post and my pink letter on the table beside my beer. First things first, I checked the dishwasher's status. Full and clean, so I began to unload, then realized that if I believed Gran's New Year's Eve theory, I would be cleaning for the rest of the year. Well, feck that, as she would say. I stopped what I was doing and sat down at the dining table, running my fingers over its many scratches and indents from years of meals and living. When I was a kid, Dad always went to the library to write. So it was Gran who collected me from school, bringing me back here to do my homework. She coaxed and bribed me, matching my stubborn refusal to learn my times tables with an even more stubborn insistence that I do.

'I was a bloody nightmare then. Sorry, Gran,' I said to the ghosts of Innisfree. If Gran was annoyed with me though, she never let me see it. I think she understood that for me there were so many more exciting things to do, to explore, rather than learn algebra. A milestone year for me was when I turned twelve and was allowed to make my own way home. Gran said that independence put years on her. Because I always found something to distract me. A poster on a telephone pole looking for a missing dog was all it took to make me forget about going home. Instead I would begin to search for clues to the beloved pet's whereabouts. I'd eventually remember where I should be and, knowing they'd be worried, I'd run all the way to the house, breathless as I stormed into the warm kitchen. I smiled as I remembered the look they always had on their faces when they saw me arrive. Love and pride, with a little annoyance thrown in, because I'd worried them with my tardiness.

'Slow down!' Grandad would say, a big grin on his face as he held up a hand to steady me, and stop me from falling and skinning my knees. You only realize how often someone was there to catch you after they are gone.

'You'll be late for your own funeral, Bea O'Connor!' Gran would shout, but she'd smile as she reprimanded me. I knew she wasn't really cross. And to milk the situation and get maximum laughs from my grandparents, I'd pretend to die, in a long dramatic fall to the linoleum floor in their kitchen, adding in plenty of moans and groans for effect. I liked to make them laugh, and laugh they did at my antics. They wrapped me in a blanket of warmth and safety, those two. Another swell of sadness threatened to topple me over. Five years gone and I could still be caught off guard. This is a truth I've learned – you never get over losing someone, you learn to live with it.

I opened up the pantry, moving the cookie jar to one side, then the cereal boxes, until I found Grandad's bottle of Irish Midleton Whiskey. This had been his hiding space ever since he moved into Innisfree. He'd take it out for special occasions. And in times of sadness it made an appearance too. When his brother died at home in Ireland in a farming accident, I saw him cry for the first time as he sipped a measure of this Midleton. I was only four or five, no more than that. I hadn't started school, because I was at home when he got the call. I crawled onto his lap as the tears fell onto his jumper and I cuddled him as he had cuddled me so many times when I hurt myself. He couldn't get home to Ireland to attend the funeral because he couldn't get time off work. And I suspect now, as an adult, money was a factor too. I poured a good-sized measure into a Waterford Crystal cut-glass tumbler filled with ice, the same way my grandad always drank it. Then I raised my drink in an Irish toast to my family and all the memories we had in this kitchen. 'Sláinte!'

As the words echoed around the kitchen, I could almost hear my grandparents answer me back, 'Sláinte, Bea.'

The smooth liquid burned my throat. But it did the trick and I felt my earlier tiredness disappear. I grabbed the post, ignored the bills and picked up the mystery pink envelope. I ripped it open and found a postcard and another envelope inside.

The photograph on the postcard was a black-and-white

fingerprint with a quote from Sir Arthur Conan Doyle, 'There is nothing more deceptive than an obvious fact.' I liked that. On the reverse was a short note.

*Dear Bea*
*When I saw this postcard, I thought of you. I hope you like it. I often think of you and wonder how life turned out for you. Do you remember the time capsule we made?*
    *Well, as promised, I have posted all of the letters to the future selves of the students in the class of 2003. It feels like yesterday that Rudy Giuliani came to visit us in St. Joseph's and you all placed your letters into the chest. I hope you enjoy reading your letter.*
    *Please give my best to your dad,*

*Warmest wishes,*
*Corinne (Dryden)*

After all these years, Ms Dryden had kept her promise. I hadn't thought about her or this letter for the longest time. Stephanie and I figured she'd chuck them all in the trash. But that wasn't Ms Dryden's style. Of course she kept them. I bet she went to some trouble to find the right postcard for each student too. I read her note a second time and felt a stab of regret. She thought of me often. I didn't deserve that. I wondered if Dad thought about her?

# 6

## *Bea*

### New Year's Day 2019

*Innisfree, Prospect Avenue, Brooklyn*

I decided to open the letter in my childhood bedroom. That seemed apt somehow. It was still decorated as it had been when I was a kid. Pink, with large white furniture, from the Olsen twins range. *Full House* really had influenced me back then. I flicked on my neon bedside lava lamp and watched the blue bubbles make their way up and down. I'd suggested to Dad that he should turn this room into a writing space, but he'd declined. He preferred to write in the New York Public Library. I think this room is another example of his stubbornness to leave things as they were. I worry about that for a moment. Was he stuck in the past? And if so, is that somehow my fault?

I flopped onto my bed, opened the envelope and pulled

out a thick bundle of pages, folded in half. My heart raced in excitement as I flipped them open and began to read words I'd written seventeen years ago.

*Dear future me*
*Hello from the past! This is Bea. You. Me!*

As I read the pages, I couldn't help but look back and wonder at my innocence. And I laughed more than once at the foolish things I'd stated. Especially the bit about saving the president. Why was I so worried about George Bush? I wondered what my younger self would say about Donald Trump ending up in the Oval Office. I marvelled at my penmanship. I couldn't possibly write like that now with beautiful flounces and twirls on every letter. I spent hours perfecting it when I was a kid. But it had only taken an instant to forget. Which was a great pity really. But in addition to my amusement at my naivety, there was sadness too. My words formed a bridge back to my childhood, to a time when I thought Gran and Grandad would live forever. And back to a time when I could talk to my mom in my head. I don't remember the day I stopped doing that, but I suppose it must have been a few years after I wrote the letter. And then I felt another rush of emotion as I remembered the day that Stephanie gave me the Mom scrapbook. She'd been such a good friend to me. The best of friends. Yet, now, we rarely saw each other.

Well, younger me, at least I never ate any brussel sprouts. But I had fallen for the dubious charms of nicotine. All because I wanted to impress a boy too. What was his name . . . Joel or Doug? No, not Joel, that was one of

Katrina's conquests. It was definitely Doug. Whatever his name was back then, he said he liked me because I was sophisticated and looked much older than the other girls that he knew. How on earth had I ever fallen for such baloney? Why didn't I say no? He showed me how to light it. I thought it was romantic. If I could go back in time, I'd tell whatever his name was to go shove his cigarettes where the sun doesn't shine.

I dropped the letter for a moment, to search my bedside locker, looking for a shoebox that served as my memory box. And in the middle of the drawer, as I'd left it, many years ago, there it was. Written on the lid, in multicoloured gel pens: PRIVATE PROPERTY OF BEATRICE O'CONNOR. DO NOT OPEN. OR YOU WILL DIE!

I giggled at the absurdity of this threat. I would have to ask Dad tomorrow if he had ever succumbed to curiosity. Somehow I don't believe he had. It wasn't his style. I opened the lid and right on top were a bundle of lip smackers. I grabbed the Coconut Cake flavoured one and gave it a sniff. Did lip balms go off? It smelt as divine now as it did back then, so I wiped a slick on my lips, smacking them together happily. Beneath that were a couple of feather pens. The stems sparkly and glittery, and the tops so soft and girly. Who was I even back then? My mom's Chanel clutch bag was filled with bundles of photographs, ticket stubs for movies, concerts and the theatre. This bag was the only thing of Mom's that I had and it was my most precious possession, as it had been hers. And there were about half a dozen notebooks in bright colours, some with butterflies on the front, others with flowers, but all with the same small silver padlock on the side. These were my detective notebooks, filled with information I thought would help me in future crimes. Back then, when I was a teen, full of angst and sorrow, I thought the padlocks were as good a security system as you could find in a bank vault. When the truth of the matter was that with the tip of a knife and a bit of jiggling, you could open them without breaking the lock.

I propped myself up on my pink pillows and began to flick through the photographs, searching for one in particular. When I was sixteen I'd received a Polaroid camera from Uncle Mike. I loved that camera; in fact it was probably in a drawer in this room somewhere too. There were dozens of photographs with Katrina, Stephanie and me posing, lips puckered for the camera, eyes sparkling with fun. I missed those days. How long had it been since the three of us had a night out together? I tried to remember and couldn't. There were photographs of other school friends too, but for the life of me I couldn't remember half their names. In one photo a girl had her arm around me and I was laughing so hard my whole body was curled up in merriment, but I hadn't a clue who she was now. I felt old. Then I came to the photo of me I was looking for – me moodily staring at the camera with a cigarette dangling from my bottom lip.

'Sorry to tell you, Bea, you don't look one bit cool!' I whispered, laughing at the state of me. I was dressed head to toe in black. I'd gone through a goth stage for a few years. It drove Gran mad and now, I could see why. The photograph must have been taken at the end of a night, I reckoned. There was someone holding up a red balloon beside my face. Judging by the skinny leopard print the arm was clothed in, it belonged to Katrina. She was and still is a demon for leopard print. Then a memory began to tickle my conscience. I started to hum the Eighties song, '99 Red Balloons' by Nena. We'd sung that song all night long! It was a party at Stephanie's house. Her sixteenth birthday party, that's right. And she kept playing her mother's old LPs over and over. We all took a shine to Nena's red balloons and when Stephanie found a pack of balloons in a drawer, she blew up the red ones. Whenever the song came on, we'd all burst into song and wave the balloons about. We thought we were hilarious. We *were* hilarious. I'm both mesmerized and appalled by the volume in my hair. It's a wonder I didn't set fire to myself when I lit my cigarette there was so much hairspray in it. Not to mention how ridiculous the cigarette looked, as if it didn't belong there. Like a prop I was using as I played dress-up with my pals.

'Would you stop if I asked you to?' On a whim, I picked up one of my sparkly feather pens and scrolled to the paragraph in my letter where I had written, under-lined, that I would never smoke. I scribbled a short note in the margin.

*When a boy called Doug tries to get you to smoke – just say no! It doesn't suit you. Trust me. With love from Bea, You, Me! x*

My barely legible scrawl stood out like a sore thumb, not a flourish or swirl in sight. I regretted the impulse immediately. It looked like graffiti on a white wall. But it was too late now. Another wave of tiredness hit me and this time I couldn't ignore it. It felt like lead was squeezing my eyes shut. The whiskey was strong and better than any lullaby. I'd sleep this crazy night away and wake up tomorrow in a calmer, less reflective mood. I dropped my sparkly pen into the shoebox, beside the cigarette photograph and letter. I fell back onto the soft pillows of my bed. Within seconds I had fallen asleep dreaming of a nameless boy who chased me down Prospect Avenue with a box of cigarettes. Only he didn't look like whatshisname, he looked a lot like a man called Dan.

I felt the bright rays of the sun on my face when I awoke at half past eight the next morning. I sat up and stretched my arms above my head. I felt great. More than great. I felt like I'd slept for a week not just seven hours or so. Mind you, I'm normally a wake-up-at-seven-a.m. kind of gal, so the extra hour and a half must have given me a boost. I could hear people mooching about downstairs. I figured that with a bit of luck there might be pancakes on the go. They were one of Dad's specialities. As I made a move to get up, my hand brushed against the shoebox of memories which lay on the middle of my bed. The lid was open. I could see my photographs and letter peeking out. I grabbed the photograph. I wanted to take a screenshot of it for Katrina. She'd laugh for a week when she saw how ridiculous I looked. But then I noticed something very strange. I blinked, once, twice, three times. My eyes refocused on the photograph until I appeared again with frizzy hair, dressed in black, and a stupid red balloon beside me, held by a leopard print skinny arm.

Exactly as the photograph had been last night.

But not quite the same.

It was like those spot-the-difference games; the photographs were identical, but not entirely.

44

Where the hell had my cigarette gone?

I laughed out loud, because it was so bizarre. Had I imagined the cigarette when I looked at the photograph the previous evening? I wasn't drunk, despite the beers and whiskey. Well, certainly not *that* drunk! And while I was tired, there has been no time in my life where tiredness caused me to hallucinate. The only logical explanation was that there were two similar photographs. One taken with me smoking and another taken with me not. I rifled through my memory box. I flicked through the photograph bundles a couple of times, but each time came up blank. I pulled back the duvet, checked under my pillows, I even crawled under the bed to make sure the missing photo wasn't playing hide and seek on me.

I found nothing.

This was getting creepy. There was only one explanation.

Dad.

He must have found me here sleeping and taken the photo. He was drunk from the partying in Farrell's and thought it would be fun to mess with me.

'Dad!' I yelled as I ran down the stairs, two steps at a time. I screeched to a halt when I got to the kitchen, waving the photograph in my hand.

'Morning, love. Happy New Year! Did you smell the pancakes? I was going to bring them up to you, let you have breakfast in bed. Such a gorgeous surprise to find you in your old bed. I miss you being here. Anyhow, pancakes will be ready in five. Lemon and sugar, or Nutella and bananas?' He kissed my forehead.

'Both,' I said. 'But don't you "morning, love" me. Did you take a photograph from my shoebox earlier?'

'Of course not. I'd never dream of opening that. You told me often enough as a kid that death would befall me if I did,' he said in a dramatic doom-filled voice.

'Back in a sec,' I said as I ran downstairs to check the studio, even though I knew I'd not been back there. I scanned the room, but there was no sign of the missing photograph. Then I spied my handbag, so ran over to check that. And to my surprise, there was no sign of cigarettes there. I ran back upstairs, ready to confront Dad. He probably thought he was teaching me some kind of lame lesson about smoking, taking them and the photo. A passive-aggressive give-up-smoking-for-the-New-Year trick.

His face, it had to be said, was a picture of shock, surprise, then amusement when I questioned him. 'What would you be doing with cigarettes? You don't smoke! Is this a New Year's Day joke? I'm a bit hungover so maybe a little slow on the uptake. It was some session in Farrell's last night. Your Uncle Mike sang "Raglan Road", had the whole place in tears. It's when he gets to that last bit, the earnestness in his voice, it breaks my heart. Reminds me of Mam and Dad.'

'They always sang it with so much heart too.'

'I even belted out "Whiskey in the Jar". You should have come. It was great fun.'

Dad was either a good liar or trying to deflect my question. 'Dad, you know as well as I do that I smoke. We've played this game for decades, me pretending I don't smoke, you pretending you don't know I do.'

'What are you talking about? Don't tell me you're having one of those late teenage rebellions. I've heard it all now.'

I felt alarm and irritation in equal measures. My voice rose an octave and I tried to keep it steady. 'I've been smoking since I was sixteen years old. You hate it. We've always pretended it wasn't happening. Admit you snuck in my bedroom last night while I slept and took my cigarettes from my handbag.' I kept the bit about the photograph to myself.

He put down his mixing bowl and stopped whisking the pancake batter. 'I swear on Mam and Dad's grave, I have not hidden cigarettes from you today or any other day. But I won't lie. I am shocked that you are a smoker. I honest to goodness never knew. Are you sure this isn't a wind-up? Did Uncle Mike put you up to it?'

I felt a wave of dizziness flash over me.

'Hey, are you OK? You look a bit peaky there.' Dad moved closer and grabbed my arm. 'You've not been yourself for weeks, if you ask me. Not since you and Dan split up.'

'No, I don't think I am OK.' I sat down, because I did feel a bit strange. My legs wobbled as another dizzy spell hit me.

Uncle Mike came into the kitchen, frowning, 'What's all this shouting about? I'm officially dying here. Hey, what's up, Bea? Is it that Dan fella? Has he upset you again?'

'She's trying to forget about him,' Dad said.

'What did he do? Was it another woman?' Uncle Mike persisted.

'He didn't cheat,' I said.

'Well he must have done something bad, because you two were as thick as thieves one minute, then boom, it's over.'

'I want to call him. But she won't have it,' Dad said.

'Her mom will never be dead with that one. Both the same, stubborn as mules,' Mike agreed.

'Hello, I'm sitting right here. I'm fine. I just got a little upset, thinking about Gran and Grandad. This has nothing to do with Dan!'

'Ah, I had a little weep myself last night too. After we all sang "Auld Lang Syne". I think that song should be banned. It's too sad.'

'Hard agree,' I said.

'If you tell anyone I cried, I will deny it forever more, of course,' Uncle Mike said.

'Your secret is safe with us,' Dad replied. 'Pancakes in five.'

'Nutella and bananas. Go heavy on the Nutella.'

Dad saluted him, then sat down beside me when Uncle Mike walked out.

'I think you and I need a chat. Take a deep breath, then slowly tell me what you are so upset about.'

I hated it when Dad got all reasonable on me. But if I was going to get anywhere, I had to do as he asked. So I copied his reasoned tone and calmly told him about the photograph changing overnight. His face went through several phases of disbelief. I placed it in the centre of the table.

'Exhibit A,' I said.

He didn't look so calm any more and there was only concern on his face as he studied the photograph. Then he placed it back on the table and took my two hands between his.

'Bea, I give you my word that to my knowledge you have never smoked. Ever.' He leaned over and felt my forehead, 'You do feel a little warm. Maybe you're coming down with something. Remember when you had that awful flu when you were six, you thought I was Sherlock Holmes.'

I smiled despite my worry. That had been a lovely hallucination. Sherlock had given me all sorts of tips on how to be a good detective.

'Don't worry, pretend I said nothing. Probably the best thing to do is to feed me pancakes.'

He didn't look so sure, but he went back to the stove and heated the pan, ready to start cooking and flipping. I told him I was going to get some air while he cooked and went out the back to our courtyard. I rummaged through the plant pot. There should have been half a dozen cigarette butts there.

Damn it. Nothing. I went back in and asked Dad if he'd been out the back yet this morning.

He shook his head, another frown appearing, 'Is there something else wrong?'

'No. The sun is out, that's all. You should go out.'

As I took a seat at our dining room table, I looked at Dad while he poured batter into the pan. He looked tired. What if there was something wrong with *him*? We had a case in work a few years back where a man, younger than Dad was, had early-stage dementia. Maybe he took my cigarettes without even realizing what he was doing.

The problem with that theory was Exhibit A sitting on the table. Had Dad turned into a photoshop wizard too? My theory had more holes in it than Uncle Mike's socks. In all my years solving cases of missing persons, the most logical answer to any puzzle was almost always the correct answer.

Which led me to only one conclusion. If it wasn't Dad losing his mind, then it must be me.

I didn't much feel like eating pancakes any more. My head was filled with only one thing: the time-capsule letter and the crazy it seemed to have unleashed when I tore the envelope open. How had my life got so messed up? I longed to turn back time to twelve months ago, when the only concern I had was over the spot that had taken up residence on my chin . . .

# 7

## Bea

New Year's Eve, 2018

*Woodside, Queens, New York*

When I woke up with a zit the size of Staten Island on my chin this morning, I felt I had no choice but to avoid my usual New Year's Eve shenanigans with Katrina. I'd happily ensconced myself on my battered sofa, a hand-me-down from upstairs when Dad and Uncle Mike went all fancy and bought an L-shaped sofa. I had all I needed – a bag of Doritos and a bottle of Corona. I figured I'd binge-watch the complete series of *Fast & Furious*. Mainly because Dwayne Johnson starred in it. The Rock gave good smoulder. I switched my phone off to avoid the inevitable mass texting of friends and acquaintances who felt the need to send a 'Happy New Year' to everyone in their phone contacts. When will they ever learn that I never respond to these? People I barely knew would appear on my screen. The responsibility of deciding to reply or not felt heavy on my shoulders. It was a minefield. But then I heard the clip-clop of heels on the stairs and Katrina burst into my living room, clearly annoyed with me. She was having none of my feeling sorry for myself and my enormous zit. She insisted she needed me as her wing girl. She was determined to tie down her on-off boyfriend, Nas, tonight. And when I say tie down, that's literally what she meant. She had no interest in becoming Nas's girlfriend, but she did have plans that involved rope later on. Katrina rummaged her way through the rail my clothes hung on, throwing jeans and a top in my direction. 'You look like slob. I will do make-up for you, hide spot and try to improve . . . well everything.'

'Hey, that hurts!' I'd complained as she yanked my hair out of its ponytail. 'I was happy here with the Rock and my beer.'

'Come out with me and I find you real Rock tonight. New York is full of them.'

'Do I have to?' I moaned half-heartedly. In truth, I was delighted she was here to drag me out. Once Katrina had worked her magic on my zit and hair, we took the subway to Woodside in Queens. Our destination, an Irish pub called Saints and Sinners. Katrina found Nas within seconds of arriving and I went to the bar to get drinks. And that's when I met him. A giant of a man, six feet seven, covered in tattoos on each of his arms. His sheer size filled the air between us. There's no other way to describe it. I felt intimidated and interested all at once. I've always been contrary.

'Howya,' he shouted, leaning down towards me.

I ignored him. He was trouble and after a decade of

only dating trouble, I wanted no part of this man. I didn't need it to be a New Year to know that it was time for a change for me.

'Whereabouts in Ireland are you from?' he shouted again. I shifted my body so that my back was turned to him. He was persistent and carried on regardless. With hindsight, thank goodness he carried on.

'You've a look of a Dub about you. Am I right? A Jackeen loose in Queens? I won't hold it against you if you are, even if you do keep beating us at football.'

And despite my head telling me to ignore him, I found myself turning towards him and shouting back an answer. 'Wrong. I'm from Brooklyn, born and bred.'

'Ah, but you're Irish. If not born there, you are still Irish. I can tell by the look of you,' he insisted.

I had to concede that it was true. I did look Irish. Fair skin, blue eyes and mid-brown hair. 'My grandparents were from Wexford. A place called Gorey.'

'I knew it! I can spot the Irish from a mile off. And small world, I'm a Wexford man myself. I'm from The Ballagh.'

Hearing the word Wexford startled me. Whenever it came up, it evoked so many what-ifs and could-have-beens. I'd lost countless hours looking it up on my computer, googling images and trying to imagine what it might be like to sit on Kilmore Quay, looking at the Saltee Islands.

'My mother was from Wexford too.'

'Go away. Now that is a bit crazy. Like buses, the Wexford folk come in threes! What part is your mam from?'

'She was from a place called Kilmore Quay.'

'A fishing village. Beautiful there. The most gorgeous little thatched cottages scattered throughout. They have the best fish and chip shop in Ireland too, although some would argue Beshoffs in Dublin is better. Not a bit of it. The Saltee Chipper all the way. On a hot summer's day there's nothing nicer than sitting on the quay, looking at the boats bob up and down on the blue water, with a paper full of fish and chips on your lap. The air is filled with the smell of vinegar and salty sea air.' He stopped suddenly, 'Sorry, I got carried away there.'

'Don't apologize. It sounds wonderful to me.' I stored away everything he said and imagined my mother licking vinegar from her fingers as she munched on a salty feast. It was a nice thought.

'Have you visited Kilmore Quay, with your mother?' Tattoo man asked.

'She's dead,' I blurted out in a strangled shout, as the Black Eyed Peas sang that tonight's gonna be a good night. I don't know why I told him that, because I'm usually good at diverting from subjects that are painful to me. But there was something about him. Something that made me want to tell him all my truths.

'Ah, I'm sorry. My mother's dead too. Shit, isn't it? Every day, but today it's more shit than any other, I think.'

He was right. I'd made a plan to run to the toilets when the DJ stuck on 'Auld Lang Syne'. I watched Tattoo Man watching me and I felt a connection to this giant of a man. A knowing, a recognition.

'I can't hear myself think here. And we'll both be hoarse from shouting. Will we go somewhere else for a chat?'

I wanted to, but I felt nervous. OK, we'd shared a nice conversation loudly over the noise of the pub, but I didn't know him. He saw doubt flood my face and quickly reassured me, 'I know what you're thinking. This fella is mad as a bag of cats. He'll probably cut me up into a thousand pieces. And if one of my sisters went off with a stranger they'd met minutes before, I'd kill them. But I'm not crazy. I suppose you can only take my word for that. But I have this hunch that you and I might get on.'

I had a feeling he might be right. But that didn't mean I could leave Katrina on her own. I was on wing-girl duty tonight.

'I suppose we could stand here all night screaming into each other's ears then swap numbers at the end of the night and hopefully go out tomorrow or the next day. But we'd probably have no voices by then. So how about we go across the road to the Stop Inn for a coffee and a chat? It's a grand little diner. Do you know it? Then we can come back here in a bit.'

I opened my mouth to say no. The whole idea was ridiculous. But instead I found myself turn into a nodding dog. 'I need to tell my friend Katrina.'

He followed me as I squeezed my way round the pub. I found her enjoying a neck nibble from Nas. Watching her mouth fall open in shock was kind of cool, as I filled her in on what was happening. It was nice to surprise her the odd time. 'I told you that you would find Mr Rock here. New York has someone for everyone. Even you. Text me every hour though.' Then she stood on tiptoes and shouted something in Tattoo Man's ear, which made him wide-eyed.

We walked across the street to the diner, which as Dan said was only a short walk from our pub. If he turned out to be an asshole, I could run back up the road to Katrina. When we stepped into the warm diner, a waiter called out in greeting, 'Dan!'

It was then that I realized I hadn't even known his name.

'You come here a lot then?' I said, nodding towards the waitress who obviously knew him.

'Where everybody knows your name . . .' Dan sang the *Cheers* song off-key. 'I suppose I'm the Stop Inn's Norm! I'd never eat a decent meal if I didn't come in here every other day.'

When the waitress walked over, Dan said, 'Howya, Denise. Give us one sec. Are you hungry, blue eyes?'

As Denise gave me the side-eye, looking me up and down, I wondered if Dan took many girls here for coffee.

I shook my head. 'Just coffee for me please.'

'Grand so. Two coffees, but we'll share a plate of chips too.'

'He means fries. Don't you?' I asked, trying to be helpful.

'I do. But Denise knows what I want, she's used to us Irish. I made the chips/fries mistake only once, the first time I ordered a burger and asked for a side of chips. Tayto, I wouldn't have minded, but the potato chips that arrived in a bowl were the blandest things . . .'

Denise leaned in, 'I have some of those goujons you like too, Dan. Big man needs lots of food.'

'Why not? Throw on some of those as well. Good woman.'

I looked around the diner as Denise busied herself pouring coffee for us into two large white mugs that were turning grey with age. The booths were burnt orange, with white Formica tables. Posters and photographs were scattered across the walls, some new, others there for decades. There was no denying there was a strong Irish influence here. As the waiter joked about how much sugar Dan was putting into his mug, I realized that Denise knew this man better than I did.

'I really am sound as a pound. Go on, ask me anything,' he said, reading my mind. I would learn over the coming months that this was a knack of his.

'Thanks to Denise, I know your name is Dan. Do you live in Woodside?'

'I do. My dad's first cousin Billy lives on 61st. He's been here since the Nineties. Got one of the Morrison lottery visas in '93. I'd never actually met him before I got here, but he put me up when I arrived green off the flight.'

'When was that?'

'Six months ago or so.'

'A New York newbie. What do you do?'

'I'm an accountant for an advertising agency. Our firm has a branch in Dublin. I worked there for five years but wanted a change. I asked them for a job over here. It took about a year for a position to come up. And here I am.'

I took another look at him. From his long, messy, dirty-blond hair that was almost too long, to the shadow of a beard on his jawline, to the black Metallica T-shirt worn over scruffy jeans. He was the most unlikely-looking accountant I'd ever seen.

'I scrub up well. I can rock a suit when I need to,' he said, mind-reading again. 'What about you, blue eyes? What do you do to earn a crust?'

'I run my own business. With my friend Katrina.'

'The girl who was playing tonsil hockey with yer man?'

I giggled. I'd not heard that phrase before, but I liked

it. 'That's the one. We run an agency that looks for missing people. What did she say to you, by the way?'

'A detective,' he said. 'I've never met one of those before. Very cool.'

'Not always that cool. Sometimes, though.'

'Please tell me you wear a trench coat.'

'Please tell me you don't have a fetish for a trench coat.' I shook my head in mock despair and he laughed. It was a good laugh, I decided.

'I like your banter. I always wanted to be a detective when I was little,' he said.

'Me too. My dad has always been obsessed with anything to do with solving mysteries. *Poirot*, *NCIS*, *Sherlock* . . . I was brought up watching them all.'

'I knew there was something about you when I saw you in Saints and Sinners. As for your pal back there, she's some mouth on her. She said she'd hunt me down and stuff my testicles in my mouth if I hurt you.'

I spluttered my coffee onto the table between us. 'She would too. Serbian, and the biggest badass I know.'

'I wondered where her accent was from. Mostly New York, but with a twang.'

'She's been in America almost her entire life, but she never quite lost her accent. She used to live next door to me when we were kids. But she has her own place now, uptown.'

'So you go way back,' he said. 'Says a lot about a person, the length of time their friendships last.'

'We've been best friends – and partners in crime, if you will – for a couple of decades. We did everything together as kids. We walked to school linking arms. We sat in the yard and ate our lunch together, swapping foods that we didn't like. Katrina taught Stephanie – she's our other friend – and me how to put on make-up. Katrina always knew much more about everything than we did. She still does.'

'It helps to have someone like that. Roger is my Katrina, you could say. My best friend from home. Knows everything.'

'Brings a whole new definition to the term "Roger that".'

He laughed at my joke and gained himself another set of brownie points.

'Well, it's good to know that you pass the friendship test with flying colours,' Dan said.

I felt a bit like a fraud. I'd not spoken to Stephanie in months. OK, I'd tried to get in touch with her and left messages several times this month alone. But still. While it could be that she was just loved up with her boyfriend, maybe there was something wrong. Of all the people she could have ended up with, she'd chosen Jimmy Del Torio from school. A complete and utter knucklehead then, and he was even worse now. I turned my attention back to Dan, pushing my friend to the back of my head, focusing on the man in front of me. 'It's my turn to ask questions. Do you still live with your cousin Billy?'

'Nah. He had feck all space. I was in the way – although, to his credit, he never once made me feel like that. But his fella and him needed their privacy. I got an apartment not far from St Joseph's Church. Close enough that I can call in for a cuppa or a beer when I want company, but not so close that we're in each other's pockets. I like it in Woodside. It has a nice vibe. Lots of different cultures all hanging out together. But enough Irish to keep any homesickness at bay.'

'My mother came to America on one of those lottery visas too, like your cousin Billy did.'

Dan raised his coffee mug in a toast. 'To Senator Bruce Morrison. Good man.'

I clinked his mug with mine and smiled.

'You've a nice smile,' Dan said.

'Don't start throwing meaningless lines my way. I hate them.'

'It wasn't a line. You were smiling and it was nice.'

'Fair enough.' And I smiled again.

'Will you tell me what made you smile?'

'The fact that if someone had told me this morning that I'd be toasting Senator Bruce Morrison with a virtual stranger in the Stop Inn, I'd have laughed.'

'Isn't life and its surprises great?' Dan smiled at me and I had to bite back a cheesy line of my own to him. Because never mind me, *he* had a cute smile. Normal white teeth, without a Hollywood veneer in sight. One of my biggest turn-offs in a man. 'Never trust a man whose teeth you can see in space' was a dating motto that had served Stephanie, Katrina and me well.

'Are you going to tell me your name?' He leaned into me.

'You haven't asked me,' I said, unsure why I felt the need to be contrary.

'I'm asking now. What's your name, blue eyes?'

I liked that he had already given me a nickname. 'Beatrice O'Connor. But everyone calls me Bea.'

'I like that name. Both versions. Suits you. I don't think I've met a Beatrice or a Bea before.'

'Named after my maternal and paternal grandmothers' middle names, which by pure fluke were the same. Both grandmothers were Irish too. But they lived very different lives on either side of the Atlantic.' I didn't add that I'd never met my maternal grandmother. He looked confused, so I explained a little more. 'Dad is second-generation Irish, born in New York. His parents, my grandparents, emigrated in the late Fifties.'

'And your dad met your mam here? You said she came over on a visa?'

I nodded. 'It was supposed to be for the summer initially, to see how it worked out. As it turned out, she never left.'

'She found the American Dream,' Dan said. 'I'm not sure I'll go back either. Some days I get so homesick I can't breathe. But that passes. And I feel feckin' lucky to be here, living this life.' He looked at me intently, then asked, 'So with that many Irish in your family, do you identify as Irish or American?'

'Both really. I feel Irish. My Irish heritage has always been very much part of who I am. I march side by side with my family in the New York Saint Patrick's Day parade every year. I Irish-danced my way through school and I can still do a pretty decent jig. I know the words of every Irish song from "Whiskey in the Jar" to "Danny Boy". And I can sing a decent rendition of "Isle of Innisfree" on command. Which incidentally is what our house is named after. Does that make me Irish?'

'I think it might,' Dan said. 'My mam used to sing "Danny Boy" to me every night before I went to sleep. A lullaby. I thought for the longest time she'd composed it herself. I think I was ten or eleven before I worked out that it wasn't about me at all.'

'Your mam sounds lovely.'

'She was. How long is your mam dead?' His voice lowered a fraction. I could only see interest and concern on his face, so I found myself opening up to him in a way I rarely did, whenever the subject of Mom came up.

'She died when I was three. Knocked down running across the street after our dog that had escaped when she opened the door to accept a parcel from the postman. Mom thought she could make it to the other side of the street but misjudged the speed of a car heading her way. Witnesses said she stopped in the middle of the road. A split-second decision to turn back the way she had come. The dog ran on to the other side. The car swerved to the left, thinking she'd follow the dog. Mom didn't stand a chance. She died shortly after the paramedics got her to hospital.'

Dan didn't say anything. No trite comments came from his mouth because he knew there was nothing to be said. He leaned in over the table between us and touched my hand lightly. Only for a moment. Then he let go, respectful of my space. We both took a sip of our coffee and let the silence find a spot to sit comfortably for a moment.

'It was breast cancer that took my mam. Two years ago. She didn't have a lump or anything. No sign that the nasty bugger was growing inside of her until it was too late. By the time she went to the doc because she was feeling off, the cancer was at stage four. Aggressive little shit. A few months later and that was it. She was gone. No more "Danny Boy" lullabies for me.'

I wondered what was worse. Losing a mother as young as I had, never knowing her. Relying on stories from family members that were scarce and unsatisfactory. Clinging to mentions of her hometown just to find a way to feel connected to her. Or losing a mother as Dan had, with a lifetime of memories to pierce and comfort at once. I didn't have an answer to that. My hand found his, as his had found mine moments before, and I squeezed it back.

Denise arrived with our food at exactly the right moment. If we allowed it, we could have taken a turn into maudlin New Year's Eve town.

'I put an extra scoop of fries on for you, Dan. And your pretty lady,' Denise said.

'They look delicious,' I said, and my stomach growled in agreement.

'Salt and vinegar?' Dan asked.

I nodded. 'Lots of it. Plus ketchup. And mayonnaise too, while you're at it.'

He squeezed a blob of Heinz onto the side of the plate, then squirted a blob of mayonnaise on the opposite side. 'Not quite the Saltee Chipper, but right now, pretty damn good.'

We both dipped our fries then bit into the crunchy golden potatoes. They were as good as any fries I'd ever eaten.

'Do you know what I'd love to do tonight?' Dan asked.

I raised my eyebrow, no idea what he was going to say. 'Steady.'

He laughed as I hoped he would. 'I'd love to go into Times Square, see that big disco ball drop.'

'It's a ticketed event. We won't get near it.'

'Ah but I know a fella who knows a fella who owes me a favour. If you want to go, I'll get us in.'

His confidence wasn't arrogance, I realized. This was a man who knew that he could make this happen.

'Katrina . . .' I said, but I'd already made up my mind. Something was happening to me. I couldn't put my finger on it. I felt an unravelling inside of me. I would follow this man anywhere. I'd lived in New York my entire life, but despite this fact I'd never been to Times Square to watch the ball drop at midnight on New Year's Eve. As a child, Dad said it wasn't a suitable place for me. And Gran and Grandad always said it was too touristy. Not to mention the cost factor, because it was expensive to get a ticket. This strange wonderful Irish man was going to be the one to take me there. And that felt *right*. Once we'd finished our food, we paid Denise and then we rode the subway into Times Square. I texted Katrina to fill her in on the new turn of events. And sure enough, Dan's friend of a friend came through and about thirty minutes before midnight we were with the lucky few, behind the barriers in Times Square. It started to rain, but Dan had that covered too and produced a hat from his coat pocket, pulling it over my mop hair.

Dan and I stood amongst the thousands of tourists in Times Square, and I couldn't help but get carried away with the excitement of the crowd as the rain licked our cheeks. When he reached over to hold my hand, as the tick-tock of the clock bounced around the square, amplified on speakers, it felt like the most natural thing in the world. We joined in with the chanting crowd, counting down the seconds towards midnight. When the sparkling ball dropped, marking the start of a new year, I held my breath until it hit the ground.

It was a spectacular moment. A once-in-a-lifetime, never-to-forget moment.

Fireworks exploded into the inky blue sky behind the

Capital One digital clock as they simultaneously exploded into my heart.

Then a saxophone began to play 'Auld Lang Syne' and Dan put his arm around me. The crowd began to sing about old acquaintances and we all swayed together in time to the music. Dan leaned down to wipe a tear from my eye that I hadn't realized was there.

'My mom.' And he nodded, understanding and unquestioning. Then the music changed and the saxophone morphed into the croon of Frank Sinatra's 'New York, New York'. The song kicked up the mood and the tempo, revellers jumped up and down, kissing their loved ones and strangers alike. And as we all sang about our blues melting away and how we were gonna make it anyhow, I looked at Dan and thought, *I've made it already.*

I've kissed many men since my first clash of teeth and lips with a boy called Spencer behind the youth centre when I was thirteen years old. And I've enjoyed most of my kisses since. But when Dan kissed me at one moment past midnight, it was the kiss that I would forever hold up as one to eclipse.

It was every romantic movie and love song I'd ever seen.

It was a sonnet, a love affair.

It was full of what-ifs and maybes.

*It was my everything.*

When Dan pulled me into him until our bodies moulded into one, I knew that I loved him. In fact I loved him as I'd never loved another person before, or would again.

And I'd only just met him.

# 8

## *Lucy*

### June 1992

*Nellie's Pub, Kilmore Quay, Wexford*

The wait to hear if we'd passed our embassy interviews felt endless and we spoke of little else every day as we waited for the postman to arrive. Our final exams diverted our attention somewhat, then once we'd said goodbye to college, it was time to pack up our things. We were all moving home to Wexford. But then, two days before we gave our keys back, two life-changing letters dropped on our front doormat. Maeve and I held hands as Michelle ripped them open, one after the other, saying nothing until she'd read them both. Then she squealed, waving the letters in front of us.

*Congratulations you have been awarded an American Visa.*

Michelle cried, Maeve cried, I cried. We opened a bottle of Blue Nun even though it was only 11 a.m. No matter how many times we read our letters, it felt surreal. I could not compute that I would leave Ireland. I'd never thought of myself as the kind of person who did life-changing things like emigrate.

'When will you go?' Michelle asked.

'As soon as possible. By the end of the month latest. We'll go home for a few weeks to pack up, say our goodbyes, have a party, then it's goodbye Wexford and Dublin and hello to the Big juicy Apple!' Maeve said. Her eyes danced with excitement.

'Mam and Dad will do their nut.' I was worried about how they were going to take it. Maeve had no concept as to the impact this would have on them.

'Tough luck. They'll have to suck it up. It's our life, Lucy. We have to live it on our own terms.'

Over the previous few years, Maeve's relationship with our parents had been quite volatile. While I loved working in the bar, she found it curtailed her social life. She clashed with Mam over everything – what she wore, from her make-up to her skirts that were too short, to her heels that were too high. It irritated me how hard Mam was on Maeve. But I could also see how often Maeve pushed my parents' buttons, just to wind them up. When she worked in the bar she spent most of the time flirting with the locals. Hamming it up if she saw Mam give her a disproving look. Dad said little, but saw everything. I knew it hurt him when any of us fought.

The pub had been my maternal grandfather's originally. He named it after my grandmother, Nellie. And when Dad married Mam, he gave up his job as a fisherman to work side by side with her. They'd given their lives to their business. Together they'd introduced a new lounge, creating an area for live music at the weekends. Dad managed the darts tournaments that ran every Friday night. Couples played for a rib of beef or a ham. And at Christmas and Easter they played for turkeys. While Nellie's wasn't a trendy pub, it was a great local. My parents greeted everyone who came in through the door by name. They made it their business to know everyone in the parish. All milestones of life were celebrated in Nellie's, from wakes to christenings and post-wedding parties. And I had grown up part of that. It meant something. To me at least.

'Go easy on them.' I was irritated at Maeve's callousness. She wasn't mean-spirited, but even I had to admit that sometimes she was thoughtless.

'Relax. You worry too much,' she replied, but when I continued to give her the stink eye, she softened. 'OK, I promise to play nice.'

Michelle's new boyfriend, Tadgh, drove up to Maynooth in a van he'd borrowed from a friend to help us move. Judging by the way they kept looking at each other, it was a good job Michelle hadn't won a visa. They were smitten, laughing and smiling, hanging on to each other's words, in the way couples do when they first fall in love. I hadn't seen Michelle like that with any other man before. And if I'm honest, a part of me was jealous. Would I ever have that for myself? Yes, I dated, but nothing had lasted beyond a couple of weeks. Maeve and Michelle said I was too fussy. I don't think that's true. More often than not it was the guy who dumped me. Mam said that I just hadn't met the right person and to have faith because he was out there, waiting to bump into me one day.

Between the three of us, we managed to accumulate a lot of stuff from our four years renting in Dublin and we filled Tadgh's van to cramming point. Once it was emptied, we stood in the flat and looked around the empty space.

'We've drunk a lot of Blue Nun in here,' Michelle said.

'We've watched a lot of *Cheers* here too,' I said.

'And kissed a few frogs and more than the odd prince,' Maeve added.

Michelle turned to us both and started to cry. 'It won't be the same, will it. You'll both go to America and get all fancy and sophisticated. You won't want me any more.'

'No!' we both cried, protesting the absurdity of the accusation.

'We're the Three Amigos,' I said. 'That's a lifelong bond. In fact, I think we need to say our motto one more time here, just to seal the deal. Are you ready?'

Their response was to stand with their hands on their hips, *Three Amigos* style. I joined them, and the three of us began our chant: 'Whenever there is injustice, you'll find us. Wherever there is suffering, we'll be there. Wherever Liberty is threatened, you will find the Three Amigos!'

We fell to the floor laughing and crying and hugging each other, each knowing that despite our protests, Michelle was right. Things would never be the same again. And I think we would have stayed there for hours if Tadgh hadn't come in and put an end to our 'dramatics', as he called them.

'I've a goo on me for some chips from that takeaway in Ashford,' he said, and we all agreed happily. It was rare that anyone did a drive to Dublin from Wexford that didn't involve a stop in that chippy. We closed the door to our flat for the last time and made our way home to Kilmore. Sitting in the back of the car, with Maeve's head resting on my shoulder as she dozed, realized that I felt scared.

# 9

## Lucy

### June 1992

*Nellie's Pub, Kilmore Quay, Wexford*

We waited until the end of the shift to tell our parents the big news. As we stacked the pint glasses into the dishwasher, emptied ashtrays and wiped the tabletops, the mood was light. Mam was singing and Dad hummed along to her. I would have put it off until the next day, but Maeve wanted it out of the way. So she sat them down and told them our news. I'm not sure what I expected. But I hadn't anticipated Mam crying. It started off like a strangled sob, but then she gave in to it and when the tears came they wouldn't stop.

We sat in silence, watching her, feeling horrendous that we had made our mam so upset. Then Dad spoke. He never took the lead in things; he always let Mam do that. 'There's no need for you both to go. You have jobs here, if you can't get work teaching. You have a home. There's no need. No need. Really no need.' He kept repeating that fact over and over. Maeve and I looked at each other helplessly. Our parents had gone into full meltdown.

'We're only going for the summer!' Maeve said suddenly.

Mam stopped crying and Dad stopped muttering. They looked at us both, one after the other. Then Mam found her voice, 'Why didn't you say so? The summer is a great idea. Travel, see the world, I wish I'd done it when I was your age.'

Dad nodded, a smile so wide on his face I felt my heart crack a little. Maeve winked at me and for a moment I believed that our plans had changed. This was a working holiday, not us emigrating. But when we went to bed, she just laughed when I suggested it.

'It's easier this way. We're breaking it to them gently. We'll go, and in September we'll tell them we're staying on a little bit longer. Then by the time Christmas comes they'll be used to us being gone. No big drama. You'll see.'

'You lied to them,' I said.

'It's a white lie, for their own good, which doesn't count.'

'I don't like it.'

'You don't like much any more, Lucy Mernagh. If you're not careful, you'll end up a right old misery guts. Look, if you want to stay here, you stay. But I'm going with or without you.'

'You'd go without me?' I asked in disbelief.

'I don't want to. But I can't force you to come with me. I'm going, Lucy. And if you have any sense, so will you.'

I contemplated staying, even suggested as much to Mam, but by this time she was fully on board the summer in New York train, and told me not to be silly. A few weeks later, we were back on the road to Dublin again, but this time in Dad's car. We'd said our goodbyes to Michelle the night before at the party our parents threw for us in Nellie's. All the neighbours came, they booked a band and Dad gave a free round of drinks to the house. Michelle asked the band to play 'Don't Go' in our honour. Everyone sang along and Mam, Dad, Michelle, Maeve and I stood with our arms around each other, half laughing, half weeping as we sang don't go, don't leave me now, now, now. I'd never hear that song again without remembering that night. If we'd stuck around and laughed a while as the song said, maybe it wouldn't have been the last time that we were all together. But maybe fate would have caught up with us one way or the other . . .

Before the night ended, I slipped outside and went for one last walk on my own through the village. A full moon shone bright over Kilmore Quay. It was as if I was seeing its beauty for the first time, as others must see it when they arrive. The inky blue water with fishing trawlers bobbing up and down on the quayside. The faint outline of the Saltee Islands in the distance, the sound of a seagull's caw echoing in the sky. We'd spent so many happy times visiting that island on Dad's boat. When we were little, Maeve and I used to dream about building houses on it, side by side. We'd marry two drop-dead gorgeous men and our children would grow up as close as we were. I saw the moon glisten on the golden roofs of the thatched cottages with their whitewashed walls.

And I swallowed an ever-growing lump in my throat as one of my neighbours shouted their best wishes as they passed by, telling me to come home soon.

*Home.*

I loved it here so much.

But I loved my sister more. Where she went, I would always follow.

I watched the moon that hung low over the water. I couldn't fathom that the next time I looked at this same moon, it would be in New York, thousands of miles away from here.

The next morning we checked into our flight with a smiling Aer Lingus steward, then walked to the entrance of the departure gates. We stood awkwardly for a moment; nobody wanted to say goodbye. Mam threw holy water over both of us, then put a small bottle of it into each of our handbags.

'Throw some over your bedroom when you arrive. And don't talk to strangers.'

'Mam, they'll all be strangers to us over there!' Maeve pointed out.

'Then talk to nobody,' Mam replied.

We promised. It was easier to agree. I knew she was fussing because she was close to tears again. We put our goodbyes off until time was stretched to its limit. We took turns to hug each other and, despite our best efforts, our sorrow caught up with us and we did cry.

'So silly,' Mam said, blowing her nose. 'We'll see you in a few months. The time will fly in.'

I hated myself then for allowing Maeve's lie to take root. But it was too late to change it now. We walked through the sliding doors and, just before they slid shut,

I saw my parents holding hands, waving to us. That image will never leave me either.

'This won't do,' Maeve said, wiping tears away. 'We're on our way to America and you'd swear we were going to Dingle or something!'

'I like Dingle.'

'You know what I mean!' Maeve said. 'Come on, let's have one drink.' She pulled me into the Gate Clock Bar and ordered two glasses of champagne. To her credit, she didn't flinch when the bill came.

'We've come a long way from Blue Nun,' I said, as we clinked glasses.

'Champagne all the way for us now, Sis. You wait and see. Anything can happen.'

'What will we toast to?' I asked.

'To possibilities.'

'To possibilities,' I replied, and we raised our glasses and sipped. 'You know, I think I prefer Blue Nun.'

'Don't you dare say that! I could have bought two bottles of the stuff for the price of these two glasses.'

And by the time we'd finished our drinks and made our way to the boarding gates, we were giddy with excitement. I'd never flown anywhere before, other than a school trip to London a few years back, so flying transatlantic was a big deal. As we settled into our seats, headphones on, choosing which movies to watch on the small screen on the headrest in front of us, I began to relax. Maeve was right. I did need to lighten up.

Landing on the tarmac of John F. Kennedy Airport was a sobering experience. We were now in another world. We went through the motions of going through immigration and collecting our baggage, almost in silence. And it was impossible not to reflect on the thousands of Irish who had arrived before us. From the Ellis Island immigrants to us now, with our futures yet to be decided. I thought about the footprints we made, as the soil on the soles of our shoes changed from Irish to American with each step we took.

Martin, our contact in New York, had given us instructions on how to get to Woodside. We found the express shuttle bus exactly where he told us it would be. Watching the tall skyscrapers on either side of us as we drove to Manhattan was surreal. We looked from one side to the other and clasped each other's hands in delight. We got off the bus at Grand Central Station and that's when it became real, as three bright yellow taxi cabs whizzed by. We were in New York!

'It's like a movie set,' I whispered, jumping to one side when a man wheeling a large battered suitcase bashed into me, shouting obscenities at us for being in his way.

'Look,' Maeve said, pointing to a Budweiser truck, rumbling over an air vent that sent smoke from the subway below into the air.

'I swear I saw that exact truck on *Cheers* last week,' I said.

'I know. Me too. Sis . . .'

'Yeah?'

Maeve turned to me, 'I know I pushed you into coming here. And I was all bravado saying I'd go on my own. But honestly, I can't imagine doing this without you. Thank you.'

I was grateful for the acknowledgement. I nudged her shoulder with mine and we had one of those smiles that said so much.

Thank you. I love you. We are in New York!

Then I spied a small cart on the corner of the street. 'Look, we can finally find out what a pretzel tastes like.' I ran over and ordered two, handing over a ten-dollar bill, crisp and new, straight from the bank that week. 'They're hot!' I said, handing one to Maeve. We took a bite each on the busy street, one hand clutching our cases, the other on the salty snack. And I was glad I had a bossy sister who always got her own way. I was in New York and I knew I had one hell of an adventure ahead of me.

# 10

## Bea

New Year's Day 2020

*Innisfree, Prospect Avenue, Brooklyn*

'Did you have to bring him?' I asked as Katrina led Karl in through the door to my studio. Karl was her pet pug, named after her favourite actor, Karl Malden. The actor was a hero back in her home country Serbia. They even had a statue of him in Belgrade.

'He go where I go. Plus, you owe me. I should be sleeping. Not getting my eight hours is no good for my complexion. Look at what it has done to you.' Katrina peered at my face then laughed as I glanced in the hall mirror to double-check that I'd not changed appearance overnight. If she wasn't my friend, I'd hate her.

'Just make sure he doesn't pee anywhere,' I demanded.

Karl started sniffing around my studio and then jumped up onto the sofa to dry-hump a cushion.

'Are you seeing that?' I asked Katrina.

'Is his normal sex drive. No big deal,' she replied. Some people have to strain to understand her Serbian accent – even though she'd been in America for most of her life, she spoke in clipped, sometimes stilted English. Because she spoke in her native tongue to her parents, her accent had never left her. A bit like my grandparents, who kept their Irish accent right until they died.

'Did you have a good night last night?' I asked.

'Not so much.' Then with an unusual display of affection, she said, 'I missed you.'

'Sorry. I just couldn't face it.' I hated letting her down.

Katrina pointed to my opened laptop. 'You working again?'

I decided it was better not to answer. I had been pulling some late nights in the office recently. While I loved working with my best friend, it meant I couldn't hide anything from her. I snapped the MacBook Air closed and gave her a look that I hoped said, *subject closed*.

It worked because she shrugged, then pulled a box from her small handbag and threw it at me, hitting me on the arm with it.

'What's this for?'

'No reason. I saw and thought of you. I think you like it.'

I peeled off the gold-and-silver-striped wrapping paper to reveal a blue jewellery box. I flipped the lid open and inside was a rose gold chain, with an oblong bar hanging from it. On one side, it had three initials, BFF. On the other side, BOC, KP. Katrina never bought things like this. Typical presents from her over the years included tequila, a tangerine and a voucher for rock climbing. I felt her eyes on me and I tried my best to hold in the tears. 'Oh Katrina, I love it.'

'Is too sentimental for me, but you have been sad, so I think, just this once I get you a present you like.'

I hung it around my neck and then clicked it closed. 'I love it.' I walked over to her and threw my arms around her. She let me hug her for a second, then pushed me away.

'Now what is the mystery that I must come here so early?'

I thought she'd never get here so that I could share my crazy out loud with her. But it was surprisingly hard to say the words. 'I need to tell you something that I know sounds totally unbelievable. I'm going out of my freaking mind here. Can you keep an open mind and just listen while I tell you what happened last night?'

'I can do that. Do I need drink for this?'

'Maybe. Actually, yes, probably. One minute.'

I grabbed two beers from the fridge and handed one to Katrina. She held it up and said, '*Živeli*,' to which I replied '*Sláinte*.' It was one of our things, toasting in Serbian and Irish. All that was missing was Stephanie's *cheers*!

'We've not done that in a while,' I admitted.

'No. We have not. But you have not been out at all since you and Dan . . .'

'I know . . . soon . . . I'll come to karaoke next week,' I said quickly to shut her up.

'Is OK. But you have to talk about what happened. What if I see him? Do I hate Dan now? Or do I feel sorry for him?'

I shrugged. I wasn't ready to get into all that. It was too much on top of my letter.

She took a long slug. 'Tell me what is code-red emergency.'

As she drank her beer, I told her everything. I showed her the letter. The photograph. And throughout it all she made good on her promise and said nothing. When I finished, she swore softly in her native Serbian, 'Kurac!'

Yes, indeed.

'I need new beer,' Katrina said.

I grabbed another two bottles of beer from the fridge.

'Normally when I have a drink, I need a cigarette. But the thing is . . . I don't want one,' I said. The look that Katrina gave me was unreadable.

'You do not smoke,' Katrina said.

'Not any more. But I did!' I cried.

She put her beer down and said slowly, emphasizing each word, 'You. Have. Never. Smoked.'

I shrugged. While I had no reason to doubt both Dad and Katrina, I knew what I knew. I tugged at the memory of the red balloon party from all those years ago, unravelling it one more time. I smoked one of whatshisname's cigarettes and we flirted, then kissed. Then the following weekend we went to the cinema to see *Surfer Dude*. And I've smoked ever since, trying most years to give up, but always failing. But even as the words and images from that party flickered through my head, it didn't feel right. It was as if I could see the end of the thread I'd unravelled but I couldn't quite grasp it. It kept moving away from me, flickering in the wind, this way and that.

'If I've never smoked before, then why am I so sure I did?' I asked.

'That I do not know. But we will work it out.'

'Do you think anyone is messing with me?'

'No.'

'OK. That was quick.'

'Well, it makes no sense that someone mess with you. Do you want a cigarette now?'

That was the strangest thing. I'd not had a single craving for one all morning. Earlier I ran to the kiosk on the corner of my street and bought a pack of Newport cigarettes and a lighter. I ran back to my studio, opened the kitchen window and sat in my usual smoking spot. And that's when things got weird again. My hand shook as I tried to connect the flame to the tip of my cigarette and I felt clumsy, unsure of what to do next. I pulled hard and inhaled the smoke, then coughed a lung up, throwing the cigarette into the sink with disgust. I'd forgotten how to smoke.

'Could I have been hypnotized while I slept last night?' Katrina's answering look needed no explanation.

'What if it's the letter then?' I asked.

She put her drink down. 'Explain.'

'Either I'm losing my mind, which I cannot accept, or my time-capsule letter is some kind of magical portal to my past self.' I rushed saying this last bit.

'You really think you can write notes to your younger self that change the future?'

I was back to shrugging again. This letter was turning me into a moody truculent teen. Katrina stared at the letter some more, then said, 'OK. Write something to your younger self now. I'll stay here and wait with you, to see what happens.'

'That's a brilliant plan!'

'I know.'

'What should I say to her?'

'To yourself, you mean,' Katrina said.

'Yes, I suppose I do. But it's as if she's a different person to me.'

The look Katrina gave me spoke volumes.

'I'll prove to you that I'm not crazy. You are not to leave my side, you are to guard the letter. That way you can make sure that I don't write anything else on it. As in, the me from here, that is. If that makes sense.'

'None of this is sense,' Katrina answered. She leaned in close to me and I smelled a waft of alcohol from her. 'I hate to say this, but I think most likely you are crazy. There are no magical letters. This is not a Disney movie.'

I sighed, nodding in agreement. I didn't believe in magical letters either.

Katrina touched my new chain. 'You are my BFF, so I must help you, crazy lady. And you are lucky, I like crazy. And if you end up in a special home, I will come visit every week and pluck the hair from your chin.'

'I don't have any hair on my chin!' I rubbed it just to make sure.

'No. Not yet. But when crazy comes, so does the hair. Trust me.' She waved a hand towards the letters. 'What will you write?'

I picked up the pages and flicked through them one by one. 'I've been thinking a lot about Stephanie. *We'll never stop being BFFs. Not till the day we die.* That's what I said here. Why aren't we friends with her any more?'

'Because she does not wish to be our friend,' Katrina said with a shrug.

'Hmm,' I said, noncommittally. My childhood love for Stephanie shone bright on the pages in front of me. And it made me feel guilty and sad that somehow I'd let her down.

'How long since we've seen her? It must be at least a year since we had a proper conversation.'

'She came out for a drink with us shortly after you met Dan. We haven't seen her since.'

'I can't believe we've left it so long. I'm not sure if I need to use the same pen to write this note.' I picked up the sparkly pen from the previous evening again. 'Better use it, to be on the safe side.'

'Yeah. In case it's the pen that is magic, not the letter,' Katrina said. I nodded, delighted she was getting into the spirit of things. Until I saw her throwing her eyes up to the heavens. 'How much drink you have last night?'

'A couple of beers and a whiskey.'

'Whiskey!' she said, cheered up by this admission. 'You are not a whiskey drinker. When you had Jack Daniels at my apartment warming party, you went bat shit.'

'I did not!' I said, outraged by the comment.

'You kissed one of our clients.'

'Ex-client,' I said. There was a difference. 'You shouldn't have invited him to the party anyhow.'

'He had sad news. I felt sorry. But you made it better for him . . .' She winked, then motioned to the letter. 'Go on . . . write.'

I scrolled down to the end of the page and wrote a note to my younger self.

*Katrina and I are not best friends any more with*
*Stephanie. We haven't seen her in a long time.*
*With love from Bea, You, Me! x*

I folded the letter in half, dropped both it and the sparkly pen into the shoebox, then placed it on the coffee table in front of us. We both stared at it, Katrina with a cushion placed in between her and it, as if she half expected it to come flying at her.

'Now we wait,' Katrina said, handing me my bottle of beer. 'I will not take my eyes off your letter.'

'You really are a great sidekick. I'd be lost without you,' I said, unable to keep a grin off my face when I saw her expression. I picked up my letter and read out loud, 'I plan to have a sidekick because all the great detectives had someone to take care of the small stuff while they went about their business being brilliant. Sherlock and Watson, Batman and Robin, Remington and Laura. Now we can add O'Connor and Petrovic.'

'For that comment, you will be paying for lunch for the next month. I am nobody's sidekick . . . I'll show you the only kick I have . . .' She lifted a pointy-heeled toe towards me, making us both squeal with laughter. As I stared at the shoebox of memories, I didn't feel scared any more. We sipped our beers in happy silence, waiting for magic to happen. As the minutes ticked on, I worried that maybe I had done it wrong this time.

'Do you think I need to be in my old bedroom upstairs to make it work again? Or perhaps I need to go to sleep, like I did last night,' I asked Katrina. I felt tired, as it happened. All of the excitement of the morning was catching up with me. The beers might have contributed to that too.

'Yes, you sleep. I watch.' Katrina picked up her phone and began to flick through Instagram.

'Do not film me on Snapchat,' I warned. She'd done that before while I had a power nap in the office. With the sound on too, so my snoring was on show for the world to see. Fifteen thousand people had watched that bloody video. I flopped back on the sofa and closed my eyes, trying to ignore the cackle of laughter from Katrina. She was enjoying this a little too much. I've always been a fan of the power nap. I'd read somewhere that the optimum time was seventeen minutes, and I found that to be true. I always woke up feeling refreshed afterwards. Sometimes when I was working late in the office on a case and felt tiredness overcome me, I'd lie my head on the desk, then close my eyes. Now, with the beer and the fact that I hadn't slept much all week, I drifted off on cue. Next thing I knew Karl was licking my face as he dry-humped my arm. As I shook him off me, Katrina sent another Snapchat comedy gold moment off, courtesy of me.

'I hate you sometimes.'

'No you don't. One moment. I check letter.' She picked it up, laughing at what I'd written. 'Nothing here except your childish nonsense. See, you are not crazy. You were drunk last night and write it yourself. Case closed. I am hungry. Let's eat.'

'That doesn't explain the cigarettes,' I whispered as she searched my fridge for food. Surprisingly, in addition to feeling relieved that there hadn't been any more blasts from my past, I also felt a little disappointed. Whatever spooky, creepy stuff had gone on last night, it must have been a one-off. I'd involved Katrina for no reason and given her ammunition to make fun of me for years.

'There is nothing to eat,' Katrina said, opening and closing cupboards and my fridge.

I shoved her out of the way and made some lunch for us both. I didn't feel like cooking so it would have to be my fail-safe comfort food: cheese and crackers. We could always order pizza later if we needed something more substantial. When I placed the food on the coffee table, I heard Katrina gasp. And she's not the gasping type as a rule.

'Relax. I'll buy you a pizza later!' I said.

'No. Look.' Katrina grabbed my arm, her red nails gripping me so tight that they were hurting me. 'I don't believe my eyes. This is too much.'

Written in red glitter gel was another message.

*Once a BFF, always a BFF!*

We screamed and jumped into each other's arms as we read the words out loud together. Katrina blessed herself and began muttering some Serbian prayer. I started the Hail Mary. Karl looked up from his new lover (the cushion) with interest.

'Please say you are seeing that too,' I said.

'Yes. I see.'

'And there's no way I could have written it myself, here, I mean.'

'I have not left letter for a second. I even took it to bathroom with me. Hang on. Except when I look for food a few moments ago. You could have written it then.' She looked at me with suspicion.

'So you think that the second you walked over to the kitchen, I took the opportunity to write this. And I am now lying about it? That's ridiculous.'

'I do not know. This is new crazy for me.'

'I swear I didn't write this. So why is this happening?' I jumped up and began pacing around my studio.

'When I was small child in Belgrade, my grandmama tell me about a sign she received from my dead grandpapa. From the other side.'

'What was it?' I felt the hairs on my arm rise.

'The sign was a chicken.'

'A chicken?' I repeated, wondering if Katrina was muddling her words up, as she sometimes did.

'Yes. My dead grandfather was in the body of a chicken.'

'Was the chicken alive or dead?' I asked, trying not to smile.

'Alive of course. And this chicken kept going peck, peck, peck at the same area in her garden, where she sowed potatoes. My grandmama decided she must dig up the potato where the chicken pecked. And that's when she found it.'

I held my breath, imagining all the possible things the chicken might have found. Money, jewellery . . .

'She found his pipe.'

Not quite what I imagined. But maybe it was solid gold or a family heirloom. 'Was it worth a lot of money?'

'It was worth nothing to anyone but my grandpapa, who never had it out of his mouth. Over the years she grew tired of the sound of him sucking on that pipe, so she buried it in the garden. You see?'

I nodded, even though I had no clue where this was going. Maybe the common link was the smoking. 'They are the same, because he smoked and I smoked?'

'No, stupid. My grandpapa was angry and he accused my grandma of throwing his pipe away. She say no. Over and over, they fought about this for years, every day, until he died.'

'So the chicken came back to tell her that she was wrong to lie? To make her feel guilty.'

Katrina tsk'd. It was never good when she made that sound. I decided to stay quiet. 'My grandmama said that the chicken came back so that my grandad could have the last word.'

I couldn't help it, I started to laugh. Katrina however was serious. 'Don't you see? These messages are your chicken, who is peck, peck, pecking. Now you must work out what *you* have to dig up.'

'I think it's telling us we have to go see Stephanie!'

'You maybe. I have no chicken telling me to do anything.'

'Listen, the chicken wants what the chicken wants. And like it or lump it, Katrina Petrovic, you are in this with me now. I'm going to ring Stephanie and then you and I are going to Staten Island to see her.'

# 11

*Bea*

January 2020

*Family Finders Agency, 57th Street, Manhattan*

My smart watch buzzed on my wrist, telling me that it was time to stand. *Where had that hour gone?* Lately, time had become fleeting. It passed me by without my knowledge, leaving me every now and then slightly puzzled and bewildered as to where it had gone. I quickly checked my phone to see if Stephanie had returned my now six voice messages and dozen text messages. Nothing. I'd read my time-capsule letter at least a dozen times every day. Half hope and dread as I scanned the pages, wondering if my younger self had written any more messages. But so far no further notes were issued or received. I stood up and stretched my arms above my head and felt a pop as one of my shoulders protested their new position. Just because my watch told me to stand didn't mean that I always listened to it and it had been a few hours since I moved more than my right hand to click the mouse. As I swung my arms around in a circular motion to further loosen them up, I began to pace my office. There was a path worn on the grey carpet from the hundreds of times I'd done this over the past couple of years. I liked a good pace.

The voices of my colleagues, light, giddy and giggling, floated inside my door. Hidden in the dark corner of my office, I became an unwitting eavesdropper. It was Friday evening which meant that the Family Finders gang were heading to Cassidy's Bar on 55th Street for karaoke night. The traditional end of the week celebration for our firm. One that I'd normally be leading the charge to. I felt a flash of guilt as I remembered my earlier promise to Katrina that I'd go tonight. A promise I had no intention of keeping.

'Is she in there? I can't see her,' Nikki asked. Our PA's voice sounded impatient. She'd be out there, lip gloss on, ready for her night out. I should have called out there and then, but instead I stepped further back into the corner. I found myself in an almost embrace with a potted plant. For the record, I felt guilty. Whatever about Nikki, Katrina deserved better. I thought once I managed to get through the holidays, I'd feel more like myself. But the reality was that I felt less like me than ever before. The thought of socializing, being with friends or strangers, filled me with a dread that I normally reserved for visits to the dentist.

'If she is not at desk, then maybe she is gone out for coffee,' Katrina said.

'Or she could have slipped out home,' Nikki said.

Katrina snorted her contempt at this suggestion. 'Bea is not home. She is always working. When I get here, she is at that desk. When I leave, she's there too.'

*Not always.* I felt annoyed at the inference that I had no life outside of this place.

'If we don't go soon, we won't get a seat. And my feet are killing me. I should never have worn these new boots to work,' Nikki said, looking down at her four-inch stiletto black boots.

'Let's go,' Katrina said, with a sigh. 'She might follow. Maybe.'

I peeped around the plant and watched her scribble a note on the board that sat in reception.

*Cassidy's. Join us. Please. K x*

'She won't come,' Nikki said. 'She'll text you tomorrow saying that she got caught up in her case and that she forgot the time.'

Nikki was beginning to irritate me with her stinging comments. Maybe this time I *did* want to go for a drink. Even as the thought entered my head, I knew it was a lie. Nevertheless, I looked out from behind the potted plant and knew it was a new low for me. I was a grown-ass woman, and if I didn't want to go for a drink, all I had to do was say so. But instead I chose to act like a kid and hide behind a plant. The absurdity of my situation struck me as funny and I felt a gurgle of laughter splutter out. I clasped my hand over my mouth so that they couldn't hear me.

'You know I've been thinking about Bea saying no to us all the time. Maybe it's time to stop asking,' Nikki said. 'We could be making her feel ever so uncomfortable, pushing her to join us every week.'

'Don't be silly,' Katrina answered, loyal as always. I took one step forward at that. But my feet didn't seem to want to go any further, and stalled. I stayed that way, like a toy robot who'd run out of battery, frozen mid-step, until I heard the front door slam shut. My heart hammered into my chest and I glanced at my watch, half expecting it to raise an alarm.

The thing was, I didn't want them to stop asking me. Nikki was wrong. I loved spending time with them. It was just. . . I couldn't finish that thought. I could run after them. Tell them, 'Of course I'm coming. First drink is on me!' Nikki would be delighted I said yes. Katrina would give me one of her knowing looks, but then she would link arms with me as we walked. In fact, she probably knew I was hiding in here right now. She missed nothing. I sometimes thought she had mystical powers.

Then again, I could stay hidden in the shadows of my office until I was certain they'd gone. They had already written me off, so no harm really. I glanced at my iMac sitting on my desk a few feet away. If I gave my case another hour, I could close it. I lied to myself that my decision to stay was for my client's sake.

I clicked open Facebook to continue my search for a client's biological mom. When it came to finding missing parents, mothers in particular, I became too emotionally connected to the cases. Katrina did a lot of the work searching for deadbeat dads, chasing up alimony or child maintenance. I took the missing parents. I suppose it didn't take Freud to work out that I had mommy issues. I might not be able to find my own mother, but I could help others find theirs. And I was close to finding my client Leah's mom, Noelle. I could feel it, as I scrolled through the photographs and posts on the screen in front of me. Pretty soon I forgot about letting down Katrina and Nikki as I got lost chasing Noelle. While she herself wasn't on Facebook, I'd found her sister, who took a lot of photographs of her cats. In her garden, on the chair, on the end of the bed, it was mind-numbingly boring – 80 per cent of my work was. But after forty-five minutes of scrolling, clicking, reading every boring comment, I got a hit. The missing piece of Leah's puzzle.

A photograph taken in 2012 had two people in it holding up a glass of champagne. Both had big, cheesy smiles for the camera. At a guess, they'd had a few glasses of bubbles already when the snap was taken. And the caption beneath the shot was, 'Surprise birthday drinks at my little sister's house! Thanks, Noelle, you are the best!' I held my breath as I checked to see if the location tagging was on. *Yes!* She lived in North Carolina. A Google search with these filters on gave me several hits. She was the secretary of a local Credit Union and her email was listed in their AGM minutes.

There is no better feeling than dialling a client's phone when you have good news to report. I explained to Leah that I'd found Noelle and that I had contact details. At first she didn't say anything. Then the sound of sobs began, soft at first, growing with each passing second. Leah had been looking for her mother for years before she contacted us at the agency. She'd all but given up on ever finding her. It felt good— Scratch that, it felt *amazing* to have helped her in some small way. Of course, Noelle might not want to meet her. And even if they did meet, they might not get on. More often than not, in my experience, happy ever afters don't come in these reunions. But at least Leah would have some answers. More than I would ever get from my mom.

I stretched my arms above my head and thought about going home. Maybe I'd grab a pizza slice on the way. I knew I had no food in the fridge and, even if I had, I didn't want to cook. My arm tingled as my watch buzzed again, this time with a text message.

Just a gentle reminder about our dinner tonight. Can't wait to see you. Love Dad.

Damn it. Our dinner had gone out of my mind completely. What was wrong with me lately? I needed to get my head back in the game! I typed another message, this one laced with guilt.

I haven't forgotten. What do you take me for? Don't answer that! I can't wait to see you too.

The sentiment was true at least. You would think that we would see more of each other, considering there was only a stairwell between us. But I'd not seen him in person since New Year's Day a few weeks back. I seemed to be letting a lot of people down lately. I ran my finger over his sign-off, *Love Dad*. No matter how many times I told him that I could see the message was from him, that there was no need for him to sign off stating the obvious, he'd always shrug and say, 'Don't take away my happiness at saying I love you whenever I can. That's what we dads do.' I added a *Love Bea* to the end of my text and hit send. I could picture him smiling as he read it and the need to see him overwhelmed me. I began logging off, closing down programmes and pages that I'd used in my search. I was about to close down Facebook when I spotted a post that the Irish Central page had shared. It was a bride on her wedding day, singing "Danny Boy" for her new husband . . . Damn it to hell, I felt fresh tears spring to my eyes without warning. Dan's song. I used to think that I might sing it to him on our wedding day. But I'll never sing that song again. It's ruined for me. I didn't have the strength to deal with the memories, so I pushed them away. Dan was gone. I'd cried enough tears to fill the River Slaney, as my gran used to say. Katrina said that it's good to cry about things we have lost. That in her country, they cry as often as they laugh. She said that I am bottling up my emotions and that they will come back to hunt me down. And slay me, if I'm not careful. I pushed that thought away too.

Then I realized that I could use my dinner with Dad as an excuse for missing karaoke this evening. I quickly typed a WhatsApp to our group chat.

Bea: Sorry for missing you earlier. It's daddy-daughter night at Mario's.

Katrina: Ah, I should have remembered. Nikki is singing badly. You miss nothing. You miss everything. Give Ryan a kiss from me.

My dad and Katrina had a mutual appreciation society going on. I made a mental note to organize a dinner for us all. I had to find my way out of this funk I was in, but I wasn't sure how. This thing with the letter and smoking, as well as not being able to get hold of Stephanie, was making me crazy. I did a quick fix of my make-up before I stepped out onto the sidewalk. My stomach grumbled at the thought of a Mario's dinner. We'd been going to this same diner ever since I was a toddler. Legend had it that Dad stumbled across it one evening while he was out for a walk with me in my stroller. I'd been a terror all day, teething and seething, causing chaos for my poor frazzled father, who was trying to get through the sadness of the first anniversary of my mother's passing. But when he walked by the diner, I stopped screaming and pointed with excitement to the bright neon lights in the window. So we went in. My dad's weary expression and the tired stoop of his shoulders inspired solidarity in Mario, himself a father. He took me into his arms and, like a child whisperer, made me forget my tantrum. I had my first taste of ice-cream that evening. Half a scoop of homemade creamy vanilla ice-cream that made me squeal again, only this time in delight. And Mario insisted that Dad try his famous meatloaf, a family recipe passed down for generations. There's a photograph of us both, taken by Mario on that first night. He had one of those automatic Polaroid cameras that printed snaps immediately. We joined the other regular customers on his wall of fame behind the till. Me, sitting in an off-white high chair, with my hair tied in two skew-ways bunches with red ribbon. Dad sitting opposite me, a proud lopsided smile on his face as he watched me tuck into a large sundae. We didn't know it in that moment, but a tradition was born. Because from that evening on, all milestone occasions for us two were celebrated with a portion of meatloaf and a scoop of ice-cream. Birthdays, graduations, anniversaries, lost teeth, new teeth, Irish dancing exams. Staff may have come and gone over the years, but the menu and Mario remained constant.

You can't walk a block in New York without passing a diner. They are as iconic to our city as the corner pretzel cart. They might all share bottomless coffee, 200-line menus and Formica countertops, but each has its own special something that differentiates it from the rest. That something was Mario himself. I've watched him over the years, as he greeted customers when they arrived at the diner's chrome doors. He has the knack of making everybody feel like they are VIP guests, important and valued. That's a gift.

Dad reckoned it was Mom who guided us to Mario's. Like an angel from above, she steered us to where we needed to be after she died. I liked that. And today it was twenty-five years since she died. And I had almost forgotten. How could I? The guilt made my stomach churn. This was another result of me burning the candle at both ends. Pushing myself to my limits, working twelve-hour days, six and sometimes seven days a week. No wonder I was forgetful. As I rode the subway to Brooklyn, I opened up my phone and looked at photographs of Dan and me, picking at the proverbial scab again. I couldn't stop myself doing this, on every commute. Mostly selfies, of us in the park, at home, in Times Square, at the parade. And in every single one, both of us were smiling.

Happy.

In love.

Well, to hell with that. I snapped the phone shut.

'Bella Beatrice.' Mario jumped up to embrace me, kissing me on both cheeks as I walked into the diner. He smelt of grease, leather and paper, a trio of smells that I'd grown to love through the decades of hugs and kisses I'd received from him. Mario treated us like family and, to Dad and me, he felt like family too. 'Come. We have your table ready. Your papa is not here yet. Are you hungry? You look tired. You look thin.' Mario ushered me towards the furthest laminated booth at the back of the deli as he tutted over my appearance. I had lost weight, I supposed. Sometimes I forgot to eat. I slid into our booth, the same one we always sat in. He'd placed a reserved sign on the table earlier, so that nobody else could nab it. 'Coffee while you wait?'

'I think I'll have a Corona tonight.'

'I keep forgetting you are not a child any more. I don't know, where did those years go. I'm getting old . . .' he muttered as he walked to the counter, asking a waitress to send a beer over. I noticed he walked slower these days and his hair was more salt than pepper. Time moved on. I felt eyes on me and looked up.

*Dad.*

His face lit up in a smile so bright that it made my heart constrict tight, then release with a kapow! I remembered all of the versions of me that had sat in this booth with Dad over the years. Happy, sad, moody, hormonal, broken-hearted, angry, indifferent and every now and then, a downright rude Bea. And no matter which version I was, Dad always had that same, bright, proud smile on his face. For the third time tonight, I felt tears rush me. I jumped up and fell into his embrace, sighing as he held me tight.

# 12

## Bea

### January 2020

*Mario's Diner, Brooklyn*

'The usual?' Mario asked, even though he knew the answer before we nodded. We never bothered to look at the menu. Coming here and not eating the meatloaf would be tantamount to sacrilege. On my seventh birthday we couldn't come here because I was at home miserable with chickenpox. There wasn't a part of my body that did not itch and I still have some scars on my arms from all the scratching. Dad cancelled our reservation because, while I was no longer infectious, I looked like I had the plague. I was devastated. Not going to Mario's felt like the end of the world. But Mario saved the day by delivering our meal to Innisfree in person. I felt like royalty that night. Dad said that his kindness sealed our loyalty to Mario forever.

We avoided the subject of Mom at first, even though this dinner was in celebration of her life. Dad was always careful to say that. Once we'd eaten and caught up on life, we'd get to her. Two plates of steaming hot meatloaf, topped with a glazed tomato sauce and a generous scoop of creamy mashed potato arrived.

'Oh Mario, that smells divine,' I told him, and he beamed at the compliment.

Dad told me all about the latest episode of *Law & Order* he'd been watching. A couch investigator, he liked nothing better than to solve a mystery and the crime shows were his favourites. I smiled as I listened to him tell me about the plot highlights and the exact moment he figured out whodunnit. And somewhere between him telling me about a body found in a dumpster and the murderer being caught by Mariska – who he'd had a crush on for years – we found our groove again. He knew me, you see. It took me a while to ease back into us, so he took the lead in the conversation until I got there too.

'It's no wonder I ended up wanting to be a detective,' I said to him, teasing, smiling. 'Goodness knows I grew up watching shows like *Law & Order* instead of Disney.'

'You loved them too!' he said. 'Are you happy, love? Has Family Finders worked out as you hoped it would?'

'I love what I do. Some days are boring, grunt work. But others, I know that I've done some good in the world. Made a difference. I think that first case I ever took was life-changing for me. A switch turned on, that I can't turn off. I don't think I could ever stop doing this now. It's part of who I am.'

That first case had taught me that some people got lost deliberately. And wanted to stay that way. When I graduated from college, I toyed with applying to the NYPD. Uncle Mike had made a good career there and, if I had made that choice, I think I could have been happy too. But then I saw an online missing persons agency looking for an administrator. I applied, got the job and almost instantly regretted it, as my first week was spent on mindlessly boring paperwork. But a few months later, I was given the chance to help on a case to find a missing wife. I spoke to her husband on the phone and he pleaded with me to find her, bring her home. I felt sorry for him; he seemed so upset and worried that she'd disappeared off the face of the earth. It took me about a month to find her. And don't ask me why I did it – Uncle Mike says I have some kind of sixth sense; all good detectives do – I decided to drive the four hours to the small apartment where she was living. I watched her as she left the building and got into her car. She was a nervous wreck, checking up and down the street constantly as she walked down the driveway. She was scared. It was obvious with every step she made. So I broke protocol and spoke to her. Our job was to find people and pass information on. Not get involved in the whys and wherefores. I'm so glad I did, though, because she explained why she had to run away. Her husband used her as a punchbag, both emotionally and physically. She told me that if I gave him her address, I would be signing her death warrant. I lied to my boss and my client and told him that his wife was untraceable. We gave him back his fee. After that, I began to think about setting up my own agency. One that brought life and colour to the clients and missing people we traced. Everybody has a story, and I guess I wanted to find out what that was.

It took me a year to get the nerve to go for it. And when I announced to my family and friends that I was going to take the plunge, Katrina approached me and asked if she could be my partner. I was gobsmacked. She was working in real estate and doing a great job too. But she hated it. She wanted to be her own boss and I knew instinctively that she would be the perfect fit for my agency. She had a great business head, unlike me. So, Family Finders was established. We started off slowly, but over the years our reputation had grown.

'No regrets, I'm glad to hear that,' Dad said.

'My only regret is that I've almost finished this meatloaf.' And when we handed our empty plates to Mario twenty minutes later, Dad said, 'We didn't enjoy that one bit,' in a joke as old as time.

Mario beamed approval and took a trip down memory lane. 'I remember that first night like it was yesterday. Your papa was frazzled. But I knew a good meal would sort him out. And you, my Bella Bea, all you needed was some of my special ice-cream. Speaking of which, you ready for a sundae now?'

'Yes please! I've been thinking of nothing else since I walked in.'

'You look thinner than the last time I saw you,' Dad said. 'You're not doing one of those silly diets, are you?'

'As if!' I said. 'I demolished a meal big enough to feed a family of three! You know me, my weight goes up and down all the time.'

Dad frowned and didn't look convinced. 'And this business with the photograph and smoking. The letter. Have you had any further . . . episodes?'

'I'm mortified about all of that, Dad. I was still drunk

from Grandad's whiskey. Put it out of your mind because all I want is to forget about it.' The relief on his face confirmed I was right to play the letter and its messages all the way down to no big deal town. Before he could question me any further, I changed the subject. 'Talk to me about Mom.' I never got tired of hearing about how they met, their love for each other, their love for me. Dad was a natural storyteller and could make any tale magical. Their love story was my favourite.

He closed his eyes for a moment as he pulled memories from the corners of his head and heart. 'She was a beauty. Like you are. And boy could she eat. She would have made light work of that meatloaf, as you did!'

'It's a skill,' I said, feeling inordinately pleased at the comparison. I gave him my full attention, hoping for a new titbit of information that I could hold close and later examine.

'Her energy burned everything off. You too! Not like your old man.' He looked down at his middle-aged paunch and shook his head in remorse.

'You look great,' I said. He might have got a little soft around his middle and had grey at his temples, but he was still a good-looking man.

'Why thank you! Your mom's voice had a soft Irish lilt. Every word was almost a note in a sentence, a song. People fell in love with her immediately. She had the X factor, whatever that is.'

'Tell me about the *Three Amigos*!' I said. This part of his story had always been my favourite.

He laughed. 'Ahh. Your mom's friends. Separately they were Michelle, Maeve and Lucy, but together they were the Three Amigos! They were like you, Stephanie and

Katrina growing up. Thick as thieves. Michelle was their neighbour. She grew up down the road from them. They had lots of in-jokes from years of messing and shenanigans. But their favourite thing to do was quote lines from the movie, *The Three Amigos*.'

In my best movie copycat amigos voice, I said, 'Whenever there is injustice, you'll find us. Wherever there is suffering, we'll be there. Wherever Liberty is threatened, you will find the Three Amigos!'

Dad smiled. 'You looked exactly like her as you said that line.'

I never got bored hearing him say that.

'I was always surprised that your mom chose to be with me. I wasn't her usual type.'

'You always put yourself down. Of course she fell for you. You're a catch, Mr Author man.'

'You're biased, but I'll take it. Thank you. I wish she'd lived long enough to see my books published. That all happened after she died. She only knew me as the aspiring writer, with big dreams.'

It was a damn shame. Since then, with the exception of Corinne Dryden, he'd not had any long-term relationships. Was it my fault that he was single all these years later? I touched my bag, thinking of the letter that sat inside of it. Never out of my sight, it felt hot to touch now, almost burning my thigh. I figured that until I tracked down Stephanie, the letter would not speak to me again. Or at least that was my best guess.

'Tell me about the wedding.' I had a photograph of them on their wedding day, framed, on my bedside locker.

'We were married a few short months after we met. At the end of a warm, sultry summer.'

When I was younger I used to imagine that I was with them at the wedding. And somewhere in my teens, I worked out that I was, in a way, as they were pregnant with me when they got married in the New York Public Library. He wrote most of his books in its Rose Room, so it was almost a second home to him. Some days, I take my lunch to go and eat on the steps of that landmark building, trying not to photo-bomb tourists' selfies. To me, there isn't a more quintessential New York City icon than the place my parents wed. So much history in one building and my family were part of that now too. It was a nice thought. After the ceremony, they went back to Innisfree for their wedding party. Gran baked a ham and made salads, with her homemade brown soda bread. They only had a few friends and neighbours in attendance. That always made me sad. They deserved a party with thousands surrounding them. Michelle at least had flown over from Ireland with her boyfriend and now husband, Tadgh.

'Why didn't Mom's family come to the wedding?' I'd asked this question dozens of times over the years, but always found Dad's answer unsatisfactory, so I kept asking it, hoping for a clue in his answer.

'Your grandfather died during the summer. And then your grandmother got sick and your aunt stayed home to take care of her. It was bad timing, that's all.'

'That must have been awful for Mom, especially not having her sister there. You said they were so close.'

'Your mom cried for weeks when she realized that they wouldn't make it. They were more like twins really, with only ten months between them. They started school on the same day because they couldn't bear to be parted.

And that never changed as they got older. It was a disappointment for us both, but we understood.' His eyes had become glassy, as he remembered.

'Don't get upset.' I grabbed his hand.

'Your mom brought so much light and joy into so many lives. And when she found out that she was pregnant – earlier than we had planned, mind you – we were so happy. Every day she'd sing to you in her tummy. I'd almost finished my first novel. As I completed an edit on a chapter, I'd read it to her tummy. It was a sure-fire way to send her to sleep!'

'She didn't like historical fiction?'

'No, she didn't. But she loved you! We were both besotted with you, long before we got to hold you in our arms.'

Maybe I should tell him that it was enough. We could get back to his recounts about *Law & Order*. The thing was, this anniversary dinner was the only time we spoke about Mom. Over the years, I'd learned she was off limits other than now. I'm not sure who made that rule up, I suppose it was Dad. Maybe it was too painful for him to think about.

I couldn't help it though, I continued to pick at our old wound. 'Tell me about the night I was born.'

'It was a wet day. A thunderstorm hovered over New York all week. Your mom was in tune with the weather, she smiled more when the sun shone. Winter didn't suit her, the rain made her melancholy. She was overdue by two weeks and the doctor said they would induce if you didn't make an appearance within a few days. We were both ready to say hello to you. We'd baby proofed Innisfree, with your gran's help and turned the spare room into a nursery. We even survived putting together your crib, without too much of a row.'

'Tell me about the day I was born.'

'Well, I'd been writing all day as I was working to a deadline.'

'You're always on a deadline!' I'd grown up watching Dad working around the clock trying to finish a manuscript or do edits. It was part of who he was.

'Feels that way sometimes, for sure. Your mom went to bed without me and I carried on working until the wee hours. And when I finally went to bed, I'd barely closed my eyes when she prodded me awake and told me she had a longing for trifle.'

'I love that phrase, "a longing for". Why don't we say that here?'

'I don't know, love. I do know that your mom used it a lot during her pregnancy. And it wasn't any old trifle she wanted. It was the exact same one that her mom used to make every Sunday for them at home in Wexford. I rang your nana Elizabeth in Ireland and she called out the method over the phone. I eventually perfected a pretty decent version. I had a bowl of it made in the fridge, because I'd gotten used to her late-night cravings. By the time I came back with a heaped bowl for her and some indigestion tablets that she was sure to need as soon as she'd eaten it, she was standing in the bedroom doorway with a puddle of water at her feet.'

'No!'

'Yes!'

As I listened to Dad relay their rush to the hospital and my mom's surprisingly short delivery, with me arriving less than an hour later, I pictured every moment as if it were a movie playing in my mind. I could feel their excitement and love as their baby daughter was placed in my mom's arms. *Me*. I brushed tears from my cheeks.

That phrase, *a longing for*. I longed for my mother more than any other thing or person in the world. I always had done and I supposed I always would.

'She loved you so much, Bea.' Dad handed me a tissue, sensing the shift in my emotions.

I nodded, swallowing back a lump. Even though I'd no memory of her and me together, other than the ones Dad shared or the photographs I cherished, I knew she loved me. I felt it.

'Do you ever wonder what life would have been like if she hadn't died?' I whispered.

Dad looked out the window of the diner, into the busy street outside. 'Every day.'

'It's so unfair. You only had such a short time with her.'

'Life isn't fair for many. But I don't regret a single thing. Because even though she left, I had you. My gorgeous girl. And that's more than many get. You have been the biggest blessing in my life.'

Then without warning, he threw in, 'I saw Dan yesterday.'

The mere mention of his name made my insides clench. Then my hands began to sweat so much that I had to wipe them on my skirt.

'I was in Bryant Park, which was packed with alfresco diners, so it's a wonder we saw each other at all. I was walking, trying to work out a sticky plot point, and we literally bumped into each other. He'd been in the café for lunch.'

I continued to ignore him, partly because it was easier and partly because I couldn't trust myself to speak without crying.

'He asked after you.'

I held my hands up. They said, *no more*. And Dad got it, because he nodded in response, but not before he said one last thing, 'He looked wretched and said he missed you. I don't know what happened, but he looked anything but happy about it.'

Mario appeared with our ice-creams and placed them gently in front of us. His eyes were glassy. He'd been listening to us reminisce. He'd heard it all over the years we'd been here, mundane to farcical, to heartbreaking confessions. A silent witness to it all. I supposed some would have found him an intrusion. But to us, he'd always been a quiet support. I squeezed Mario's hand in thanks. I guessed he'd timed the ice-cream to save me from any more Dan questions. We ate in silence and I watched Dad watching me, worry making his forehead crease. I felt a wave of love flood me again. I owed him so much.

'Thank you, Dad.'

'For what?'

'For everything. I know how many sacrifices you've made for me throughout my childhood. I don't think I've been a great daughter recently. I'm sorry I've not spent much time with you.'

'Can I ask a favour and then we'll call it quits?' Dad asked.

'Sure.'

'Will you give work a miss for the weekend. It's your company, surely you can take a few days off? Spend some time with all of us. I think Mike is off this weekend. We can con him into making a roast for us all. He misses you. We both do. Let us spoil you.'

I went through all the possible excuses I could give him as to why I couldn't do as he asked. I wasn't sure I could survive a full weekend without breaking down and telling him everything, the reason Dan and I split up. And I'm not sure I'll ever be ready to share that.

'Please, love. I'm lonely.'

*Oh Dad.*

'I'm not watching *Law & Order* all weekend,' I said.

His smile of gratitude nearly finished me off. 'And I'm not watching *Long Lost Family* either.'

'Deal!' he said with a grin, and all at once I was back to Dan again. We'd only been together a few months, but I'd decided it was time for him to meet my family, so I asked him to join me on our annual march in the St Patrick's Day Parade.

'If you can promise me that nobody will say the words St Patty's Day in my earshot, I'll think about it.'

'Any self-respecting Irish person would never utter such nonsense. We all know a patty is a burger, or short for Patricia, not Patrick and certainly not somebody who has the power to banish snakes,' I said, with the mock seriousness that the subject deserved.

'In that case, blue eyes, you've got yourself a deal.'

# 13

## *Bea*

### St Patrick's Day, 2019

*Lexington Avenue, Manhattan*

'You're late,' I said to Dan, as he ran the last few steps towards me. I tried to be cross with him. And failed. The mere sight of him made me feel happy.

'Ah, sorry, love. But this poor fecker fell walking up the subway steps on Lexington. I wasn't surprised he fell, 'cos he was wearing four-inch platform heels. Mad-looking yokes. There he was, face planted, his stuff all over the place. And everyone carried on walking, moving to one side to avoid stepping on him. They didn't even glance in his direction. That can't be normal!'

'Sounds about normal to me,' I said. Dan was still naive to New Yorker ways. That would change. It always did.

'Well, you should have seen this fella's face when I

leant down to help him pick his bag up. He went white. I swear he thought I was trying to mug him.'

'You've got to be careful. There's a lot of eccentric people around. Especially on the subway. He could have turned on you.'

'For what? Helping him get back on his feet? Don't be daft. We all need that every now and then. He was delighted once I assured him I was neither thief nor threat. Nice fella as it turned out, a bit of craic I'd say. Toby, from Nebraska, but living in Queens now like myself. We only live a block from each other. He said he might see us later for a pint. I told him we'd probably be in Saints and Sinners this evening.'

I marvelled that Dan could make a friend with a random subway guy as quickly as this. 'I've commuted on the subway my whole life and I've never ended up arranging to meet someone for drinks while doing so.'

'Ah you're not living at all, Bea. Sure half the fun of the commute is the bants you have with the randomers. Last week I met this fella who rides the subway all day. Talking away to himself, he was. About the house he was going to buy up on a hill, can't remember the name of it, giving out about Trump and his orange face. He didn't stop talking from Woodside to Grand Central, not once. I was in stitches laughing at the stuff coming out of his mouth, couldn't help myself. But he didn't seem to mind me laughing. He joined in too. Satisfying, that laugh was. He always waves at me now when I see him.'

Over the past few months since I became Dan's girlfriend, I'd seen the effect his laughter had on those in our company. It was an impossibility for anyone to remain poker-faced when something tickled his fancy. He had one of those belly laughs that came from the very core of him. Loud, dirty and infectious.

'Do me a solid and remember you're not in Wexford any more, Dan. New York has a bite. That's all I'm saying.'

'Well if someone tries to bite me, I'll have to bite back. Besides, who's gonna take on me?' He posed Popeye style, flexing his not inconsiderable muscles. He was right, of course. Most would run away from a fight with Dan.

'You're a good man,' I said, then leaned into his embrace for a hug. I felt a shiver of shame as I realized that had it been me who passed that man on the steps, I would have probably walked on by; most New Yorkers would. But not my gentle giant. If I'd followed my first instinct when I bumped into him on New Year's Eve in Saints and Sinners, I would have missed out on getting to know the most decent, kind man I'd ever known.

'Where have you gone, blue eyes?' Dan asked, bringing me back to him.

'I was thinking about chips, if you must know,' I said.

'The Stop Inn,' he said with a smile. 'We'll have to go back there again soon. Denise was asking after you only yesterday.'

We turned onto East 74th Street and I slowed my pace down to a gentle stroll. 'Jackie Kennedy Onassis lived here,' I said, pointing to the red-brick, pre-war building we were about to pass.

Dan stopped to take a better look. 'That's mad to think that Jackie O must have walked on this very pavement. My mam would have got such a kick out of that. She loved her. Said she was the epitome of a lady. And sure, at home in Wexford, we all have a special place for that family. There's a museum in New Ross, a place called

Dunganstown, where JFK's family originated from. He visited there a couple of times. I'll take you one day.'

He threw that in casually, but I caught the quick side-look he gave me to see my reaction. Which incidentally was to grin like the Cheshire cat. 'My grandparents cried for weeks when JFK was shot. Gran was hanging laundry on the line in our garden, the radio on in the background. And they interrupted a song to say that shots had been fired at the president's motorcade. She said she dropped the basket of clothes to the ground and ran inside, calling for Grandad.'

'A sad day. We better get a move on. We'll be late,' Dan said, grabbing my arm and moving us along.

'Nervous?' he asked, grinning from ear to ear.

'No. Of course not,' I denied. His grin got wider and to my annoyance one jumped onto my face in response to his. I moved to the side of the busy street so that a group of kids, no more than fifteen or sixteen, could pass us by. All of them were dressed head to toe in green, their faces painted green, white and orange.

'Half the city is wearing green today,' Dan said. 'I've never seen anything like it.'

'St Patrick's Day is a big deal over here. Wait till you see the pubs later on. There won't be a single one in the city that's not bedecked with the Irish flag. And by the way, does anything ever bother you?' I envied him his ease. In the three months since we'd known each other, he'd never shown any signs of stress. I, on the other hand, seemed to live in a state of perpetual stress.

'Ah sure, life is too short. You worry too much, blue eyes.' He leaned in and kissed me. And all thoughts of my family and friends, who were only a few minutes' walk away, disappeared. I lost all perspective when Dan kissed me.

'The only thing I'm worried about is remembering everyone's names. I've been running through them all as I travelled over here on the subway.'

'Don't worry about that. Everyone is chilled and will be delighted to have you with us. Dad is looking forward to meeting you. He's been at me for ages to bring you home to meet him.'

'Are you sure it's a good idea me coming today, though? You said marching in the parade together is a family tradition. Will they be pissed off, me landing on them?'

'Not at all. They're dying to meet you. Fresh Wexford blood! If only Gran and Grandad were alive. I think this would be the happiest day of their life. They were beside themselves when Dad married a Wexford girl. Now their granddaughter is dating a Wexford man. They are up there in heaven throwing a party, I bet.'

'I love hearing your stories about the two of them.' Dan reached into the inside pocket of his coat, then held up a copy of Dad's latest novel, *The Mystery of Breanna Bay*. 'I've nearly finished it. And I'm really enjoying it. More than I thought I would, to be honest. I'm normally more of a Stephen King man.'

'You didn't have to read one of Dad's books!' I was touched that he would do so.

'Course I did. He's your dad. It would be rude not to.' He touched the side of my cheek, a gentle caress. A promise. 'His dedication to you at the beginning gave me a lump in my throat.' He opened the book and read it out, in a whisper. *To Beatrice, the one who makes me strive to do better, every day.*

'Every single one of his books has a dedication to me, always with the same words. He says I'm his lucky charm. His four-leaf clover.'

'Seriously cool. I can't imagine anyone ever dedicating a book to me. The closest I've ever been to an author is when I bumped into Eoin Colfer coming out of the jacks in the Crown Bar at home in Wexford. Or at least I think it was him. I had a few scoops on me at the time, so I wouldn't like to swear to it,' Dan said with a grin.

'Dad used to read his books to me when I was a kid. I'm officially jealous!'

'Remind me again who else is marching with us and who do I need to impress?'

'My Uncle Mike is a tough nut to crack. Suspicious of everyone. But when he's on your side, he's all in. There's a strong contingent of Wexfordians living in New York and most take the time to march. You might even meet someone you know. It always amazes me how small our world is. Nearly every year there's a reunion of some sort. Oh, and they'll all want to talk to you about home. Uncle Mike follows Irish politics closely, be warned. We try not to let him talk about politics at family dinners, 'cos he can get so irate.'

'Noted. Did you say you have some cousins coming too?'

'I do. Second and third cousins that we see for weddings and funerals. To be honest, now that my grandparents are gone, there's less reason to keep in touch. You'll get to know them in time, but I won't confuse you now with their names. Watch out for Nancy though. She'll be all smiles, but she'll also be watching you like a hawk. She was my gran's first cousin and they were close.'

'Noted. I'll watch my p's and q's with them all, but especially Mike and Nancy! Don't worry. It'll be grand.'

And Dan smiled again, the relaxed smile of someone who has always had it easy. He grabbed my gloved hand and pulled me along, towards the gathering crowds at the end of the street. The parade route began every year at East 44th Street and ended at the American Irish Historical Society at East 80th Street. New York police officers, firefighters, schools, marching bands, majorettes, and associations representing every county in Ireland, took part every year. People travelled from all over the world to be here, with 150,000 people marching.

I scanned the large group ahead of me, all wearing purple and gold sashes, the Wexford colours. I saw the Kehoes, Gallahues, Howlins, Longs and Murphys. Some of the group I only saw on this one day each year, others were family friends. Dad spotted us first and shouted out my name, alerting the group I was there. Word that I was bringing a boyfriend must have filtered down to everyone, because they all had their eyes on stalks as they took in my date. And I suppose it was newsworthy because in my twenty-odd years of marching with this gang, I'd never brought anyone before.

Dad reached us first and hugged me quickly, before shaking Dan's hand.

'Mr O'Connor. Delighted to meet you,' Dan said, sounding more formal than I'd ever heard him before. Then all of a sudden, we were surrounded. I watched cousins pump his hand up and down. Then the circle around him widened as the rest of our association came over to clap him on the back and ask what part of Wexford he was from. When Dan told them he was from

The Ballagh, they started shouting out people's names to him, asking him if he knew such and such. Delight resonated when he confirmed that, yes, he did know their cousin, aunt, neighbour, old school friend. This ritual was something I'd grown up with. It was a deep-driven need to find a connection to home that only an immigrant understood. I listened as friends began to tell Dan where their roots lay in County Wexford.

'Rosslare.'

'Screen. The Ballybeg Road. Do you know the Martins?'

'The Ballagh. On the Curclough Lane. D'you know it?'

'I'm a Bree woman.'

Dan answered each one and laughed with everyone as they discovered they had mutual friends. Six degrees of separation as the saying went, unless you are Irish and then it was reduced to two. I looked around for my Uncle Mike. He was standing back, taking it all in.

I called out to him and pulled Dan by the hand towards him.

'So you're the guy that's been keeping our girl away from home?' Uncle Mike said, looking up at him. 'She said you were big.'

'Hello, Mr O'Connor. It's a pleasure to meet you.'

'You've manners. That's a start, I suppose,' Uncle Mike said. 'Do you play rugby? You have the look of a rugby player.'

'I don't, Mr O'Connor. Sorry about that.'

'Hurling?'

'I have done. But I'm not that good,' Dan admitted.

'Don't worry about that. We need some new players for the league. I'll add your name down. I don't think we'll have a jersey your size though.'

Nancy who'd been hovering, nodded her head in agreement. 'He'll be a double XL I would say. Wasn't that Flynn boyo a double XL?'

'He was. But he never gave us back the jersey when he left.'

'The bollix,' Nancy said.

That made Dan laugh. Nancy always took people by surprise. She was petite and looked like butter wouldn't melt. But she had a mouth like a fishwife and was the fiercest woman I knew.

Nancy held up a sash and said, 'This one is for you, big fella. But I want it back. Don't stick it in your pocket for a souvenir to show your mammy back home.'

'His mam is dead,' I whispered, mortified, mouthing sorry to Dan. But he didn't look in the least put out. In fact he looked quite smitten with Nancy.

'Is she? Ah, God love you,' Nancy said, pulling him in for a hug. Then Uncle Mike reached over to pat him on the back. So much for worrying about how they'd get on. Seeing my family and Dan connect made my insides melt. I was continually surprised at how much Dan meant to me, in such a short space of time.

'I'll be needing a ladder!' Nancy said to Uncle Mike over her shoulder. Then she reached up to place the sash over Dan's head. He bent his knees to help her out, as if he was being knighted by the Queen of England. She smoothed the silk over Dan's chest, and then when she was satisfied that it looked OK, she turned to me and said, 'I like him. He'll do.'

Uncle Mike called for attention and the group silenced, moving closer to him. 'For the newbies here, welcome. We are delighted to have you with us. The parade begins at 44th Street, then we'll march up Fifth Avenue – make sure and bless yourself as you go by St Patrick's Cathedral on 50th Street – then we'll go all the way to 79th Street. We finish at the American Irish Historical Society on East 80th Street.'

Nods of approval rippled through the group. Parents called out for their kids and the O'Connor clan claimed our spot, side by side. To my surprise, Dan was promoted to carry the flag up the front. I could tell he was chuffed and I was delighted with how well it was all going.

'The Taoiseach, Leo, he's here,' Dad said.

Nancy silenced us all and said, 'Remember everyone, if you get the chance to talk to him, ask him about the new children's hospital. Poor Ann is beside herself waiting for a date for little Conor's operation. It's a disgrace.'

'I love how invested you all are in what's going on over in Ireland,' Dan said. 'And I can see why you love spending time with your family. They're fun.' I felt happiness swell inside me. He liked them and they liked him. And even though the wind was so sharp it whipped my face, it could not take away the smile. Dan was not only coping with the banter being thrown his way, he was thriving on it. It was as if he'd known everyone for much longer than the fifteen minutes he'd actually been in the O'Connor clan's company. It boded well for the future.

We marched up Fifth Avenue and I watched his eyes greedily take in every detail of the buildings on either side of us. From the outdoor plaza of the Rockefeller Center where you could hear the delight of skaters whizzing by, to the iconic blue of Tiffany's flagship store, the opulent Plaza and Trump Tower hotels. Tourists and New Yorkers alike stood behind fences and waved at us, cheering if they recognized kinship in the colours of the sashes and flags. The sounds of bagpipes and the purup-a-pom-pom beat of the drums bounced around us. As we passed St Patrick's Cathedral, Nancy gave us all the nod, so we blessed ourselves as instructed.

When I was a kid, my grandparents would take me here to light candles for special intentions: a sick relative at home or to remember the dead on anniversaries. And I always thought the cathedral looked like a fairy-tale castle. The two stone towers stood at 330 feet high and when I should have been praying I'd be imagining Rapunzel throwing her hair down from them. Gran told me she dreamed that one day I might get married there too. She had it all planned in her head, telling me that it should be at Christmas so that way we'd have the spectacular Saks light show that illuminates the avenue every night and the backdrop of the Rockefeller Christmas tree for photographs. Then she'd laugh and say, 'All we have to do is find you a decent man and we're all set. I'll keep lighting candles for you, Bea. The right one will come along, I promise.'

I looked at Dan, who was now shaking hands with the Grand Marshal Brian O'Dwyer, who had wandered over to thank us for marching. And I wondered if perhaps Gran's wish had come true.

As we passed the TV cameras, Dan turned to look at me. 'Funny, I wasn't feeling in the least bit homesick until I saw the RTE crew.' I watched his face soften and his eyes glisten. And I wondered what it must feel like to be him. I'd never left America. I'd visited many states in our country with Dad over the years, on road trips and vacations, but that was as far as we'd gone.

'The longest I've ever been away from home is three weeks. I can only imagine how much you must miss Wexford. Is this very different to the parades you had at home?'

'There's a parade every year, but it's mainly GAA clubs, boy scouts and girl guides, that type of thing. Not on a scale like this. The parade in Dublin is bigger, similar to this, I suppose.'

'Did you go every year?' I asked.

Dan shook his head. 'Only until I was about eleven or twelve. Then we all got a bit too cool for school. Not even the bribe of ice-cream and chocolate could make us go for Mam and Dad. So they gave up asking.'

'Why haven't you ever been to Ireland?' he asked suddenly.

I shrugged. It was a hard question to answer. I looked at Dad, who was marching a few feet away from me, chatting to the Kehoe family. Gran and Grandad went back and forth every couple of years, when I was young. Once or twice, discussions were held about me going along with them, but it never panned out. Dad would always find an excuse as to why I couldn't go – school commitments or work commitments for him. Then he would book somewhere exciting to take my mind off it. I've been financially independent for several years, so I could have gone on my own buck. But something held me back. What was it? Fear, I think. Yes, that was it. Fear of finally finding my mom's family, where she began her life, and not finding traces of her there. I felt Dan's eyes on me, questioning. 'I would like to visit one day. It would be cool to see where my mom was born. See if I can find any family left.'

'You haven't spoken about your mom since the night we met,' Dan said.

That's because it hurts too much, I thought. But I didn't say that. He must find it strange, because he on the other hand spoke about his mam all the time. I felt like I had known her. And I mourned her loss, as strange as that sounded. I flashed a smile at my boyfriend and decided to do what I always did when faced with a subject I didn't like to discuss. I changed it. 'We're almost at the end! And I don't know about you, but I'm starving!'

Once we reached the end of the parade, people dispersed pretty quickly. Most had plans in various pubs around the city, or in their own local suburb. The O'Connor clan always headed to the Fitzpatrick Hotel for the full Irish breakfast. Sausages, bacon, eggs, white and black pudding, toast, butter and tea.

We filed into the hotel lobby, walking over to the open fire that blazed in the library off reception. Shane Cookman, the hotel manager, knew our family well and greeted us all like we were his own family.

'Brennan's bread and Kerrygold butter. My mouth is watering already, Shane,' Dad said, as we followed him into the restaurant and took our seats on either side of a long table that had been reserved for us.

'One of the few places in town where you can get the real deal. You'll learn that a lot promise you the full Irish, but not everyone delivers. A taste from home, I guarantee it,' Uncle Mike told Dan.

'You know what I miss the most. A decent cup of tea,' Dan said. 'No offence, but it's impossible to get one over here.'

'You just need to know where to go,' Nancy said, tapping her nose conspiratorially.

'They only serve Barry's here. Isn't that right, Shane?' Dad called out.

Shane nodded enthusiastically. 'I've trained the staff myself. They know how to make a decent pot of tea. I'll stake my reputation on it.'

'But is it a pot? None of this bag in a mug business,' Dan challenged.

'A pot. With boiled water. That's half the problem, I've found. Most don't boil the water at all.'

'We'll all have the full Irish, Shane,' Dad said, looking around the table quickly to make sure that there were no renegades looking for pancakes or some equally non-Irish option. There wasn't. Nobody dared.

'You won't believe it,' I threw in. 'I was in Duke's diner last week and ordered tea.'

'They always have Barry's,' Dad said.

'Not last week. They gave me Lipton's. Knew the second I saw the colour of it,' I said. The table responded with the right amount of indignation that this news deserved.

'Out of order. Did you send it back?' Dad said.

'I did. Then I told the waitress to bring me the good stuff. She looked a bit puzzled. Barry's tea, I explained, and she still looked clueless. So I walked over to the counter myself and looked underneath where I knew it was hidden.'

'Was it there?' Uncle Mike asked.

'Of course it was! The owner is Irish – he always has a stash of the good stuff hidden.'

'Well, here at the Fitzpatrick we don't hide the good stuff, we give it to everyone,' Shane said with perfect timing, a pot of tea in each hand. 'I made them myself. So don't even think about complaining.'

This was one of my favourite days of each year. A chance to connect with old friends that we rarely saw the rest of the year. And a chance to remember Gran and Grandad, because they were wrapped up in all of our memories. But I'd never been so happy as I was this year. Watching Dan laughing with my family and friends, it was as if he'd always been with us. He fitted in here, I realized. And I wondered, if I went to Ireland with him as he suggested, would I fit in over there? I'm American Irish and proud of that. I wouldn't choose to live in any other city in the world. I am where I am meant to be. But I'd also spent my entire life feeling homesick for a place that I'd never actually visited. Maybe it was time to address that.

# 14

## Lucy

July 1992

*Woodside, Queens, New York*

I wasn't sure I would ever get used to not waking up in Ireland. The first few moments were the most peaceful part of my day, before my brain kicked in and remembered that I wasn't at home in Kilmore any more. The homesickness came in waves, a physical reaction to a loss that only emigrants could understand. I'd shower and get dressed, watch Maeve put pop tarts in the oversized toaster as we listened to the sounds of sirens and trains outside our window. I felt like we were actors in a play, pretending to live here in this strange city. At any moment the curtain would fall, we'd take a bow and then put our real clothes on. Despite this, somehow, I survived our first month in New York. I hadn't worked out if I liked it or not yet. Getting the subway to Woodside on that first day we arrived was a panic. We couldn't work out which train to get. Uptown or downtown made no sense and everybody was rushing so fast, it was impossible to find someone to help. New Yorkers move at a different pace to any other species I know. In the end we approached a couple of Chinese tourists, who had their heads buried in a map. They were friendly and helpful, with a better knowledge of the subway than us. Thanks to them we got on the correct train and managed to get off it on 61st Street as instructed. And as we stood on the walkway, looking down onto the street below, we saw the Stop Inn right in front of us, where our contact Martin had told us to wait for him.

'Our first American diner experience!' Maeve said, opening the menu when we took a seat in one of the laminated booths.

'I'm not very hungry,' I admitted. Somehow or other, since we'd left Ireland we'd been continuously snacking and looking through the hundreds of items on the menu, I felt overwhelmed by the choice. I thought about the small blackboard that sat above the bar at home in Nellie's:

> *Soup of the day*
> *Roast of the day*
> *Mixed Sandwiches*
> *Apple tart*

I stifled a sob, knowing that my sister would possibly kill me if I told her I missed Mam's apple tart, less than twenty-four hours since we'd had a slice.

'I couldn't eat a thing either. But let's choose what we'll

have tomorrow for breakfast. Because we have to come back for pancakes.'

We finished two coffees before Martin arrived, red-faced and panting from running several blocks to get to us. 'Sorry! Got held up in work. You must be Maeve and Lucy?'

He was as nice as we'd been told by Michelle. And insisted on buying our coffees, telling us all about the local nightlife, hotspots where the Irish tended to hang out. Then he took us to the flat he'd found for us. It was in the apartment block he lived in and had become vacant soon after we got our visa offers. When he emailed us to tell us about it, we gratefully paid our deposit via a bank draft. We knew we were in the lucky position of having somewhere to go straight to, rather than starting off in digs or a hotel.

Our new home was small. It took a bit of getting used to, compared to the much more spacious flat we'd shared in Dublin. But it's funny how quickly you can adapt to your new normal. And it had everything we needed. Two small bedrooms, with one bathroom and a decent-sized kitchen-cum-dining room and living room. It was sparsely furnished, with the bare minimum. But that didn't worry us as we'd already, after one week, managed to make it homely. Maeve bought a large framed poster of a baby harp seal, lying in a blanket of icy white snow, with huge black eyes, looking sorrowfully at you, so no matter where you moved in the room, its eyes did too.

'It reminded me of the seals from the Saltee Islands. I thought it was a little bit of home for us, right here.' She loved those seals, we both did, reminding us of the times we went boating with our dad as kids.

Martin advised us not to go down the compare route over here. 'Nothing is the same in New York, so the quicker you accept that, the quicker you'll settle in. Dive all-in and commit to the New York state of mind, otherwise you'll be in no man's land between here and there.'

It was good advice, but I wasn't as good as Maeve at implementing the rule. Because I kept missing the silliest things from home. Take, for instance, our fireplace. I mean, how ridiculous was that? I'd spent years begging Mam and Dad to get central heating because our house was always freezing. We'd wake up most mornings with an ice-block for a nose. The only sanctuary from the cold was the sitting room, where the open fire always made the room toasty. You'd open the door to that room and a wave of heat would flash over your face. And within minutes you'd feel like you were in a sauna and have to run outside to cool off. Plus there was the pain-in-the-neck chore of going outside to get coal and logs. Once or twice, when Mam and Dad ran out of money and in turn fuel, the fire went out and we had no choice but to layer up with jumpers and mittens. Maeve and I would sit in our bedroom, teeth chattering with the cold and bemoan our horrendous life. So why on earth did I miss that blasted fire now?

I envied how fast Maeve adjusted to life here. She strode across the sidewalk with a confidence that I wasn't sure I'd ever possess. The noise, the smells, they were all alien to me. I kept reminding myself that it had only been a week, so it would be unfair to make any judgements yet.

'You ready?' Maeve shouted into my bedroom.

'Coming,' I said, as I ran down to the hall.

Maeve looked so beautiful she made me gasp. We always shared our clothes and the dress she had on now was actually mine. Maeve had a knack for accessorizing clothes; she'd add a belt, scarf or jewellery and suddenly the outfit would look as if it had been styled for a fashion shoot. 'That looks so much better on you than it does on me.'

'You're not looking too shabby either, Sis. Look at the legs on you! I've huge calves, I can't get away with jeans like that,' Maeve said kindly. I was delighted with the compliment. I was wearing a pair of skin-tight faded blue jeans that I'd always felt too self-conscious to wear at home. But over here, I felt a little more daring. We were heading to Gobeen's Bar for the night, to meet Martin and some of his friends. Maeve had been right about the men. For her at least. We'd only been here two days when she announced she had a date with some guy called Toby. He was meeting us there too. I liked him. He was funny and very handsome. And she was besotted. But Maeve always was at first. The only problem was that the flame usually burned out quickly for her. I'd seen it hundreds of times.

I, on the other hand, hadn't been exactly mobbed, as Maeve had promised would happen when we got to New York. I had been on a few dates, but dating American style was a whole new ball game for me. The rules were different here than in Ireland. I'd worked out that American men liked to date a lot, but that didn't neces-sarily mean that you ended up as boyfriend and girlfriend. At home, a guy asks you out, by the end of the date, you are an item, official, exclusive. There wasn't any big conversation around this. Here it was more common that people dated multiple partners at the same time. I wasn't sure I liked that.

Another thing that was different here was work. We'd both managed to get waitressing and bar work within a week of arriving in Queens. It didn't pay much; we worked for tips. But I lost my first job after two weeks. Not because I did anything wrong, but because the owner's son's friend needed a job. Last in, first out. I moped for a day, then dusted myself off and went in search of new employment. I got lucky in the fourth place I tried – the Woodside Steakhouse. I liked it there. It had red brocade-covered walls and regular entertainment. Customers were encouraged to sing too and it wasn't unusual for someone to jump up and give a verse of 'Carrickfergus' or 'The Mountain Dew'. And I'd learned pretty quickly that if I sang 'Danny Boy' the tips were proportionately higher for every verse I belted out. The manager liked me too. On my first day, I'd proved to him that I could change a keg, sing and carry five platters of food at once. Plus the customers liked my Irish accent. Most were Irish immigrants and loved having a chat about home. That part was the saving grace for me really. The community of Irish in Queens was a force to be reckoned with. They stuck together and there was a strength in that.

Long term, my plan was to look for a teaching job. But for now, I agreed with Maeve that we should just enjoy the summer. The rest of our lives could begin later.

'I wonder how Mam and Dad are?' I asked.

'Fine. Same as they were yesterday when you called them!'

I looked at my watch and worked out the time at

home. Mam would be in the kitchen preparing dinner. There'd be a ham sitting in a saucepan of water, steeping, to extract all the salt. Dad would be chopping logs to make sure we had enough in for the next day. Maybe polishing his Sunday shoes, ready for Mass the next day. Homesickness punched me in the gut. I longed to hear their voices. But it was so expensive to phone them, a dollar per minute soon made a dint into our rent money.

'You OK, Sis?' Maeve asked, concern wrinkling her nose.

A tear escaped and I shook my head. 'I miss Mam and Dad. I miss home.'

She led me back into the sitting room and we sat down, side by side on the couch.

'Me too. Over five thousand miles away from them and I've never got on so well with them. I've had more conversations with them on the phone than I've had in years at home,' she said. 'It will get easier. The first month is the hardest, everyone says so. Trying to get used to a new country . . .'

'I miss Mam's fry-ups,' I said.

Maeve licked her lips. 'Galtee sausages and rashers.'

'The bacon so crispy it falls to pieces when you cut it.'

'And Batchelors beans,' Maeve said.

'With a knob of Kerrygold butter in them.'

'Two eggs, cooked in the fat of the rashers.'

We sat in silence thinking about Mam's full Irish fry that we'd had every Sunday morning as long as we could remember. We'd taken it for granted. Sometimes giving out that it never changed. 'Remember the time we asked Mam to make French toast for a change?' I said.

'She went ballistic. "It's far from French Toast that you were both reared!" she said.'

'So instead she threw some Pat the Baker bread into the frying pan and gave us fried bread, with a fried egg on top. "That's Irish toast," she said!'

We both laughed at the memory.

'Tell you what, let's go to the Stop Inn tomorrow morning for the full Irish. They have Galtee sausages.'

'I don't like their grits. Grits have no place on an Irish fry,' I grumbled.

'We'll insist they hold all grits,' Maeve said. She leaned in and with her thumb rubbed my running eyeliner away.

'Do I look a state?'

'You look beautiful.' She pulled me into her arms and hugged me close. 'If by the end of the summer you still hate it, we'll go home.'

'You'd do that for me?'

'Of course. I couldn't stay here without you, Sis. It's always been you and me together. And that's the way it has to stay. I won't force you to be here, I promise.'

And suddenly I felt OK, the weight of fear that had been pinning me down disappeared. Just knowing that we could go home again took the pressure off. 'I'm going to try harder to settle in.'

'You're doing great,' she insisted. 'It's only been a few weeks. Now come on, let's head to Gobeen's before Toby thinks I'm a non-runner and starts chatting up someone else.'

'He wouldn't!'

'Ah but he would. He's a flighty one. Half the reason I like him. Can't beat a bad boy.'

I felt a rush of love for my sister. There were times she

drove me around the bend, but those moments were eclipsed by the fun we had together. I also knew that, as much as I missed home and my parents, I could never leave Maeve. She wasn't just my sister, she was my best friend.

# 15

## Lucy

### August 1992

*New York Public Library, Fifth Avenue, Manhattan*

'You'd get lost in your own bedroom,' Mam used to say to me. She'd have a right laugh at me now, because I'd just managed to walk around in circles for the past twenty minutes. A couple of months in New York and I still couldn't get my head around streets and avenues and the way they ran. Which way was East and West, Uptown or Downtown? I seemed to always have my head stuck in a map, but truth be told, I usually just guessed which way to go. And there was a fifty-fifty chance I'd get it right. I was meeting Maeve for lunch in Junior's, a diner on Broadway. And in another five minutes, I'd be officially late. Rumour had it that they served cake in a milkshake and we both wanted some of that. We had promised to take a photograph to send back to Michelle.

Somehow or other, I'd managed to end up in front of a large building on Fifth Avenue. As I took in the steps that ran up to tall pillars and a grand entrance, I realized that I knew this building. Or at least it looked familiar to me. I took a step backwards to get a better look. I'd seen it in a movie. And just as the name of the movie came to me, a voice said, 'I'm trying to work out if you're a *Ghostbusters* or *Breakfast at Tiffany's* fan?'

I turned to my left and a guy about my own age was watching me watching the building. And he was freaking me out, because he was reading my mind.

'You're a tricky one. No doubt you are about the right age to be a *Ghostbusters* fan. But there again, you look like a Hepburn fan. You've got a look of her. Bet you've been told that before. So it's *Breakfast at Tiffany's*, am I right?'

I shook my head and tried to work out which way to walk next. Was Broadway up or down? I was pretty sure it was up. But east or west? My head hurt, trying to work it out.

'*Ghostbusters!* You've surprised me!' he smiled. He didn't look like an obvious threat. In fact, he reminded me of home, which was strange, because he had a strong New York accent.

'I never said I was a fan. I just recognized the building from the movie. Which was, as it goes, only average.'

'You're Irish,' the man said, a smile breaking out across his face. 'Me too.'

'I don't think I've heard that accent anywhere in Ireland.'

He laughed and I found myself smiling too. He had a nice laugh. It was strong and full, unapologetic. I liked that.

'My parents are from Ireland. I was born here. But that's just geography. I feel Irish in here.' He tapped his heart.

'I've never seen *Breakfast at Tiffany's*. I didn't know it was filmed here,' I said.

'Here and lots of cool locations around New York. You should watch the movie. It's not half bad.'

I looked at my map and searched the page until I found Fifth Avenue. I was standing in front of The Public Library of New York.

'You going in?' he said, 'There's lots of really cool things to see inside. It's open to the public.'

'Not today. I'm on my way to meet my sister. If I can work out how to get there.'

He moved in closer. 'Where?'

'A restaurant on Broadway. Junior's.'

He made a face, then said, 'I'll show you. It's not far.'

My first instinct was to say no. This guy could be the Son of Sam's grandson for all I knew. But he had an honest face. And I found myself thanking him and following him as he made his way to the right.

'What you have to remember is that Manhattan is actually a grid. Fifth Avenue, where we are now, separates the east and west sides. The street numbers increase as you head away from Fifth; if you remember that, you'll be OK. Streets are east–west. Avenues are north–south.'

'I don't think my brain handles directions well. When you explain it like that, it sounds easy. But I'm the kind of person who gets lost at home. Honestly, I'm not joking.'

'Well, it's a good job I walked out of the library when I did.'

I looked at his brown leather satchel, slung diagonally over his shoulder.

'Do you work in the library?' I noticed a flush cross his face.

'I'm a writer. Nothing published yet,' he said the words in a rush.

'That's really cool. I was rubbish in English, could never get my head around creative writing.'

'What do you do?'

'I've not long graduated from university back home in Ireland. A teacher's degree. But for now, I'm waitressing.'

'Around here?'

'No. The Woodside Steakhouse.'

'I know that place. By the number 7 subway on 61st.'

'That's the one.'

'There's a lot of Irish in that area. You should try Shane's Deli for breakfast. Decent!'

'I'll remember that. We've been hanging out in the Stop Inn a lot.'

'Because they sell Barry's Tea.'

'Yes!' I laughed. I stole a glance at him as we walked, or rather he walked and I trotted to keep up. I felt a trickle of excitement make its way around my tummy. It wasn't that this guy was that good-looking, but there was something about his face that was charismatic.

'What do you write?' I asked as we weaved our way through the tourists in Times Square. My eyes were still on stalks whenever I wandered up here, taking in the digital billboard signs for Coca Cola, Sony and Maxwell. A man approached opening his jacket to reveal rows of watches and chains. I shook my head, because I was still too scared to stop and ask how much the bling was. But

I could already see some of those going into a parcel for Mam and Dad.

'Fiction. I'm working on my first novel. A detective series set in the Wild West. I've had some interest from an agent, when I sent in a couple of sample chapters. Now I need to finish it. I can't believe I told you that! I haven't even told my family about the agent's interest.'

'Your secret is safe with me. Congratulations.'

'See that TKTS booth? That's where you go to get discounted tickets for Broadway,' my new friend and tour guide told me. We continued walking for a few moments more, then he stopped and gently touched my arm to guide me out of the main thoroughfare. 'We're here.'

I looked up and saw a huge red neon sign, saying Junior's. There was a queue with the concierge for a table and I spotted Maeve near the front of the line, her eyes agog as she watched me arrive with a strange man.

'Thank you. Honestly, I'd probably have ended up in Central Park if I was left to my own devices.'

'My pleasure. Happy to help you find your way around New York, anytime.'

Now it was my turn to flush. We stood in silence for a moment. It felt awkward and I searched for something to say, anything to fill the quiet. 'Do you like cheesecake?' Of all the things I could have said, I chose that. *Mortified.*

'Yes!' he answered. 'All of them. But my favourite in Junior's is the Brownie Explosion cheesecake. If you like chocolate, it's pretty good.'

'I'll remember that.' Maeve was now waving at me and pointing to a waitress. 'Looks like we've got a seat. I'd better go. Thanks again.' I walked towards the entrance, the unusual aroma combination of onions and sugar wafting its way towards me.

'Wait! I'm Ryan O'Connor. What's your name?'

I turned back and smiled. 'I'm Lucy. Lucy Mernagh.' Then I walked into the restaurant.

'What is going on! Who were you with?' Maeve demanded when I joined her in our booth.

'His name is Ryan. He's a writer.' I liked how his name sounded when I said it.

'Details! I need all the details, Sis!'

'I met him about fifteen minutes ago. I was lost. He offered to bring me here. That's it.'

'Are you seeing him again?'

I shook my head and realized that I wished more than anything that he was one of those American boys we'd heard about back home, who asked you for dates at the drop of a hat. 'He never asked.'

'His loss,' Maeve said. 'He was OK-looking, I suppose; you wouldn't throw him out of the bed for eating Tayto crisps, but he's no Tom Cruise.'

I looked out through the plate-glass windows, hoping that he might be still standing there. Stupid, I knew. The waitress came over and smiled brightly at us. 'Which of you gals is Lucy?'

I looked at Maeve and she quickly pointed to me, saying, 'Her!'

My heart started to race.

'Then this is for you, honey. A dishy-looking guy handed it to me. Nice manners too. He's a keeper.' She placed a slice of cheesecake onto the Formica table in front of me. 'This is the brownie explosion cheesecake. He's paid for it.'

My hands shook as I unfolded a piece of notepaper with frayed edges, ripped from a notebook.

*I'd love to take you out on a date. My number is 718 555 4314. Give me a call, please! I'm free tonight, or any other night this week. But please say tonight. I really enjoyed meeting you, Lucy. Yours, Ryan*

I passed the note to Maeve, so that she could read it. There was something about the way he ended his note, with Yours, that made me blush.

'I told you that the men over here love the Irish women. You need to call him right now and tell him that you'll see him tonight!'

'Oh no, honey. Make him sweat. Eat your cheesecake, then call him in an hour. Never does to be too needy,' our hovering waitress said.

'I like your style,' Maeve said. 'We'll have one of those cheesecakes in a milkshake yokes, please, this one is sorted it seems! And two coffees. Thank you.'

'You got it.' And the waitress was off, sticking her pen behind her ear.

'Now, missus, you need to tell me everything! Start from the beginning and tell me it all, every single word he said. Wait till Michelle hears about this,' Maeve said.

And for the first time since I arrived in New York, I understood Maeve's excitement. All of a sudden, I didn't feel so homesick. Rather than longing for my phone call with Mam later on, I was longing to call this strange guy with the lovely smile.

# 16

## *Bea*

### January 2020

*Georges Street, Staten Island, New York*

Katrina and I took a seat on a bench on the outside deck of the Staten Island Ferry. We were heading to Stephanie's apartment on Georges Street. She'd moved over to the Island a little over a year ago. Now, with the benefit of hindsight, I could see that the move was not just a move from the city, but also from our friendship.

Most native New Yorkers avoid the starboard side of the ship, because that's where all the tourists go for the best views of the Statue. But I loved watching the city through their eyes. Every avenue, park and yellow cab is a movie set for the New York newbie. Grandad said to me once that living in New York was a choice. That there were easier places to live, with lower rents and a slower pace of life. But nowhere else in the world could give you the colour that New York did. I didn't understand what he meant at the time, but the older I get, the more I get it. The colour comes from the woman who wears a fur coat and pearls every day as she walks her miniature poodle through Central Park. Or the guy standing in line for a coffee and sandwich at the deli, people listening. The Tony Stark skyline that always takes my breath away. The street artists, the commuters, the diversity, the energy.

My grandparents once talked about moving 'home to Ireland'. And they always said it that way. Home to Ireland. They went as far as going over to look at possible retirement properties a few years before they died. But it was only then that they realized that, while they loved Ireland and it would always be their first love, it was no longer the love of their life. I've never forgotten what Grandad said: 'I was home, but not really home, because I realized that I could never go back. New York is home now.'

'This sea air is not good for my hair. What will people think,' Katrina said, pulling her hat further down over her hair to stop it whipping around her face.

'No one is looking at you,' I said.

'People always look at me. It is my burden and blessing to be so beautiful. Tell me again why we are going to see Stephanie when it's clear she doesn't want to see us. Your call to her didn't go exactly well?'

'Look, it's a case of bringing the mountain to Muhammad. As for my call, well she left me no choice but to ring her through the Facebook app. She refused to return my calls, texts or WhatsApp. Did I tell you that she'd unfriended me! Isn't that awful? Has she unfriended you, did you check?'

'She has. I noticed that a few months back.' Katrina shrugged, showing her indifference.

'How can you not be bothered by that? The three of us were such great friends. I know our lives have moved on in different directions, but for goodness' sake, we've history.'

'You and she were the big friends. I've always suspected she put up with me because of you.'

'That's not true!'

'Really? If you were not in the middle, then we would not be friends, that is truth. Like it or lump it. And the reason she does not like seeing us any more is because we are her mirror.'

'What are you going on about?'

'We told her that she should finish with Jimmy last year and she swore she would. But of course, she took him back. She knows we think she is weak. She knows she is weak.'

I had a feeling that Katrina had hit a nail on the head there. 'Friends should be there for each other, no matter what. OK, maybe we don't approve of her relationship with Jimmy, but that doesn't mean we can't be in her life.'

'I'm not sure she feels the same way.'

'Well, judging by the way she spoke to me when I called her on the Facebook messenger thingy, you're right.'

'Very technical.'

'You know what I mean! She only answered the call because I caught her off guard. Katrina, it was awkward as fuck. She wasn't very chatty. She even made me introduce myself. "Who is this," she said, as if I were nobody. She made me feel like the most unimportant person in her life.'

'Rude. I hope you told her that.'

'No. I was like a fool saying, "It's me – Bea, from St Joseph's." And when she still didn't answer, I ended up losing my temper and said, "Oh for fuck's sake, Stephanie. It's Bea. Your supposed BFF!"'

'What did she say then?'

'She sighed. I asked her "How have you been?" She gave me clipped one-word answers. I swear, I've wracked my brains, Katrina, trying to think of anything that you or I have done to make her treat us like this. I even went back through our WhatsApp conversations to see if I'd said anything to offend. When I asked her if I'd upset her, she laughed and muttered, "Everything doesn't revolve around you, Bea. Some of us have lives of our own."'

'Ouch,' Katrina said. It *had* stung.

'Then she told me she was busy. I got annoyed, asked her why she was being so snarky with me. She let out a snigger at that, but she didn't sound one bit amused. She started shouting at me that we'd not spoken for months. That it made no difference if I'd upset her or not. That she had no interest in chatting to me. And that she had a life to get back to. Then she hung up!'

'Remind me why we are wasting our time going over to see her. Most likely she will slam door in our face!' Katrina said.

'No shit, Sherlock,' I said. 'Do me a favour though, play nice today. We need to go in softly-softly. I have this feeling that she's in trouble. And my letter said I'd never stop being her BFF. I want to make sure she's OK, that's all. I owe her that much.'

'Maybe. But you know better than anyone that some

people do not want to be found. Stephanie ghosted us for a reason. Maybe we should leave it.'

I shook my head. If Katrina wanted to back out of the visit, I couldn't stop her, but I was not leaving Stephanie's until we'd had a proper conversation. The letter wanted me to find my childhood best friend and build some bridges. And damn it, I was going to do that.

'Speaking about your letter. Have you had any more messages from the beyond?' Katrina tried to sound spooky, but the look of worry on her face disconcerted me. Not a lot worried my friend. Maybe I shouldn't share the latest development. It would only make me look crazy.

'Tell me,' Katrina insisted. She gave me one of her stares. She had this way of looking at you that demanded full transparency. A big advantage for us when we were in full-on detective mode, interviewing someone. Not so good for me right now. I pulled the letter from my bag and admitted, 'I had a new message this morning.'

'This should be first thing you tell me,' Katrina grumbled.

'I know. Sorry. I'm still getting my head around all of this. And I'm worried that you'll think I'm cracked . . .'

'Your worry is justified. You are cracked. But that matters not. I still need to know all new letter-related developments.'

'And you won't laugh?' I asked.

She made a sign of a cross over her heart, like we used to do as kids when we made a vow to each other. 'Cross our hearts, hope to die, stick a needle in our eye . . .'

I handed her the third page. 'Look at the bit where my younger self spoke about her wish to find someone to love, who looked at her in the same way my grandad looked at my gran in their wedding photograph.'

Katrina read out loud the message that was written in the same fancy script.

*Am I hot? Am I married to a really hot guy? I better be!*

I pointed to the message scrawled under it. 'I wrote that bit after I'd received her message.'

'I can see that,' Katrina said. She read it, then looked at me, then went back to the letter again. Finally, she read my response to my younger self out loud, breaking into snorts of laughter as she did.

*Happy to confirm I am smokin' hot. We are not married, but we date loads of cute guys.*

'Smokin' hot!' Katrina squealed again, clutching her stomach. My first reaction was that it wasn't that funny. But watching her laugh made me look at the message through her eyes, and then I saw the funny side of it. I couldn't help but join in, gently at first, but within seconds we both erupted into full-blown hysteria. I felt tears roll down my face as Katrina kept repeating, 'Smoking hot!' Then she pretended to burn as she touched my arm. That made us both howl even louder. I think I even peed a little.

'You must never tell her the truth of your frown lines. You must lie to her.'

That should have made me cross but only made me laugh even harder.

'And who are these hot guys you are dating?' Katrina demanded.

'I'll have you know that I flirted with the barista in Starbucks earlier today. Totally gorgeous he was.'

'It's not just the letter-writing you are imagining,' Katrina muttered. Then she pointed to my lady bits and said, 'If you leave that any longer, it will close up.'

'How rude! It's only been a few weeks.'

'That is enough time to freeze up. Dan is hot guy and he would go back with you in a moment.'

'Have you been talking to him?' I snapped. I didn't want him talking to my friends or family. Especially Katrina.

'I see him around. He misses you.'

'He has no right. You have no right. It's over between us and having you and Dad and everyone going on and on about it only makes it harder for me!' I felt temper crackle its way through me, the flames growing inch by inch.

'Hey, calm down!' Katrina said, putting her hands over mine. 'If you say it's over, fine. But you look sad all the time. To us, it's as if you want to be with Dan. And he wants to be with you.'

'We can't snap our fingers and get over each other. But it's over for a very good reason.'

'That's the thing, you've never told us what the reason is.'

'Yes I did!' I was getting really pissed off now. It was so tiring going over and over the same thing with them all.

'No you didn't,' Katrina persisted. 'You have been vague.'

'I don't love him enough. It's as simple as that. I realized he wasn't the one.'

'The one what? That is most ridiculous thing you have ever said.'

'Well, I'm sorry my feelings don't work for you, Katrina! But you and everyone else are going to have to get over this. We are finished.'

'Fine. Then you have to stop moping. If he is gone, so be it. It is time to find new man. Or woman, I do not care.' She began eyeing up everybody in our vicinity. I took a firm hold on her arm in case she decided to grab one of the tourists snapping photographs of the Statue of Liberty and the Manhattan skyline beside us.

'I'll go back to Starbucks tomorrow and wink at the barista. OK?' I showed Katrina my very best wink, which made her smile again. I didn't like us fighting over Dan. They were friends, we'd all partied together a lot. But this was our new status quo and she had to get her head around it. By the time the ferry slowed down as it made its way into the harbour, the subject of my ex was dropped. We headed to the gangway and disembarked, following the tourists and New Yorkers out of the terminal building. The walk to Stephanie's apartment was only a brisk twenty-minute stroll and as it was such a nice day we decided against a cab. The closer we got, the more nervous I felt. When we arrived, I took a deep breath, then pushed the buzzer to 7B.

'Hello.' Stephanie's voice came through the intercom. A good start, she was home at least.

'Hi! It's Bea and Katrina,' I said, holding the button down to speak. I had no idea if she would let us in and it went quiet for a while, except for the sound of our breathing as we waited for her response.

'This is ridiculous,' Katrina said, and she buzzed the

intercom a second time. She said a little more forcibly than me, 'We can wait here all day, Stephanie. Or you can let us in, so we can all continue with our lives!'

Stephanie's response was of the four-letter word variety, but the door swung open all the same. We ran inside before she changed her mind. When we got to her front door she was waiting for us. But to be honest, I nearly didn't recognize her. Judging by the '*Kurac*' that Katrina whispered, it was the same for her too. Stephanie was thinner than I'd ever seen her before. Almost to the point of being underweight. Her collarbone stuck out and the baggy oversized T-shirt she wore only accentuated her small frame.

'Sorry for barging in unannounced,' I said.

'She did try to call. Many times,' Katrina added.

'Be nice,' I whispered. Katrina's comments earlier about the state of their friendship were not unfounded. I couldn't deny that they'd always had an up-and-down friendship. 90 per cent of the time they were fine, but every now and then they'd clash and a row would erupt. Gran always said that they competed for my attention, but I could never see that. It was ridiculous, because I loved both of them equally. Stephanie walked into her apartment, still without saying a word. As she left the door open behind her, we took it as an invitation to follow her in. Our second shock of the day was seeing how messy everything was. There were dishes in the sink, unwashed mugs of half-drunk coffee on the floor, laundry spilt onto the floor from the couch, books and magazines in piles on every surface available. I caught Katrina's eyes and she mouthed 'She's lost it!'

I was worried. The Stephanie I knew was one of those

annoying people who had a place for everything and everything in its place. I'd watched her once on her hands and knees scrubbing the white kickboards. I mean, who did that?

I sat down beside her at the small dining room table. 'Oh Stephanie, honey, what's wrong? Tell us. Let us help.'

'What do you care?' she spat at me. And I mean, literally spat. I don't think I've ever been so shocked by a reaction in my life. It was as if she hated me.

'Of course we care!' I protested, wiping a little bit of spittle from my cheek. I leaned in to grab her hand, but she pushed me away as if my touch stung her.

Katrina joined us at the table and with more tenderness than I'd ever heard in her voice before, said, 'Whatever is wrong, we are here to help. We are your friends.' I smiled my gratitude to Katrina. I knew I hadn't imagined their friendship. Stephanie sighed a sigh worth a thousand sighs and then closed her eyes. I looked at Katrina and mouthed, 'Bet it's Jimmy.' It was always Jimmy.

'Is it Jimmy?' Katrina decided to take the bull by the horns.

'What have you heard?' Stephanie cried. Her face paled even further.

'We haven't heard anything. But this . . .' Katrina motioned the chaos in the room around us, '. . . is a hint that you are upset. And if past history is anything to go by, he's been up to his tricks.'

Stephanie picked up a newspaper from the table, then pointed to an advert in the *New York Times*. 'There's no point in hiding this. It's only a matter of time before you find out.' Katrina and I read in silence, and with every word my heart broke a little more for my friend.

### *Rita Gregory engaged to marry Jimmy Del Torio*

*Harry and Connie Gregory of Cypress Lane,
New Haven, Connecticut, announce the
engagement of their daughter, Rita, to Jimmy Del
Torio, son of Carlos and Meghan Del Torio of
Windsor Terrace, Brooklyn, New York.
The future bride graduated from Penn University
in New York with a degree in business studies.
Ms. Gregory works in marketing. The future
bridegroom graduated from St. Joseph High
School, Brooklyn, New York. He is the co-owner
of Del Torio and Molloy Real Estate.
The couple plan to marry in 2021.*

# 17

## *Bea*

### January 2020

*Georges Street, Staten Island, New York*

'He didn't even have the decency to tell me himself. I had to find out about his engagement from my mother. I have never been so humiliated in my life.'

What could we say to this? Jimmy had two-timed Stephanie constantly ever since they began dating in high school. I'd never liked him as a kid. His ability to charm people seemed to get stronger with time, but I'd not forgotten that day he'd showed me his true self when he tried to kill a bird. No matter how many times he broke Stephanie's heart, she always forgave him and took him back. Then two years ago, he'd announced on Facebook that he was in a relationship with a woman called Rita. And we all thought that was the last straw for Stephanie. For a while it did appear that she had reached the end of her Jimmy tether. When she texted us both to tell us about Rita, Katrina and I packed a weekend bag, picked up supplies from Target, then arrived on the doorstep of her uptown apartment. We drank tequila, we ate pizza and Chinese takeaway. We called Jimmy every name under the sun and even had a cleansing ritual where we burned all of his things in Stephanie's metal bin. We set the fire alarm off, which caused a bit of a hullaballoo when the whole building had to be evacuated. But it made her laugh and for a while it looked like we had our Stephanie back. When we left her, she was strong and resolute, ready to start a new chapter in her life. Less than a week later, she messaged us to tell us that Jimmy had called, begging her to meet him for a coffee. Only to chat, she insisted, to give him back his Prince CD collection that she'd borrowed. We knew she would take him back. Damn it to hell, we were right. The problem was, the things that Katrina and I had said about Jimmy could not be taken back. We'd both been honest about how we felt, neither of us holding back on our thoughts. Which basically boiled down to the fact that Jimmy was a class-A arsehole.

After that, Stephanie started to filter her conversations with us. She rarely mentioned Jimmy, and that meant she was hiding a big part of her life from us. Our friendship could not withstand that. When she announced she was moving to the Island, it was the final nail in the deterioration of our friendship. She was embarrassed that she'd taken back someone who treated her so badly. And we were embarrassed for her. That's a whole lot of embarrassment.

'Go on. Say it!' Stephanie shouted at us both. Her anger was distressing to see.

'I'm so sorry,' I said. And I truly was.

'I'm sorry too,' Katrina said.

Stephanie looked thrown by our comments. 'That's not what you both want to say. Go on, just say I told you so, get it out of the way.'

We both kept quiet. There was no joy in being right here.

'I tried to stay away from him. I know you both think I'm weak, but you don't understand what it's like for me. He's got a hold over me. When I see him, it's like he's the magnet and I'm the tin.'

'We know,' I said.

'Don't think I'm unaware how weak and pathetic I am!'

'We never thought that,' I said. But my words sounded thin and transparent. Katrina and I had dozens of conversations where we'd used those very words over the past year.

'Tell us what happened,' Katrina said.

'When he started to date Rita, I meant it when I swore that we were over. I was sick and tired of playing second fiddle to other women. That was a first for him, publicly stating he had another girlfriend. Up until then, he'd said he never wanted to be exclusive with anyone.'

'Jimmy "I don't like labels" Del Torio,' Katrina said. We'd given him that nickname years ago. I couldn't count the amount of times we'd listened to Stephanie complain that once again he refused to tell everyone that they were dating. I held my breath, expecting Stephanie to get annoyed by Katrina's comment. But to my surprise she merely nodded.

'Yep. That's Jimmy to a T. Remember when you guys

moved in with me? We'd be sitting at home, having a drink, eating pizza and I'd have to sit on my hands so I wouldn't open Facebook just to look at him. At them. Together.'

'I remember. Once or twice we had to confiscate your phone. No good ever comes from social media stalking,' I said. I should know that. I'd done enough looking at Dan's Instagram feed for the past few weeks. Today he'd shared a photograph of Central Park, and it felt like a secret message to me. Silly.

'But the pull to break that promise was too strong. I can remember watching myself "like" a photograph of him on Facebook, in a kind of out-of-body experience.'

'Let me guess, a few minutes later he was sliding into your PM's,' Katrina said.

Stephanie nodded. 'I wish I didn't love him. He's ruined my life! But I can't seem to get him out of my system. From that very first day in high school, when he smiled at me, flashing his big, white teeth – whiter than mine – I was bedazzled by them, by him, by the sheer chemistry that fizzed between us. My mam said afterwards that a man with teeth that white couldn't be trusted. She was right. But it was too late for me by that point.'

'We're not fifteen any more, Stephanie,' I said to her. 'You can't keep doing this to yourself. Jimmy is never going to change, you know that. He showed you who he was over ten years ago. I know you kept telling us we didn't know him like you. But honestly, to be so cruel as to get engaged and let you find out like that? When he knows how much you love him. It's unconscionable.'

Stephanie welled up again and we sat in silence for a moment.

'It's not just Jimmy who is a shithead though. I know-ingly kept seeing him, sleeping with him, while watching him on Facebook and Instagram with Rita. What does that make me?'

'So much drama,' Katrina said, shaking her head. 'We need drink.' She walked over to the fridge and rummaged around until she found a bottle of wine. 'No beer, but this will do.' She opened the bottle and poured three glasses, handing one to each of us.

'You can't beat yourself up about this. You have been dating him for a decade and he kept you dangling. This is all on him, as far as I'm concerned,' I pointed out.

'He swore that he was going to leave Rita. He said he wanted me and nobody else.'

'He had his cake and he was eating it. He wanted the best of both worlds. Why would he leave her, when you would have him too?' Katrina said.

'I'm so pathetic. I hate myself. I wish I could . . .'

'Could what?' I asked, the hairs on my arms rising in worry.

'Disappear. I don't want to be me any more.'

Katrina and I looked at each other in alarm. We inched our chairs closer towards her.

'You don't want to be the Stephanie that hurts right now. There's a difference. But you are a kind, funny, lovely person that is loved by so many.'

'Not by Jimmy?' she whispered in a question, almost to herself as much as to us.

'No, not by Jimmy,' Katrina agreed, and I nodded too. Our chairs moved another inch towards her. I put my arms around her tiny frame from one side, then Katrina did the same from the other.

'We love you though,' Katrina said as she brushed a tear away from her face. A big softie at heart, who hid that behind what could be abrasive comments. I felt a sudden rush of love for these two women, my BFF's, *my amigos*.

Stephanie slumped into our arms. It was a physical give and an admission that she needed us. We sat like that for a long time, in a tangled knot of friendship. We cried. We cursed Jimmy and Rita and every man who had ever hurt us. And it was cathartic.

Katrina topped our drinks up and remarked that we'd need to do a booze-run soon, when the bottle emptied.

'I've tequila in the freezer,' Stephanie said.

'That'll do.' Katrina jumped up to get it.

'I've told him so many times that it was over. I'd wallow in my misery, then cave in, late at night, and message him. It was always so idyllic when he came back to me. He was so kind and gentle with me. So passionate. But this time, I know it's over. Even I have my standards and I can't pretend any longer that I'm OK with being his emotional punchbag. It's just . . I don't know how I'll live without him.'

'You made the choice to get into the relationship so you can make the choice to get out of it too,' I said.

'I had an affair with married man,' Katrina announced as she walked back to us.

'Shut the front door!' I said, as Stephanie screamed one of her 'Oh-My-God's.

Katrina smiled, delighted with our shocked reaction. 'I met him at a conference in Boston a year ago, at the bar in the hotel. He was younger than me. I told him he was too young, but he said that while he might be younger, he was also what I would like. He was right because I did like. I liked it when his hand touched my shoulder, sliding down my arm in a gentle caress that promised so much more. I liked it when he said my name, a whisper in my ear. And I liked it when we fell into a hotel room less than an hour after we met and had sex.'

'I think I've read that story in one of my Harlequin romances,' Stephanie said.

'Very funny,' Katrina said.

I could not believe that Katrina had withheld this information from me. We confided in each other, always. I shoved away the thought that this wasn't strictly true any more for me.

We *all* had our secrets.

'I told myself that I hadn't known he was married. But that was a lie. He didn't hide the jewellery that laid a claim on him by another. He never mentioned her and I didn't ask. Not that first night, anyhow. I suppose our affair began like a fantasy and I kept it like that.' She shrugged in her Katrina way. 'I wish I could go back to the beginning. I would still sleep with him. That was inevitable. But I'd leave it at that one time. No expectations, just sex. Pure and simple. Well, maybe not so pure.'

'How long did it go on for?' Stephanie asked.

'About six months. I am ashamed of it. I should not have disrespected his wife. Which is why I do not speak of it. But I'm telling you now, so you can see that I understand how easy it is to get sucked into a situation.'

'Wow,' I said, taking another drink. 'Who knew my two best friends were such harlots?'

They clinked glasses with each other.

'Is it over now?' I asked Katrina.

'I did not like myself when we were together. So yes, it is over.'

'That's how I feel too. I've spent most of the past ten years feeling guilty. I can't keep doing this to myself. Going over and over the past year. I made a mistake, I paid highly for it. And now it's time to draw a line under it.'

We all clinked our glasses to that too.

'It's OK for you,' Stephanie said to me. 'You have Dan. Even though I've only met him once, I could tell he is the perfect man.'

'Before you say any more on that subject, you should know that they broke up,' Katrina said.

'No!' Stephanie was clearly shocked by this news. 'What happened?'

'Do not start the war. She won't talk about it, other than to say it's over,' Katrina said.

I tried to zone out my friends as Katrina told Stephanie how amazing Dan was and how foolish I was to let him go.

'What did he do? Did he turn out to be a cheat too? Is that it?' Stephanie asked.

'What makes you think he was to blame? Maybe it was me. Maybe I realized that I didn't love him any more.'

'And that would be fine if she had not spent weeks moping since then. There are weird things going on with Bea,' Katrina told Stephanie.

'Hey, I'm right here!' I wasn't comfortable with the way the subject was changing from Stephanie's love life to mine.

'You need to tell Stephanie about the time-capsule letters,' Katrina said.

I tried to kick her in an effort to shut her up, but I got the leg of the table instead. Bloody well hurt too.

'Are you talking about those letters from school? I'd forgotten all about them until mine arrived in the post. My letter was basically a love letter stating how much I loved Jesse. You know, from *Full House*.'

'You wanted to move to San Francisco to be near him!' I remembered.

'I should have done that. Maybe then I wouldn't be in this situation.'

'Can I see your letter?' I asked.

'I threw it in the bin. God, do you remember that day? Rudy Giuliani came to the school and we all had to tell him what we'd do if we were mayor for the day. What was in your letter?'

'Mine was full of things about you, Stephie, and our friendship. How we'll always be...'

'BFFs forever,' she finished, giving me a shy-smile. *Progress*.

'Speaking of the letters, Bea's one is magic.' I gave Katrina a look that I hoped she understood meant *Keep your mouth shut*. She responded by sticking her tongue out at me.

'What are you going on about?' Stephanie looked confused.

'Nothing,' I answered quickly.

'It's OK. I'm used to you both having secrets, leaving me out of things. Some things never change.' Stephanie chucked back a shot of tequila, gasping after she'd swallowed it.

'No one is leaving anyone out. But if I tell you, you'll only think I'm crazy.'

'Hey, you haven't judged me for being a fool about Jimmy. Hit me with your worst crazy.'

'You haven't heard what she's got to say yet. You better refill our shot glasses.' Katrina held hers out.

I realized I wanted to tell Stephanie. It felt good to have the gang back together again and I didn't want there to be any secrets between us. 'Do you remember the night of your sixteenth birthday?'

'Of course I remember.'

'I had my first cigarette that night.'

'Did you?' Stephanie asked. 'I don't remember that.'

'I did,' I said firmly.

'Funny, I don't remember you as a smoker in school. Me, I was the proverbial under-the-bleachers smoker.'

'Well I did. I only gave up recently.'

'If you say so.' And then Stephanie and Katrina gave a look to each other that basically conveyed that I was indeed crazier than Joe Exotic, on a good day.

Stephanie had been my last hope to remember that I had been a smoker before the letters arrived. The unravelling thread I'd been trying to hold onto for days began to flutter away from me again.

'What is it?' Stephanie asked, alarm on her face. Now it was me who needed comfort.

'I thought that there was a cover-up. That you were all in on it together.'

'I don't understand,' Stephanie said.

'Welcome to my world,' Katrina replied. 'Wait till she tells you about the messages.'

'Either I'm losing it. Or . . . my letters have magic powers.' I waited until Stephanie stopped giggling when she realized I wasn't joking. Then I told her everything.

From New Year's Eve, up to the last message I'd received this morning. When I'd finished my tale, Stephanie exhaled a long breath, then said to Katrina, 'That is bat-shit crazy.'

'It is too much weirdness for me to deal with on my own. So you cannot disappear again. I need you.'

'There's a sentence I never thought I'd hear you say, Petrovic!' Stephanie said. She refilled our glasses with tequila and we clinked once more.

Then Stephanie held her glass up towards us both in a toast: 'To BFFs and all their weirdness.'

'BFFs and their weirdness,' Katrina said. They both looked at me.

'BFFs and their weirdness and dirty affairs,' I added, sticking my tongue out at them both. And as they happily toasted to that, I felt a little lighter. A problem shared really was a problem halved. Somehow, now I didn't feel so bad. I had two friends who were on my side, despite the obvious crazy town I had found myself in.

'I'm glad you're here. I've kept you away for so long because I couldn't bear to have you judge me,' Stephanie admitted.

'We never judged you. Him, yes. But not you. But we did worry about you. We still do,' I said.

'Promise us that it's over this time, though. Really over?' Katrina asked.

Stephanie nodded, with a look of sorrow on her face that made me want to cry. She loved this man. And I understood what it was like to say goodbye to someone you loved. While it might be the right thing to do, it didn't make it any easier to cope with.

# 18

## Bea

February 2020

*Family Finders Agency, 57th Street, Manhattan*

'You busy?' Katrina asked. She carried on hovering outside my door until I nodded to the chair in front of my desk. We had only one hard and fast rule in the agency: no interrupting when someone's head was down working on a case, unless it was code red.

She sat down and looked at me closely. 'Something else is going on with you. I have not worked out what it is yet. But I will.'

'You don't think the letter stuff is weird enough?'

'No I don't.' Katrina knew me better than anyone else. She was the keeper of all of my secrets. She was also an excellent investigator because she missed nothing. Time to deflect.

'You know everything, oh friend of mine. There've been

no more messages from the letter, so I reckon that's the end of all that nonsense.'

'Just like that?'

'Yes. Just like that.' But there was one problem with my master plan. No matter where I placed the letter, I couldn't stop thinking about its contents, over and over. Last night I'd tossed and turned for hours, my mind bombarded with flashes of highly charged arguments I'd had with Corinne, Dad's ex-girlfriend, when I was a kid. Those moments are the ones that I'm most ashamed of. The things I said and did to her were awful. And for what? Because I was scared that Dad loved her more than me.

'I say piss and shit, Bea. You are hiding something else. The frown is bigger on your face now. More creases. And you are not done with the letter. Do not tell me what you think I want to hear.'

'Jeez, you know how to make a friend feel good,' I said, while simultaneously trying to uncrease my forehead. That was harder than it sounded.

Karl jumped down from her lap and started sniffing my plant pot.

'I swear to God, if he pees over there again . . .'

Katrina ignored me, not giving one hoot about Karl and his habit of cocking his leg whenever the urge hit him. When I suggested that she leave her dog at home when she came to work, it hadn't gone down well. 'Where I go, Karl goes.' The only exception to that was on Fridays, when he stayed at home because of our weekly trip to Cassidy's for karaoke. 'For what it's worth, I think letter is not finished with you. There is more you must look into.'

'Another chicken hunt?' I said.

'Yes. The letter sent you to Stephanie. Maybe it needs to send you to someone else now.'

'Well as it happens, I do keep thinking about Corinne,' I said.

'I liked her. For a teacher, she was OK.'

'I liked her too. But the dating-my-dad bit, not so much. I was such a bitch to her.'

'You were. I think maybe she is your new chicken. But you must forget for now, because we have new client. Olive Spadoni. She looks like she's living on her nerves. My money is on her being a crier. Can you take?'

Katrina hated the criers. 'Send her in. And thank you, Katrina, you're always here for me. I appreciate your concern. But I'm fine.'

'Maybe you fool others with your "I am fine" rubbish. But I see. You have not been fine for weeks now. And I'm not talking about Dan. We will talk soon, before your forehead turns to old lady. Oh, I think you will need these.' She threw some tissues at me, then smirked as she walked out. I didn't mind crying, per se, but it did make my job harder to get to the truth in between all the boohoos.

I stood up to greet the woman who walked in. I guessed she could be anything from forty to mid-fifties. She was dressed in jeans, a sweatshirt and sneakers, so that gave her an air of youth. But there were lines on her face that hinted she'd lived a life. Time to find out exactly what her story was.

'Hello.' I smiled and ushered her in to take the seat opposite mine. 'I'm Bea O'Connor, one of the investigators here at Family Finders Agency. How can I help?'

'Hello.' Her voice was so low, I had to strain to hear her. Her hands shook as she pulled a notebook from her handbag and flipped it open. 'M-m-my-y son suggested that I, erm, write things down. That way, you know, I won't forget. Er, is that OK with you?'

The poor woman was a bag of nerves. I held my own notebook up and waved it at her. 'I think that's a very good plan. I always do the same. How about we start with the easy stuff. What's your name?'

'I can manage that I'm sure. I'm Olive Spadoni.' She smiled hesitantly, but it was a start.

'OK, Olive, how can I help you?'

'I'm looking for my husband. Ted. He's been missing since September 2017. The police have stopped looking for him. They've done all they can, but they came up blank with every line of enquiry they pursued. But how can I just give up? We were married for over fifteen years. I don't know what else to do. So I thought I'd come here. Can you help me?'

'I'd like to try. Can you tell me the details behind his disappearance and we can take it from there.'

The relief on the woman's face gave me pause for a moment. I wondered what Olive had been through over the past couple of years. While I've often thought of my mom as kind of missing, in a way I've always known where she was and what happened to her. Not knowing must be another level of pain. 'You've come to the right place, Olive. We help people find everyone from birth parents to high school sweethearts. We have access to every public record in the US and many countries overseas. And our success rate, while not quite perfect, is not far off it. You're in good hands.'

I waited for the tears that Katrina had predicted, but Olive took a deep breath and visibly pulled herself together. Good for her; she was made of sterner stuff than she looked on first appearance.

'Let's start with the basic facts. I'm going to need to see all of your husband's documents: birth certificate, etc.'

She passed me a bundle of documents and I leafed through them one by one. Birth certificate, driving licence, bank details and a copy of his last mobile phone bill, which was dated August 2017.

'Tell me about the last time you saw Ted . . .'

'Nothing remarkable about it. Another normal autumn day. He left the house a little earlier than usual for his job, I suppose. At half past seven I was still in bed. Half asleep when he leaned in to kiss me goodbye. He always did that, every morning. I didn't even open my eyes as he walked out the door. I kick myself now, for trying to hold on to that last moment of sleep. If I'd looked at him, maybe I'd have noticed he was upset.'

I nodded in sympathy. I could imagine how that haunted her now. 'I take it you don't know what he was wearing that morning.'

'I'm sorry. The police have been through this with me so many times. But his usual attire was slacks, with a shirt and jumper. If he took a bag with him, it must have been one of his gym bags. All our family suitcases were still in the attic.'

It probably didn't matter at this point. It wasn't as if he'd still be wearing the same clothes three years later. 'When did you realize he was missing?'

'That evening. He didn't come home from work at his usual time of half past six. He was an accountant in a big multinational. We started our evening meal without him. That felt strange. We always ate our evening meal together.' She swallowed and then leaned in to me. 'I'm doing this for our son, Teddy. He turns fifteen soon. When I asked him what he wanted for his birthday, he said he wanted his dad to come home. He's asked me for the same thing for Christmas and for his birthdays ever since Ted went missing.'

'That must be difficult. For both of you.' I looked at the photograph in the file that Olive had placed in front of me. A moment captured in happier times, with the three of them standing in front of a lake, their faces brown from the sun. Ted in the middle of Olive and Teddy, an arm slung over their shoulders. The perfect family, wide smiles and eyes bright with happiness. Sometimes the camera *does* lie.

'You make a beautiful family.'

'That was taken the summer before Ted disappeared, on Lake Michigan. We went camping for a few days. I look at that photograph now and try to see hints in his face of anything that might give me a clue as to where he is. But I honestly can't see anything but happiness at what was a lovely day.'

'Sometimes life blindsides us, Olive. There are no hints or warnings.'

'That's for sure. The feeling of uselessness has overwhelmed me, shackled me, I suppose. But I'm sick of crying at home, worrying about the what-ifs and the whys. It's time to be proactive. Be brave. That's why I decided to come here. Maybe you can succeed where the detectives can't. Teddy deserves to have his birthday wish granted.'

I shoved a lump back down my throat for this kid that I'd never met. I knew what it felt like to only want a parent for a gift. How many years had I sat on Santa's knee at the mall and wished for that very same thing, even as I asked out loud for an American Girl doll or a bike. All I wanted was my mom – an impossible wish, even for Santa.

Gently I teased the rest of Ted's story from her. He'd called in sick that morning after he left their home. He'd not seemed ill the previous evening, so this surprised her. His phone went to voicemail. His family members and friends, including the bowling team he played in a league with, all came up blank. Nobody had heard from or seen him. She rang their doctor and the local hospitals. At 10 p.m. she called the police and reported him missing.

From what she'd told me, everything pointed to this man disappearing on purpose. 'Is there any chance that he would choose to go away?' There was no way to sugar-coat that question. I hated asking, but it had to be done.

'I thought we loved each other and our life together.'

Over the years since I got into this business, I discovered that sometimes there are several truths in a marriage. Just because Olive believed hers was fairy-tale happy, didn't mean that Ted felt the same way.

'How far did the NYPD get in their investigation?' I decided to steer the subject to safer ground.

'The NYPD Missing Persons Squad found Ted's car, with his phone inside, parked at the Greyhound bus station at the Port Authority. But the case grew cold after that. It's as if he disappeared off the face of the earth,' Olive said. 'Oh, and I ring all hospitals in the state every

Monday morning. Just to double-check that he hasn't turned up there with amnesia.'

'In my experience, amnesia is rarely the reason that someone is missing. It's the Hollywood answer, but in real life . . .'

Olive smiled at this, but it was one of those smiles that are without any humour. 'I suppose I can't believe that he's left us on purpose. But I don't believe he's dead either. He used to come home from work every day at half past six, and it's the darnedest thing, we still watch for him through the living room window at that time. I can't stop myself. But we can't go on like this. It's taking a toll on Teddy and me. We need to know what happened. So that we can stop looking out that window.'

'I promise you I'll do everything I can to help you move on.'

I double-checked all the information she'd given me and questioned her again on the last conversation she'd had with Ted the evening before he disappeared. There didn't seem to be any red flags in anything she'd shared. Nor did I think she was holding anything back. We went through the financials and Olive signed a contract. As she stood up to leave, I asked her one last question: 'When is your son's birthday?'

'April ninth.'

That was it then. My case had a deadline. 'Let's see if we can make this birthday wish come true for him.'

I respected and understood that Olive didn't want to hide from the truth any more. There was a lesson in that. I was driving myself crazy trying to ignore the letter one minute then scanning every word closely the next. I needed to make a decision and own it. Either I threw the letter into the trash, like Stephanie had done with hers, or I embraced it in all its weirdness. If my life had taken a turn into Marty McFly town, then I needed to know that. I thought of Corinne and Ryan, my dad, as a couple. And knew that because I wanted the impossible then – my mom and dad to be together – I had made it my business to make life difficult for them both. A visit to Corinne Dryden, Dad's ex-girlfriend, was long overdue.

# 19

## Lucy

### August 1992

*Times Square, Manhattan*

We'd watched a lot of romantic comedies as teenagers and young adults. *When Harry Met Sally*, *Pretty in Pink*, *Moonstruck*, *Mannequin*. We loved them all. And as we cheered on the various couples to their inevitable happy-ever-after, I'd dream about finding a guy like the ones we saw on the big screen. Ever since Ryan bought me that cheesecake in Junior's, I felt like I was the leading lady in my very own movie.

I called Ryan later that evening. He answered the phone after one ring and shouted with delight when I said hello. His obvious delight that I rang was infectious and I found myself giggling like a twelve-year-old. We arranged to go out the next evening. He arrived to collect me from our apartment on time, to the minute. He came in and didn't flinch when Maeve interrogated him, insisting she had to make sure he wasn't a bad hombre.

'Bad hombre?' Ryan asked, looking more than a little puzzled.

'I'll tell you later,' I said. 'That's enough, Maeve. I haven't put all your dates through this much! Fair is fair.'

'That's different. I can take care of myself.' Then she turned to Ryan and all signs of merriment were gone, replaced with her very best stern face. 'Lucy is special. You need to take very good care of her. Or you'll have me to answer to. I can't have a bad hombre hurt my sister.'

My respect for Ryan grew when he responded, with appropriate earnestness, 'I give you my word.'

'That's good enough for me. Go. Have fun.'

'You look like your sister,' Ryan said as we walked towards the subway.

'I hear that a lot. There's only ten months between us. Irish twins, as the saying goes.'

'So the two of you are close?'

'Extremely. I don't have any memories that don't include her.'

'What's the bad hombre thing about?'

'From the movie, *The Three Amigos*. We're slightly obsessed with it.'

'I'll have to check it out.'

'Where are we going?'

Ryan's face broke into a grin. 'I knew I had to pull out the big guns for you. I want tonight to be perfect. So I've got tickets for a show on Broadway! I noticed you looking at the billboard signs when we were in Times Square.'

I felt like Vivian in *Pretty Woman*, on her way to the opera. That was until I found out that the show was *Cats*.

I hated cats. I had a phobia of them. It started when I was about four or five and my cousin Huey threw one at me. It landed on my head and scratched my face as it tried to claw its way to the ground. I never got over that. I didn't want to say anything to Ryan because he'd obviously gone to a lot of trouble and expense to get the tickets. But all the same he noticed that I wasn't enjoying myself. At the interval, when he pushed me, I confessed that the cast dressed as cats were freaking me out. Despite roaring with laughter, he grabbed my hand and we left. Just like that. No drama. No recriminations or disappointment.

We walked to the View Lounge, a rooftop bar in the Marriott Times Square. Ryan had a beer and I ordered a cocktail called Top of the View. And with the most spectacular of views, we chatted with so much ease, it was as if we'd known each other our entire lives rather than a few hours. Ryan told me about his book, and his obvious passion for his work was lovely to see.

'My parents own a bar at home. Nellie's,' I said.

'What's it like?'

'If you could think of the complete opposite of this.' I waved my arm around the chic surroundings, with huge glass windows. 'That's our Nellie's. It's a family-run business, been in the Mernagh family for generations. Nellie was my grandmother. We've got open fires, a long bar in the lounge and a smaller snug for the locals who just want to drink and not be social. I miss it.'

'I've got an idea. Fancy coming to my local? It might

be a little nearer to Nellie's than this. But I have to warn you, some of my family might be there.'

'I'd like that a lot.' And even though I suppose I should have been nervous at the thought of meeting his people, I wasn't. It felt right. As we walked across the street towards the subway, he reached down for my hand, and that felt right too. My hand seemed to fit inside of his, like the last piece of jigsaw sliding into place.

He told me about Farrell's on the journey. How his parents went there most weekend nights, and how they never missed a Sunday evening. Because that's when the Irish papers arrived, flown in on an Aer Lingus flight. Along with their Irish friends who lived in the neighbour-hood, they all congregated to catch up on the news at home as a group. They'd swap gossip they'd learned during the week, from phone calls or letters. They discussed Irish politics and sport. The pub played all the Irish GAA games too, hurling and Gaelic football. Ryan told me that by the time he was thirteen, both he and his brother Mike were regulars, sitting in the young 'uns corner, drinking sodas.

As soon as we walked into the bar and heard people laughing and chatting, I knew I'd found somewhere I could relax in. It wasn't Nellie's, but Ryan was right, it was a hell of a lot closer to it than the stylish The View. We made our way to the bar and he ordered two beers, which were poured into large styrofoam cups. That was a first for me, but I learned that these cups had been a tradition in Farrell's for decades. His brother Mike spied us fairly quickly and came over, curious to meet me. I liked him. He was one of those men who had no sides to him. You got what you saw.

'You must be pretty special,' he shouted into my ear. 'Ryan has never brought anyone to Farrell's. Ever.'

I looked at Ryan in surprise. And dared to hope that maybe I *was* pretty special.

'What did Dad say to us, when we started to date?' Mike put on a thick Irish accent and said, 'Don't shit on your own doorstep lad.'

Ryan looked a bit worried, but I thought it was hilarious.

I had a great chat with Eddie the owner too and we swapped landlord horror stories. He promised he'd call in to Nellie's next time he was in Ireland and down Wexford way.

By the time I left the pub, I was in deep. And he hadn't even kissed me. Ryan called a cab for me, and insisted he accompany me back to my apartment.

'Can I see you tomorrow?'

'I'm working the lunchtime shift.'

'We could do breakfast. Have you been to Pershing's yet?'

'No. Sorry, should I have?'

'Yes! It's a New York institution. Meet me at Grand Central Station at 8 a.m. The restaurant is opposite the clock. We can have a few hours together before you need to get ready for work. OK?'

'It's a date.' Then we both grinned, charmed with ourselves and each other. Eventually I had no choice but to go inside my apartment. I think I might have floated in. I was glad that Maeve wasn't there because I didn't want to talk about the date yet. I wanted to savour and keep it all to myself. I fell asleep thinking about Ryan and when I awoke the next morning, he was my first thought. And when I realized I wasn't in Ireland any more, unlike the other mornings, I smiled. I was in New York and I understood why so many fell in love with this wonderful, vibrant city. Last night, I'd developed a mighty big crush on it myself.

When I got to Pershing's, he was waiting for me. And we did another moment of staring at each other, with cheesy grins. I thought he was going to kiss me hello, but then he kind of steered himself backwards again. There was a short wait for a table, but I loved watching the Manhattanites rushing in and out, picking up coffees and bagels from the takeaway area. Always rushing. The speed that people moved in New York still surprised and worried me slightly. Our server led us to our table, in the centre of the restaurant, which was another architectural gem. No Fifties diner, this place. It was elegant and very grown-up. I looked at Ryan and tried to work out if he got lucky by choosing a restaurant that was so me, or was it possible that he actually got me?

'So what do you recommend?' I asked, looking through the menu.

'Pancakes. Or the omelettes.'

'My mam makes omelettes for dinner every Friday night. With chips on the side. That's French fries to you!'

'Hey, I know what chips are,' Ryan said. 'I grew up in an Irish home, remember. One of my mam's pet peeves is the wrong use of crisps or chips on a menu. Over thirty years here and she still calls the trash, rubbish and our sneakers, runners. As she says, what do you do when you put your runners on. You run!'

'I think I'd like your mam. She sounds fun.'

'She is. But she's no pushover either. Surrounded by

men, as she says, she has to be tough to keep us all under control.'

'Yesterday I was in JCPenneys. It was so cold, I needed to get some warmer clothes. Anyhow, I asked a member of staff where the jumpers were. And the look she gave me! 'Jumper! There's a jumper? Where?' she screamed as she looked out to the window. Took me ages to persuade her that there wasn't anyone suicidal and all I wanted was to buy a sweater!'

We both laughed and it was easy, fun. 'Don't get Mam started on the whole footpath versus sidewalk debate. That drives her mad.'

Our food arrived and the stack of blueberry pancakes Ryan had recommended was delicious. We tucked into our food in a happy silence, and I was glad that he wasn't one of those types who felt the need to chatter all the time.

'I got a letter yesterday,' he announced suddenly. 'I've been accepted into the New York Police Academy.'

'Wow,' I said. 'Sorry. That was a bit uncool. But it does sound a bit wow to me. Is it a big deal?'

'My parents are delighted. Mike is too. He's already in the NYPD.'

'What's involved? Was it hard to get in?'

'I had to do a written exam. There was also medical and psychological screening. Lots of paperwork to submit. They ran a background check and I had a formal interview. It took a while and, to be honest, I didn't think I had a chance in hell of being accepted.'

'So this is a celebration breakfast,' I said. He smiled, but this time it didn't reach his eyes. Somehow he didn't seem very enthusiastic about it.

'How long does the training last?'

'Six months. The training bureau is here in Manhattan, so good enough for me. I can commute from home every day. That's handy.'

'Can I ask you something?'

'Yeah, sure.'

'Do you want to be a cop?'

'Why do you ask that?'

'It's just, when you talk about writing and your books, your whole body lights up. You don't seem as buzzed about this career move.'

'You don't miss much,' he acknowledged. 'My parents want me to do this. They've been pushing me to apply for the academy for years. Dad says I need to start a career.'

I wanted to say a lot more to him, but I also knew that I barely knew him. It wasn't my place to give him career advice. Who was to say that becoming a cop wasn't the right move for him?

When we finished our meal, Ryan asked, 'Have you been in Grand Central Station?'

'Course.'

'But I bet you've not really seen it. There's a lot more to this place than a train station.'

When we walked into the centre of the concourse, he said, 'I like it here at this time. It's quiet. In another twenty minutes, you won't be able to move with all the commuters. I often come in here for a coffee while I wait for the library to open.'

'It looks different when it's empty,' I admitted, looking around the room. In fact it looked almost like a church in this light, with large windows shooting early morning sun onto the floor.

'Look up,' Ryan said, touching my arm to stop me.

The ceiling was the most magnificent I'd ever seen. It took my breath away. 'That's absolutely stunning. I can't believe I never noticed it when I was in here before!'

'Here's a little bit of useless trivia for you. Jackie O helped save this place, when they wanted to knock it down in the Seventies. She had to go to the Supreme Court to make sure it didn't fall prey to a wrecking ball.'

'What a travesty that would have been.'

When I looked back down, he was watching me and our eyes met. For a brief second we were the only two people in the world, as commuters faded to ghosts around us. Ryan felt it too, I could see it in his eyes. We were both moving together towards an inevitable moment, the agony and the ecstasy was waiting to know when.

Ryan pointed to the clock that sat on top of the information kiosk. 'That has four faces and it's worth about twenty million dollars. And the clock on the facade outside is a Tiffany one.'

'It's a hidden gem, isn't it? We've walked by here loads of times, but I always assumed it was another boring train station.'

'I know! And it's got a few secrets up its sleeve.' He grabbed my hand and we ran through a passageway towards the food court. 'This domed area is pretty special. Stand here and put your ear to the wall.' I made a face, sure he was making fun of me, but he insisted that I should trust him. He ran across to the opposite corner of the vaulted archway and leaned into the wall too, so I placed my cheek against the cold marble.

Then I heard a whisper. It was Ryan's voice. And

somehow, it was in my ear, whispering my name over and over. 'Lucy. Lucy. Lucy.'

I looked across at him in shock and he laughed, shouting across to me, 'This is the Whispering Gallery. Some crazy acoustic stuff going on, but it means you can communicate in whispers from one side to the other. Go on, try it. Whisper into the wall!'

With all the wonder of a child, I leaned in and whispered, 'You are full of surprises, Ryan O'Connor.'

His whisper came back almost immediately, 'I would like to surprise you every day, if you'll let me.'

I looked over to him, but his face was still leaned into the wall, waiting for my response. 'I don't think you should accept the NYPD offer. I know I have no right to say this to you. I know it's none of my business. But I have this instinct that it's the wrong move for you. That if you take that job, you'll never finish your novel and find out what that agent thinks.' I finished my long whisper, breathless and also embarrassed. There was silence from him. I didn't dare look at him. I'd spoken out of line. I should have kept my opinion to myself.

'What if the agent doesn't like my book?' his whisper came back.

'I don't think that's the question you need to ask. What if the agent *does* like it?'

His sigh transferred across the magical dome and caressed my cheek.

'I think that, somehow, you know me better than any other person alive and I've only just met you. I've not even kissed you yet.'

I felt heat travel through every part of my body and I moved away from the wall, towards the centre of the dome. As Ryan came towards me, I felt the hairs on my arms rise in attention to the possibilities of the question. It was as if the earth was shifting on its axis and it thrilled me. It was time for the inevitable.

'Can I kiss you, Lucy Mernagh?'

My answer was a sigh, but he understood it and in a second I was in his arms. He kissed me, a kiss worthy of every romantic comedy I'd ever dreamed I could be part of. And I knew that there would never be another man for me.

I was his and he was mine.

# 20

## Lucy

### September 1992

*Innisfree, Prospect Avenue, Brooklyn, New York*

An invite to Innisfree came within a week of our first date. Mike had told their parents about me and they insisted I visit. His mam, Peggy, had received phone calls all week, following my evening in Farrell's. She was disgusted that most of her friends had met me before she had. I begged Maeve to come with me. But she had a date with a Dutch guy called Eric who lived in the apartment next door to us. He'd been watching her with puppy eyes ever since we moved in last month. I felt sorry for him, because I knew she wasn't really interested in him. Every time he bumped into her, which I reckon he orchestrated with intent, he begged for a date. And every time she laughed, flicked her long, shiny hair and said no. Until she found out that he worked for a talent agency. This was serendipity for him because Maeve had decided a week previously that she wanted to be an actress. It was a fad. Like the time she wanted to be a pop star. We'd queued for hours so that she could audition for a TV show in Dublin. Only for her to be knocked back because of the not so little issue that she was, like me, without a note in her head. Maeve was one of those people who took notions and couldn't be dissuaded from them, until the next notion hit. So it was exit stage left for Toby and enter stage right for Eric.

'Imagine the possibilities,' she'd told me, when I expressed surprise at the news.

'I can't. Enlighten me.'

'Well, he must get to all the cool parties. And you never know who I'll get to meet there.'

'Please be nice to Eric. I think he really likes you.'

'I'm always nice,' Maeve said, and I couldn't help but laugh. She was incorrigible.

I changed my clothes three times before I settled on my denim pinafore, with a short-sleeved white T-shirt underneath. Ryan must have been watching out for me, because he was at the front door before I was halfway up the short path to Innisfree.

'Your home is beautiful,' I said. It looked so different to any home I'd ever been in before. A three-storey brown-stone with beautiful bay windows in the front. I thought about our cottage at home, with the low ceilings and small, odd-shaped rooms, which I'd always considered beautiful too. They were so different it was impossible to compare them.

'Never mind our house, you're beautiful,' Ryan said, then gave me a quick kiss.

I flushed again and wondered when I'd stop feeling like a teenager in his company.

'Everyone is in here.' He led me into a large open-plan sitting room. It had high ceilings edged by intricate coving, and was filled with well-worn and lived-in furniture, which to me made the room picture-perfect.

His mam was tiny, one of those women who made you feel awkward standing by them. She was no more than five feet and from a distance looked much younger than her years. She wore her long hair in a loose bun; coupled with her jeans and sweatshirt, she could have passed for a woman half her age. It was only as I got closer to shake her hand that I noticed the fine lines around her eyes and mouth. Ryan was like his dad. Tall and lean, with the same eyes and smile.

'You're very welcome to Innisfree, Lucy. I'm Joe. And this is Peggy.'

'Thank you for having me. I got you something.' I handed a gift bag to Peggy. I'd called to The Butcher's Block earlier that morning as I decided an Irish care package might be a nice gift. The Butcher's Block was a supermarket in Sunnyside, Queens, and a mainstay for every Irish immigrant living in the locale. They stocked everything from Kimberley Mikados to Batchelors baked beans.

Peggy opened the bag and whooped, holding up one of the items in the bag like a trophy. 'Kerrygold butter!'

'Well, you might as well have given her a bar of gold!' Ryan said. 'Kerrygold butter was and has always been a special treat here. We didn't get it every day growing up, because it's expensive, but on special occasions we looked forward to it.'

'Peggy is making colcannon and ham for dinner today. And I know what I'll be doing with that butter. A great big knob is going on top of the mash,' Joe said.

'The ham is glazed, ready to go into the oven. I better get on with it if we're to eat in an hour.'

'No better cook than my Peggy,' Joe said with pride.

'I miss my mam's dinners. I don't think I paid enough attention to her over the years. I'm afraid I've never quite mastered her knack at cooking, so this will be a treat for me.'

'Irish grub was the thing I missed most from home when I first got here. But then I met Peggy and that saved the day,' Joe said.

'Last week, I paid four dollars for a packet of Knorr meal maker because I had a goo on me for my mother's shepherd's pie. She always makes it with one of them,' I said.

'Sometimes when homesickness takes over every part of you, a taste from home is the only medicine needed,' Peggy said, patting my hand. 'If you ever want anything that your mam cooked for you, tell me and I'll do my best to recreate it.'

And I could see that her offer was genuine. Right now, in this house with the O'Connor family, I felt the closest to being at home since I'd arrived in the USA. She examined the rest of the items from the gift bag. 'And Cadbury's chocolate, Brennan's bread, Barry's tea! Ah, love, that's very good of you.'

'I thought you might like them more than a bunch of flowers.'

'You thought right. Joe, get our guest a drink. I'll have a glass of wine. I'll be out in a minute, once I've got the dinner sorted.'

'Can I help?' I offered.

'Not at all. But the offer is appreciated.'

We took a seat on the sofa that was as comfortable as it looked. 'Is that an original fireplace?' I asked.

'It is. I know it's more fashionable to have central heating with radiators, but you can't beat watching the flames flicker and ebb,' Joe said.

Mike walked in, wearing his uniform. 'Yo!' he called out to me.

'Hi, Mike.'

'What time are you on at?' Peggy called from the kitchen. 'Dinner will be ready in forty mins or so. Ryan's Lucy brought Kerrygold with her.'

'That's lit! I've got time for dinner.'

I felt ridiculously happy at being called Ryan's Lucy, and curious at how excited Mike was about Irish butter. 'I get why your parents miss certain foods from home. I do myself. But how come you guys crave it so much, when you were both born here in New York? I thought you'd be all peanut butter and jelly sambos, or pancakes with an extra side of pancake.'

'Ha! I'm partial to a good PB&J. But while we might not have been born in Ireland, we all grew up Irish,' Ryan said.

Joe handed me a glass of wine, then Peggy joined us. 'How are you enjoying living in Woodside?'

'I found it difficult to adjust at first. Everything is so different to where I'm from. Things move at a different speed there. It's taken me a while to catch up. My sister, Maeve, she's settled in quicker than me.'

'It gets easier. The first year was the hardest, but when you find your own, meet like-minded people, then it kinda falls into place,' Joe said. His accent had a strong hint of Irish, dancing with the New York twang. I wondered if that was how I'd sound in a few more years.

'My eyes were on stalks when I arrived, but for you back then, it must have felt like a whole new world,' I said.

'Don't get him started. Dad loves telling his immigration story,' Ryan warned.

'I'd love to hear it.' I meant it. I settled back further into my seat, sipping my white wine.

'I left home in 1955. And while I hated saying goodbye to my parents and brothers, I couldn't wait to leave. There was nothing for me in Ireland but hardship. And sure, we Irish know how to leave when there's an economic crisis. It's in our DNA. I had sixty dollars in my back pocket and very little else. But I was lucky. I had somewhere to go. There's a saying that New York was built by the Irish. Well, my Uncle Richard, who gave me this house, was part of that. He left Ireland in the Twenties, made a few bob working as a sandhog in construction. But he never got married.'

'He was a good man and would have been a good father, if he'd had kids,' Peggy added.

'He would. A lot of my childhood memories are dust now, but I have a vivid one that's never lost colour. Uncle Richard came home to Ireland to visit my gran, who was dying. A few hours after he walked into her small bedroom to say hello, she said goodbye to us all. Uncle Richard looked so handsome, all dickied up in a fancy grey three-piece suit. Half his suitcase was full of candy and Hershey's kisses. We'd never tasted anything like those treats back then. When he was leaving, hot tears burnt my eyes. I'd not cried when my gran died, but it was all I could do not to start sobbing when he shook my hand goodbye. I asked him to take me back with him. He laughed and said, "You can't leave your mam. She'd kill me!" But he never forgot my request, and when I was eighteen he wrote to Mam, enclosing the money for my boat fare. It would have taken me half a lifetime to save that sum up. Richard wanted someone to take care of him in his old age. He'd bought Innisfree and he was lonely here. He made it clear that he'd leave his house to me when he died, if I took the chance of a lifetime and came over.'

'I can't imagine what that must have been like for your parents, watching you leave,' Lucy said, thinking of her own parents standing in Dublin airport, her mother clutching a bottle of holy water, her dad clutching her mam.

'It was a different time. They understood. Dad told me to pack my things and never look back. He hadn't been working for nearly a decade. And I had no fear in those days. I was all spit and muscle and thought I could take on the world. Mind you, two days into the journey and I didn't feel so invincible. No aeroplanes back then, just the boat to Ellis Island.'

'I never got seasick once,' Peggy said. 'But I've always had a stronger stomach than Joe.' When they smiled at each other, I could see a lifetime of love pass between them. I felt Ryan's eyes on me and I wondered if he was wishing for a lifetime of love with me, as I was with him. My face burned at the thought.

'Did you meet on the boat?' I asked.

'No, Joe was in New York for over a year before I arrived. My cousin Colm was living in Brooklyn and promised to send the fare to me once he had it saved. I could have gone to London, but once I saw *Rebel Without a Cause*, I thought I'd have a better chance at meeting a James Dean over here than I could in England!'

We all laughed as Joe brushed his white hair back into a quiff and pouted.

'Some rebel,' Peggy said.

'Tell Lucy how you met,' Ryan said. 'Serendipity throughout this story.'

'Lucy doesn't want to be listening to that . . .' Peggy protested.

But I quickly told her that yes, I did want to hear. The more time I spent with this family, the more charmed I was.

'Colm sent the fare over, earlier than we anticipated, because a friend of his loaned him the money. I was to join Colm at his boarding house in Brooklyn, which was run by a Cork woman. Anyhow, there were no phones back then – your generation have it much easier than we did. All I had was a scribbled address in a small notebook. Colm couldn't take time off work to meet me off the boat. But I figured if I managed to cross the Atlantic on my own, I could make my way to Brooklyn too.'

'Was the boat journey awful for you?' I asked.

'Boring. Grey. Wet. But it suited my mood. I spent most of the passage lying in bed, reading, trying not to cry as I thought about my mam and dad at home. My last image of them was pierced into my brain, and I kept hitting play on it, over and over. Her wringing her apron, a blue one, in her hand. Him in his work boots, crying. I'd never seen my dad cry before.'

Joe reached over and held his wife's hand as her eyes

filled with tears. She looked at me and said, 'I never saw my dad again. He died before I got home ten years later.'

The room quietened as the depth of her loss filled us all.

'The impact of bereavement, on those who leave and those who are left behind, is hard to understand, unless you've been through it,' Ryan said. 'There's an emptiness that can never be filled. No matter how many cups of Barry's tea you pour into it.'

'You always had a way with words. That's why I'm glad you've decided to follow your dream to be an author.'

'Yeah, you'd make a crap cop, in fairness,' Mike agreed.

'I believe you've helped him make that decision,' Peggy said to me. 'Thank you.'

I flushed again, amazed that I'd had such an impact.

'Now where were we? That's right, I got the subway to Brooklyn. Got off at 15th Street as Colm told me to do, in his letter. But I got horribly lost when I stepped out onto the street. I ended up at the entrance to the park, and Colm hadn't mentioned that. I walked back up the street towards the subway again and couldn't work out whether to go right or left. I thought to myself, what would my dad do? I could hear his voice in my head saying, You've got a voice, you've got two good feet, now go find someone and ask them for directions. And that's when I saw Farrell's pub opposite. It had an Irish shamrock in the window. So I went in.'

Joe jumped in again, their double act perfectly in sync. 'What Peggy didn't know was that Farrell's was a male-only pub back then. For decades women weren't allowed in the bar, unless they were chaperoned. Women sat at a table at the back, and their date would order a drink for them.'

I made a loud tutting noise to let him know how much this annoyed me.

'I know, I know. But it was a different time, Lucy. Anyhow, back to the story: Peggy walked up to the bar, and asked for a glass of water.'

'I had very little money and, to be honest, I didn't understand the currency. But I was thirsty and tired.'

'I looked up and saw Peggy standing there, pretty as a picture in a green woollen coat with a brown hat perched precariously over her red curls. She had two big, battered brown suitcases, one in each hand – they were almost the size of her. Lacey, a Donegal man, pissed as a fart, shouted at her to get out. He was outraged at her audacity, asking for a drink. I shouted at him to hold his whisht. I could tell she was fresh off the boat. We'd all been there at some point.'

Peggy continued, 'Farrell himself was behind the bar and, without a word, he poured a glass of water into one of his styrofoam containers. I could feel the whole pub's eyes on me as I drank it. But as strange as it might sound, this pub comforted me. It looked like home with its hammered tin roof and Guinness on tap. Then this handsome man sitting at the bar asked me, with great kindness, if I was lost. I couldn't believe it when I heard his voice. He was a Wexford man. You can't mistake the accent. The first person to speak to me in New York and it was someone from home. I never felt so relieved in my life. I told him I was looking for my cousin Colm Long and then he started to laugh.'

'I said to her, you're Colm's little cousin Peggy!' Joe said.

'I was gobsmacked.' Both were now wearing matching

smiles. 'And then I found out that it was Joe who lent Colm the money for my boat fare.'

'I walked Peggy to her boarding house, of course. And stayed with her until Colm got home that evening. When I went home that night I knew that I'd marry Peggy one day. As sure as I was standing, I knew it.'

'You got a bargain, Joe O'Connor. A bride for the price of a boat fare,' Peggy replied.

'I sure did, my love. I'd gladly pay it every day for the rest of my life. And it would still be a bargain,' Joe agreed.

I turned to Ryan and said, 'You couldn't write that!'

'I did as it happens,' Ryan said, 'The only thing I've had published was a short story about how these two met. The *Irish Echo* paid me twenty dollars for that story. Mam and Dad have the story framed and hung on their kitchen wall!'

'Tell Lucy about Shirley MacLaine,' Mike said.

'I love that movie *Steel Magnolias*,' I said.

'Well, would you believe that I've met her! It must have been mid-Seventies, because the kids were small and we had left them with a sitter. It was my birthday, I was sitting at the table for the women, Joe was at the bar, ordering a drink for us both, when in walks Shirley MacLaine.'

'She was a beauty,' Joe said. 'Very glamorous. And she had something about her. A steel in her that made you think that you couldn't or shouldn't mess with Shirley.'

'What was she doing in Farrell's?' I asked, trying to work out why any Hollywood actress would stop by a small Irish pub in Brooklyn.

'She had a friend from the neighbourhood. Well, she decided she wanted to order her own drink, so she sashayed her way up to the bar and placed her order!'

'Everyone was in a tizzy. The whole place scandalized and delighted all at once,' Peggy said.

'The bartenders were a bit star-struck. But they served her. Shirley became the first unchaperoned woman to take the honour of being served at the bar. Or so the story goes,' Joe said.

'Well, sorry, Shirley, but I got there first! OK, it was only water, but I was still served unchaperoned over a decade before!'

'Go Peggy!' I shouted and everyone cheered along. 'I love hearing stories like this,' I whispered to Ryan. 'Your family are really, really great. Thanks for inviting me.'

He looked at me so intently, I felt warm inside, as if a milestone had been passed for us. 'I knew they'd love you as much as I do.'

'Your parents were meant to be, weren't they?' I said.

'We're meant to be too, Lucy Mernagh,' Ryan whispered to me. 'Like Dad said, I know that as sure as I'm standing here.'

'Sitting,' I said, breathless with emotion.

'That too,' he replied, and even though everyone was watching us, he kissed me.

# 21

## *Bea*

### May 2000

*Innisfree, Prospect Avenue, Brooklyn, New York*

I was eight years old when I noticed that when Dad bought a new shirt, it meant a new woman was on the scene. They never lasted though. He'd ditch his shirts and go back to his tee-and-jeans combo. Gran complained regularly that she never got to meet any of his girlfriends. Dad would say, when someone is special enough to bring home, I'll bring her. Every now and then, even though the dates never made it as far as Innisfree, I'd get to meet them. Dad would take me to the park by the swings, or maybe to the cinema. And then he'd feign surprise that he bumped into his 'friend'. I never minded those dates, because usually they meant I was spoiled with treats. Both Dad and his date had a vested interest in my approval. I milked the situation, with extra cream and sprinkles on top too. And even though I knew nothing about romantic love, I could tell that the woman was always way more into Dad than he was into her. And if I'm honest, that's how I liked it. I was Dad's most important person. I didn't want that to change for anyone.

I was nine when Corinne Dryden changed from being my teacher to my potential stepmom. It started when our class did a series of bring-your-parent-to-school days. I was so proud to bring Dad in. The only kid in school who had a parent who was an author. And he'd become a *New York Times* bestseller with his fourth book by that stage, so he was a little bit famous too. Ms Dryden was so impressed with his talk that she asked him to help out with the school's creative writing group. She was worried that St. Joseph's was too heavily invested in its football and basketball teams and there wasn't enough emphasis on the children who lived in their imaginations. Dad had been asked to do talks like this before and he would always say no, he was too busy. But he didn't hesitate to say yes when Ms Dryden asked. I noticed a change in him almost immediately. He took to whistling as he moved around the house. Sometimes at dinner he had this goofy look on his face. He dropped her name into conversation whenever he could. We'd be eating toast for breakfast and he'd say, 'Corinne said we should try this bakery on the corner of 51st and 4th.' I'd relay everything he said to Katrina and Stephanie and we'd analyse the comments.

'They are having the sex,' Katrina said. We'd gasped at this, because back then we weren't really sure what sex was, but we knew it involved nakedness and kissing. The thought of my dad being naked with anyone made me want to vomit. About a month after the talks began, he sat me down to tell me that they had started to date. It shouldn't have been a shock or a surprise. But it was. And I didn't like it. I felt a shadow of foreboding, and even though I knew there was no reason to feel so threatened, I did. Self-absorbed as I was, I think I knew that this was different to any other relationship he'd had.

Then one day, I came home from Stephanie's where I'd spent the day watching *Full House* episodes back to back, and I found Corinne in our kitchen chatting to Gran and Grandad. Dad was clearly delighted with himself, standing beside Corinne with the same goofy expression. To my shame, I'd shouted, 'What's she doing here?' Then I ran to Katrina's house next door to complain.

Dad was patient and kind, telling me he understood that I needed time to get used to the transition of Ms Dryden being not just my teacher, but also his special friend. He was adamant that I had to get used to it all the same. He told me that he was in love with her. All of a sudden, she was in Innisfree every single day.

Things began to change far too quickly for my liking. She began to stay overnight at weekends. And that brought change. I didn't like change. She suggested that we switch our normal Saturday-morning pancake breakfasts to egg-white omelettes. And to my horror, Gran agreed with her. I'd begun to watch *Law & Order* with Dad by this stage too. But whenever Corinne was with us, we seemed to watch a lot of the TLC channel.

I hated to admit it, but it wasn't all bad. Corinne was fun. Like one Friday afternoon she suggested we try to make a chain of Lego that ran all the way around Innisfree. We clicked in pieces, one by one, for hours. We didn't stop for dinner; Gran gave us burgers that we ate cross-legged beside the stairway. When we ran out of Lego before we reached my bedroom, Corinne ran next door to the Petrovics's and persuaded them to give her their box of Lego. I think that was one of the most fun nights I'd ever had as a kid. Grandad got his camera out to take a photograph of me putting in the last piece. And I called Corinne to get in the photo too, alongside Dad and me.

I'm not sure when I got used to our new normal, but one day it didn't bother me to see Corinne sitting at the kitchen table. And I began to look forward to watching TLC with her. And there were other benefits too. I now had an inside track to solving algebra problems. The O'Connor brain did not do well with hypotheses, Grandad always said. Corinne helped me, but never made it seem like it was work. And then she talked Dad down on more than one occasion when he was too overprotective, letting me take some steps of independence, tentatively. Katrina, Stephanie and I wanted to get the subway to the Rockefeller Center to see *The Today Show* being filmed. We'd heard that NSYNC were due to be there. Dad said no; he always said no. Gran was no use, throwing holy water at me whenever I asked to go anywhere outside of Brooklyn. But Corinne stepped in and suggested that it was time to give me some freedom. And she talked Dad around. NSYNC never did turn up but we three did end up on TV, in the background of several shots. Things were good and I thought we could continue in this vein. But life wasn't like that. Life moved on and demanded that we all move with it.

The problems began the night Corinne joined us in Mario's, for our annual anniversary dinner for Mom. And maybe if Dad had spoken to me about it, rather than springing her on me, I would have taken it better. But instead, one minute it was Dad and me, the next she was slipping in beside Dad in our booth. And it wasn't only me who was surprised. I could see Mario was taken aback too. The meals in Mario's were supposed to be for the two of us. We never asked Gran or Grandad. Uncle Mike once hinted he'd like to come, but Dad knocked that on the head immediately. For the first time that I'd sat in our booth, I felt awkward and uncomfortable. When Mario took our order, Corinne said meatloaf gave her indigestion. Dad shushed me when I protested her choice of a green salad with grilled chicken. I mean, that was completely against the whole ethos of our evening. My surprise changed to hurt then. He could see it, but avoided eye contact with me. Then when it came to dessert, she skipped our usual sundaes too. She said she wanted coffee and somehow her tone made Dad and me feel guilty. My shock and hurt then stepped aside to make way for outrage. It flew over me like a tsunami and drowned out every other emotion. If Dad noticed, he decided not to do anything about it. Instead he held her hand, on the night that was supposed to be in honour of my mom. I had to get up to go to the restroom to stop myself from throwing cola over the two of them. As I passed him, Mario pulled me to one side.

'It's good to see your dad happy, no?'

'No.'

'It's not good?'

'I'm mortified for him. Look!' I pointed towards them, where they were nose to nose, giggling like a couple of teenagers.

'Give him a break, Bella Bea. He's been on his own for so long. Can you let him off this once?'

I shrugged. I wasn't sure I could, so I wasn't going to promise anything.

'It's tough being a parent. You'll find that out one day. But isn't it true that your dad has always done everything in his power to put you first?'

Reluctantly I agreed. Even though I didn't feel like being nice about Dad right then.

'Maybe you can put him first now?' Mario urged. 'Please.'

And because he looked so earnest and asked so nicely, I agreed to try. But that was before I knew what was coming my way when I got back to our booth.

Corinne said, 'Shall we tell her?'

Dad replied, 'You tell her.'

To which Corinne said, in true comedy gold, 'No, you tell her.'

I knew instinctively that whatever they wanted to tell me wouldn't be good news for me, so I kept my mouth shut. Once they stopped giggling, Dad announced that he'd proposed to Corinne. She held up her hand that now was bejewelled with a large solitaire diamond.

I was twelve years old and I had never been so devastated by a single piece of news in my life. Corinne reassured me that nothing would change for a while. But the plan was that Dad and I would leave Innisfree and move into her house when they got married. I watched Dad watching me. I refused to say a word. And when Mario brought our sundaes over, I told him I felt sick. It wasn't a lie. The evening lay in tatters on the Formica tabletop between us. I could see hurt in both Dad and Corinne's face. They wanted a blessing I could not give. I vowed there and then that I'd never leave Gran and

Grandad. Dad could do what he wanted, but I would not go with him. He didn't care that, if we moved, I'd never see Stephanie or Katrina.

'Nothing will change,' Dad said in an effort to reassure me. But that was a lie and they both knew it. Dad was oblivious to my sadness, caught up in his love for Corinne. As the days went on, I resented every single smile or moment he shared with her. I began to feel like an intruder in my own home. When Corinne tried to help me with my homework, I brushed her away. The maths tutoring that I once enjoyed now felt like it was laced with conde-scension. Dad and I fought almost every day. If he said white, I said black. If Corinne tried to side with me, I'd tell her she wasn't my mother. Then when Dad told me that I was acting like a child, I replied, 'yes, I am a child.' Sometimes I ignored them. I spent nearly a week not uttering a word to either of them. Corinne accused me of being passive-aggressive, which I suppose I was. But throwing grenades at her became sport to me.

It all came to an ugly head a few months after their engagement. The tension had been building up for a long time and it was inevitable that something would give. The proverbial straw that broke the camel's back was in her reorganization of our sitting room. She moved the furniture around, 'to improve the feng shui'. Gran and Grandad thought it looked great and were full of compli-ments about her knack for making a room look good. She'd gone shopping with Gran and they'd bought a new throw to cover the stains on Dad's lazy-boy chair that had seen better days. And new cushion covers now replaced those that had been in the room as long as I could remember. The thing was, Dad had said to me once that Mom used to prop me against one of those big pink cushions and she'd play with me, tickling me or massaging me. Now the pink cushion was green.

'That was Mom's favourite cushion!' I yelled.

Corinne had looked stricken at this and turned to Dad, 'You should have told me. I'd never have changed the cover if I'd known!'

'Your mom didn't have a favourite cushion,' Dad said.

'She didn't, love,' Grandad added.

'Yes she did,' I shouted.

'I'm sorry. I don't remember. Can we get the cover back?' Dad asked.

'I gave them to the charity shop on Windsor Square,' Gran said. 'Joe, go down and see if you can get it back.'

My grandad stood up and promised me he'd find the cover, even if he had to knock on everyone's door. I wanted to crawl into a ball and cry. Not for me, but for my poor mom who'd died and had lost everything, including her one true love. I looked from one to the other and saw the worry and love on their faces. And I felt my anger begin to slip away, until I noticed something else. The biggest act of treason. The framed photograph of my mom was gone.

'Where is it?' I cried. I looked at Corinne, knowing it was her fault this had happened. I told her she might take my dad, but she'd never take my mom. I'd pushed too far, because Corinne snapped. She shouted back. Why must I always assume the worst of her? What did she have to do to prove herself to me? She'd not touched the photograph.

Dad told me to calm down. But I was beyond reason at this point. Snot and tears streamed down my face. And

I pushed Gran away when she tried to put her arms around me.

'I moved the photograph,' Dad admitted.

I couldn't believe my ears. 'How could you do that, Dad? Mom was the love of your life, but now you've met someone else you are going to pretend she never existed? What's next? You want to get rid of me too, because I remind you of Mom too?'

'Stop that this minute!' Dad shouted. He'd never raised his voice to me, in all the years of mishaps and mayhem that had ensued throughout my childhood. 'The photograph is in your room. On your bedside locker. Now, you need to calm down.'

I couldn't contain my rage. His words and efforts to placate me only lit a fuse. I threw the new cushions from the sofa across the room. Corinne told Dad that he needed to nip this in the bud. She told him that he needed to put her first the odd time, if they were to ever work. If Grandad hadn't held me back, I would have jumped on top of her at that. From my vantage point, it had been the Corinne show for far too long.

'Don't make me choose between you both,' Dad warned Corinne, and as soon as he said that, I knew what I had to do. I wanted him to have to choose between us. Because I knew I could win. Dad had always been fiercely over-protective of me. If anybody so much as threatened the safety of his girl, he went all alpha male. I walked by Corinne and tripped myself up. I hit the ground hard, the thud ringing through the room. There was shocked silence, until my screams pierced the air. Dad got to me first and I whispered to him, 'She tripped me up, Dad. On purpose.'

'Don't be silly, love. Corinne wouldn't do that.'

Corinne's face was aghast and she denied it, saying she loved me and would never harm me. I cried and put in an Oscar-winning performance, begging Dad to take me to my room, away from her. And as he half carried me back to my bedroom, I threw my final grenade at Corinne. 'Why would you deliberately want to hurt me?'

As I lay in my bed that night, I could hear them arguing. I heard tears too. They played music so I couldn't make out the words, but I did hear Dad saying that he had to put me first. Everything he'd done was to protect me. Corinne said he was making a mistake and that lies always catch up with you. I pulled my duvet up higher, over my head, to drown out her words. I didn't want to listen to them any more. I had this nagging feeling of guilt that I didn't like. I knew deep down that I'd behaved appallingly, but I didn't want to admit that to anyone else.

The next morning Dad told me that Corinne and he had split up. There would be no wedding. She would come for her things that weekend.

The final battle had been fought and I'd won.

The funny thing was, after she left, the feeling of victory didn't taste very sweet. Dad and I both missed her. And things were never quite the same at home after that.

# 22

## *Bea*

February 2020

*Brooklyn Heights, Brooklyn, New York*

I walked up and down the tree-lined avenue three times.
As soon as I got close to Corinne's house, my courage
deserted me at the last minute. I made my way down
Orange Street, walking towards the water and stopped
to take in the view of downtown Manhattan and the
Brooklyn Bridge. Tourists took selfies of themselves and
the sound of their merriment as they posed filled the air.
The bridge felt like a connecting portal to another world.
It linked Brooklyn to Manhattan over the East River. And
more than that, I'd learned through my grandad that it
also linked many cultures. When I was a kid, about seven
or eight, Grandad woke me early one summer's morning
and told me we were going on an adventure. I jumped
out of bed and got dressed quickly, without question.

Grandad was full of surprises like this and his excursions never disappointed. We drove to Vinegar Hill, a neighbourhood named for an Enniscorthy landmark, to honour the many Irish who lived there. Once he parked up, Grandad took my hand and then we strolled towards the Brooklyn Bridge pedestrian walkway. The views of the Manhattan skyline were spectacular, the city skyscrapers nestled against a pink sky. We stopped to watch a bride and groom pose as a photographer took snaps.

Grandad shouted his congratulations to them and they told us that they'd got married the day before, but they were doing their official photographs today at popular landmarks.

'When I married this one's grandmother in 1961 a friend of ours gave us a blessing. It goes something like this . . .' Grandad said, clearing his throat, 'With the first light of sun – Bless you. When the long day is done – Bless you. In your smiles and your tears – Bless you. Through each day of your years – Bless you.'

Time stood still in that moment, as his strong voice filled the air between us and the young couple. With their arms wrapped around each other, I saw the woman's eyes brim with emotion. They shook Grandad's hand and thanked him. I felt emotion that I couldn't understand yet. My throat tightened and I was embarrassed that I felt like crying. I was too young to understand why I felt so emotional. But now I know. It was *pride*. My grandad was a man who could take a moment of his day to stop with strangers and recite a beautiful blessing, making their day a little brighter. That was his superpower. He made all of our lives brighter with the small and the big moments we had by his side.

I placed my hand inside his again and we continued our walk across the bridge. His hand was calloused and the skin was hard from years of manual labour. But I never felt as safe as I did when I held it. 'One day, you'll get married, and please God I'll be there to recite that blessing to you too, Bea.'

I liked the idea of that very much.

As we continued our walk across the bridge, Grandad told me about the many Irish who had helped build the famous suspension bridge that stretched across the water to Brooklyn. At least twenty had perished as the structure was built. He told me about the time that P. T. Barnum, the circus man, brought twenty-one elephants over the bridge to prove how strong it was. I jumped up and down and wished that I'd lived back in the 1880s so that I could have seen the spectacle myself.

'Why did you bring me here this morning, Grandad?' I asked.

'I wanted to tell you something important. Show you too. You see the foundations of this bridge were laid by Irish immigrants who came off the famine ships in the 1860s. It was the toughest of jobs and the saying went that only the hungriest would go anywhere near work like this. But we Irish have always been made of strong stock.' He touched a steel pole, then took my little hand and placed it onto the steel beneath his. 'There's a heart-beat running through this, the heartbeat of every immigrant who helped to build this city. I'm part of this heartbeat, your father is and so are you too. We're Irish, but we're American too. That's a powerful combination. Don't ever forget that.'

I closed my eyes and I could feel vibrations make my

hand tremble. And even though I was young and knew very little about the world, I understood what Grandad was sharing with me. I was part of something bigger than myself. I was born in New York and I stood on the shoulders of my ancestors who helped to build the city that I called my home.

Now, over twenty years later, I watched the sun bounce off the steel suspensions and I thought of all those who had gone before me. And the legacy they had left behind them. When I died, I wanted to leave something tangible behind me too. I wanted to have made a difference. Even though I wasn't in the slightest bit hungry, I grabbed a slice of pizza from Dellarocco's and had an impromptu picnic on the grass at the waterfront. As I watched tourists take photographs, I almost persuaded myself that I should abandon my plan to find Corinne Dryden and go back to my studio. I still wasn't sure why I was doing this.

Stephanie had queried if I was planning to orchestrate a reunion between Corinne and Dad. I thought about that for a moment too. Was it possible that they could fall in love again? This time without any interference from me. Was it possible to make Dad's world a little better *now*?

My phone buzzed and I opened a WhatsApp message from Katrina. It was a photo of a chicken, pecking at the ground. I sent her back a photo of a hairless cat I found on a Google search. Cats creeped out Katrina and the ones with no fur gave her nightmares. I smiled in satisfaction as she responded with a one-finger emoji.

But the message spurred me on. I couldn't procrastinate any longer. I made my way back to Corinne's brownstone.

Smoothing down my hair, I wiped my face to make sure that there was no pizza sauce on it. Then I rang her doorbell.

'Please don't be in, please don't be in,' I prayed to myself. But the door opened anyway and suddenly there she was. Older, her hair with streaks of grey through it, lines around her mouth and eyes. Yet she was also the same and, looking at her, I felt regret. I hadn't realized until this moment how much I missed having her in my life.

'I don't know if you remember me, but my name is . . .' I began.

She choked out a cry of surprise, then pulled me into her embrace. Corinne felt soft and as she held me tight, and the years fell away like leaves on a tree. She whispered into my hair, 'Bea O'Connor. My little Bea.'

So she did remember me after all. I felt a rush of relief. We all want to leave an imprint on those we meet in our lives, don't we?

'What am I like, leaving you standing on my doorstep! Come in.' She opened the door wide behind her and I followed her into her home. The hallway was bright, with black and white flagstones and sunshine yellow painted on the walls. It suited her. Warm, cosy and inviting. Exactly as I remembered her to be. We went through to her kitchen and she poured water into a kettle and then flipped the switch on. She kept stealing glances at me and I suppose I was doing the same with her too. 'I'm going to make some tea. Or maybe you prefer coffee?'

'Tea would be great. Thanks.'

'So how are you? You look well.'

I hesitated for a second and she raised an eyebrow. I quickly told her I was good.

'I've thought about you so much over the years, Bea. Tell me first of all, what did you grow up to be?'

'Do you remember Katrina Petrovic?' She nodded, so I continued, 'Well we are co-owners of the Family Finders Agency. We help find missing people.' I felt a stab of pride telling her this.

'Yes!' she said, punching the air, responding as I hoped she would. 'I always thought you'd end up doing something like that. You and your dad were obsessed with every possible crime show on TV back then.' She frowned for a moment, then cleared her throat to ask the question that must have been on her mind the second she saw me. 'How is your dad? You're not here to tell me bad news, are you?'

'No! He's fine. He's working on his fifteenth novel, almost at the end of the first draft. He's still addicted to *Law & Order* in all its forms.'

She smiled as I told her this. But it was one of those smiles crammed full of sadness. I'd seen Dad smile like this many times. Hell, I'd done it too. I spotted a small chicken figurine sitting on the edge of the Belfast sink in her kitchen. It felt like a sign. I found myself thinking about ways to initiate a meeting between them. Maybe my letter did want me to sort out a reconciliation.

'Thank you for the time-capsule letter.'

'It took me some time to track down a fair few from the class. You were easiest of all. You always said you'd never leave Innisfree. And you haven't. Good for you.'

'Did you read them?' I asked. I was embarrassed by my comments about her in them and crossed my fingers behind my back, as I used to do as a child, wishing she hadn't.

She looked offended by the question. 'Of course not! They were sealed when you put them in the time capsule and they were still sealed when I forwarded them to you.'

'I'm sorry.' And I was sorry. Not just for my unfair accusation, but for so much more.

'You've nothing to be sorry about,' she answered, understanding that my apology had many layers to it.

'Dad still thinks of you,' I blurted out, testing the waters.

'Is that why you're here? Ryan sent you? After all this time?' She seemed surprised.

'Dad doesn't even know I'm here, I promise you. But I know he misses you. He was never the same after you broke up.'

'It was such a long time ago,' Corinne said. 'I'm sure he's moved on. I know I have.'

She turned away from me as she busied herself making the tea. Had she moved on? I sneaked a look around her kitchen. I couldn't see any signs of another man.

'While it's wonderful to see you, I suspect you are here for a reason. What do you need from me, Bea?'

I flushed. I'd forgotten how direct she was.

'Gran always used to say that you got what you saw with Corinne. That there were no sides to you. She really liked you. She was cross with me, for ages, after you and Dad split up.'

Corinne's face softened. 'I loved your gran too. I wasn't close to my mother; she was the complete anthesis of your gran, cold and distant. I remember when your dad said to me that he wanted to introduce me to his family. I was so nervous. Not just meeting you, his only child, but also meeting his mother who he lived with! I was even more afraid when he told me that your mom hadn't got on well with Peggy. But within a few minutes of meeting, I felt like I'd known her my whole life. I often think of her and her gorgeous scones.'

'With Kerrygold butter . . .' I said as my mind digested the latest titbit I'd learned. My mom hadn't got on well with Gran. That was news to me.

She placed a pretty flowered plate onto the table in front of me, with a couple of stacks of chocolate chip cookies. Then poured the tea into two mugs.

'You must miss your gran.'

'Every day. And Grandad too.'

'I went to their funerals. It was a beautiful service for both. A packed church, which was no surprise to me. They were much loved and respected in the neighbourhood.'

I looked at her in surprise. I hadn't known she'd been there. 'I didn't see you at the wakes. You should have said hello.'

'I didn't want to intrude. I could see the pain you were all in. Especially for your grandad's, so close after losing Peggy.'

'I don't think I've got over either of their deaths. I miss them both so much. And it's funny, but since I received the letter from the time capsule, they've been in my thoughts even more. I don't have a memory from my childhood that doesn't include them really.'

'That's understandable.'

It was time to fess up and face the music. 'Upon mature reflection, I suppose on occasion there were times back then that perhaps didn't cover me in glory.'

Corinne didn't say anything, just carried on stirring her tea with a tiny teaspoon.

I wasn't sure how to begin and all my rehearsed speeches flew out of my brain. There wasn't a correct way to own up to a bad deed, I supposed. 'In school I used to scrape my chair loudly on the ground because I knew it irritated you.'

'You used to stick your tongue out at me too,' she said with an easy laugh.

'You were my favourite teacher.'

'Until I started to date your dad and then the battle lines were drawn.'

'I was so angry back then and it was unfair of me to take it out on you.'

'Please don't worry about it.'

'I have been worrying and I need to tell you something. That night you and Dad rowed, when you made some changes to the sitting room. I did something bad.'

'We all have moments that we regret, Bea. And that evening is one of them for me too,' Corinne said, taking me by surprise.

'But you didn't do anything wrong. It was all me. I mean, as well as the way I spoke to you, I tripped myself up on purpose. I pretended it was you, because I wanted to make Dad choose between us. I was a complete and utter spoiled brat. So if anyone should regret that evening, it's me.'

She took her time responding. The silence filled the air between us and as the seconds added up to a minute, I felt sick. I wanted her to shout at me. Maybe give me a slap. Not a hard one, but a little one would help to make me feel less guilty. Goodness knows I probably deserved it.

But all she said was, 'I knew that.'

'There is no excuse for my behaviour. I was angry with

you and Dad, because I felt blindsided by you both. It wasn't only the cushion; Mario's had always been our thing. But I never wanted you to split up. I really am sorry that I did that to you. It wasn't just Dad that missed you afterwards. I did too.'

'At one time I thought you might have been the daughter I'd never had. I would have loved that. I need you to know that I would never have changed that cushion, had I known how precious it was to you. Your gran asked me to give the place a spruce up, as she called it.'

'Grandad always used to say that there were three sides to every story. Yours, mine and the truth.'

Corinne smiled as she topped up my tea.

'Please accept my apology. It's important to me that you know I'm sorry for being such a little cow.'

'Oh Beatrice, I really appreciate you coming here to say that to me. But there was no need.' She leaned over and gave my hand a squeeze, to reaffirm that she meant it. 'Your dad never believed for one second that I tripped you up. He saw how much I loved you. He knew that I could never hurt you like that.'

'But you fought, I heard you. And then you left . . .' I said, confused by what she was saying.

'Yes. But that was for a very different reason. Your trip was the catalyst to the inevitable. We would never have married. I saw that as time moved on after our engagement. I don't think your dad really loved me, Bea.'

I felt a weight of responsibility fall from my shoulders. Followed quickly by curiosity. 'If it wasn't my fault, then why did you split up?'

'You need to ask your dad that,' she replied.

There was something about the way she said this, coupled with my nose for spotting that there was more to this story. 'I'm asking you, Corinne. Why did you and Dad really split up?'

# 23

## Bea

February 2020

*Brooklyn Heights, Brooklyn, New York*

She sighed. Then shrugged. 'It's not my story to share. All I can tell you is that I had my reasons. I found out about something your dad had done that didn't sit well with me. I asked him to . . . fix it. He wouldn't. That's what we fought about. So I left. But as I said, there was more to it than that row. We had been fighting for months before that. Some relationships are just not meant to be.'

My head began to spin with this revelation. I couldn't imagine a single thing that my father could have done wrong. And I had seen a lot of sick shit over the years through my job. 'Can you tell me what it was he did?'

'As I said, you need to ask him that.'

'OK, I will. But you are wrong about him not loving you. I think he did. And he still might.'

She started at this and her eyes filled with tears. 'I loved him. But I don't think I was the love of his life. Do you remember making the Lego tower? I often think of that evening. It was the most perfect night, wasn't it? Or maybe I'm remembering with rose-tinted glasses.'

'No, it was perfect.'

'I meant it when I said I would have loved to be your stepmother. You were such a great kid with an imagination that I was in awe of. Fearless too. It was a privilege for me to be part of your life, if only for a short time.'

Memories that I'd long forgotten, shoved down deep inside of me, burst to the surface. Shopping trips together to buy my first bra. The gift she'd left on my bed the day I got my period for the first time – a hamper filled with chocolate, aspirin, a furry hot-water bottle, a Judi Curtin book and a phone. There was a note attached to this, where she'd written that I should call her, day or night, if I needed her. And the affection she gave me. Years of hugs and tender touches, even when I shrugged them away.

'I pushed you away. But you kept coming back. You were so patient with me. I'd forgotten how much you'd done for me. I think I buried how important you were to me, because it was too painful to live with what I'd done. Corinne, you *were* my stepmother. In every way that mattered. I didn't realize how important that was until now. I'm an idiot,' I said.

She brushed away a tear with the back of her hand. And in that single tear, I felt a trickle of hope grow that maybe it wasn't too late for us. Maybe there was still time for Dad and her. A second chance.

'Is there someone special in your life now?' I asked.

She shook her head.

'Then you should call Dad. Maybe it's time you both reconnected. Perhaps get back together again.'

I could imagine it too. The two of them pottering around this house or Innisfree. They could be happy together. Drinking Barry's tea, reading books, watching TV.

But she put a pin in that dream, until it blew away to nowhere. 'Our time has passed. There are some things that are not meant to be. We are one of them.'

'I don't agree. I think you should meet him for a coffee. If for no other reason than to catch up on each other's lives.'

'No.' She was polite but firm. 'Don't press me on this matter again, Bea. That was a hard time for me back then. I mourned the loss of your father and you. But I've moved on. Let that be the end of it. But it is good to see *you*. I'd love it if we stayed in touch.'

'I'd like that too.' And I realized as I said it that it was very much true.

'What about you? Are you dating anyone?'

'I split up with someone before Christmas. Dan. He was . . . I thought he would be my forever. But it didn't work out.'

'You're still in love with him,' she said. Another statement.

And unlike every other time Dan was brought up by Katrina or Dad, I didn't deny anything. Corinne handed me a tissue and I mopped the tears that began to fall. 'Damn it! Sorry. I'm an emotional mess.'

'Love sucks sometimes. Do you want to talk about it?'

While I didn't understand much about what was going

on in our lives right now, I knew I didn't want to talk about Dan. It was too hard. 'I've got some things to work out in my life right now. Things have been difficult.'

'I'd like to help, if I can. At the very least, I'm a really good listener.'

'Thank you and I'll remember that. When I received my letter on New Year's Eve, it seems to have started a chain of events. The things I said back then, well, they've made me ask some tough questions about my life now. They've opened up a can of worms. To be honest, the worms are spilling everywhere!'

'So that's why you came here.'

'Yeah. It feels like my letter is pushing me towards something. I know that sounds crazy.'

I snuck a peek at Corinne but she didn't look weirded out by my words, merely reflective. I told her about Stephanie and our recent reconciliation.

'Well, that makes me even more grateful that I didn't lose that time capsule over the years! I'm pleased that you two are friends again. In many ways the friends we choose are even more precious than family, because they're the ones we choose for ourselves. I'd never thought about the time capsule project as a means for you students to make amends for mistakes. How interesting!'

I wondered what she'd make of the letters if I told her that they were active, alive, magical. Remembering my dad's face though, I thought it better not to tell her that.

Corinne made a fresh pot of tea and we sat there for another hour, chatting about our lives. She no longer taught; she'd taken early retirement the previous year. But she was still busy, volunteering in the local youth centre. Corinne was my kind of people. The type of person

I'd happily spend time with. I would spend the rest of my life regretting that she wasn't a more permanent part of it. We swapped each other's cell numbers and promised to stay in touch.

As we hugged each other goodbye, she said to me, 'As you've been busy reflecting on life and relationships, I wondered if you had ever thought about getting in touch with your mom's family in Ireland?'

I looked at her in surprise. 'Over the years, I've thought about it. Dan and I planned to go to Ireland together, but that's off the cards now. Dad reckons we should leave it.'

'What about your aunt? And your mom's best friend? From what I remember Ryan telling me, they were close. I bet they'd love to meet you.'

'I've had the odd card from Michelle, but my aunt is some kind of recluse. She's never been in touch.'

'Well, if someone isn't physically in your life, that doesn't mean they don't think about you often. You can take my word for that, Bea. Maybe you should reach out to her too.'

'What if she tells me to get lost?'

'Then you get lost. But she won't. If you take the time to visit her, she'd love that. Think how nice it would be to understand a little bit more about your mom's life in Ireland before she emigrated to America. You're an investigator, Bea O'Connor. It's time you investigated your own life to find out a little more about your heritage.'

'I don't think Dad would like that.' In fact I knew he wouldn't. He always got a bit antsy whenever I spoke about Mom's family.

'You're not a child any more, Bea. It's time you did

what you want, not what your dad wants. You could have cousins galore over there, all waiting to open their arms to you. Take it from me. You turning up here today unannounced – well, you've made my day.'

There was so much to think about as I walked back towards my car and drove home to Innisfree. I went straight to my studio and pulled the shoebox of memories out from my bedside locker, where it now lived. I felt like I was missing something so obvious that when I worked it out, I'd kick myself. Corinne hinted that there was something Dad was hiding from me. But what? I picked up Mom's handbag again – it was a knock-off Chanel, I know that now, but she'd loved it. And the only thing of hers that Dad kept after she died. I flicked through the photographs, one by one, hoping for a clue. But I found nothing. As I placed the photos back, I noticed a small pocket inside the main inner pocket that I'd never seen before. How had I missed that? I reached my two fingers into it and found a note. I didn't recognize the writing, so I looked down to the end and saw that it was from my mom's friend, Michelle.

*You have made a mistake. And you have learned in the most painful way that secrets always come out. But you can't hide from this. It will never go away and you are going to lose everything if you don't fix it. Please. You have to try.*

*Love*
*Michelle*

What the actual? What had my mom done? I ran up the stairs calling for Dad as I went.

'Hey, love. What's wrong?' Dad asked.

'I've found a letter in Mom's handbag.' I shoved it at him. As he read it, a bead of sweat formed above his lip. 'What is Michelle talking about?'

'I have no idea. Those three were always fighting about something or other.'

'And I thought they were the Three Amigos. United. Best friends forever.'

'Well they were. But like you, Katrina and Stephanie, they fell out every now and then. I honestly don't remember what this was about. Probably about us getting married. Michelle thought your mom was too young. Throw it in the bin. Forget about it.'

'No!' I screamed. 'My mom touched that note. And you want to chuck it in the trash?' I was hurt and angry at once. I hadn't felt this way towards my dad since that horrible night with Corinne.

'I can't talk to you when you're like this,' Dad said, walking out.

I went back to my studio and opened up a WhatsApp video message chat with Katrina and Stephanie. We had a newly formed message chat group, The BFFs, which was busy with audio and video messages every few minutes.

'I've been to Corinne's and now I've had a row with Dad!' I was shaking.

'Calm down. You look shit, Bea. Are you feeling OK?' Stephanie said.

'I'm angry. So no, I'm not feeling OK. I swear, Dad has just lied to me, he's such a crap liar.'

'Sit down,' Katrina ordered. 'Get a cold drink and tell us what happened.'

I filled them in on my visit with Corinne first of all. 'Honestly, she was really cool. She said that it wasn't because of my actions that she and Dad split up. The time flew by. I'd forgotten how much I enjoyed her company.'

'I hope you didn't tell her I'd been doing the dirt with Jimmy Del Torio while you drank all that tea.'

'She wasn't that shocked. She said you were always a dirt bird,' I joked.

'Stop! You better not have. I have secrets I could share about you, Bea O'Connor. Starting with how you used to stuff your bra with toilet paper.'

'She still does,' Katrina said. 'So what happened with Ryan?'

'Corinne said that I should find my mother's family in Ireland. The way she said it made me think there was more to her suggestion. I had a look through my shoebox and found a note hidden in Mom's handbag.' I read the note to them both, then told them about Ryan's reaction to it. 'What do you think?' My emotions were still running too high and I couldn't get my thoughts straight.

'I think the chicken is still there, pick, pick, picking away,' Katrina said.

'And by the sounds of it, the chicken had better get its passport ready. You need to go to Ireland,' Stephanie added.

I opened the top drawer of my locker and pulled out my passport – updated last year, as it happened.

And that brought me right back to last year, when I was running towards Dan, with the passport in my hand . . .

# 24

## Bea

### October 2019

*Eataly, Flatiron, Financial District, Manhattan*

I ran three blocks, arriving at the entrance to Eataly out of breath. 'Sorry!' I managed to get out as I bent over, trying to catch my breath. 'But look, my passport arrived.' I reached into my rucksack and pulled out the post that had arrived that morning. He'd asked me to make sure it was updated, so that if we came across a cheap flight to Ireland, we could take advantage at a moment's notice.

He looked a little less annoyed seeing my passport. But his usual grin that he wore whenever we were together wasn't there. 'You're always late, I expect that from you. But twenty-five minutes? I have to be back in work in fifteen minutes.'

I've always been forgetful, some would say a bit flaky. I know I've a problem with timekeeping. I make resolutions all the time to do better. But then I'd say screw it and be back to square one.

'Don't be cross with me. You know what I'm like. And what's that saying? Better late than never.'

'I don't mind you being a few minutes late, but this is taking the piss, Bea.'

Shit, he was really cross. And I hadn't done it on purpose. 'Honestly, I'm sorry, Dan. I was about to leave the office, but I felt a bit weird. Think I might be getting the flu. So I had to sit down for a bit.'

He felt my forehead, in that time-tested way of checking someone's temperature. 'You don't feel hot. Do you feel nauseous or anything?'

'I did for a while. But I'm fine now.'

'I think you're overdoing it at work. Part of your charm is your forgetfulness, but you've been scattier than normal these past few weeks. Maybe you should take a few days off.'

I hated seeing Dan's forehead wrinkle in worry. I reached up to smooth out the lines.

'Don't be trying to divert my attention,' he said, but he was smiling now, so I leaned in and kissed him.

'Stop it, woman,' he growled in my ear, 'or I'll be late for the afternoon's appointments too.'

'I could be persuaded to take a couple hours off,' I said and that's all it took. He threw a few dollars down for his coffee and we grabbed a cab to his apartment, to hell with the expense. I had to hold my hand over my mouth to stop the giggles when he rang his boss to say he was feeling ill. That afternoon was one of the best of my life. Just the two of us in his bed, making love, napping, then making love again. When I was with Dan, all my worries disappeared and the world became small and perfect, with just the two of us in it.

As we ate Chinese takeout from boxes, sitting cross-legged on his double bed, we discussed my always being late. I tried to dodge responsibility and told him that it wasn't my fault. 'It's Dad who's to blame.'

'This I've got to hear,' Dan said, laughing. 'Go on, plead your case.'

'Well, he's always written whenever the muse strikes him. And honest to God, this was mostly late at night. Which meant that he often slept through his alarm. We'd wake up with Gran shouting up the stairs to get a move on. Even though we lived only a few blocks from my school, I never quite seemed to make it in time before the first bell. You can't blame me for that.'

'Maybe not, but you can't blame your dad for you being late today!'

'No, but my point is that, because of my childhood, I grew up thinking that all times scheduled for meetings, or get-togethers, were approximate rather than set in stone.'

'I bet that made your dad popular over the years,' Dan said, trying without success to make his chopsticks behave.

'Dad always says that forgetfulness is a family curse! So, Dan Heffernan, next time you want to complain about my timekeeping, please remember that it is my burden to live with this curse. I rest my case!'

'I'll remember that. But maybe I've just the thing that can help.' He jumped up and pulled open his jocks and sock drawer. 'I bought you this for your Christmas present. But feck it, have it now. I'll buy you another present.'

Like a child at Christmas, I reached over greedily for his gift. I loved surprises.

'It's the best on the market. With all the latest thinga-majigs,' Dan said, as I looked at the Apple Watch he'd bought me.

'I love a good thingamajig and this thingamajig is very generous. I can't believe you bought me this. It's too much.'

'Only the best for you. And look.' He pointed to an icon of a heart on the packaging. 'It can detect if your heartbeat stops!'

'That's a cheery thought.'

Laughing, he said, 'You can thank me if you fall over, and this brings the paramedics to save your life.'

'Now all you have to do is tell me that it can make me a Nespresso in the morning when I wake up. Please let it be so.'

'But that's what I'm here for,' he said. 'In fact, I could do that every day for you, if you want.'

It was a good job I wasn't wearing the watch yet, because my heart stopped beating. 'Did you ask me to move in with you?'

He nodded.

I thought about Innisfree and how I swore I'd never leave there. Could I? For Dan?

'You're thinking about Innisfree,' he said.

Goddamn it, how did he do that? 'Yes.'

'Well, I'll move in there if you want. If your dad and Uncle Mike don't mind. All I want is to be with you. And I don't mind where that is.'

'Can I think about it?' I asked.

'Take as long as you like.'

# 25

## *Bea*

February 2020

*Irish Center, Long Island, Manhattan*

I had a lead in the Ted Spadoni case so I was on my way
to the Irish Center. Earlier, I filled Katrina in on where I
was at. We often bounced things off each other when we
were reaching a brick wall. And this missing guy, Ted
Spadoni, was proving difficult to find. It was as if he'd
vanished off the face of the earth three years ago. He
hadn't withdrawn any money from their joint bank
account. He left his phone behind him. I'd checked all
public and private databases to see if he had applied for
a job anywhere in the country and that was another
blank. If he was alive and working, it was under the
counter, cash in hand. I'd pulled in another favour from
Uncle Mike, and asked him to look through the case file
for me. Sometimes a fresh pair of eyes can spot some

detail that was missed first time round. And I was interested to see if there was any additional information there that Olive hadn't been told about. But he hadn't uncovered anything new either.

'So it is time to put skip-trace hat on, no?' Katrina said.

I laughed and agreed it was, pretending to don a cap for her. Skip-tracing was the term used for tracking down someone who had skipped town.

'Something tells me that there isn't foul play involved here. Ted wanted to leave. If I can find out why, maybe I can find out where he is in time for his son's birthday.'

'So you start with phone records,' Katrina said.

'I've already begun cross-referencing every number he's called and received over the previous six months before he disappeared. These are family numbers that Olive has given me.'

Katrina nodded as I showed her that over 70 per cent of the numbers listed had been eliminated. 'That leaves me with approximately two hundred numbers to check out.'

'Start with this one,' Katrina said. 'He calls it most Friday nights. Why?'

I dialled it there and then, but it turned out to be the local pizza takeout. 'It would have been too easy to find a trace on my first attempt. Nobody is that lucky.'

We continued eliminating the numbers one by one, each bringing us down a further dead end. If Ted was making calls to plan his escape, it wasn't on this phone.

I scribbled a note on the file. Second phone? Then a number jumped out at me and struck me as strange. 'He's Italian, right? So why is he calling the Irish Center on

Long Island so much?' I showed Katrina the highlighted entries. 'That is odd,' she agreed.

'I don't know why, but I've got a hunch this is important. It's time for a trip down memory lane for me, I think.'

As I made my way to Long Island to the Center, a flood of memories resurfaced. My childhood weekends were either spent there at a Fèis, a traditional Gaelic arts and culture festival, or watching Dad and Uncle Mike play hurling. Then, if I was lucky, Dad would buy me a Crunchie chocolate bar, a favourite treat of Gran's, and in turn for him, and then me. And I thought of my mom again. How had she felt, being so far from home? She was younger than me when she came here. I realized that I knew little about her early life. Corinne was right. It was time to dig deeper. Maybe if I understood more about her, I might understand a bit more about myself. *Maybe.*

'Hello,' a voice I recognized called from behind me when I walked into the lobby. Mary had worked in the Center for decades. I turned towards her and her face lit up in recognition. I wasn't sure what I was looking for. But my inbuilt antenna that I was on the right track was on high alert. I looked at the noticeboard that listed events. An author reading, a play, a ceilidh. Adverts for tin-whistle and Irish dancing classes. A book club. Orientation for new immigrants.

'Bea O'Connor! I haven't seen you for years. Look at you, all grown-up now. You look wonderful. Pretty as a picture, you always were.'

'Thanks, Mary,' I said. 'You look great too. Do you have a minute? I'm trying to find a missing person and

I'm following up on a lead that links him here.' I handed her my business card, which she read then pocketed.

'Course I do. We'll be more comfortable in my office. Will you have a cup of tea?'

I nodded and watched her as she took out her Barry's tea from a press to make a pot.

As I breathed in the scent of the tea, I felt another wave of emotion hit me. 'Gran always made her tea in a china teapot. A Duleek one, I think it was. It was a wedding gift. God, she loved that teapot. Sorry, I'm rambling!'

'Ramble away. There's nothing nicer than tea made in a decent teapot. My granddaughter bought me a new-fangled fancy one from the Martha Stewart range. I can't take to it at all! Now, tell me about this missing person of yours.'

I pulled up a photograph of Ted Spadoni on my phone and showed it to her. She looked at it for a minute, then nodded. 'I never forget a face. And I've seen thousands of them come in and out of here over the years. But names, they never stick. Ted Spadoni was here all right, a regular for a while. He was in our book club.'

I had hoped for a lead. This was a bundle of them, all gift-wrapped up as one. Olive never mentioned a book club membership and certainly not at this centre. My palm itched as it sometimes did when I was getting close to a new truth.

'You need to speak to Deirdre who runs the book club get-togethers. Let me get you her number. She might be able to tell you a bit more about him. She's not here today, but you might be lucky and get her at home, if she's not visiting her daughter. She takes care of her grandchildren on her day off sometimes.'

Mary scribbled down Deirdre's number. I drank the last of my tea, then said my thanks and goodbyes, making promises not to leave it so long the next time.

Luck was on my side; Deirdre was home and told me to head over to her place in Queens. Thirty minutes later I was drinking my second cup of Barry's of the day.

'Yes, I remember Ted. A nice man. Friendly.'

'When was the last time you saw him?' I asked.

'Oh, it's years since he was in the book club. Let me think. He was with us for that book about the *Titanic*. One moment. I have a notebook and keep a track of all the books we read.' As she rummaged through her handbag I looked around her living room, which was stacked with books in every possible spare inch. Against the wall, on top of the mantelpiece, on the sofa where I sat.

'Here we go.' She smiled triumphantly. '*The Girl Who Came Home* by Hazel Gaynor. He loved that one. I can still remember him talking about it and how it was the first book he'd read in years that made him emotional. Have you read it?'

I shook my head but promised to rectify that as soon as possible.

'Back to that last book club meeting. When was that?' I said, gently returning Deirdre to the question at hand. I could see that it would take very little to have her talking books all afternoon.

'It's written down right here.' She showed me her notebook.

*July 2017*
*Book of the month, The Girl Who Came Home.*

A couple of months before he went missing. 'Was he there for the August book of the month?'

She flicked a page on her notebook and sighed. 'No, it appears he wasn't. Now that I think about it, he did send me an email telling me that he was leaving the book club.'

'Is there a chance you still have that email?' I asked, feeling excitement build. We'd been through his email account but there most definitely had not been any mention of a book club membership.

'I could look for it in my inbox.'

'That would be great.'

'Right now?' she asked, looking a bit put out.

'Yes, if that's possible.' She became flustered by my pushiness, so I threw in some emotional blackmail. 'His son turns fifteen in April and he wants his daddy back. There might be something in the email that helps me find him.'

'Oh, the poor boy. So young to be missing his father. I didn't realize he had a son. What did Paula say when you spoke to her? She must be in an awful state, assuming they are still together.'

Who the hell was Paula? 'Sorry, I'm not sure I know who Paula is. Was she in the book club too?'

Deidre gave me a look of annoyance. 'I'm not sure you're much of a detective, dear, if you haven't even spoken to his girlfriend!'

You dirty old dog, Ted Spadoni. I shook my head in amazement. In his photograph, he looked like butter wouldn't melt. 'Do you know Paula's second name?'

'Yes.'

'Can you tell me?' I tried to keep the irritation from my voice. It was like pulling teeth with this one.

'Quigley. Paula Quigley. She left at the same time as Ted. She decided to move back home to Ireland. Tipperary, I think she said. Paula couldn't settle over here. She wanted to be closer to her parents who were getting on in years. That's nice, isn't it. I wish my son was as thoughtful. He's only up the road but I don't see him from one end of the year to the other, not unless he's looking for money. Now, my daughter is another kettle of fish. I see her all the time, because she wants me to mind her kids. I don't know where we went wrong. Are you good to your parents? I bet you are. You seem like such a nice girl.'

I took a steadying breath. 'Yes, I see my dad a lot. Are you certain Ted went to Ireland with her?'

'As sure as you are sitting there now. They were sweet together. It was Paula who brought him into the book club. She'd been a member for about eighteen months before he joined. I'll see if I can find that email. And there will be one for Paula too.'

She made her way to her dining room table where a laptop was hidden amongst several stacks of books. As it whirred back to life, I thought about Ted living it large in Ireland, reading books with his Irish girlfriend, while his wife and son mourned him. It infuriated me. Now I wanted to find him just so I could hit him. Olive said that she didn't believe he was dead. Somehow though, I didn't think she had any clue that this was what he was up to. And poor Teddy Jr. Any joy at finding out his daddy was alive would soon fade when he realized that he'd left him without so much as a backward glance.

'Here we go,' Deirdre said, surprising me at how quickly she'd found the email. I peered over her shoulder and sure enough there it was. It didn't say much, other than he was leaving New York, but the email address was different from the one I had on file, given to me by Olive. I took a screenshot of the email on my phone. Then Deirdre pulled up the last email she'd received from Paula, which spoke about her sick mother and the need to be closer to her. I took another screenshot of this email and then thanked Deirdre.

*Not long now, Ted. I'm coming to get you.*

As I strolled back towards the subway, I spied a comic book store. On a whim, I walked in. When I'd googled magical letters, my head hurt as I fell into a rabbit hole of websites about time portals. But often, linked to the stories I read, were comics. I had no clue what I was looking for or expected by stepping inside, so I just walked along the rows of graphic comics, bright, colourful and surprisingly dark. There were dolls and figurines too, some I recognized and others new to me. Stephen King's Grady twins from *The Shining* made me scurry away from that aisle with speed.

'You look like you could do with some help.' One of the sales clerks walked towards me; he looked no more than fifteen years old. I felt ancient.

'Just browsing. I'm interested in comics where the hero can effect change, by say, writing to their younger selves.' I half expected him to start laughing at my ridiculous question.

'Ah, Ray Bradbury wrote a short story in 1952 that coined the phrase, *The Butterfly Effect*,' he answered without a smirk or smile. 'A small change can make much bigger changes happen. A butterfly flaps its wings in Chicago and a tornado occurs in Tokyo.'

'Oh! That makes sense.' Was that what had happened with my sage warning to my younger self about smoking?

The clerk made his way towards the back of the store and I followed him as he continued his lesson. 'In Bradbury's story, a group of hunters go back in time to hunt a T-rex. And the idea is that they will only kill a dinosaur that was going to be killed anyhow by a falling tree. But one of the hunters gets his freak on and runs away, stepping on a butterfly as he runs. He alters the world as a result.'

He handed me a comic. 'EC Comics, illustrated by Al Williamson. Another classic. And you might want to check out the 2007 graphic novel *I Killed Adolf Hitler.* Classic Grandfather Paradox.'

'What's that?' I gave him my most winning smile, so he didn't lose interest in me and my questions.

'Say your grandfather is an asshole, maybe he knocks you about. You go back in time to shoot him. Only you don't kill him. You just cause him brain damage, which in turn causes him to be the asshole in the now. Or you do kill him, but then you are no longer born. Whatever way you look at it, you can't change the past.'

'What about the future? Can you change that by altering a choice we made in the past?'

'Give me an example.'

'What if I tell my younger self not to start smoking.'

He smiled. 'You can't change the past. If you hopped into a time machine and took the cigarette from your younger self's mouth, you'd still find a way to smoke. The past has already happened and it can't unhappen, no matter how hard you try to stop it.'

'But what if I'm not talking about a time machine.'

'What are you talking about?'

'Say I wrote something in my teenage diary. And my sixteen-year-old self read it and listened to me. The past is altered and so is the future. What then?'

'Oh then you're into what's called Plastic Time territory. Where you can make small changes to history, but any big events will be met with resistance.'

'So this diary in theory could change small things. But if I tried to save my mother's life, for example, it couldn't do that.'

'Exactly. Basically, you've got to ignore everything that Marty McFly taught you about time travel. Fun movie, but nonsense. Listen, I'm due to go on my break now. Do you want these?' He held up the two comics.

I didn't but felt obliged to buy them as he'd been so helpful. As I walked back to the office, I thought about his words. If I believed him, my magical letter couldn't exist. But that felt wrong too.

I felt surer than ever that my letter was pushing me towards something.

Stephanie led me to Corinne.

Corinne led me to my mother.

Now where does my mother want to lead me?

# 26

## *Bea*

February 2020

*Innisfree, Prospect Avenue, Brooklyn*

I found Dad, eyes closed, in his thinking lazy-boy chair. He sat there to tease out plot lines in books, always had done.

'Hi, Dad.'

He opened his eyes and we looked at each other warily, as we figured out if we were still angry with each other. I decided I wasn't and I suppose he did too, because he offered to make us both lunch. I followed him into the kitchen and watched him as he made us both a roast beef sandwich. I'd not eaten since breakfast and my stomach growled in anticipation.

'To what do I owe this pleasure? It's not like you to call in midweek.'

'Do I need an excuse?' I said. But even as the words

left my mouth I knew that they were a lie. I had come here for a reason, but now that I was sitting beside Dad, with his rapt attention, I couldn't find the words to ask him. So instead I told him about Ted and his secret life in Ireland.

'That poor woman,' Dad said, looking horrified by the story. 'So what happens next?'

'I'm going to get a location for him in Ireland. Confirm that it's really him before I break the news to Olive and her son. I can't imagine how horrific it will be for them to find out that he's done this to them. I mean, fair enough he fell in love with another woman. But be a man and break it off with your wife. Don't just disappear!'

'He must have had his reasons,' Dad said. 'These things are never as cut and dried as they might look from the outside in.'

I thought about Corinne. Was he thinking about her too? I decided that now was as good a time as any to find out. 'I need to tell you something. I went to see Corinne. But we ended up fighting yesterday before I had a chance to tell you.'

He started to choke on a mouthful of his sandwich. His face turned tomato red and it took him a brimming glass of water to calm down.

'Sorry, Dad,' I said, genuinely upset that I'd nearly choked him to death. 'I didn't mean to give you a scare.'

'No, it's fine, love. Just that I haven't heard her name in a long time. How is she?'

'She looks brilliant, Dad. Happy. Still living in her gorgeous brownstone in Brooklyn Heights.'

'Why did you go to see her? I'm not sure I understand. Is it to do with the time-capsule letter she sent you?'

'Kind of. But I also wanted to apologize for my behaviour that night she left. Remember when I tripped.'

'I don't understand, love. Why the need to bare your soul after all these years?'

I thought about that and wondered how much I should share with him. I didn't like to keep secrets from Dad. But I wasn't sure how I could break the news to him about temporal paradoxes in my letters. Even with his writer's imagination, I figured that would be too much for him. I also knew that the best thing to do was tell him as much of the truth as possible.

'The letter has made me reflect, I suppose. On what I wanted back then and who I am now. And Corinne was a big part of my life then. I didn't realize how big at the time, but now I do. She never tripped me up that night Dad.'

He nodded. 'I knew that. And she did too.'

'Yeah. She told me. You know, I always thought that you broke up because I made you choose between us. She said that you'd not been getting on for a long time before that. And that there was another reason why you fought that night. That I should ask you what that was.'

He shrugged and then sighed. 'We had been fighting for a while. Little things adding up to one big thing, I suppose. The crazy thing is that now I can't remember most of them. At the time they seemed so important.'

'I got the feeling that there was something specific though. She said I should ask you, that it wasn't her place to say.'

He closed his eyes and for a moment I thought that was his way of saying subject closed. I felt my temper snap. But before I had the chance to yell at him, he spoke. 'We fought about your mom that night. Corinne felt that my past with your mom had too strong a hold on me.

She said that it was strangling me. She wanted me to let it go, to move on. It was an impossible situation.'

'Is that what the moving of her photograph was about?'

Dad looked sad as he continued, 'We fought about that photo a lot. I told her that it made me sad to look at it. She couldn't see why I didn't move it.'

'I never knew it made you sad.' I tried to remember if Dad had ever expressed this fact to me, but I was pretty sure he hadn't. I felt like I was missing something here. I might have been a kid back then, but Corinne had never struck me as the kind of woman who worried or fretted about my mom. I suppose it was possible that I'd just not noticed. 'Do you miss her, Dad?'

'All the time,' he replied, and for a moment I wasn't sure who he meant. Mom or Corinne. Maybe both.

'Do you regret splitting up? I remember you moping around the place for ages afterwards.'

'I loved her. And I missed her for a hell of a long time. But maybe it was for the best. Maybe I'm not the type who gets to be with someone for more than a year or two at most.'

That was so profoundly sad. It made tears sting my eyes. I picked up his notebook and pencil – he always kept them to hand so he could jot down ideas for his next novel. I scribbled Corinne's cell number down. 'You should visit her. If only so you can get some closure. I think you both could do with that. I'm really glad I went. And I'm going to stay in touch with her.'

'Maybe I will.'

'Dad, there's something else I've been thinking about. Mom's family in Ireland. Why didn't we stay in touch with them?'

His face changed at this question. Hardened. Was that anger too? 'Don't put that on me, Bea. It wasn't anything I did,' he said firmly. 'They chose to stay away.'

'And why was Mom buried over there and not here?'

'Her choice.'

'You talked about that?' This seemed weird to me. A young couple discussing burial plans at the start of their life together. Had she an inkling that she was going to die?

'We'd been at a memorial service for one of the Farrell's gang. He'd been flown home for his burial. Your mom told me that she wanted to be sent home too, but that we should cremate her to make it easier. She was quite insistent. Of course we never thought for a second that it was something we'd have to worry about for years to come. But a few months later . . .' He didn't finish.

'So she was cremated here, then sent home?'

Dad nodded. 'I had to honour her wishes.'

'I wish she had been buried here. It would have been nice to have somewhere to visit over the years.'

'Yes, it would,' he agreed, his face softening again to the one I was used to. He found this subject difficult. I felt uncomfortable making him feel uncomfortable. But I needed to tell him my plans.

'I'm going to get in touch with my aunt. She might not want to have a relationship with me, but I want to ask her about Mom. And I'd like to meet Michelle too.'

Dad looked less than impressed with my plan.

'Mom had a life in Ireland for over twenty years before you met her. And I want to find out about that. Corinne thought it was a good idea too.'

'That sounds like something Corinne would encourage

all right. Look, you're an adult, I can't stop you. But I think you're making a mistake. She won't want to see you.'

'Maybe. But it's my mistake to make. I'm a grown woman, Dad. Old enough to make my own mind up.'

I noticed a fleeting expression on his face. Was it fear? What on earth could my dad be afraid of?

'What are you so scared of?' I asked.

'Of you getting hurt. But most of all, of losing you.'

How could he think I'd ever leave him for my Irish family? 'Oh Dad. You don't ever have to worry about that. You've got to trust me. I know what I'm doing.'

And all of that was true except for the last part. I had no clue what my next move should be. But somehow I felt that, whatever it was, it would be life-changing.

# 27

## *Bea*

### February 2020

*Family Finders Agency, 57th Street, Manhattan*

Olive Spadoni arrived at the agency, a frown creasing her forehead. I had no interest in prolonging her agony. I could only imagine the myriad of things going through her mind.

'We've found Ted. He's alive.' That was the most important piece of information to impart.

I let Olive enjoy the relief that this gave her, knowing that any joy she felt at her husband being alive and well was about to be squashed by his ugly, cruel infidelity.

'I cannot believe it. He's OK? Well?' Olive asked, tears flowing down her face.

I nodded. In rude health, from what I could gather from my intel.

'Wait until Teddy hears this. He's going to be so happy.

You said you'd find him before Teddy's birthday and you did.'

While that might be true, I didn't much feel like celebrating.

'Where is he?' she asked. I wondered when the penny would drop that if he was alive and well, why wasn't he at home with her and their son?

I glanced at Katrina, who looked pensive as she stroked Karl on her lap. This was a part of our jobs that we both hated. Imparting bad news to clients.

'Ted has started a new life in Ireland.'

The woman was predictably confused by this information. She shook her head, over and over, as if that might make it untrue. 'That makes no sense. We have no family in Ireland. Or friends. What is he doing there?'

'It appears that Ted is in a relationship with another woman. She's called Paula Quigley and she's Irish. They are living in Co. Cork.'

This time a louder denial, 'I don't believe it.'

'I'm afraid it's true.' I explained how my investigation had led me to the Irish Center and their book club. And how I eventually found Paula. I passed several screenshots of Paula's social media, which spoke about her boyfriend and their love for each other.

'How do you know it's him? I mean, there must be hundreds of Ted Spadonis. Is there a photograph of him in any of her posts online? Something to confirm their relationship?'

'Your husband has been quite careful to ensure he's not photographed.'

'I don't understand why he would do this to us. Fine, he fell out of love with me. But we have a son. And he loves Teddy. I'm sure of it. Why not set up home here with this woman? Why lie and run away?'

I had no answer to that.

'Your husband is the only one who can answer those questions,' Katrina said.

I passed Olive a contact sheet with his new address in Ireland. Getting that had been easy. I contacted Paula via email, pretending I had found a piece of her jewellery in the Irish Center. She gave me her address so I could forward it to her.

'What should I do?' Olive asked. Her face had gone a paler shade of white.

On cue, Nikki came in with a glass of water for her and we watched as she shakily accepted it, taking a small sip.

'I can't tell Teddy this . . .' She motioned to the pages we'd handed her moments before.

'At least he will know that his father is alive.'

'He must be sick. Amnesia. Something like that. Or maybe the woman, this Paula, is blackmailing him.'

'It's possible,' I said, before continuing as gently as I could, 'but it's also possible that he chose to live a new life without you both, but was too cowardly to tell you.'

I could only imagine what was running through the woman's head right now. It was a lot of news to take in.

'What would you do?' Olive asked us. 'If you were faced with the same news.'

'I would cut his balls off. Then feed them to Karl,' Katrina said, making her fingers scissor-like, then stroking a sleeping Karl on her lap.

'Katrina, not helpful,' I said, but thankfully there was a ghost of a smile on Olive's face now.

'That does sound tempting,' Olive said.

'What you need to do is take a little time to think about your next move. You've had a shock. It's a lot to take in. But you can't hide from it either. Eventually you will need to make contact with him,' I said.

Olive shook her head. 'I can't do that, not until I have all the information. I need you to go to Ireland. Find out why he left. What his life is like over there.'

'I think it might be better if you went. Or perhaps call him. We'll be here to support you.'

She shook her head. 'No. Not yet, at least. I want to know all the facts before I speak to him. Will you go?'

I looked at Katrina questioningly. We'd travelled as part of our investigations before, but the furthest we'd been in the past was Canada.

'You would have to cover all costs for flights and hotels. Plus the usual daily rate. And if we go, it would be for at least five days; it's too far to go over and back in twenty-four hours,' Katrina said, trying to put her off.

'Money isn't an issue. I'm willing to pay for all expenses and up to a week of your time. Before I speak to Teddy, I need to know what kind of asshole his father really is.'

I noted that she didn't refer to him as her husband this time.

'Will you excuse us for a moment?' I said, then nodded to Katrina to follow me to my office.

'I don't want to take this case for the wrong reasons,' I said. Katrina understood. She knew that I planned to get in touch with my aunt. And this trip was giving me the perfect opportunity not only to call her, but to visit her in person.

'Your chicken has led crumbs all the way to Ireland.

You said you want to find out about your mother. This is way you can do it, at same time. You cannot *not* do this.'

I felt a tremor of excitement build up inside of me. It did appear that the universe was sending me to Ireland.

'If nothing else, I'd like to visit my mother's grave. Maybe lay some flowers on it.'

Katrina nodded.

'What about our cases here? Can you manage without me?'

'I will be going with you. I am not letting you do this on your own.'

I didn't even pretend to put up a fight. I was grateful for the offer. I knew I did not have the strength to do this on my own.

'We can't charge Olive the full rate, not when I want to go anyhow. How about if we charge her for the days we spend over there working on the case? But we cover our own costs.'

'That sounds good. We have had a good year in the business, so we can afford this. And money does not matter. I think you will need me, so I go.'

I pulled her into me for a hug.

'Is fine,' she replied. 'Good luck telling Ryan though.'

'He'll be upset.'

'Maybe. But this is your life. I'll get Nikki to start looking at flight options.'

# 28

## *Lucy*

### September 1992

*Woodside, Queens, New York*

When the phone rang early on Saturday morning, I knew that something was wrong. Call it intuition or sixth sense, but as I climbed out of bed, leaving a sleeping Ryan behind, I felt a shiver ripple its way through my body. Whoever was on the end of the line, they weren't calling with good news.

Mam's voice, tearful and hesitant, gave me relief for a few seconds. If she was talking on the phone, then she was OK. But then she delivered the news that I was not ready to receive. I don't suppose anyone would ever be ready for this kind of news.

'There's no easy way to tell you. I'm so sorry. Dad had a heart attack, love. He died on the way to the hospital. The paramedics did everything they could to save him. I'm so sorry, love. I'm so sorry.'

People say all the time that their knees buckled beneath them. Maeve and I spent a large amount of our spare time watching Maury Povich and laughing at his guests, who always fell to their knees when they received bad news. But I understood now. Because I had to hold onto the countertop to stop myself collapsing. Ryan walked into the kitchen, still in his boxer shorts, stifling a yawn. But as soon as he saw my distress, he ran over to my side.

'What is it?' he whispered.

'Lucy, are you there? Say something,' Mam asked.

'I'm here, Mam.' Here in New York, thousands of miles away from my family, away from my dad, who was now dead. I felt dizzy from the pain and even more so, the guilt.

'Father Kelly said we can delay the funeral for two days, so you can both come home. I need you, Lucy. I need both my girls.' Then she broke down in sobs so loud that I couldn't understand another word. A neighbour of ours, Eileen Doyle, took the phone from her. She said I should call back when I'd organized flights. And then she hung up, leaving me standing with the phone receiver in my hand.

The whole thing felt surreal, I wasn't even sure whether I had imagined the call. I turned to Ryan and said, 'I don't trust that I'm not asleep. Pinch me.'

'You're awake,' he said, cupping my face in his hands, so tenderly that it made me want to weep. 'Is it bad news from home?'

I nodded, but I couldn't tell Ryan before I spoke to Maeve. I wasn't sure how I'd find the words though. And as if the very thought of her conjured her up, my sister walked into the kitchen rubbing her eyes. 'Did I hear the phone ring? What time is it? Ah here, it's only six o'clock in the morning. On a Saturday! Oh for goodness' sake! Who was ringing us this early?'

'Mam.' I couldn't look at her. How was I supposed to impart the pain that was attacking me right now onto my sister?

'Classic Mam! She'll never get used to the time difference. Last week she rang in the middle of the night. I suppose we should celebrate this as an improvement!' Maeve began pulling mugs out of the press and filled the kettle. 'Coffee. I need lots of it. That was some session in Saints and Sinners last night, wasn't it? Mad craic.'

I moved closer to her.

'You look awful, Lucy. As white as a ghost. Go back to bed and sleep your hangover off.'

'Dad had a heart attack last night.'

Maeve turned towards me, alarm and fear on her face. Years fell away and she looked like a small child again. 'It's the bloody cigarettes. How many times have we told him to give those up? But he won't be told. How bad is it? Is he in intensive care in Wexford Hospital? Or did they send him to Waterford or Dublin?'

I wished I could go back in time and ignore the phone. I wished I could run away from all of this pain. I wished it could be anyone else but me to break my sister's heart.

'Say something, for goodness' sake, Lucy! How bad is it?' Maeve shouted at me. She swiped at the tears that were spilling down her face.

'He . . . he died,' I whispered.

The coffee jar fell from Maeve's hand and landed with a clatter on the floor.

I felt Ryan's hands on my arm and I heard him say how sorry he was. Maeve was rooted to the spot by the kettle, like a deer in headlights. I moved towards her and we looked at each other, taking in the pain mirrored in the eyes in front of us.

'Was it our fault?' Maeve whispered, and I honestly didn't have an answer. Dad had been so upset with us when we said we were leaving. And he'd held on to that ever since. And now he was gone.

'Poor Mam. She must be in an awful state,' Maeve said.

'Sit down. I'll make the coffee,' Ryan said, and he gently guided us towards the sofa. We sat side by side in silence for a few moments and then I felt Maeve's hand reach for mine. I pulled her into my arms and we cried for our daddy that we loved and would miss for the rest of our lives. Life had changed in an instant now that he was gone. We didn't know it, but our mam would never recover from the pain of his loss. A light switched off in her when Dad breathed his last breath and, over the coming weeks, the darkness would spread like a virus.

The next few hours went by in a blur. Ryan booked flights for us both for that night. It was an overnight flight and we would arrive early the next day into Dublin airport. Michelle called to say she would collect us. Dad would be waked at home, as was the traditional way to mourn the loss of a loved one in Ireland. Eric arrived, with takeout from the Stop Inn. I was glad Maeve had him. I watched him, how he was with her. He was in love with her, I could tell. And Maeve seemed to like him a lot. Maybe her sadness would bring them closer together.

I rang the Woodside Steakhouse and asked for some

time off. I was worried they'd fire me, because I'd only been there a short time. But Mick, the manager, was incredibly understanding. 'It's an emigrant's worst fear, that long-distance death call. Your job will be here when you get back, Lucy, don't let this be a worry for you.'

Maeve and I packed our bags. We only seemed to have cute tops in bright colours, it all seemed so inappropriate. I was grateful for the black knitted sweater I'd bought only a few weeks ago in JCPenneys. Ryan borrowed his dad's car and drove us to the airport. Peggy had called earlier and told me she'd have Mass said in St Sebastian's for Dad. Eric came to the airport too, and I marvelled at how much had changed for us two sisters in such a few short months. When Ryan hugged me goodbye, I had that same feeling I'd experienced earlier that morning when the phone rang. Dread and fear.

'I'm afraid,' I told him.

'That's only natural. I can't imagine how it must feel to go home, knowing your dad won't be there. But remember this: I love you. I'll be here waiting when you get back.'

'I love you too.' And we kissed a sweet, lingering kiss of goodbye.

The flight home passed in a dazed blur. The Aer Lingus stewardess was kind and gentle with us when we explained that we were going home to a funeral. I'd dreamed of going home many times over the previous months, of flying over the green fields of Ireland. But the pain of loss and dread dulled any joy I might have had, returning home.

Michelle was in Arrivals waiting for us, as promised. She ducked under the chrome barrier and ran towards us both, her two arms open wide to pull us close. The Three Amigos back together again and for a moment, as we clutched each other, we could pretend that everything was OK.

'Tadgh offered to drive, but I wanted to come on my own, so we could chat properly.' I liked Tadgh, but it was never the same when he was with us. The drive to Wexford was bittersweet. We went from chatting excitedly about our lives, sharing titbits that we'd not mentioned in letters or emails, to crying as each mile brought us closer to a reality we were not prepared for. Ireland looked different somehow. The fields of green were more vibrant and when we drove over the bridge into Wexford Town, I felt a lump the size of a lemon in my throat.

By the time we got to Kilmore, both Maeve and I were emotionally overwrought.

'I'll have to double-park. The place is bananas busy,' Michelle said. 'I'll get Tadgh to help me bring your luggage in. He's here somewhere. You go on in.'

We looked at Nellie's pub, a black wreath pinned to its front door. We'd done the same when my grandmother died and, at the time, I'd thought to myself, one day we'll use this wreath for Mam and Dad. And I'd felt wicked for thinking it. It had never occurred to me it would be this soon.

But, it's always too soon to lose someone you love. We couldn't wait to see Mam, but the walk into our home where Dad was no more felt like our own hellish green mile.

There were about a dozen neighbours queuing to get into our cottage. Dad was a popular man from the village and it appeared everyone had come out to pay their respects at the wake. As they spotted us, a murmur of sympathy ran down the line.

'Ah, it's the girls.'

'Lucy and Maeve.'

'God love you, girls.'

'So sorry. He was a good man.'

We'd hear hundreds of well-intended genuine offers of sympathy over the coming days. At first I didn't know what to say in response, but I copped on quickly that all that was needed was a nod of thanks or a squeeze of someone's hand. They moved aside to let us walk into our hall. Mam's friend, Eileen, was waiting for us, a tea towel in her hand. She had taken control of the kitchen and was co-ordinating tea, coffee, mixed sandwiches and cakes for the many visitors who were calling every hour. She wasn't a naturally warm person, but she had a good heart. 'I'm sorry for your loss, girls. Your dad is laid out in the sitting room. Your mam is there with him. Tea will be waiting for you when you're ready for it. I'd say you both must be wall-falling after the flight. They don't feed you at all on the planes, do they? Awful muck, from what I've been told.' Then before we could offer any response, she shoved us through the door into the room that we'd always referred to as the 'good room', only used for Christmas and special occasions.

I was disorientated at first because it looked so different. The furniture had been pushed back against the walls. Chairs from the lounge in the pub were lined up in rows around the mahogany coffin that sat in the middle of the room. Maeve gasped, so I gave her hand a reassuring squeeze. A sea of faces, sad and full of compassion, looked up at us. More sympathy was proffered. I searched for

Mam, missing her at first because her head was low, as if bowed in prayer. I'd thought about our reunion many times, and how I'd run into her arms. She'd laugh and cry; we both would. And it would be one of those happy moments that we'd never forget as we reconnected with each other. But that was just a dream. Now, in the harsh reality of the good sitting room that was now a funeral parlour, I felt unsure. Should I go to her, kneel, then place my head in her lap and cry? Or go to the open coffin, to see Dad for one last time before we put him in the ground? In the end, Maeve made the decision for me. She crouched down to her hunkers in front of Mam. My legs took root, forgetting how to move. When Mam looked up, it was my turn to gasp. She had always looked young for her years, but now she was all of a sudden an old woman. I stood, awkward on display in this strange setting. And when I should have been thinking of my father, all I could think of was Ryan and how much I missed him. I wished he were there with me, his strong arms around me, ready to catch me if I fell.

'Say goodbye to your dad. He looks so peaceful. Like he's sleeping.' Eileen Doyle walked over to me, taking matters into her own capable hands. She pushed me again until I was beside him. I kept my eyes lowered, taking in the shine of the polished wood, the gleam on the brass handles. Mam had chosen well. I would have to tell her that later on. Dad liked dark furniture. Mam loved pine but he could never stand it. I was glad she'd given him what he wanted in this concluding life choice. I ran my hands lightly across its surface and tried to find the strength to look at my lovely daddy.

I felt the eyes of the mourners on me, watching for a

response. Not unkindly or anything, as it's human nature to rubberneck. Impossible to look away from raw pain, no matter how intrusive it is. I wished I had the nerve to ask Eileen to clear the room. Surely I deserved some privacy in this moment? I turned back to look and Maeve and Mam were still in each other's arms. It felt like time was stretched; it could have been seconds or minutes.

'It's OK, love,' I heard Dad's voice whisper to me from wherever he was. 'It's only a body. I'm up here with your gran.'

'Oh Dad,' I sobbed as I looked inside the coffin. They had dressed him in his good suit, the one he'd worn to our graduation earlier this year. His shirt looked like it had been taken out of a packet. I remembered Dad saying to Mam that he'd never get the wear out of a new suit when she'd insisted he buy one. In a million years, I'd never have thought this would be the next time he'd put it on. The thought made me want to run from the house and get back on the next flight to New York. I didn't want to be here. I felt ill-equipped. Even though I was now a young woman, an adult who had lived on her own for years now, I became a child once more.

Eileen said he looked like he was sleeping. Peaceful.

I wanted to cry 'bullshit!' Dad looked like he was dead. Gone from me. From all of us. We'd never hear his laugh again or listen to him tell one of his tall stories to the punters in the pub, or yell out to everyone that it was time, gentleman and ladies, please, have you no homes to go to.

I touched his face. It felt waxy and cold. And my fingers left a mark on the make-up that the undertaker had placed on him.

After a few moments, Maeve and I swapped places. I knelt down to take Mam into my arms. She'd lost weight since we'd left. And her face, once rosy and full, looked gaunt and grey. We didn't say anything to each other, we just keened in a lament for a special man. Two seats appeared and everyone shuffled down so Maeve and I could sit on either side of Mam. The room fell silent for a while, as friends and family gave us our time to get used to this new normal. Then Ned Doyle, Eileen's husband and a long-time friend of Dad's, spoke.

'There isn't a man in the county who could run a table quiz like Denis Mernagh.'

A ripple of affirmations ran through the room.

'A fountain of useless information, your dad,' Ned went on.

'He read so much, that's why,' Mam said. And everyone nodded because it was a well-known fact that on a quiet day in the pub you'd find Dad behind the bar, glasses perched low on his nose, a book in hand.

'If he was here now, he'd be telling us all about why wakes were invented. How many times did he tell us that story?'

'Every funeral we were ever at, he'd bring up the pewter tankards,' Eileen said.

'Aye. He'd say, people used to get lead poisoning from drinking stout in them. The poor old feckers would fall into a catatonic state and everyone thought they were dead, only to get the fright of their lives when they'd rise from the dead! Denis would laugh for ten minutes then, tickled by the image,' Ned said.

'He'd say, if it wasn't for a wake, half the country would have been in the ground back then!' Eileen said, and a ripple of laughter started and stopped just as quick.

Then Paudie Murphy, another regular from Nellie's, started to laugh. 'Sorry,' he said, holding his hand up. But he had the fit of the giggles and couldn't stop them.

'What's so funny, lad? Spit it out!' Ned said.

'Do you remember the episode of *Only Fools and Horses* when Rodney and Del dressed up as Batman and Robin for a fancy dress party, which turned out to be a wake?'

'Dad loved that episode,' Maeve said, smiling. And as people shared stories, it helped to cut the tension a little. We somehow got through the wake. And in turn the funeral the following day. At times it felt like we were the walking dead ourselves, because all three of us were in a trance. We showered, dried and combed our hair, wore our best clothes and stood at the door to greet people who called to pay their respects. But we were not really present, we were just going through the motions. Nellie's closed but opened on the day of the funeral for a private function, so neighbours and family could say their goodbyes to Dad in the way the Irish do best – with song and story.

It felt good to be back in the bar. It was and always would be a big part of my life. And it was a comfort to be pulling pints, pouring shots of vodka and gin into ice-filled glasses. Hugh, Dad's right-hand barman, tried to get me to sit down. But I needed to work. It helped me forget that once this was all over, one fact would never change. I would never see my father again.

Maeve got pretty drunk as the night progressed. As bad as I'd seen her in a long time. I think it didn't help that neither of us had eaten more than a bite of an odd sandwich in days. We lost our appetites at the same time as we lost our father. Then things got messy. Maeve made a clumsy pass at one of the Jones lads. I'm not even sure which one. He was only eighteen years old. He seemed happy enough to go along with Maeve on whatever journey she had in mind for them. But his mother wasn't as pleased. She'd shouted, a little too loudly I felt, that Maeve should pick on someone her own age. Maeve responded by downing another shot of vodka and orange juice. But I'd seen the hurt in her eyes and I knew what she was doing. She was trying to forget in the only way she knew how.

I didn't have much time to worry about Maeve, because Mam needed my attention more. We were due to go back to New York two days after the funeral but I couldn't see how we could leave Mam. Apart from anything else, she would be in no fit state to manage the pub. We'd need to appoint a manager. Dad trusted Hugh and he seemed like the obvious answer to our problem. But getting Mam to agree to that was another matter. She didn't want to make any changes. And at the same time, she wasn't fit to be in charge herself. My plan was to sit her down, once the funeral was over and try to make her see the sense in taking on some help.

It was quiet the day after we buried Dad. Our cottage was cleaner than I'd ever seen it. Eileen and some neighbours had given it a head to toe, as she called it. The fridge was chock-full of meals, all ready to be popped in the oven. The kindness was overwhelming and I knew that I'd spend my life forever grateful.

Maeve came into our kitchen, red-eyed and a little shamefaced, which put her in a mood. 'I hate this coffee!

Why doesn't Mam have a filter coffee machine, for goodness' sake?'

'Because Mam doesn't drink coffee. Sit down. I'll make you tea and a bacon sandwich.'

'Did I make a holy show of myself?'

'Not at all,' I lied. 'Everyone was locked by then, so nobody noticed.'

'I'm mortified. What was I thinking?'

'You were upset. Give yourself a hall pass.' I placed her food in front of her. 'But we need to chat, Sis. Mam isn't coping.'

'We have to make her eat. She's a bag of bones,' Maeve said.

'Maybe now that the funeral is over, she'll eat. She's still asleep. But we need to talk about Friday. I don't think we can go back and leave her. Not yet.'

Maeve threw her sandwich down and I thought she was going to burst into tears. 'No way, Lucy. If we don't go back, we'll never get away. I am devastated for Mam, I really am. But we can't stay. We just can't.'

'I want to get back to Ryan, believe me I do. But how the hell can we leave her in the state she's in? We can't go.'

'What about work? They'll fire us. And then what will we do? We have rent to pay at the end of the month.'

'I know. It's not ideal. I'll call Mick in work later today. I'll have to hope he understands.'

'You might as well put me in the ground beside Dad if you make me stay here any longer. I'm not like you, Lucy. I'm a selfish wagon, I know I am. But I have to go back on Friday. Besides, think about it: if I go back and work lots of overtime, I can take care of the rent. It doesn't make sense for us both to stay.'

There was no point arguing with her. When Maeve made her mind up, that was it. So I let her go. Mam's relief and gratitude that I was staying behind made the pain at not seeing Ryan for a bit longer easier to bear. Maeve told Mam that she'd lose her job if she didn't go back. And she said she wished she was as lucky as I was, with a forgiving boss who was happy to extend compassionate leave. It frightened me sometimes how easily Maeve could twist the truth to make it suit her. But again, I figured it was kinder this way for Mam.

# 29

## Lucy

### October 1992

*Woodside, Brooklyn, Manhattan*

My few days at home had turned into almost a month. We'd phoned each other twice a week. But it wasn't the same. I missed Ryan's smell, his touch, his voice. And our phone call last Friday had seemed stilted. He was quiet and it was only when I put the phone down that I realized he'd hardly said a word. Had I babbled on too much about the changes I'd put into place at Nellie's? I began to fret, worried that every day I stayed away from Woodside was a step away from Ryan. Mam and I had had a lot of heart-to-heart conversations over the previous couple of weeks, late into the night. And when I told her that I loved Ryan, she encouraged me to return to New York. She understood that I had to be with him. She'd a lifetime of love with Dad and she wanted the same for me. It was incredibly generous of her, because if she'd put the guilt on me to stay longer, I'm not sure I would have had the heart to leave.

And during the transatlantic flight back to New York, I realized with surprise that it wasn't just Ryan and Maeve that I couldn't wait to see. I missed New York too. The bustling crowds impatient to continue their day, the coffee-cart guy on the corner of 61st by the subway, who never forgot that I liked two sugars and creamer with my morning coffee, walking and watching both the tourists and locals as they took a bite out of the Big Apple, the fact that the city truly never slept as we piled into a diner for fries and shakes after a late night in Saints and Sinners. New York had got under my skin. I had fallen in love with its charms as so many others had done before me and I acknowledged to myself for the first time that Maeve wasn't the only one who had no wish to return home to Ireland. I felt the same way.

As I pushed the airport trolley in front of me, it almost tripped me up, I moved so fast. I scanned the crowd in Arrivals for my boyfriend and my stomach flipped with nervous anticipation. What if he'd gone off me? Out of sight, out of mind.

But then I saw him. Standing by a potted plant, shuffling on his feet in the way he did when he was nervous. He looked in my direction and called out my name, his face breaking into that gorgeous smile I loved so much. Every doubt disappeared.

This was Ryan. My Ryan. My love. I left the trolley behind and ran to him.

'I've missed you so much,' I said, reaching up to kiss his face, over and over. I couldn't get enough of him. I wanted to feel every part of him against me.

'Oh Lucy. You have no idea how hard this has been for me. The longest month of my life! I'm no good without you,' he sighed into my hair and time stood still as we held each other. 'Are you OK? You look thin.'

'I'm fine. Or at least I am now.' I tried to push the thought of my weeping mother from my mind. Would she ever forgive me for leaving her? 'Where's Maeve?'

'I wanted to have you all to myself. So she said she would meet us at the apartment. She mentioned something about giving it a clean.'

'Impossible. That one hasn't done any cleaning in over five years.'

He laughed and spun me around in a circle, making me feel like one of those girls I'd watched in romantic comedies throughout my teens.

'I was glad when she said she'd stay put. Don't be cross at me for not wanting to share you.'

'How could I ever be cross with you?' I said, kissing him again. 'Oops, I'd better get that.' I pointed to my discarded trolley that was causing an obstruction. He ran over and grabbed it and as he pushed it towards the bus terminal, I linked my arm through his. I had a month of missed embraces to make up for.

As I sat beside Ryan on the bus, it struck me how much had changed since I'd arrived in New York earlier that year. 'The last time I flew into JFK, it was with Maeve and we hadn't a clue. We sat on this bus feeling like green eejits from the country. When we spotted our first yellow cab, we squealed. We'd only seen them on TV or in the cinema before. Now I feel like I'm seeing old friends.'

'I love it when you say eejit. Best word in the world,

that is. I don't know why the Americans don't adopt it as their own.'

'It's even better when you put fecking in front of it. Satisfying.'

'There's no real equivalent in American. Idiot or fool, I suppose. I've made a decision, Lucy. I shall only say eejit from now on,' Ryan proceeded to say the word over and over, making me giggle and the couple across the aisle from us stare. We were in giddy form, happiness fizzed up between us like a newly opened bottle of pop.

'How's the novel going?'

'I've only managed to do another five thousand words this month. You're my muse, Lucy. I write faster when you are around!'

'Well I promise not to leave you again so,' I said. 'Tell me all the other news. How's Mike, and your parents?'

'They can't wait to see you. They want you to come over for lunch on Sunday. They had Mass said for your dad again at the weekend.'

They were so good. They'd had at least four Masses paid for to my knowledge. But that's what you did when you couldn't be there for someone in person. Since we'd been in New York, I'd attended four memorial services for a family member of one of the Irish diaspora who couldn't get home for their loved one's funeral. A lot of people were in the States illegally, so they daren't leave. A high price to pay for living in the land of opportunity and dreams. I supposed I was lucky that I could travel back and forth, without any penalty.

'The other big news in the O'Connor house is that Mike asked Eugenie to marry him yesterday. She said yes. I think they're planning a summer wedding.'

'Oh, I'm so happy for them both. But crikey, that's quick! Your mam must be over the moon! Is she buying a new hat already?'

'Beside herself. And already thinking about the wedding party. She was afraid Mike would never ask anyone that question, he's been such a player when it comes to women. I know I shouldn't say anything bad about my brother, but honestly, the amount of women I've seen come and go over the years . . .'

'He loves Eugenie. Maybe he just needed to meet the right woman.' I wasn't sure Eugenie loved him though. There was something shifty about her.

'Mam thought her only hope for grandchildren was with me. I could never see myself getting married, having a family. Not until I met you, that is.'

I couldn't breathe; my heart hammered so loudly I was sure he must hear it. He picked up my hand and held it between his. 'Lucy Mernagh, I could spend the rest of my life with you.'

'I could spend the rest of my life with you too,' I replied breathlessly. Was he going to propose, here, on a slightly musty-smelling bus?

But before I could work out if that would be a good or a bad thing, he went on. 'I'm not going to propose. Not here, anyhow. You deserve much more. But brace yourself, Lucy. I've got plans for you. For us. The forever kind.'

'I like forever plans,' I whispered, then leant up to kiss him again. It was the happiest moment of my life.

Once we arrived in Penn Station, we jumped on the subway to Woodside. *To home.* And that was another moment of realization for me. I had never thought of our apartment as home until this moment. I walked in the door and smelt a whiff of lemon. Maeve had been cleaning. 'Hey, Sis. I need to go away more often. The place looks great!'

She didn't move towards me, she hung back at the cooker. 'Don't be getting any ideas that I'll do this on a regular basis.'

I recognized the look on Maeve's face. Shame. I'd seen it many times over the years. She was guilty and I knew why. I had been a bit peeved when she'd left me to take care of everything at home. But I'd long since forgiven her. 'You have nothing to feel bad about, Sis.' And that only made her look even more pained. 'You can't beat yourself about what's done. And it's all OK. Mam was all right when I said goodbye, better than I thought she'd be.' This was true. She'd given me her blessing to return here, along with another liberal douse of holy water. To my surprise, before I had the chance to tell Maeve any of this, she burst into tears. She must have been living her own hell, worrying about what was going on at home. I ran over to her and pulled her into my arms, shushing away her tears.

'I'm so sorry. I'm so, so sorry,' she repeated, over and over again.

'We'll go back home together soon, maybe for Christmas. Or Mam might surprise us all and come over herself. Michelle said she'd bring her, so she'd have company on the flight. They both want to meet you, Ryan.'

Maeve cried even louder and I looked over her shoulder to Ryan, mouthing my apologies. To my surprise he looked tearful too. He was such a softie.

'Listen, you two, I've had a month of tears at home. Pull yourselves together. I'm going to have a shower. Wash the flight off me. But I'm starving.'

'I think all we have here are pop tarts. I forgot to shop, sorry,' Maeve said.

'Some things never change. How did you survive without me this past month? I have a real goo on me for a Stop Inn special. The dirtiest burger they've got. But can we make it a takeaway? And remind me to fill you in on the big romance between Michelle and Tadgh. If he hasn't proposed by Christmas, I'll eat my hat. Pour me a glass of wine, will you, Ryan? I reckon I've about two hours before I'll fall in a heap, so why don't we make them count.'

'That I can do,' Ryan said, breaking into a grin. 'It's great to have you back.'

I sang the whole way through my shower. I was back with my two favourite people in the world. And I knew that only good things were coming my way.

# 30

## *Bea*

### February 2020

*Aer Lingus Flight EI107*

I couldn't quite believe that sitting on one side of me was a sleeping Katrina and on the other a sleeping Stephanie. It was Katrina who had suggested that Stephanie join us both. And she said yes, in an instant. This trip could not be better timed for her, a chance to escape the fallout of her messy break-up. Despite feeling exhausted, I couldn't stay asleep for more than ten minutes. But the in-cabin movie selection was excellent, so I decided to catch up on several movies I'd not managed to see in the cinema. I flicked through the movie channel, looking for inspiration for my next watch. Then I saw it: *Circle of Friends*, the movie based on a novel by Maeve Binchy. And I remembered another time I'd watched this movie, cushioned by the arms of Dan. We were in my bed, late one

Sunday morning, both a little hungover from the previous night's St Patrick's Day party at The Still. We both thought the movie was charming, well maybe me a little more than Dan. But he pretended to love it too.

'I'm going to take you to my home in Ireland one day. My parents will love you. And my sisters too,' Dan said. It was the first time he'd spoken about our future in any way.

'When?' I asked, realizing that I'd quite like to do this.

'I don't know. Maybe one summer. Every bucket list should include a drive along Ireland's Wild Atlantic Way. Maybe we could do it together. Visit my dad in The Ballagh for a few days. Then head off, just the two of us.'

'I could go and visit Mom's grave.' It was impossible for me to think about Ireland and not think about Mom. They were a package deal.

He pulled me in closer towards him and held me tight. 'Maybe we can find a way while we're there to commemorate your mom.' Dan scrunched his face up as he thought about this. 'I don't know, like plant a tree that would grow and live on in her memory. That's off the top of my head, but we can work on a better idea.'

'I'd like that,' I whispered and the love that had been growing in me for Dan took root inside every part of me. And I knew that love would never leave me. I kissed him to seal the deal. 'We have to stay in cute B&Bs, rather than big hotels though. I want to see Ireland, not the touristy parts.'

'Well, you're lucky you have me, blue eyes, because I know all the good spots. Consider me your free Irish tourist guide.'

I knew I was lucky then, and I still know it today. I wondered what Dan would make of me finally travelling to Ireland. Without him. I'd daydreamed at one point that we would make the trip part of our honeymoon. I should never have thought such a thing. Because when a girl begins to think wedding bells, it's tantamount to shooting yourself in the foot. In the end, that's exactly what I did, bang, bang, bang. There would be no honeymoon in Ireland with Dan. No cute B&Bs. I left my memories of Dan locked away in that compartment in the back of my mind. Then I flicked the channel to the TV shows section and watched re-runs of *Frasier*.

It was cloudy and grey as we made our descent. The patchwork green quilt that I'd heard about from Gran throughout my childhood couldn't be seen. Our luggage came out without any issue, we made our way to the car-hire company and sorted out the paperwork. Katrina managed to get us a free upgrade, hinting that we might join the cashier for drinks later that night in somewhere called Gibney's. I was riding shotgun, with Stephanie in the back. We had a Ford C-MAX people carrier. It looked new and was perfect for our trip.

Stephanie used Bluetooth to connect her phone to the car's stereo system and her holiday playlist filled the car – a hits of the Nineties compilation. The perfect soundtrack for our road trip.

'LeAnn Rimes!' We all shouted as she began to sing along to 'Can't Fight the Moonlight'.

'You OK?' I asked Katrina, when I realized she had yet to start the car.

'Yes. It's a gear shift. I just need a moment to work it out.'

'Should we swap it for an automatic?' I asked. 'I'm sure they'd let us swap.'

'Who drives a gear shift these days anyhow?' Stephanie asked.

'In Serbia, I drive gear shift.'

'You were twelve when you left there!' I said.

'Do you remember all those times your grandad made us drive his cars?' Stephanie asked at the exact moment the memory came to me too.

'Oh my God, the fun we had with the street parking laws!' On Wednesday mornings, to allow the street cleaners in, you couldn't park on the left-hand side outside Innisfree. And then on Thursday afternoons, you couldn't be on the right. If you were caught parked at those times, they would tow you and also give you a hefty fine. Between Grandad, Mike and Dad we had three cars, but two of them weren't working half the time, their batteries dead as doornails. So Grandad would call up the stairs to me when it was time to move the cars. And with him pushing, me behind the wheel, I'd steer the car to its new parking spot.

'I used to sit in the passenger seat with you. Oh Bea, I remember it like it was yesterday. Your grandad was so lovely,' Stephanie said.

'He was. I'd give anything to have the chance to move a car for him now.'

'What would he think about you being here?'

'He'd be happy. And most probably be driving the car by now!'

'Cheek! We're off!' Katrina said as the car started and we began our two-hour drive to Wexford. We'd tossed a coin whether to head to Cork to find Ted first, but in the end this felt like a better option. Top priority for me was to find my mother's grave in Kilmore. Then, after that, we would visit my aunt. I decided not to give her any advance warning. That way, she couldn't make an excuse to be unavailable. Our PA Nikki had booked a hotel in the area for two nights. Then we'd head to Cork. Our next move after that would be dictated by how elusive or co-operative Ted was.

There wasn't much to see on the motorway. The grey tarmac of the road matched the grey skies. But then half an hour south of Dublin the Wicklow Mountains said hello. As did the sun, which poked its head out through the clouds. The sunny south-east earned its nickname. I felt a wave of emotion begin to build. This was the Ireland I'd dreamt about for years, the Ireland I'd felt a connection to. The Ireland I'd sung about with every note of 'The Isle of Innisfree'. We continued along the M11, watching strange place names whizz by us on green road signs. Enniscorthy. Ferns. Camolin. Blackwater. Castlebridge. Then finally we saw the signs for Wexford town.

'I know we ate loads on the flight, but I'm starving,' Stephanie admitted. It was nearly noon and the previous night's dinner long forgotten.

'Why don't we find somewhere to eat in Wexford town, before we head to our hotel in Kilmore Quay? The satnav says that's only about thirty minutes from here,' I suggested.

Katrina turned off the N11, making her way along the Estuary. We spied a large car park beside a cinema and decided to stop there. It was cold, but as the sun was still shining we set off for a walk along the waterfront. A couple of dozen dog walkers and families with buggies made their way up the quay. A railway line ran parallel to the quay on one side, with the water on the other, fishing boats bobbing up and down. We didn't speak; I assumed the girls were like me, taking in the charming maritime town beside us. It couldn't have been more different to Manhattan; instead of skyscrapers dotting the skyline whichever way you looked, there were only a couple of church spires. We continued walking until we reached an area called Crescent Quay. We paused to take a look at a bronze statue of Commodore John Barry. A plaque told us that the USA had given the statue to Wexford in the 1950s. A fair swap for my grandparents, I thought. When I read that the Commodore was originally from Tacumshane, I started to laugh as another memory popped back.

'Did Grandad ever tell you his bus story?' I asked.

Stephanie and Katrina shook their heads.

'Grandad worked for the Metro bus line when he first came to New York. Back then, the driver would have to announce what the next stop was. Next stop Lexington. Next stop Times Square. So on and so forth. Well, this day, about a year after he left Ireland, he spied someone in the rear-view mirror. Someone from Tacumshane, like on this plaque. Grandad used to play hurling against the guy he spied, back when he was a young fella. So he said into the microphone to the whole bus, "Next stop Tacumshane."'

'He was so funny,' Stephanie said. 'I bet they went for drinks afterwards too, knowing Joe.'

'Apparently Grandad brought him home to Innisfree that night and they partied until the early hours. Singing, telling stories about home.'

We made our way up Harper's Lane, then turned left

into the cobbled South Main Street. The paths were narrow on either side of the small road. We came across a small restaurant with an Irish name we struggled to pronounce, Cistín Eile. When in Rome, Stephanie said, so we went in. The small restaurant was as charmingly Irish as we could ever have wished. Irish phrases adorned the painted walls. *Is maith an t-anlann an t-ocras.* Our waitress taught us how to pronounce the name of the restaurant and also the phrase, which translated to 'hunger makes a great sauce'. We all chose bacon and cabbage, because the waitress said it was one of their specialities. And when the food arrived, we all agreed that this was the most delicious food we'd ever had. I'd grown up in a house that served bacon and cabbage with mashed potatoes every other Sunday. But Gran never made food like this. The glazed bacon was served with a mustard sauce, buttery cabbage and the most divine champ potatoes.

'Erm, no offence to your gran, but this beats any bacon and cabbage I've eaten at Innisfree,' Stephanie said. I felt guilty just nodding in agreement.

'We need to come back here,' Katrina said, all but licking her plate clean. We left happy and replete. And a little surprised at the quality of the local artisan food we'd eaten. Friends had visited Ireland over the years and they'd come back with nothing but praise for their visit, with one exception: the food! But if this was a taste of what we could expect in the future, then I was all in.

We made our way back to the car, this time walking along the cobbled Main Street, as opposed to the quay. I linked arms with Katrina and Stephanie, me in the middle of the two of them, as we'd done so many times since we were kids. We passed a couple of buskers, who were belting out an Ed Sheeran song. We stopped and sang along for a few minutes. I realized that this was the first time I'd felt properly happy in weeks. And I felt a little bit of hope grow that maybe there could be more fun moments in my future. We passed several boutiques that looked like they could rival the small ones I loved in SoHo. We stopped to chat to a man who was walking his six dogs, all dressed in their Sunday best. We left Wexford and the scenery changed as we left the main road and made our way towards Kilmore. We whizzed by green fields dotted with hay bales and rust-coloured gates. We all squealed when we spotted our first thatched cottage. Stone walls lined the road, which began to get considerably narrower the nearer we got to Kilmore Quay. Katrina slowed down to almost a crawl.

'How do you pronounce Quay?' Stephanie asked. 'Is it key or kay?'

'Key,' I said. And in my head, I heard Dan's voice saying it.

We spotted our hotel, the Coast Kilmore Quay at the edge of the village.

'So many thatched cottages,' Katrina said. Some of which were dirty brown with weather-worn age, others stood out proud with a new vibrant golden thatch that glimmered in the sun.

'That's my favourite. Look over there!' Stephanie said, looking at a small whitewashed cottage with pink clematis flowers draped across its front like a feather boa. We spotted several pubs, including Kehoe's and Kilmore Quay Lodge. There was a large marina which had large and small fishing boats berthed, with thick twisted ropes and brightly coloured fishing crates, sitting in a pile on the concrete deck.

'Any sign of Nellie's?' Stephanie asked.

'It might be on the other side of the village,' I guessed. And then we saw it. A small whitewashed building ahead on the right-hand side.

'It's small. But kind of quaint. I like it,' Stephanie said. 'Look, that must be the car park over there.'

Katrina parked the car and I realized that I couldn't move. My legs felt like they were now detached from my body and would not cooperate.

'What's up, Bea?' Stephanie asked. 'You've gone white.'

'This feels big, girls. Like the biggest thing I've ever done. I'm shitting myself.'

'You've nothing to be nervous about. You are a decent, lovely person. And it is always a good thing when you meet family,' Katrina said.

'My mother grew up in that house.' I pointed to the small cottage that stood beside the pub. 'That's the family home. Or at least I think it is.'

'It's so quiet,' Stephanie said. I looked up and down the small village street and not one person was to be seen.

'So different to Brooklyn. I can only imagine what that must have been like for her when she got to America. It must have been such a gear change,' I said.

'Do you want to go in now?' Katrina asked.

I wasn't ready. Not yet. 'Can we go back to the hotel first? Check in. I'd like to walk over to the graveyard too. See where my mom is buried.'

'I noticed a shop on the way in and they had bunches of flowers outside it. We could pick some up to put on the grave,' Stephanie said. She was always so thoughtful. I'd have thought about flowers when we were standing by the grave and it was too late to buy them.

'I'm glad you guys are with me.'

'BFFs until we die.' Stephanie said, and Katrina didn't even throw her eyes up to the heavens.

The hotel was small but charming. We had a double room each. I tried the bed out and was pleased to note that it was comfortable. The receptionist couldn't have been more helpful and told us that afternoon tea was being served in the bar, if we fancied it. We were still stuffed from our earlier lunch but promised to check it out another time. We took an hour to freshen up then met in the lobby.

'You can smell the lobster, can't you?' Stephanie said as we strolled up to the harbour and watched the colourful boats bob up and down on the water.

'How you know it is lobster. Not hake. Or cod,' Katrina asked. Sometimes she was contrary purely to wind Stephanie up.

'Because it smells like lobster. That's why,' Stephanie said.

'I love the sea. Isn't it the only place in the world where you can stand and be,' I said, before their debate took root.

'Be what?' Stephanie asked.

'Be anything you want. The possibilities are endless, looking out to that vast ocean.'

'Well, if that's the case, I don't want to be pathetic any more,' Stephanie said.

I turned towards her, the wind whipping my hair across my face. 'Hey, enough of that kind of talk.'

'I met Jimmy's fiancée the other day,' Stephanie said.

'Shut. The. Front. Door!' I said. 'Where, what, how? Details!'

'I just bumped into her. I was in Macy's in Herald Square, picking up some bits for the trip. And as I came down the escalator from women's into accessories, she was standing there, looking at me.'

'Shit,' Katrina said.

'Yes. Shit. I thought she didn't know who I was, but I was wrong. The look she gave me was horrible. It was pure loathing. Like I was the dirt from her shoes.'

'You are not dirt, Stephanie,' I said, appalled that she would call herself that.

'I'm not sure about that. I rarely thought about Rita when Jimmy was in my bed. And when I did, it was as if she wasn't real. She was like a character from a book. But she was sure as hell real as she squared up to me in Macy's.'

'What did she say?' Katrina asked.

'She said that I was pathetic. Then she asked me a question. "You knew he was engaged and you made a choice to accept second place. What does that tell you about yourself?"'

I reached down to clasp her hand. Stephanie looked out to the ocean and continued, 'I had no answer. Because she was right. I had allowed myself to be second best.'

'You made a mistake. You loved the wrong man. Stephanie, you deserve to be number one in someone's life,' I said.

'Maybe I don't deserve anything more than being on my own.'

'This isn't all on you,' Katrina said. 'You were not the

cheater. You were single. Jimmy is the one she should be angry with. Right before she kicks his sorry ass to the kerb.'

'Do you think she'll do that?' Stephanie asked.

'Please tell me that you are not hoping he'll go to you, if that happens, and marry you?' I asked.

She didn't answer my question, which worried me. 'I used to think about a future with him, the fairy-tale ending with him.'

'Prince Charming doesn't say to Cinderella, "Wanna be my mistress?", does he?' Katrina said, blunt but with unavoidable truth in her words.

'No, he doesn't. And to answer your question, Bea, I'm done with Jimmy del Torio. There have been too many lies. Too many excuses. And with every mile the distance between us grew as we flew across the Atlantic, I realized that I didn't even like him any more. It was as if he was some bad drug I was addicted to.'

'Like my cigarettes,' I said.

'You never smoked,' they both replied.

'Whatever,' I said. I knew what I knew.

'Let's go buy some flowers,' Stephanie said, and we linked our arms once more.

# 31

## *Bea*

### February 2020

*Kilmore Quay, Wexford*

Stephanie emerged from the shop with four bunches of flowers in her arms. 'I bought one for the grave and one for each of us too. We can put them in our hotel rooms. I can't tell you the number of times Jimmy bought me flowers as a sorry excuse for yet another disrespectful no-show. Or a bribe for a booty call. I've decided that, from now on, I'm buying flowers for myself. I'm officially done with men.'

'Me too,' I said, pushing Dan's face from my mind.

'Me *not*,' Katrina said.

We walked past Kehoe's pub and found St Peter's Church, sitting prettily amongst the thatched cottages. It had a bell tower on its roof and I thought about the person whose job it was to ring that every Sunday before

Mass. Had any of my family done that? My mother? My aunt? The porch had a large stained-glass window of Jesus standing above a boat with fishermen. The quotation underneath it said, *I Shall Make You Fishers of Men*. Poems in mahogany and gold frames lined the brick walls, offering hope and encouragement to the parishioners who had prayed here. One called 'The Optimist Creed' made me stop and pause. It spoke about the importance of being strong so nothing can disturb your peace of mind. And to always look on the sunny side of life. And one line said that you should promise to make all your friends feel that there is something in them. I looked at my two best friends and made that vow. For as long as I could, I would think only of the best, work only for the best and expect only the best. We left the church and made our way to the old graveyard and began to wander through it, weaving in and out of the gravestones, looking for the final resting place of my Mernagh family. Pretty quickly we found my grandparents' grave. It was a grey granite Celtic cross, with the Mernagh family name written across its base.

*In Loving Memory of*
*beloved husband and father*
*Denis Mernagh*
*7.12.1951 – 5.9.1992*
*And his wife,*
*Elizabeth Mernagh*
*01.10.1949 – 12.07.1996*

'This has to be my grandparents. The names and ages seem right.'

'But your mom isn't mentioned,' Stephanie said. 'Was she definitely buried here with them or somewhere else on her own, I wonder?'

'Her ashes were supposed to be here. Dad said that was the plan.'

'Maybe they didn't add her name onto the gravestone,' Stephanie said.

My response to this was to burst into tears. Disappointment crushed me. To have come all this way from New York to Wexford only to find Mom missing, was too much. I sank down to my knees and sat on the granite stone that ran around the perimeter of the grave.

'Don't cry,' Stephanie said. 'She might be somewhere else. In her own grave. We'll look. Quick, Katrina, help me find her.' They both began to run up and down the graves, flowers in their hands, flashing colour as they went.

But there was no sign of my mom's grave anywhere. 'Maybe they scattered her ashes somewhere special,' Stephanie suggested, in a last-ditch effort to save the day.

'I wwwant my mom,' I sobbed as Katrina and Stephanie joined me on the granite kerb. They let me cry my grief out, only breaking the silence to offer words of comfort. And eventually, I only felt hollow inside. I wanted to explain to them how I felt. But it was difficult though to put into words the pain and loss of not having a mother in your life. 'I don't know what she smells like. Gran used to say when she smelt lavender that it reminded her of her own mother. She had a thing about spraying lavender onto her pillowcases. But I don't even have a smell to remember my mom by.'

I ran my hands over the grey and white pebbles that

blanketed the grave. Were her ashes scattered here? Did part of Mom linger in this atmosphere, coated to stones, the rock, the ground? I closed my eyes and tried to sense her.

I heard birdsong.

I heard the rustle of leaves in the breeze.

But I couldn't find my mom here.

'How is it possible that I miss someone I didn't even really know? Every damn day of my life I've wondered what might have been. And now, now . . .'

'Now what?' Katrina asked gently.

'I need her more than I've ever needed her before. Everything is so messed up. Dan. The bloody letter and its messages. If I could have any wish in the world, do you know what it would be? It would be to feel her arms around me, holding me, telling me that everything is going to be all right.' I rocked myself back and forth on the cold kerb.

'We can't give you that wish, but we're here for you. We might not be your mom, but we are your sisters in every way but blood,' Katrina said. She placed her arms around me.

'We're not going anywhere, Bea. Whatever you need from us, we're here. We'll work out what's going on with the letters. And I know your heart is broken about Dan. We can see that. But maybe if you talk to us, let us in, we can help with that too.' Stephanie added her arms around Katrina's.

'I honestly would be lost without you both. I'm lucky to have so many people who have always been on Team Bea. I just wish it didn't feel like I'm fighting a losing battle.'

'You are not losing anything. I will not let you,' Katrina said, so fierce I nearly believed her.

'Being here is heartbreaking. It's making you sad. That's natural. But you'll bounce back. Look at me! Who would have thought a few weeks ago that I'd be in Ireland right now. Having fun,' Stephanie added.

I reached out to hold each of their hands. 'When you go back home, you both need to do this. Hold your moms' hands. Then make sure she knows how much you love her. So she really feels it.'

'Now I'm crying . . . again!' Stephanie said.

'I need a drink,' Katrina said, wiping her eyes with her coat sleeve. 'Oy. Bea you have a little . . .' she pointed to my nose, which now had a line of snot dribbling from it.

'And of course I've no tissue,' I wailed.

'Always the drama with you. Use this,' Katrina said, pulling one of her gloves off and handing it to me. I blew my nose into it. It was quite satisfying actually. The suede was lovely and soft. I handed it back to Katrina. She peeled the second glove off and threw it at me, 'No, you keep both. I insist.'

This made Stephanie giggle, followed by Katrina, then me.

Friends are magicians. They have the power to turn tears to laughter in an instant.

# 32

## Lucy

### November 1992

*Woodside, Brooklyn, Manhattan*

I settled back into life in New York with ease. Despite my heartache at leaving Mam behind, it felt right to be back. Brooklyn had become my home. I returned to work at the Woodside Steakhouse, but while I liked it there, I knew it was time to think about my future here in New York. That meant it was time to explore working in the education sector. I wanted to teach.

Weekends were spent with Ryan at Innisfree. It was busy, but in a good way. Joe and Peggy had an open-door policy and loved to welcome in friends from the neighbourhood. Most of which were the Irish diaspora, or other immigrants. They'd built a tribe for themselves and I liked being part of it. They all but canonized me when I brought them a hamper of goods from home that I'd packed in my luggage. Barry's tea, a thirty-pack box of Tayto crisps, half a dozen bars of Tiffin chocolate, packs of Kimberley, Mikado and coconut creams, plus some fig rolls.

'You are the sweetest, kindest girl. Ryan is a lucky guy that you got lost that day outside the library,' Peggy told me.

'She didn't react with as much enthusiasm as this when I gave her diamond earrings for her fiftieth birthday,' Joe said, pretending to sulk, as he opened the Mikados.

They always invited Maeve to join us too, but she didn't enjoy Innisfree as much as I did. I think Peggy reminded her too much of home and Maeve wanted to leave every bit of Ireland behind her. It was different for me. I loved being part of the Irish community. I'd even agreed to help Peggy with the St Patrick's Day parade the following year.

I rang Mam every couple of days and she tried hard to put a brave face on her heartbreak. But during our last call she had cried for ten minutes. She'd been to Dad's month's mind, a Requiem Mass celebrated in memory of someone a month after their death. I shared my distress with Peggy, who sympathised and understood. She suggested that I write to Mam: 'Letters from home have been a blessing to me. When I left Ireland, I wrote to my mam every single week and she did the same to me. And when she died, I found all of my letters in her bedside locker tied up with a big, thick red ribbon. She kept every single one of them. Dad told me that she'd read them at least a dozen times each. Sometimes out loud to friends or family when they visited.'

My first attempt wasn't very good. It felt stilted and

strange to put my thoughts onto paper. But Ryan helped me, coaching me to open up about my day and the things I'd experienced. Once I thought about the letters as a form of journaling, it was easier and the words came from somewhere. Maeve preferred postcards and sent lots of funny ones that she found in souvenir shops. Michelle had proven herself to be a good friend, despite our distance. She visited Mam every Sunday after Mass. Michelle would take her some brown bread, or a tart, and they had a coffee together. I wondered if Mam read my letters to Michelle. It was a nice thought. Michelle planned to coax Mam out of the house with a promise of afternoon tea in the Ferrycarrig Hotel. She hadn't left her cottage since Dad died. And the change of scenery might help.

We'd spoken about her selling the pub when I was at home with her, sorting things out. But it had been in the family for four generations so it was hard to imagine it ever not being a Mernagh business. But even with Hugh now appointed manager, I still wondered if there was any point holding on to it. If we sold, then Mam could officially retire. She could take up a hobby, maybe an art class. When we were kids, she used to draw cartoon characters for us. Sometimes, late at night in the moment before my eyes closed, I allowed myself to daydream of a future house for Ryan and me. We'd have two spare bedrooms. One for a nursery and one for Mam. I loved that daydream. I smiled as I imagined Ryan and me painting the house, room by room. Sunflower yellows and kingfisher blues.

I began to sense that Maeve was not as happy with Eric as I was with Ryan. She'd been acting strange over the past few days. I thought she was avoiding Ryan and me, but when I suggested that to him, he reckoned I was overreacting. I didn't believe it was coincidental that she stayed in her bedroom whenever we were in the apartment. I'd seen this with Maeve before. When she didn't want to discuss something, she hid. When she turned down a chance to go for a drink in Saints and Sinners at the weekend, I decided it was time to confront her. I didn't care if she wanted to finish things with Eric. The heart wants what the heart wants. And while I liked him a lot, I was pretty sure she didn't love him. I also wanted to make sure she was not holding on to silly guilt about Mam. I hovered around our apartment, waiting for her to come out of the bathroom. She'd been in there for at least twenty minutes. Then I heard the unmistakable sound of her being sick. This worried me because she'd been sick the day before too, insisting it was food poisoning from a kebab she'd bought from a street vendor.

I felt a bit light-headed as my head began to thump with the conclusions that were flying around. I knew I was doing a two-and-two-makes-five leap, something I always tried to avoid. But as I heard her being ill, I remembered her pale face from the past couple of weeks. And this jolted me. I kept my eyes locked on the bathroom door until she came out, red-eyed and pale.

'What are you doing lurking there, Lucy?' She was startled to see me outside, waiting.

'Are you pregnant, Maeve?' I hadn't meant to be so direct. But the words were out before I could stop them.

She looked around me and I thought she was going to make a run for the door. 'Maeve. It's OK. It's only me. You can tell me anything, you know that. Are you pregnant?' I softened my voice, trying to coax the truth from her.

Two fat tears fell in synchronicity, landing with a plop onto her breastbone. She didn't answer me, but moved her head in the slightest of nods.

'How long?'

'About six weeks.'

'Is it Eric's?' They were on and off, dependent on her moods. I hadn't seen much of him since I got back from Ireland.

She walked past me into the kitchen and put the kettle on. 'I'm going through our stash of Barry's tea like nobody's business. It's the only thing I can stomach at the minute.'

'We can get more from the Butcher's Block. Have you told Eric yet?'

'No, and I'm not going to. Not yet. Not until I figure out what I want to do.'

'Abortion?' I asked in a squeak, and wanted to kick myself for sounding so scandalized. This was 1992 and if my sister wanted an abortion she could bloody well have one. 'Sorry, Sis. That sounded like I was judging you. I'm not. Whatever you want, I'm here for you.'

'Don't worry, Lucy. I'm judging myself enough for both of us.'

It was as if time had gone backwards and she looked no more than twelve or thirteen again. My poor, scared sister. I couldn't fathom a world where Maeve was pregnant. Not now, just as she was living the life she'd dreamt about in New York. Plus, she was so clued in when it came to birth control. We'd talked about safe sex and both vowed never to get caught out. How the hell had this even happened?

'I am considering an abortion. I have to. Because if I have this baby, it will ruin so many lives.'

'If you decide to have this baby, then it will be a good thing.'

She didn't look so sure.

'Eric will understand and support you, whatever you decide to do. I'm sure of it. I've seen the way he looks at you. He loves you, Sis.'

'I know. And I like him a lot. But I'm not in love with him. I wish I was.'

'You can't force yourself to love someone.' And I thought about Ryan and once again thanked the stars that had brought him into my life. If I got pregnant in the morning, I'd tell him straight away and I knew he'd be by my side, whatever I decided to do.

'I think Eric will want me to have an abortion. He can't stand his sister's kids. They wind him up.'

'Parents always say that other people's kids wind you up, when your own never do. So don't worry about that. Plus, you have to forget about that now. You have to work out what you want. Do *you* want this baby?'

She looked at me, her eyes wide, brimming with tears. Then she put a hand over her tummy and said, 'I can't believe I'm saying this. I'm so scared I can't sleep or eat. But yes, I think I do want this baby.'

I smiled and brushed her fringe away from her wet face. I expected as much from her. 'Well then, that's decided. You always said you wanted to be married by the time you were twenty-five, so that you could start a family. You're mixing things up a bit by having a baby first. That's all.'

She smiled through her tears and clasped my hand, bringing it to her lips and kissing it. The tenderness of the caress made me cry too.

'I don't deserve you.'

'Yes, you do. We always get through anything life throws at us. Together. Now let's make a plan. First things first, you need to go to the doctor and find out how far along you are, OK? Then we can work out what the next step for you should be. Don't you worry, Maeve, I'll be with you through it all. I promise.'

'You always are. You're the best sister I could ever have. You didn't even want to come to New York, yet you came, for me.'

'But look what I got in return for that leap of faith. I love Ryan so much. If I think about not being with him, it breaks me out in a cold sweat. I'm the one who should be thanking you for making me come with you. It's turned out to be the best decision of my life.'

As the kettle began to whistle its way to boiling point, Maeve started to sob. 'I can't believe I'm saying this. But I think I'm going to go home to Ireland. To Mam.'

'Shh. Don't make any hasty decisions yet. Let's take this one day at a time, okay?' And as I held her, I wondered what would I do, if she did go home? Could I stay here in New York on my own, with Ryan? And to my surprise, I realized that yes, I could.

# 33

## *Bea*

### February 2020

*Nellie's Pub, Kilmore Quay, Wexford*

We'd been parked outside Nellie's pub for over twenty minutes. But every time I tried to open the door to go in, I chickened out.

Katrina was getting impatient, and I couldn't blame her. 'Enough already, Bea. We either go back to hotel or we go in. But this car is too cold.'

I looked at myself a second time using my iPhone camera as a mirror.

'You look fine,' Stephanie said. 'You'd never know you had been crying earlier in the graveyard. Me, I always look like I've an eye disease after a good boohoo.'

'I know I have to go in. And I want to. But I'm scared. What if she doesn't want to speak to me?'

'Then we leave. And you will always know that you

tried. You are no worse off than you are now,' Katrina said.

'Plus we're right here with you. You're not on your own,' Stephanie said.

'OK. Let's do it. I need a code word for let's get the fork out of here though.'

'I vote chicken.' Katrina said, winking.

'Ha ha, very funny.'

'Right. Chicken. Fork out of there. Got it,' Stephanie said.

I dawdled behind them as they walked in and, when I hesitated at the door, Katrina grabbed me by the collar of my coat and yanked me inside.

'Thanks,' I said, using as much sarcasm as I could muster.

The pub was dark, despite being mid-afternoon. Low wooden beams lined the ceiling. A long mahogany bar ran from one side of the room to the other, with bar stools in front. It was empty except for one man who sat at the end of the bar, nursing a pint of beer. Stockton's Wing were singing about a beautiful affair in the background.

'I love that song! Your gran was always playing that when we were kids.' Stephanie said.

I gulped back some tears. It felt like a message from Gran. She was here with me, in spirit. It gave me strength in a strange way.

'I don't see any bar staff,' Stephanie said, looking up and down the room.

'Herself will be back in a minute,' the man at the end of the bar said to us, his eyes still focused on the pint he nursed in front of him.

'Thank you, sir,' Stephanie answered.

'Not from around here by the sounds of you.'

'No, we're visiting.'

'Well, you are very welcome to Kilmore.'

'Thank you,' Stephanie answered, our resident spokes-woman. We took a seat at a small round table beside the lit fireplace, a welcome warmth. Beer mats were scattered across its scratched surface. As I ran my hands over the uneven surface, I tried to imagine my mom sitting here, doing the same thing. I shivered at the realization that there was a strong possibility that *this* had happened. From what little I knew about her childhood, she had spent a lot of time in this pub.

'It feels like we're on the set of a movie, doesn't it?' Stephanie said.

I understood what she meant. The decor looked like it came straight from the set of *The Quiet Man*. I thought of the tourists I'd watched in New York throughout my life, taking everything in with wide eyes; this time it was us. A tall black post with a set of black-and-white road signs stood at the end of the bar. Directions to Dublin, Waterford, Kilkenny and Belfast were displayed. And there was an eclectic array of antiques hanging from every wall. An old telephone, a typewriter, a contraption that looked like it belonged on a farm and some oil lamps. The walls were painted a rich plum and as my eyes adjusted to the light I noticed that, despite the room being dark, it was spotlessly clean.

And I liked it. The decor felt comforting. Even though I'd only just arrived, I felt quite at home here. I closed my eyes and imagined my mother walking through this bar. She must have done so, hundreds of times throughout her childhood and early adulthood until she left Ireland. The flames from the fire cast shadows on the wall, for a moment I saw her. My hands began to shake and my head pounded once again. A bloody headache that I could not shake off. I ignored it and pulled my mom back to my mind's eye.

The Mom of the photographs I had grown up looking at.

The Mom of my dreams.

The Mom I craved with every fibre in my body.

I'd spent my childhood trying to find ways to feel connected to her and, sitting here in Nellie's, I'd finally succeeded.

No sooner had that thought left me than a door opened behind the bar. A woman walked in and said something to the beer-drinking man. Time slowed down, Katrina and Stephanie disappeared and the only person left in the room was my aunt.

I knew that it wasn't Mom, no matter how alike they were. My head knew that. But head and heart are two different things and, for a moment, I allowed myself to dream that a ghost I'd longed for had finally arisen.

'Oh jeepers, look, she's off again,' Stephanie whispered to Katrina, then began to root around her handbag for a tissue.

My aunt turned her attention to us and shouted from her position behind the bar, 'Sorry to keep you waiting. What can I get you, ladies?'

Stephanie shouted back, 'We were happy to wait. Could we have three bottles of Corona please?'

'Sure. Glasses or by the neck?

'The neck is great.'

'I'll drop them down to you.'

I listened to their exchange as if I were out of my body, a passer-by listening in on another's conversation.

'You look just like her,' Katrina said.

'If Mom hadn't died, I think that's exactly how she would look today.' I watched her as she prepared our drinks order. Her hair was shorter than in the photographs I'd seen of her. There was one taken of my mom and her in their apartment in Woodside, cheesy smiles for the camera, wine glasses in hand. I loved it. Dad had taken it one evening before they went out for the night. Now my aunt wore her hair cut into a short, blunt bob, with a long fringe that she kept tucked behind her ear. She was still slender and pale I noticed, as she emerged from behind the bar and brought our drinks over. Did my mother have a similar gait to her? Physically, they could have been twins. And it took my breath away. I felt anxious and exhilarated all at once. She placed our Coronas on the beer mats.

'Where you girls from?'

'New York,' Stephanie replied. 'We arrived earlier today. We're staying in the Coast Hotel.'

'It's nice there. You'll be very comfortable.' Then I felt my aunt's eyes on me. I looked up and our eyes locked. She went paler, if that were possible. I realized I wasn't the only one seeing a ghost.

'Hello,' I said, in a croak.

'Hello.'

Stephanie uttered an 'Oh. My. God.' to which Katrina hissed, 'Be quiet.'

'You look just like her,' my aunt said.

'So do you.' I felt weak.

'It's so good to meet you,' she said, her voice filled with emotion.

I lost my voice and couldn't say anything in return. This was the most surreal moment of my life.

'Are you all here on holidays?'

I looked at my friends and tried to convey to them that I needed their help.

Katrina handed me my Corona and ordered me to drink. 'Bea, you need this.'

'I'm Stephanie and this is Katrina,' our spokeswoman chipped in.

'It's really nice to meet you both.' She turned back to me. 'Bea. I like that. Suits you more than Beatrice, I think.'

'Thank you. Is it OK that I'm here?' I was relieved that my voice had come out sounding normal enough. The sharp, cold beer had done the trick.

'More than OK.' And to prove her words, she smiled at me. It's funny how a smile can change a face. She didn't look so scary now. 'Is it just the three of you visiting?'

I took this as code for is your father here too? 'Just us. I have some work to do in Cork. But we decided to come here first of all.'

My aunt smiled as she looked at the three of us, one by one. 'Good friends are everything. You three remind me of . . . never mind.' She didn't finish.

Reading her mind and thinking she'd like it, I recited the quote from *The Three Amigos*, 'Whenever there is injustice, you'll find us. Wherever there is suffering, we'll be there. Wherever Liberty is threatened, you will find the . . .' I paused, thinking that this could be a Hollywood moment for us as she'd finish the last part. Oh how we'd laugh. But she left me feeling foolish with the unfinished ending dangling in the air between us. She held her hand up and I wasn't sure if she was commanding me to stop speaking or offering it as an apology.

'I'm sorry. Dad said it was something you and my mom and Michelle used to say. I didn't intend to upset you.'

It appeared I had struck a nerve. I wasn't sure why, though. She seemed to pull herself together and turned back towards me, 'No, it's me who is sorry. You gave me a shock, that's all. You sound so like her. Despite your accent being all wrong.'

'Dad always says the same whenever I say that line. I've watched the movie dozens of times, because he said Mom loved it so much.'

'When we were young, we used to quote lines from that movie verbatim. It was our code. You took me by surprise. I've not heard it for the longest time.'

'How is Michelle? Are you in contact with her still?'

'We see each other all the time. She's busy with her life as the wife of our local councilman and they have four kids, aged from eight to eighteen. But she's not changed really from the girl she was then. She's been a good friend to me.'

'Are you married?' Stephanie asked.

'No.' I'd wondered the same thing myself many times and had half hoped that I might find a room full of cousins here. But it appeared that this side of my family was destined to remain small. We fell into another silence and it wasn't one of those comfortable ones either. The air was thick with the unsaid. All of the times I'd dreamt of meeting my mother's family, it had never gone like this. Maybe Dad had been right. I should have left the past in the past.

'I'm glad you still are good friends with Michelle,' I said; anything to break the silence. 'I'd be lost without Katrina and Stephanie.'

'Best friends forever,' Stephanie gushed.

'Nothing lasts forever.' A wince flew across my aunt's face as she whispered that.

Once again I felt like I was missing the punchline in a long joke.

'Pint when you're ready!' the man at the bar shouted, raising his empty glass in the air.

'I'll be with you in a sec,' she called back. 'Why are you in Ireland, Bea? You've never come before.'

'I wanted to see where Mom came from. Understand a bit more about her life. Dad has told me everything he knows, but as he was only with her for a short time, I feel like there must be more to her story. I hoped you and Michelle could fill in the gaps.'

'Lucy! A man could die of drought here!' The man shouted again.

My Aunt Lucy stood up and walked back to the bar to serve him.

# 34

## *Lucy*

### November 1992

*Woodside, Brooklyn, Manhattan*

I was gone for a few moments. But sometimes it only takes that to change the course of your life.

We were out of bread. And as toast and tea were all Maeve could manage, I ran across the road to the local market to buy some more. I'd watched her fall apart little by little over the past couple of days. I was prepared to do anything I could to make things easier for her. She'd made me swear not to tell anyone about the pregnancy. And I understood that, because if she did decide to terminate, then there was no need for anyone else to know. But it was a burden to hold it on my own, with nobody to talk to about it. I wished Michelle was with us, because she would have made it more bearable for us all.

Ryan knew something was up. He kept asking me what

was wrong when he called. I'd cancelled a couple of planned dates, which I hated to do, but I couldn't leave Maeve. She needed me. I would never break my promise to Maeve, so I asked him to trust me that I'd tell him when and if I could. He'd told me on the phone earlier that a scene he was writing wouldn't cooperate and he needed a break from his manuscript. If I were truthful, I needed a break too. I planned to tell Maeve that I was going out for a few hours later on. But Ryan took matters into his own hands and called to see me while I was out shopping. As I turned onto the corridor to our apartment, I could hear raised voices. I thought it was Eric and Maeve at first, that she'd finally told him about the baby. But the nearer I got to the door, I realized it was my boyfriend shouting at my sister. They had always got on well together.

'How do you know?' Ryan shouted.

'Because I always used a condom with Eric!'

My key to the front door hovered in the air in front of the lock. I tried to make sense of what they'd said. She must have told Ryan she was pregnant. But that didn't explain why she had to explain herself to him. Was Ryan more traditional than I realized? Did he disapprove of her being pregnant? That didn't feel right. But if it was, we were going to have a major problem. My hand shook and I couldn't get the bloody key to cooperate for me. It kept missing the lock. The funny thing is, if I'd been steadier of hand, I wouldn't have heard the next bit. I would have walked in and they could have made some excuse to explain their argument. And I've no doubt that I would have been gullible enough to believe them.

Because they were my boyfriend and my sister. Why would I ever doubt anything they said to me?

As I tried to open our door, Ryan said, 'We can never tell Lucy. It would kill her.'

Those words steadied my hand and, open sesame, the key slid into the lock. The room silenced. They watched me as I threw the groceries on the kitchen counter. I could almost hear their thoughts bounce across silently to each other, 'What did she hear? Don't say a word. LIE!'

'You can never tell me what?' I asked. I was surprised how strong my voice sounded.

They looked at each other and then back to me.

I saw the guilt that Maeve had been wearing for weeks mirrored on Ryan's face. A thousand scenarios rushed through my head. But I pushed them away. I loved Ryan and he was going to propose to me. He'd hinted as much. We were going to buy a house, somewhere near Innisfree. And Mam would come and stay, to help take care of her grandchildren. We'd have three. Two boys and a girl. I had our future all worked out. Ryan was a big part of why I was willing to give up my beloved Ireland, leave my heartbroken, grief-stricken Mam on her own. And this scenario, whatever it was, was not part of that.

Ryan looked at Maeve in desperation, 'Please . . .'

*Yes. Please, Maeve. Don't say something that will tear my life apart.*

But she ignored our pleas and said the words that somehow I knew were coming. 'I'm so sorry, Lucy. I'll never forgive myself, not to the day I die. But the baby is Ryan's.'

# 35

## *Bea*

February 2020

*Nellie's Pub, Kilmore Quay, Wexford*

As my Aunt Lucy sorted out a pint of Guinness for her customer, I messaged Dad to tell him that I'd met her. I watched three dots appear and then disappear beside his name. I had almost finished my bottle of Corona by the time he came back to me with a short message: 'That's great, tell her I said hi.'

My something-was-off radar was ding-ding-dinging like crazy.

'I bought you another beer,' Lucy said, rejoining us. 'And I'll join you too, I think.' She lifted her bottle up and gulped a third down in one thirsty swig. She liked beer too. It pleased me more than it should.

'You know, if you'd given me a hundred guesses as to what I'd be doing today, sitting in a bar, drinking a beer with my niece and her friends, wasn't one of them,' Lucy said.

'I know the feeling. I'm sorry if I gave you a shock, turning up out of the blue.'

'It's fine. It's a good shock.' There was a quiet confidence about her. She was cool and I liked her vibe.

'How's Ryan?'

'He's good. He said to say hi. I just had a WhatsApp from him.'

'He was a good friend to me the summer I spent in New York. I've followed his career. I'm glad things worked out well for him with his books.'

'He's a good man.' I cringed inwardly. My chitchat was appalling. We fell into another awkward silence.

'You said before that you came here to find out more about your mom? After all this time, why now?'

That was a big question and difficult to answer. 'I put Mom, and I suppose you too, in a box under my bed. And I left you there, occasionally peeping in every now and then. It was time to take you all out of the box. I've spent my life trying to make a connection with a ghost. And it's not enough any more.'

'I get that.' Lucy said. 'And I'm happy to help you fill in some of the blanks.'

'When I was small, I wanted to be like her so badly. I used to ask Dad and my grandparents endless questions about all parts of her life. What was her favourite colour? When they told me it was blue, that meant blue became my favourite too. Dad said she loved anything by Whitney Houston or Celine Dion. My Spotify list became filled with power ballads from the Nineties. What perfume did she wear?' I blurted all this out in one breathless rush.

Lucy smiled and didn't seem phased by my questions. 'Maeve did love blue and she used to sing "Where does my heart beat now?" every morning in the shower. Off-key, I might add.'

'Bea has a lovely voice,' Stephanie said.

'You must get that from your dad. He used to sing a lot back in the day. At parties and things in Innisfree. Do you still live there?'

'Yep. Dad and Uncle Mike too. I'm in the basement. Dad converted it to a studio apartment for me a few years ago.'

She smiled, 'I loved that house. I had a lot of happy times there with your grandparents. They were like second parents to me for a while.'

'What did Maeve smell like? Bea is particularly interested in hearing that.' Stephanie said, trying to be helpful, but making me sound like a crazy woman.

Lucy jumped up, telling me she'd be back in a moment. She ran behind the bar and out the door towards, I guessed, her home. And was back in less than a minute, clutching a bottle in her hand. 'Opium Eau de Parfum, by Yves Saint Laurent. Maeve wore this every day. Ever since she was sixteen. She thought it smelt sexy and provocative. And it did on her. When I tried it, it felt like I was playing dress-up with my mam's things. On the days when I can't stop thinking about her, I spray some of this into the air and it brings her back to me.'

I sprayed the perfume onto my wrist and inhaled the spicy scent and for a moment, it brought my mom back to me too. 'Why did Mom emigrate to America? Was she unhappy here in Ireland?'

Lucy shook her head. 'Nope. She, we, had a great

childhood. We lived next door to the pub, in a small cottage. It's my home now. It never felt small to us. Because we had this place. Nellie's. But Maeve always wanted to travel. We used to go to the flicks every Saturday afternoon with Michelle. We didn't have multiplex cinemas back when we were kids, so there was only one option. But we didn't care what the movie was, we still went regardless.'

'What kind of things did you watch?'

'We all loved anything set in America. *Big* with Tom Hanks, *Bill and Ted's Excellent Adventure*, *E.T.*, *Back to the Future*! They were all hits with us because they were so different to the life we had in rural Ireland. Everything about America seemed especially exotic. Maeve wanted a piece of it more than Michelle and I did. I think, sitting in the middle row – always the middle – that's where she first began to daydream about emigrating.'

'It was the opposite for me. I used to dream about moving over here to Ireland when I was little. I asked Dad often could we come to visit, but there was always a reason why we couldn't make it.'

'Life has a way of getting in the way,' Lucy said.

'Dad said you both trained to be teachers.'

'Even though I was ten months younger than Maeve, we started school at the same time. We always did everything together. I don't think we really knew what we wanted to be when we left school, so we decided to do an Arts degree.'

'Did you like university?'

A look came over Lucy's face, of nostalgia and happiness. 'One of the best times of our life. We shared a flat with Michelle. And we lived on Pot Noodles, instant coffee and Blue Nun wine. Oh and Jammie Dodgers. Your mom loved the jam and cream ones.'

'I don't think I've ever had one!'

'You haven't lived,' Lucy said with a smile. 'We partied hard, but we worked hard too.'

'Did Mom have a boyfriend back then?'

'Nobody serious. Her first love was this eejit . . .'

'Dad loves that word. He uses it a lot.'

'I remember that,' Lucy said. 'Well, Irish idiots or eejits as we call them, there was a fair whack of them around here. Maeve fell for this guy called Tomas. He liked to refer to himself as the "T-man". I mean, that alone should have warned her that he was an . . .'

'Eejit . . .' I said.

'Exactly. But she couldn't be told. She wasted a whole summer on him and his shenanigans. Until she caught him red-handed with Gorgeous Gloria.'

'Gorgeous Gloria?'

'Yep. That's what we called her, at least. She was fierce, glamorous and always looked great. But she'd been dumped by her boyfriend and her self-esteem must have taken a hammering, 'cos she lowered her standards – and her knickers – for the T-man.'

As my friends and I laughed, I realized that I had relaxed. I was enjoying myself, chatting to Lucy. She was everything and more that I'd hoped she would be.

'Was she devastated by his cheating?'

'Her ego was damaged, but that's all. She didn't love him. But we did have to go through a week of her mooning around the flat, looking miserable. Then we heard about the Morrison visas and over a bottle of Blue Nun – we were partial to it because it was cheap – we decided we'd go for it. We applied thinking we wouldn't have a chance in hell of getting one. But fate was on our side. Both Maeve and I were pulled out of the visa hat and got our green cards.'

'What about Michelle?'

'No, she didn't get one. But she didn't mind. She'd fallen in love with Tadgh – her husband – by then.'

'And my mom met my dad that summer?'

The same pinched look came over her face again. Should I just ask her what the issue was? I was afraid it might spook her.

'Yeah. They met that summer.'

'Were your parents upset when Mom married an American?'

'Dad had died by then. And Mam wasn't well. She never got over Dad's death. But she had grown used to the idea of us living in New York. She knew that, for Maeve in particular, there was nothing for us in Ireland. There were hundreds of thousands unemployed here at the time. A lot of people bailed out, like we did.'

We both fell into silence here. Not awkward, more sad, because neither of us needed to say what we were thinking. Mom's future was shortened because of her move to the US. If she'd stayed in Ireland, she would most likely be alive now.

'It was life-changing for you all,' I said.

'You could say that.'

'Dad said you two were close.'

'She was my other half. My life. My almost twin. I miss her, Bea. Every day of every week of every year, I miss Maeve. The pain never goes away.'

'I miss her too. I'm sure you think that's stupid as I didn't know her. But I feel like I did.'

'Of course you do. She loved you. With every ounce of her being, she loved you. From the moment she found out that she was pregnant.'

'The thing is, Lucy, I don't understand why you didn't stay in America to be with her, with me?'

'It was complicated. I loved your mom, but I had a broken heart. I couldn't stay in New York. Plus Mam needed me.'

This was news to me. Dad had never mentioned any hearts being broken. 'I'm sorry to hear that. Even so, it must have been hard for you to say goodbye to Mom.' My instincts were pushing me to keep peck, peck, pecking.

'It was the toughest, most heartbreaking goodbye I've ever made.'

'Do you regret coming home, or was it the right thing to do?'

'You ask a lot of questions,' Lucy said.

'Sorry.' But I wasn't in the least sorry. I wanted to know everything.

'Tell me about your life,' Lucy said, switching lanes. 'Do *you* have a boyfriend?'

'No.'

'She could have. A guy from Wexford called Dan loves her and she loves him,' Katrina said.

'Tell me more.'

Katrina and Stephanie started spilling their guts, telling Lucy all about Dan and how good we were together.

'Sounds like you two had a good thing,' Lucy said.

'For a while, yes.'

'I'm sorry it didn't work out.'

'Me too.'

The door to the bar squeaked open and we all watched

a tall, sandy-haired man enter. He walked over to us and flashed a smile at each of us. 'Howya.'

We all chorused hellos. He propped his elbow on Lucy's shoulder as he gave the three of us the once-over. Stephanie and Katrina both sat up straighter and started to mess with their hair, the way they did whenever a good-looking man was in their vicinity.

Gran used to have this saying, about something taking the wind out of her sails, when she was surprised.

Well, the wind was whipping up a storm.

This stranger turned to Lucy and said, 'Are you going to introduce me to your friends, Mam?'

# 36

## *Bea*

### February 2020

*Nellie's Pub, Kilmore Quay, Wexford*

'This is my son, Mark.' She swallowed and then added, 'And this is your cousin, Bea. She's Maeve's daughter. These are her two friends, Katrina and Stephanie.'

He took meeting us in his stride, as if meeting long-lost cousins happened every day of the week. The rest of us though were all having loud reactions. Katrina gasped. Stephanie had another Oh-My-God moment. And Lucy went silent and pale in the way that I'd already learned was her thing. Me? Well, I forgot to breathe for a moment, and it was only when I felt light-headed that I exhaled a loud, rasping breath.

'Great to meet you.' He held his hand out to shake mine. Then he laughed out loud, one of those laughs that belonged to the confident. It was a nice sound. 'Feck that.

It's not every day I get to meet a new cousin. Give us a hug.' He pulled me into his arms. I felt awkward and shy. Katrina and Stephanie shook his hand and said their hellos. And all the while Lucy watched me. Why the hell hadn't she mentioned a son earlier?

I've spent my life being told that I'm the image of my mother, and my aunt too. I've always taken it as the highest compliment. It was a badge of honour to look like them. Growing up, Dad always grumbled, insisting his DNA was in me somewhere. And if anyone said I looked like him, he'd whoop with delight. Genetics were a funny thing. Dad was the image of Grandad, who by all accounts was the image of his own dad. When they were out and about, people would say, 'Well you can't deny him, Joe!' Almost identical features, down to the cleft on their chin and the cowlick in their hair that refused to be tamed, no matter how much product was used.

'I'm parched. Can I have a beer, Mam?' Mark asked.

The curious thing was, he didn't look like Lucy in the least.

'Sure. I'll get another round. Hugh, he's our bar manager, will be here in a minute. I called him to give us time to chat,' Lucy told us.

'I'll give you a hand carrying the drinks,' Stephanie said.

'Me too,' Katrina added, leaving me on my own with my cousin.

'It's crazy how much you look like my mam,' Mark said, peering at me closely.

'You, however, don't look like her in the least.'

A shadow passed over his face. 'I must look like my dad, I suppose. Not that I've ever met him.'

'I know how much that sucks. I never knew my mom.'

'Yeah it does, right? My dad might as well be dead, I suppose. Because Mam doesn't know who he is.' He leaned into me and whispered, 'Don't say this to her, she's doesn't like to talk about it. But she had a one-night stand with a guy and never got more than his first name.'

'I won't say a word. Will you excuse me? Back in a minute.'

I walked over to the bar, a gunslinger reaching for her weapon.

'The shit is about to hit . . .' Katrina said.

'The fan . . .' Stephanie finished.

'So not just me then?' I asked them.

'Nope. Not just you,' Katrina replied.

'You OK?' Stephanie asked.

'Nope.' I turned towards Lucy and told her that I needed a word.

Lucy handed the drinks to the girls, then motioned for me to follow her out the back.

'I was about to tell you about your cousin, when he arrived home.'

'Were you going to tell me why the hell my cousin looks exactly like my dad? Because I can only think of one explanation for that. And that cannot be.'

# 37

## Bea

### February 2020

*Nellie's Pub, Kilmore Quay, Wexford*

'You don't understand,' Lucy said.

'So explain.'

'You can't tell Mark.'

Lucy looked desperate. And so she should. 'Why not? The guy deserves to know the truth. He's just said to me that he doesn't know who his father is and how much that sucks. But *you* know who his father is. I want to hear you say it. Mark's my brother.' Silence. 'Answer me!' I demanded.

'Yes. But you don't understand.'

'So you keep saying. How could you do that to my mom? Your own sister!' I was so angry I wanted to hit her. I took a step backwards because I was afraid that I might actually follow through with what I was thinking.

'Will you let me explain? Please. I deserve the chance to do that.'

'Does my father know about Mark?'

'No!'

I didn't know whether to be relieved or sad about this. It would be horrific to think Dad had ignored his own flesh and blood for all this time. But how bloody sad that he'd missed out on seeing his son grow up. I'd always wanted a brother. And all along I had one.

'What age is Mark?'

Lucy flushed red, two dark splashes of shame on her cheeks. 'He's twenty-seven.'

The same age as me, which could only mean one thing. 'You had an affair with my father. What kind of a woman does that make you!'

Lucy slumped onto the sofa behind her, her head hung low. 'It wasn't me who had the affair.'

'What does that even mean?' My hands felt clammy and my heart began to race.

'Ryan was *my* boyfriend. We were together for months before he married Maeve. He loved *me*, not her. We had a life together, a planned future. He was going to propose. Then my dad died and Maeve and I came home to the funeral. Mam needed me, so I stayed on, but Maeve went back to Brooklyn. While I was here, taking care of my mother, they slept with each other. I had no idea. And when I returned to New York, they didn't say a word.'

The shock felt like a hard slap across my face. My knees began to shake and I fell beside my aunt on the sofa.

'Ryan broke me, Bea. When I needed him to be strong, to put me first, he jumped into bed with my sister. I was so excited to see him. I'd missed him more than I could ever have imagined was possible. And all the while he had betrayed me in the worst way. I was oblivious to it all, letting him back into my bed.'

My father had always been a man of honour. I couldn't equate the man I'd known my entire life with this version Lucy shared with me.

'Maeve found out she was pregnant. I assumed it was her on-off boyfriend's baby. But then one day I walked in on her and Ryan during an argument, and they had no choice but to admit that they'd slept together. Just the once, a drunken mistake, by all accounts. Ryan called in at our apartment for a notebook he'd left there. He found Maeve crying. They had a drink together, one thing led to another, blah, blah, blah.'

I could hardly believe what I was hearing. For my whole life, I'd thought I was the result of a great love story. When all along it was a drunken illicit fumble.

'They stole my future on that night. They both cried and begged me to forgive them. Ryan said it was me he loved and he'd spend the rest of his life trying to make it up to me. Maeve said she'd move out, she'd leave Brooklyn. She said she'd do anything to make it right. My head literally melted as I listened to them both run through scenarios that might make me forgive them.'

I couldn't imagine the horror my aunt must have gone through – all at the cruel hands of my parents. I'd come to Ireland to find the ghost of my mom. But it appeared in her place I'd found a brother.

'I did consider forgiving him. I loved him. And I thought maybe we could get through it. But I also knew my sister. She loved her unborn baby. And Ryan's family would want to know his baby. And I knew Ryan too. He would want to do the right thing and be part of the baby – your – life. How could I deny you a family – and Ryan's family was one of the very best. I moved out and stayed with my manager Mick, from the Woodside Steakhouse that I worked in. And eventually, after a few days of sleeping on his sofa, I realized that there was nothing left for me in New York. I came home to Ireland. I told Maeve and Ryan that I never wanted to see them again. I meant it at the time. They hurt me so much.'

'I'm so sorry.'

'What are you sorry for? You didn't do this. This was all on them. It was the worst time of my life. I didn't eat or sleep for weeks. Mam wasn't much use to me either; she was still in a heap about Dad.'

'Then you found out you were pregnant?'

'I didn't realize it for about two months. I thought I was feeling so shit because of the break-up.'

'Why didn't you tell Dad when you realized?'

'I was angry. And more than that, I was ashamed. How the hell had we become a family where two sisters were pregnant by the same guy? It was like a bad episode of *Jerry Springer*. I told Michelle and she persuaded me to tell Ryan, but the very day I was supposed to call him, we received a wedding invitation from Maeve. She wrote a letter begging me to come over, to be her bridesmaid. She said that, for the baby's sake, she and Ryan were going to give it a shot together. It was the last nail in the coffin of our relationship. She not only stole my love, but now she was taking my wedding day, getting married in the New York Public Library. The pain turned to paranoia after Mark was born. I worried that if Ryan and Maeve found out about him, they would try to take him from me, add him into their perfect family life in Innisfree.'

'This is so messed up.' I stood up and paced the small room. 'I need that drink.'

'Me too. But I can't go out there yet. I need a minute.'

'And Mark really has no idea?'

'None.'

'I can understand why you kept it to yourself at first. But for nearly thirty years? I'm baffled.'

'When you tell enough lies to yourself, you start to believe them. I told anyone that asked that I didn't know who Mark's dad was. This scandalized everyone into shutting up and not asking any further questions. Then Maeve died. The grief was horrific. Mam died a few months later. She went to the grave never knowing the truth.'

'Shit. That must have been an awful time.'

'I can't explain the devastation. No words would ever do that justice. But when you have a child to take care of, you have to just keep on going. And that was a blessing because, without Mark, I think I would have been unable to go on.'

'And you've never considered telling Dad since then?'

'Truthfully, when Mark was young, I was so busy, I didn't have the time to think about Ryan or you. I was a single mam, juggling this pub and a baby. For years I didn't catch my breath. It was only when Mark made his First Holy Communion that I stopped to realize what I was missing out on. As your aunt, I should have been there for all of your big and small moments too. I left Mark with Michelle and I went to New York. I waited outside your school gates until you came out. And I followed you home. You played hopscotch on the sidewalk with another little girl for a bit. I think it was Stephanie actually, looking at her now.'

'I can't believe you were so close to me and I had no idea.'

'Then I saw Ryan with his arm around a woman. They took you to the park and pushed you on the swings. You looked like a happy family unit and I decided it was selfish to break that up. Too many people had lost so much, I didn't want to add to the mess.'

'I wish you'd spoken to me. We could have had a lifetime together. I could have known Mark.'

'It was hard to walk away. I could see, even from a distance, what a great job Ryan had done with you. Your mam would be so proud of you, I know she would.'

'I'm not sure how I feel about her right now. She's been on a pedestal for me, my whole life. And now you've . . .'

'Knocked her right down,' Lucy finished. She didn't look happy about that. 'I want you to know that your mam was my best friend and I loved her more than anyone else in the world. That's why her betrayal hurt so much. But she was a good person, Bea, I swear to you. She was decent and funny and kind. She was too impulsive though and sometimes had this self-destruct button.'

'Do you think, if she'd lived, you would ever have made up?'

'I'd like to think we would. But I have to be honest, maybe we wouldn't have. I felt like I had too much to lose to risk making contact with your dad. There again, she would have come home at some point and if she'd seen Mark, like you, she would have known.'

'You have to tell them. They have a right to know. I know Dad was a dick to you – and that's going to take me a while to forgive – but Mark is his son. Ryan has always been a good father to me. Mark deserves to have a relationship with him. Take it from someone who has missed their mother their whole life: it never goes away, Lucy. It's always there.'

Lucy wiped tears from my face. 'I'm so sorry, Bea. Not only for everything you've said. But also because me staying away meant that I wasn't there for you. I should have been.'

'You can be here for me now . . .' And the thing was, I knew that I needed her.

'I'd like that. I'll tell Mark. But it has to be when we are alone. I can't have him hearing this with an audience. It's too painful. I know it's time to tell Ryan too. I promise I'll do it. Just give me a few days.'

'We're heading to Cork to work on that case I'm on. It should only take a day or two. We could call back before we go home.'

*Home.* I realized that I desperately wanted to go back to New York, my home, my Innisfree. So this was what homesickness felt like. 'Where's Mom's grave? I couldn't find it earlier.'

'We didn't bury your mom's ashes, we scattered them in a spot she loved. I can take you there when you come back.'

I nodded and all of a sudden felt bone-tired. I'd had enough. My headache was back and I wanted to grab the girls and go back to the hotel. Away from the emotional hits that I'd taken. And I wished that my big gentle giant Dan was here, to scoop me up in his arms and carry me back to the hotel. I missed him with every part of my being and ached for the pain I had caused him. I may not have slept with his brother, but just like my parents did to Lucy, I broke his heart. Lucy said she thought Dad was going to propose, just as I thought Dan was going to for me...

# 38

## Bea

### June 2019

*Central Park, Manhattan*

'This had better not be a cheesy horse-drawn carriage ride-through-the-park surprise,' I said to Dan as he dragged me into the park at West 72nd Street. It's not that I didn't love Central Park – I mean, what's not to love – but I had my heart set on the movies tonight. And Dan's suggestion of a walk in the park threw me.

'Trust me, I've got a surprise for us,' Dan said.

'In my experience, whenever someone says those two words, "trust me", it's time to run. Add the word "surprise" and I'm out of here.'

'Oh you of little faith. Not much further, we're almost at Literary Walk,' Dan said. I noticed he gripped my hand a little tighter in case I did decide to bolt.

Did he just say *Literary Walk*? Dan wasn't a big reader.

I suppose there could be a play on. Shakespeare in the Park. Then a thought struck me.

Was Dan going to propose? We'd been together six months and the love word had been bandied about many times. And I meant it sincerely when I said it. I had no reason to doubt his sincerity either. I loved this man with my whole heart. But that didn't mean that I was ready for a marriage proposal. Sweat began to trickle down the small of my back as the thought now acknowledged took root.

'What's going on, Dan?' I felt a shiver of anxiety nip. Whatever he was up to, wasn't good. We passed the skaters and several joggers passed us. A group of tourists were watching a friend get their portrait sketched and a man with a white-painted face mimed his way out of a locked room, before passing around his beret for change.

'Slow down! I don't have your bloody long legs!' I moaned at Dan. I had to take three strides to keep up with one of his.

'Hear that?' he asked.

'Yes!' It was the sound of a violin playing. Had he organized a musician for the proposal? I glanced down at my jeans and T-shirt combo and wished I'd worn my green tea-dress instead. I'd contemplated it, knowing we had a date after work, but I was too lazy to sort out fake tan for my white legs. Did it matter what I wore, though? Probably not.

'Boom, boom, boom, boom . . . La da, la da da, boom, boom, boom, boom . . .' Dan made nonsensical words up as he sang along to the music. I recognized the violin's melody, I'd heard it before but in a million years would never be able to name it. 'Where is that music coming from?'

'You'll see. One sec,' Dan said, then he tapped his nose in a very annoying way. It made me want to give him a dig. I did not like being kept in the dark. But on the off-chance he was going to propose, I thought I'd better not hit him before. In case it changed his mind.

And that's when I realized that I wasn't against the idea. In fact, if I were honest with myself, I looked forward to it.

When I spotted the large crowd ahead of me, for a second I wondered if my family and friends were hidden within, ready to witness the big romantic moment. But then the music made sense as I realized what the group were watching.

'Tango!' I cried.

'I know, isn't it mad?'

Dancing counter-clockwise around Shakespeare's statue were about forty couples. There were two speakers sitting on a bench, blasting out the music. The low sun cast shadows on the asphalt pavers as it said its goodbye to the day.

Dan said. 'I stumbled across them last week and ended up watching the dancers for nearly an hour. What do you think?'

'It's . . . it's wonderful!' I exclaimed.

'Oh thank goodness!' Dan said. 'I hoped you'd like it. Look at those two over there!' He pointed to a couple who were in their seventies, him short and round, her tall and graceful, both with Snow White hair. She had a black lace dress, which was slit to the top of her thigh worn with black strappy sandals. He had a red shirt on, with black braces attached to black slacks, the crease crisp and firm down the middle. Their bodies were sculpted to each other, yin and yang dancers. I couldn't take my eyes off them as they swayed to the music.

There were others, like us, who were there to watch the dancers. A group of girls giggling, with one in the middle wearing a white veil and a sash that told us all she was the bride-to-be. I felt myself flush. How silly was I, thinking Dan was about to propose?

'It would make you want to join in, wouldn't it?' Dan said.

I shook my head. 'I've not a step in my body! I'd love to dance like that, but I'd ruin it for everyone if I tried to milonga.' I watched a woman, about my age, hook her legs around her partner's in fast succession. Another woman stroked the floor with her pointed toes.

'I thought you'd say that. There's a free lesson for beginners in a few minutes and we're going to give it a go. Come on.' Dan dragged me again, this time to the Ann Reinking London plane tree. Dan nodded at a man, who turned out to be Leo, our instructor.

'For tango, you need patience and discipline,' Leo said.

I was in trouble. I was not known for either.

Leo took his partner into his arms, then said, 'Let's learn the basic tango step. Take your partner, now walk, walk, walk.'

We watched them move forward, three times, and we gave it a go. I stood on Dan's feet three times, but to his credit he didn't complain once.

Over and over we tried this, until we had the walking part pretty down pat.

'Now we do the sidestep and close,' Leo said. 'Drag those feet in on the close, caress the pavement as if it were your lover.'

'Oh my,' I said to Dan, who tried not to giggle.

'Now we put it together. Walk, walk, walk, side, close, but we say, Slow, Slow, Quick, Quick, Slow.'

'So two slow walks, one quick walk, a quick sidestep and a slow close?' Dan asked.

'That's it!' Leo said. 'Well done. For a man who is so . . . big, you are very light on your feet!'

'Teacher's pet,' I said, sticking my tongue out at him.

'Lift your ribcage,' Leo said to us both, then he manoeuvred our bodies into the correct position. 'You must learn how to move through the core of your body. Bend your knees, lift your ribcage, hold your head dramatically to the left, that's it!'

And then, to our surprise, as we moved in hold, slow, slow, quick, quick, slow, something clicked. We stopped muttering the words to each other and began to dance without thought. I cried, 'I bloody love this!'

'I bloody love you!'

'And I bloody love you too,' I replied.

Leo appeared and said, 'Ah the young lovers. The tango is often referred to as a three-minute love affair. I think for you two lovers, it is more than that. A forever love affair, yes? Now place your cheeks together. And sway to the music. Yes! Just like that!'

We were the second-last couple to leave in the end, dancing our way from dusk into twilight, until we were under a blanket of stars, twinkling in the sky. We vowed to each other and Leo that we would come back. Every week. And while we didn't end up going every week – life was too messy and complicated for us to keep that commitment – we went often enough that it became ours.

Our couple thing.
Until we were not a couple any more.
You can find *the one*.
You can fall in love.
And then you can lose him, all in the space of one year.

# 39

## Bea

February 2020

*The Clongibbon House, Mitchelstown, Cork*

After we left Nellie's pub and said our goodbyes to Lucy and Mark, we called into the restaurant in our hotel for food. Watching Katrina and Stephanie's faces as I filled them in about Dad and Lucy was comical. They literally did a jaw-drop. But once we'd finished our food, I think jet lag, or perhaps the day's revelations, caught up with me. I had an early night, leaving the two ladies in the bar drinking gin in large fishbowl glasses. I liked seeing them together – laughing, happy.

As we drove towards Cork, I switched back to work mode, trying to forget illicit affairs and secret brothers of my past and my now. Stephanie had another jaw-drop moment as we discussed the Ted Spadoni case. 'I thought

I was bad with Jimmy. But leaving a wife and child behind? That's cold.'

'I can't begin to imagine how confusing it is for them. One minute he's there, next he's gone,' I agreed. And I realized that confused was a word that could describe how I felt right now too. I just didn't get why Dad had hidden this part of his and Mom's story from me. I felt betrayed on Lucy's behalf, on Mark's and mine too. If Dad had been honest with me, I'd have reached out to Lucy earlier and maybe then I'd have got to know my brother. And aunt. I liked her. She was the kind of person I could happily spend time with, and that had been taken from me.

I pushed the thoughts away again. I had a job to do, and for Olive and little Teddy's sake, I intended to give that 100 per cent. I pulled the file on this case from my handbag, then flicked it open. 'It's Thursday, so our scarlet pimpernel Ted should be in work. I think to be fair to his girlfriend and child, it's fairer if we approach him on his own. Also, we might get more out of him that way.'

'She might not know about his wife and son. God help her,' Stephanie said.

'She might not. There's a lot of that going around, isn't there? Secrets and lies in families. But I promise, Stephanie, we'll be respectful of all parties, no matter what.'

Google Maps didn't let us down and directed us into Mitchelstown in County Cork without a single wrong turn. Katrina drove slowly down the Main Street, parking up when we found a free spot.

'The town's famous for its cheese, according to their

tourist information,' Stephanie told us, reading from her phone. 'And it has a castle. I like castles. I think I'd quite like to live in a castle one day.'

'It would suit you.' I scanned the street, trying to get my bearings. 'I think Ted's office must be up there on the right.'

Stephanie decided to explore the town while we went to confront Ted. I had no idea what to expect from him. He was an enigma to me. What kind of man leaves a family behind? Would he show any remorse? I had to assume that it was unlikely. We climbed the stairs to the accountancy firm, which was based over a dental practice. The receptionist told us we were in luck, when we explained that we needed an accountant but had no appointment. When Katrina told her that we particularly wanted Ted Spadoni as he was American, like ourselves, she was so convincing, I half believed her. Within minutes we were seated in a small meeting room, with a round walnut table in its centre. Ted walked in, smiling like a car salesman, his arms open wide as he welcomed us. I disliked him on the spot.

'Fellow Americans, I hear!'

'Nice to meet you,' I said, shaking his hand. 'I'm Bea O'Connor and this is my associate, Katrina Petrovic.'

'Would you like tea or coffee?' he asked. The genial host. I would enjoy wiping the smile off his face.

'No thank you.' I slid my business card across the table towards him. 'We own a missing persons bureau, called the Family Finders Agency.'

He paled, his smile changed into a frown as he shifted in his seat and tugged at his tie. I couldn't help but feel satisfaction, watching him get uncomfortable. Well, he needed to buckle up, because I planned on making his day a lot worse.

'What are you doing here in Mitchelstown?' he asked. His eyes darted from Katrina to me. Like a rabbit in headlights.

'We represent your wife, Olive, and your soon to be fifteen-year-old son, Teddy.'

Like a bouncy castle deflating, he slumped forward onto the table in front of him. We gave him a moment to digest what was happening. He looked at the door – I assumed to double-check it was closed and to hide his guilty secret from his receptionist. Or maybe he was thinking about bolting.

'Olive paid us to find you, Ted. For years they've worried that you were in trouble somewhere. Calling hospitals every week. Watching the door, hoping that you would reappear. Praying for a miracle that was never going to come true. Because you were not hurt or suffering from amnesia. You were living the life here in Ireland. Not giving a shit about your family, who haven't slept a full night in over three years.'

'It's not what you think.' His face now had two bright red blotches on his cheeks.

'Tell us how it is,' I said.

'I had to leave.'

'This I have to hear,' Katrina said.

'Olive is a great woman. But we'd grown apart for years, long before I left. We were little more than room-mates.'

'That happens,' I said.

'Yes, it does,' Katrina agreed. 'But there's a thing called divorce. That's what sane people do. You tell Olive you want to leave. You make sure your son knows he is loved.'

'It wasn't that easy.' His voice had begun to sound like a high-pitched whine. 'I didn't mean to fall in love with Paula. At first it was merely an emotional connection.'

'Oh the old emotional infidelity card! If we had a dollar for every time we've heard that one.'

'It's true. I didn't sleep with her. Not for months. But she made me feel alive. And young. And loved.'

'Hard to resist,' I said.

'Yes!' he screamed, missing my sarcasm.

'Again, these things happen. But what doesn't happen, Ted, is a husband making it look like he's been abducted by aliens, or lying in a downtown morgue. That's not normal behaviour. Why not tell them you were alive?'

'I didn't know what to say.' Then he started to cry. Big loud racking sobs.

If he thought his crying was going to garner any sympathy from either Katrina or me, he was very wrong.

'Pathetic coward,' Katrina said, the only comfort he was likely to get from her.

'Does your girlfriend know about Olive and Teddy?' I asked.

He shook his head, wiping his nose with a pocket handkerchief. Then he looked to each of us in turn, begging, 'You can't tell her. We have a life here. A daughter. And she's pregnant with our second child. It's a boy. Due in three months! You can't tell her.'

'We have no interest in upsetting your girlfriend. But she does have our sympathy. Poor woman, being married to a spineless man like you.'

'What do you want from me?'

'That's up to Olive. For now, you need to wait.' I left him to cower under Katrina's scowl.

I rang Olive, who was waiting for my call. We'd been in touch several times already on WhatsApp.

'He's not being held against his will. Nor suffering from any illness that would excuse his actions?' she asked and, as delicately as I could, I told her the truth. It always amazed me how strong people can be under the most extreme situations. And Olive proved her strength when she outlined her wishes to me.

'Right, here's what you are going to do, Ted,' I told him. 'First, you need to book a flight to New York for tomorrow.'

'I can't just get up and leave. I have responsibilities here!'

I was astounded at the irony of this comment. 'As I said, you'll fly to New York tomorrow, then go straight to Olive's house.'

Katrina looked up from her phone, 'Aer Lingus have seats available down the back or up the front. You're in luck.'

'Olive will tell Teddy that you have been found in Ireland. She will explain to him that you suffered a concussion, leaving it a bit sketchy on how and where. But you can spend the eight-hour flight coming up with plausible details. She does not want Teddy to know that you abandoned him. You can explain that you have made a new life in Ireland. But you must let him down as gently as is possible. Olive is adamant that you find a way to make sure he knows none of this is his fault. Her solicitor will have divorce papers ready for you to sign when you arrive.'

'And then what?' He looked resigned now.

'Then you get to come back here and continue playing happy families. But at least your son can sleep at night knowing you are alive.'

'And what if I refuse?' he said, jutting his chin out.

'You have no choice. Because if you don't go, if Olive doesn't call us tomorrow evening and tell us that you went straight to her house to see your son, then we'll go to see your girlfriend and we will tell her everything. We're not leaving Mitchelstown until we know you've done the right thing.'

He started to cry again. It was hard to feel anything but contempt for a man who treated people who loved him in such a callous manner.

'Teddy will hate me.'

'Yes, he will. From what I gather, he's a clever lad. I'm not sure you'll be able to spin him a tale that he'll believe. But Olive wants to try. You will have to live with the consequences of your actions for the rest of your life. At least now he can leave the limbo he's been in, hoping for a miracle, watching the door, waiting for it to open to show Daddy is home.'

The fight went out of him as quick as it came. He was the deflated bouncy castle again. 'I'll book my flight. I'll make this right somehow.'

'The only way you can do that is to go back in time. And we all know that's impossible.' We stood up. We were done here. 'Remember this: we will be staying in Mitchelstown until we get confirmation that you have seen Olive and Teddy. We fully intend to take out a full-page advertisement in the local newspaper, if we have to, and expose what a dick you really are.'

'The *Evening Echo* newspaper looks like a nice one to start with. I'll get working on finding out how best to submit our story,' Katrina said, her head down in her phone again. 'Or maybe a radio interview might be more effective. There's a few we could choose. Cork's Red FM. Classic Hits. Life FM Cork.'

'Thanks, Katrina. I can see it now. They would love to help us reunite our clients with their missing father and husband.'

He put his hands in the air, then yelled at us. 'Stop. I get it. I can't lose what I have here. I love my life here. I'll do as you ask.'

'You OK?' Katrina asked, as I clasped the handrail for support as we climbed down the stairwell.

'I think I'm getting the flu. I feel a bit dizzy, that's all. I'll be OK in a minute.'

'You seem to get dizzy a lot these days,' Katrina said.

'Jet lag,' I countered. 'Let's find Stephanie.'

A quick phone call to our friend and she told us she'd found us somewhere to stay. We made our way to the Clongibbon House Hotel and found her in the bar, sitting with four lads, who were laughing as she regaled them with stories about New York. When she saw us, she waved us over.

'She's half-drunk,' Katrina said, taking in Stephanie's glassy eyes and flushed cheeks. I reckoned she was right.

'But at least she's not thinking about "I don't like labels" Jimmy Del Torio,' I said.

'I've checked us in! I've even brought your luggage in and it's in your rooms.' She passed a key card to each of us. Then she called for the barman, Pat, as if she'd known him her whole life.

The four lads introduced themselves – John, Seamus, Lorcan and Donal. All locals who insisted on buying us a round of drinks. Three large fishbowl glasses arrived, filled with gin, but this time with raspberries and mint thrown in too. They tasted delicious and most welcome after the meeting we'd had. A deserved treat. Stephanie's new friends were farmers and had been at a cattle sale in nearby Fermoy. They were celebrating because they'd managed to sell their stock.

'Eighty spring-calving cows sold!' Lorcan said. And we all cheered, clinking glasses.

'Fifty spring-calving cows sold!' Seamus said. More cheering.

'One hundred black-and-white herd sold!' John said, and we went wild cheering. This was the best fun.

'What about you?' I asked Donal.

'I'm a sheep farmer.' Which made us all howl with laughter.

Stephanie gushed about how much she liked pretty little lambs. I figured she liked more than lambs, judging by the way she kept touching Donal's arm and fluttering her eyelashes at him.

After our second drink, Pat the barman dropped wooden bowls in front of us, filled with French fries, cocktail sausages and chicken goujons.

'We didn't order these!' Stephanie said.

'On the house, girl!' He winked. 'Do you want some more salt for those chips?'

'I'm never leaving here! I love Cork!' Stephanie said, which resulted in a further round of drinks and clinking of glasses. The evening went by in a whirl. A trio of musicians set up in a corner of the pub and began to play music and sing songs. Lorcan went over to the musicians and invited himself to sing a song. He told the pub that his song was to welcome the Yanks to Cork. His choice was a pretty good rendition of 'American Pie'. Everyone seemed to know the words, so I guessed it was one of his specialities. Demands were then made for the Yanks to sing too, so the musicians took a break, leaving the stage to us. Katrina stood up, phone in hand as always, and hit the backing track for her karaoke special, 'Single Ladies'. Stephanie pulled me up beside her and we became her backing singers. We even did the iconic dance moves as we told the four lads to put a ring on it. As we danced together, the three of us became Beyoncé and my heart exploded with love for my girls. I'd missed this. All thoughts of letters, Dan and secrets of my past went, and all that was left was messy, drink-fuelled fun with my best friends. We fell into a big hug together at the end, me in the centre of the two of them, laughing as we heard the pub clapping and cheering.

'You are some singer like,' Lorcan said to Katrina.

'I am,' she agreed.

'We should do a duet. We'd fucking kill it.' They began to scroll through her backing tracks, looking for another number to sing.

Then 'Macarena' came on and Stephanie insisted we all get up to dance to it. As we swivelled our hips to the music, I thought, this is what happiness is – silly moments, dancing with best friends, not caring how we looked.

When the song ended, there was another drink waiting for us, courtesy of the lads.

'Do you sing, Donal?' Stephanie asked.

'If he does, he's never given us a single bar of a song in all the sessions we've had!' Seamus said.

Donal ignored their remarks and called over to the musicians, who were about to start playing again. 'I'll sing this for Stephanie from Staten Island.'

The guitarist began to strum a number I've known my entire life, a song I've heard a million times.

'Oh Danny Boy, the pipes, the pipes are calling . . .' Donal sang, in a clear baritone that made the bar silent, customers calling for quiet, there's a singer in the house. If you knew 'Danny Boy', then you knew that the song had power, no matter where in the world it was sung. It quietened things down. And its power now was that it made me want my Dan. With every fibre of me, I wanted to be back in his arms again. Why had I ever let him go? He was, is, would always be, the love of my life. I brushed a tear as it escaped and gave myself a stern talking to. This was not the place to fall apart. And whether I liked it or not, we were not together for a very good reason.

I watched Stephanie. Her eyes were locked firmly on Donal as he sang. She looked like she might burst with happiness. And I realized that I'd not seen her that happy since we were kids. Yes, the six or more gins she'd had helped with the general euphoria, but she had a glow about her. One of those happiness glows. When Donal finished singing the last note, she ran over and kissed him on the mouth. This made the crowd clap and cheer even louder. I turned to Katrina to have a 'what the actual' moment, but instead found my jaw dropping because she was playing tonsil hockey with Lorcan. Their plans to duet had taken a serious new turn. John nudged me, hope on his face for a hat trick.

'I'm going to bed,' I said.

'For real? Jaysus, I like you American girls! Come on so. Lead the way.' He jumped up from his bar stool.

'Hold on a minute, Romeo. *I'm* going to bed. On my own.'

'Fuck it. Knew it was too good to be true.' He downed the last of his pint.

'There's a couple of girls at the end of the bar who've been looking your way for ages. Why don't you try over there?' I told him.

Delighted with himself, he picked up a fresh pint, then sauntered down to them.

'Tell the girls I've gone up to bed,' I told the last of the four lads.

'No bother. They'll be safe with the lads. Donal and Lorcan are sound out,' Seamus replied.

'Good to know. But I'm not so sure they'll be safe with Stephanie and Katrina,' I winked as I walked out.

My room was really nice, with white bed linen. I flopped onto the bed and turned on the TV, to see if I could switch off my brain for a few minutes. Tom Cruise jumped from one tall building onto another tall building, with the usual bad guys giving chase. *Mission Impossible* something or other, I guessed. A perfect distraction. I dozed off and awoke an hour later with a thumping headache and a dry mouth. It was midnight and I could hear the distant beat of music downstairs in the bar. I wondered if the girls were still there singing their hearts out. It was possible that they might even have company in their rooms. It would be so much less complicated if I could have a one-night stand with one of the farmers. Maybe then I could forget about Dan. Did I do the right thing in finishing with him? I picked up my phone and looked at the message I'd received from him only yesterday.

> Saw your dad yesterday. Cannot believe you are in Ireland. I'm pissed, Bea. Not just because I was supposed to take you there. Because you shouldn't be anywhere but home right now. When you get back, I don't care what you say, I'm coming to see you.

I could picture his face as he wrote the message, flushed with anger, pacing up and down the floor of his apartment. I flicked back through the two dozen or so messages he'd sent over the last month, all variations of him pleading with me to see him. My vow that I'd stay away, that I'd keep him away from me was crumbling by the minute. Doing the right thing was impossible.

# 40

## Bea

### February 2020

*The Clongibbon House, Mitchelstown, Cork*

Katrina and Stephanie didn't surface for breakfast. I figured they needed time to enjoy their hangovers. Once I'd polished off a hearty full Irish, which was all kinds of wonderful, I went back up to my hotel room. Gran and Grandad were in my thoughts today. The buffet I'd just had fun with would have been heaven to them. My appetite had been a bit up and down lately, but four slices of the white soda bread on offer, toasted, with Kerrygold butter alongside local sausages and bacon, was now top of my list for my last-ever meal.

I went for a walk, strolling down one side of the Main Street, then back up the other. I stopped in a small gift shop and picked up some trinkets. A silk scarf for Corinne. A tweed peaked cap for Uncle Mike that I thought he'd enjoy wearing down in Farrell's for the craic, as he'd say. He could pretend he was gentry or something. I found a book about Irish literature that I thought Dad would enjoy, and a small plaque that said, 'Don't upset the author, you may end up dead . . . in their next novel!' I bought both, even though I was annoyed with him.

I checked in on Ted too, to make sure he was on his way. He confirmed he was standing in line for pre-immigration clearance in Dublin Airport. I had a sneaking suspicion that I couldn't trust him. He sounded very unsure about what time he would arrive at Olive's. Ted Spadoni had all the hallmarks of a man about to do another runner. And there was no way I was going to put Olive through one more evening of a no-show. I called in a favour with Uncle Mike. He was always helpful on troublesome cases. When Ted walked into Arrivals, Uncle Mike would be waiting for him, in uniform. He promised me that he would personally drive slippery Ted to Olive's.

When I got back to the hotel, I found the ladies in the lobby waiting for me.

'I'm going to need details.'

'He is good kisser,' Katrina said with a shrug. 'We kiss. We sing. We kiss some more. I say goodnight.'

I turned my attention to Stephanie, who was practically dancing on the spot with excitement. 'I slept with Donal. Three times!'

We whooped and high-fived her, delighted at her delight. This was clearly a big deal for her.

'I've never had a one-night stand in my life!' she said, as if she'd read my mind. 'In fact, I've only ever slept with Jimmy.'

'That is so tragic,' Katrina said.

'I know,' Stephanie agreed.

'Tell us everything,' Katrina said.

'I didn't mean to sleep with him. I said he could come up for a nightcap. We took brandies up with us.'

My stomach felt a little queasy just thinking about how much drink they'd had after we left.

'And then we started to kiss. And he was so tender. Not one bit pushy. And we talked for ages. He wanted to know everything about me. I think I shared more with Donal in one evening than I've done in my entire relationship with Jimmy.'

She looked like she might cry, so I quickly changed the subject. 'You are not allowed to ruin this moment by thinking about he-who-does-not-like-labels.'

She took a deep breath and shook her shoulders, as if she were literally shaking him off her. 'Last night felt right. And I thought, why not?'

'Too right,' Katrina said. 'You did good.'

Stephanie beamed at this. 'Donal has asked me to go to see his farm. Do you mind if I disappear for a few hours?'

'Not at all. We have to stay here till this evening to make sure that Ted follows through and gets to Olive's. By the way, Katrina, I have Uncle Mike lined up to meet him at the airport.'

'Good call. I think we should make our minds up to stay here another night. Then we can drive to Wexford in the morning. Gives you one more night with lover boy,' Katrina said.

We checked with the hotel and they happily extended our stay for an extra night. 'There's music on in the bar again, ladies,' the receptionist said. Katrina groaned, 'I need to go back to bed. That OK?'

'Of course. And Stephanie, remember you are to stay at Donal's as long as you like. But keep us posted.'

'What will you do?' Stephanie asked me.

'I think sleep is a nice idea too. I haven't had an afternoon nap since I was a kid, but I'm thinking they should be mandatory for adults. I must be getting old, I can't deal with hangovers any more!'

Donal arrived a few minutes later and Katrina and I warned him to look after our friend. He nodded so earnestly, assuring us of his only good intentions, that we all joined Stephanie in her newly formed "I love Donal" fan club.

'Good to see her happy,' Katrina said as we walked back to our rooms. 'I would like to see you happy too.'

'Me too.'

'Any more messages from your younger self?'

'Yes. As it happens there was one this morning when I checked. But I'll tell you about it after your nap.'

'Sleep can wait. Show me now.'

Katrina followed me into my bedroom and I picked up my letter, flicking through to page three.

*Are you in love? Does it feel wonderful?*

'You haven't answered yet,' Katrina's voice was gentle and soft.

'Because I don't know what to say.'

'Why did you and Dan break up? No more telling me that it is too painful. I want the truth.'

'I can't tell you, Katrina. Because if I do, it will change everything and I'm not ready for that.'

'Is it for good reason?'

I nodded, unable to trust myself to speak.

'You know that you can tell me anything. If I can believe that your younger self is leaving messages to you, then I will understand anything you tell me about Dan and you.'

I lay down on the bed and Katrina lay beside me, until we faced each other.

'I'm so tired, Katrina. But I will tell you soon. OK?'

'OK. For now, we sleep.' She reached over and held my hands between hers. With her touch, her support, her friendship, I always felt stronger. I closed my eyes and Katrina began to sing a lullaby that I hadn't heard in years. When we were fourteen, I burned my hand making hot chocolates for us both. And I cried for so long, she began to sing a lullaby her mother sang to her when she was a child, about a butterfly. '*Leptiriću, šareniću, hodi k' meni amo, Evo imam lepu ružu, pomiriši samo.*' I fell asleep listening to Katrina's pretty voice now, just as I had when we were children. And I dreamed we were kids again with no more to worry about than our homework or which boy we were crushing on.

I awoke four hours later with the sound of my phone beeping a new call. Katrina was asleep beside me still, so I nudged her awake. 'It's Uncle Mike.' I put the call on speaker.

'Mission accomplished. Gave him quite the fright when he saw me standing there at baggage claim. I didn't like him one bit. Little weasel tried to talk his way out of going with me. Giving it loads about his crazy Mrs. But I had none of his bullshit and drove him straight there. I stayed outside until he left. He was there for about an hour all in all. The cheeky bastard asked me for a lift when he came out. I told him to do one. But I called up to see if Olive was OK once he was gone.'

'He's unreal!' I said.

'Yep, anyhow Olive was in a bit of a state so I made her some coffee. The kid was crying, but he tried to hide it in front of me. Didn't want to be a wuss in front of a cop. I've seen it before. So I told him it takes a real man to cry, to own his feelings. I hope that was the right thing to say.'

'It was the perfect thing to say. Thanks, Uncle Mike. I owe you.'

'You are a good man,' Katrina added.

'I told Olive she could call me if she needs anything. I'm gonna go get some grub now. You guys all right over there?'

'Having a great time. We had a session in a pub last night in Cork. We all sang it out for hours,' I said.

'Good for you. It's quiet without you, Bea. Your dad is fretting. He said he'd not heard from you for a day or two.'

'I bet he is,' I said, unable to keep the sarcasm from my voice. He'd sent a few text messages but I'd ignored them. I wasn't ready to talk about Lucy and her revelations yet.

'He, um, he wondered how you got on with Lucy. How is she?'

'Good.'

'Um . . .'

'Spit it out, Uncle Mike.'

'Did she . . .' he trailed off, leaving the question unfinished.

'If you want to know whether Lucy told me that she was Dad's girlfriend before he and Mom got it on, then yes.'

Uncle Mike sighed. 'She had it rough back then. I always liked Lucy. She was a great woman. More suited to your dad than Maeve ever— Shit, maybe I shouldn't have said that.'

I tried to formulate my thoughts. I'd believed my entire life that Mom and Dad had a fairy-tale love that was cut short by the cruel hand of fate. Had they even loved each other in the end, or was I the only reason they'd married?

'Honestly, love, forget I said that. You know I talk a lot of baloney at the best of times,' Uncle Mike said, his words spilling out in a rush.

'It's fine, Uncle Mike. I have a lot of questions for Dad. But they can wait until I get home.'

'Will you just message him to let him know that you are OK?'

'I'm not having a conversation about this on text. I want to see his face. But you can tell him you've spoken to me, if you want.'

'Tell Lucy I said hello. I really did like her. She didn't deserve what happened. It wasn't right. Mom and Dad loved her too. It took them a long time to get used to Ryan being with Maeve and not her.'

'I think she'll appreciate hearing that. I owe you a dinner for today, by the way.'

'I'll hold you to that. But let's make it lunch and a pint in Farrell's. We can get merry then stagger our way home to Innisfree together afterwards.'

'Sounds good, Uncle Mike. Love ya.'

'Your dad is going to get such a shock when he finds out about Mark,' Katrina said when I hung up.

'I wonder has Lucy told Mark the truth yet?' I flicked through my WhatsApp again, to see if she'd messaged me. There had been nothing from her since we left. There was unfinished business in Kilmore Quay and I had to sort it out before I left.

I found Olive's contact details, then hit call. 'Hi, Olive. It's Bea and Katrina here. Are you OK?'

'Hi, ladies. It's been the worst day and the best day, if that makes any sense. Seeing him was so strange. Years of praying for him to walk in through our front door, and when he does, all I want to do is hit him.'

'I would have done so,' Katrina said. 'Hard.'

That made us all laugh, if only for a moment.

'Teddy didn't know what to do at first. He stood by my side, shy and unsure. But then he ran towards Ted and they both cried a while as they hugged each other. And I went over and hugged them both too. Even knowing what I did. We all clung to each other like we were hanging onto a life raft for our dear lives. I realized that, as much as I hate him, I'm still relieved he's alive. For Teddy's sake.'

Katrina made a face, so I threw a cushion at her. 'That's understandable. What happens now?'

'He told Teddy that he'd had a fall on his way to work three years ago, cracked his head and had concussion. He had an elaborate tale of hitchhiking across America, before finally meeting a group of Irish who talked him into visiting them in Cork. And then he said that he'd fallen in love with someone else. That he believed he was single and would never have made a life in Ireland had he known the truth, etc, etc.'

'Did Teddy believe his dad?'

'Not at all. Teddy said there were more holes in his dad's story than in some of his socks. He's a smart kid.'

'So what happens now?'

'He signed the divorce papers. It's straightforward enough. I keep the house. Whatever savings we had are long gone. And he's going to start to pay maintenance.'

'That's something at least. Will he stay in touch with Teddy, do you think?'

'Who knows? Teddy asked him when he would visit again. He said he wasn't sure. Teddy also asked if he could visit Ireland. His father was cagey in his response. I don't hold out much hope. His Irish family don't know about us here. And he wants to keep it that way.'

'I wish it were a Hollywood ending, with me bringing you home a concussed husband, but life is rarely like that. We're staying a few more days in Ireland, on our own buck. But when we get back, I'll be in touch. You call me if you need anything further. And for what it's worth, I've learned that secrets always have a way of coming out.'

'That's for sure. And at least my son and I can now sleep at night. The truth, though hard to hear, will be easier to bear in the long run, rather than us both living in false hope, as we were. We couldn't go on like that.'

*False hope. The truth easier to bear.* Olive's words bounced around my head, making me dizzy.

# 41

## *Bea*

### February 2020

*The Clongibbon House, Mitchelstown, Cork*

Watching Stephanie say her goodbyes to Donal made me quite emotional. They both promised to stay in touch on WhatsApp and on social media. Judging by the long lingering kiss they shared while Katrina and I waited in the car, her phone would be buzzing before we left Cork.

We decided to do some sightseeing on our way back to Wexford. Our first stop was in Cobh. Gran had a great-great-uncle who died on the *Titanic*, which famously set sail from here. It was a small charming seaport town and the weather gods were on our side. As we looked at a cruise ship in the distance, I remembered Stephanie's obsession with a childhood programme. 'Remember Zach and Cody? You loved those twins!'

'Oh. My. God. I was sure I'd marry one of them.'

'You used to say that we'd live on a cruise ship, in cabins beside each other. Just like the one in *The Suite Life*.'

'And you used to say that you could solve all the crimes that occurred there.'

'Well, if you decide to do that in the future, don't leave me behind. Sounds a lot like fun to me,' Katrina said, and we linked arms, in the way that we did. We stumbled across a Heritage Centre and decided to go in. We learned a little more about Annie Moore, the first Irish immigrant to walk through Ellis Island into New York. As we made our way around the exhibits, it struck me that my two friends and I, were all descendants of immigrants. Stephanie's mother was from the UK, Katrina was born in Serbia, and of course I was both the daughter and granddaughter of Irish immigrants. Maybe that was part of why we were such good friends. We each understood the challenges and privileges that came from being a child of someone who left their home and loved ones for a better life. Dad always said that he felt an added pressure on his shoulders to succeed. The sacrifices Gran and Grandad had made, leaving their homes and families behind them couldn't be taken in vain. And then I remembered that morning on Brooklyn Bridge with Grandad, when he spoke about the tangible legacy of the Irish who helped build New York City. Their heartbeat, their DNA could be heard in buildings and bridges alike, if you listened hard enough. And I felt pride for each and every one of them – the Irish Americans who had prevailed.

As we continued our drive through Waterford and onwards to New Ross, I wondered would I ever have the chance to visit Ireland again. Here, with the girls, anything seemed possible. As we whizzed by green fields, the words of the many Irish ballads I'd grown up singing, came to glorious life. When we realized that President John F. Kennedy's homestead was only a short diversion off our route to Wexford, we decided to visit that too. My grandparents loved him and Jackie so much, I couldn't let the opportunity pass. And Dan had mentioned it a few times to me too. JFK's great-grandfather sailed from New Ross in 1848. If he'd not survived that journey, then there would have been no Jack Kennedy. Now that was a sobering thought. The Kennedy Homestead was bigger than I expected, with a pretty farmhouse nestled between smaller slate-roofed cottages and outhouses. One of which had holes in the walls, where tourists had picked stone souvenirs to take home with them. A little piece of the Kennedy magic. The museum had a dedication plaque that read, *The Kennedys who went away and the Kennedys who stayed behind*. And I thought of Lucy and Mom getting on a flight to New York and leaving their parents behind. I thought of Gran and Grandad and of my Great-Great-Uncle Richard whom I'd never met, yet still had a place in my heart, because he gave us all Innisfree. I felt profoundly sad, thinking about the many tears that had been shed by both immigrants and the families who lost them to the promise of a better life in a new world. But there was pride too. OK, we weren't presidents, but we had done all right. More than all right. Dad was a successful author. Uncle Mike was a respected and decorated cop, who not only risked his life in the terrorist attacks of 9/11 but every day since then on the streets of New York. That meant something.

The three of us left New Ross, each quiet, lost in our thoughts. Stephanie's head was bent low, eyes on her phone, messaging Donal.

Katrina broke the silence. 'It makes you think, doesn't it? Am I successful? Have I done enough to make my family in Serbia proud?' Katrina asked.

Before I could respond, Stephanie leaned forward in her seat and said, 'If I were your family, I would be ever so proud of you. In fact I often wish that I was more like you are, Katrina.'

'How so?' Katrina looked back in surprise.

'You are beautiful. Confident. Clever. Funny. Fearless. And you are co-owner of a business that is thriving. I would think you can safely say that you are a success. Serbia should be proud.'

'Well, maybe not as successful as Karl Malden. But close enough,' I added, which did as was intended and made Katrina laugh.

'Speaking of Karl, I miss my dog,' Katrina said. 'Nikki sent photo today of him humping her H&M fake-fur coat. Funny.'

'Poor Nikki. She was kind to offer to take care of him,' I said.

'Never mind Nikki, think of the poor coat,' Stephanie said, giggling. 'What would you like to do when we get to Kilmore Quay?'

'I want to eat fish and chips on the quay, looking at the Saltee Islands. The night I met Dan, he told me about a place there.'

I could feel both of their eyes on me, surprised that I'd brought Dan up voluntarily.

'Then we shall do that,' Katrina said.

'What if Lucy hasn't told Mark? Will you tell him yourself?' Stephanie asked.

I'd thought about this a lot over the past twenty-four hours. And considered all the possible outcomes. Should I stay quiet and let sleeping dogs lie? Or finally empty the proverbial can of worms. 'If Mark doesn't know, then I won't tell him. But if Lucy doesn't tell Dad, I'll have to do that. Because he deserves to know the truth. Then he can come over to Ireland himself and let the cards fall where they fall.'

'I think that's fair,' Katrina said. 'Hey, Stephie, how's farmer boy?'

Stephanie gushed; there was no other word for it. 'He just messaged me from his tractor! Isn't that so . . . so . . . manly!'

'You should have stayed in Cork until tomorrow and gone straight to the airport from his place. We wouldn't mind,' I said.

'No way,' Stephanie said immediately. 'I made the mistake once of putting a man before my friends. Never again. I'm on holidays with you both. And while it was fun to be with Donal, it was a holiday romance. That's all.'

'You could try long-distance with him?' I said.

'That would never work. We'll chat on WhatsApp for a few more days, then I'm sure it will all fizzle out when he's at the next session in the Clongibbon. I bet a lot of tourists pass through Mitchelstown.'

'Maybe, maybe not. I think he likes you as much as you like him,' Katrina said.

'They all like you at first. I'm not going to get carried away. It is what it is. A gorgeous memory to take home with me.'

'And they do say the best way to get over a man is to get under another. So at least that mission was accomplished,' I said.

'Six times. I'm well over, you could say,' Stephanie boasted with a giggle.

'You need to get under a man quick,' Katrina said, jabbing me in my side.

'The very next one I see, I'll be sure to work on that.'

'Or maybe the truth is you do not want to get over Dan,' Katrina added.

'Maybe. But what we want and what we get are not always the same thing.'

I didn't say any more, I just let them discuss between themselves all the reasons why I still loved Dan. I closed my eyes behind my glasses and allowed myself to pick one of my favourite memories from my Dan box. I hit play and watched us both dance a slow tango in Central Park, and as we moved slow, slow, quick, quick, slow, I drifted off to sleep.

# 42

## *Bea*

February 2020

*Nellie's Pub, Kilmore Quay, Wexford*

We were welcomed back to the Coast Hotel in Kilmore as if we were family returning. This time we did accept their offer of scones and homemade jam in the lounge. If there was a more delicious taste than that combination, I don't know what it is. Every mouthful reminded me of my grandmother. Saturday mornings, standing by her side, at first on a step, helping her knead the dough. I'd sit on the floor cross-legged and peer in through the glass door of the oven, watching the scones rise tall. Then I'd sit impatiently waiting for them to cool on a wire rack. Gran was famous in the neighbourhood for her scones, a recipe she brought from Ireland. One that her mother had learned from her mother.

'Why don't I bake?' I asked as emotion threatened to undo me.

'Because you are not Martha Stewart,' Katrina said.

'But I'm letting down Gran. She taught me how to bake scones, in the same way her mother taught her. She said it was something she brought from Ireland and left in New York.' Tears sprang to my eyes, taking me by surprise.

'Oh honey, what's wrong?' Stephanie asked.

'I have never made scones on my own. Not even once. What is wrong with me?'

'You can make them when you go home,' Stephanie said.

'But what if I never have children to leave the recipe to?' I said, letting the tears fall freely now.

'Stop! You are only a baby yourself. No one has children until they are forty any more. You've got over a decade to find a man, marry and have kids. I promise you, you'll get to teach someone that recipe,' Stephanie said, picking up a napkin and dabbing my eyes for me.

I sniffed back more tears and wished my gran were here right now, to hold me and tell me that everything was going to be OK. I caught Katrina's eye. I felt her watching me a lot lately and I knew I worried her. I blew my nose into my napkin and apologized for being so silly.

'When we go back to Brooklyn, I would like to learn scone recipe. Do you remember the day when we arrived in Prospect Avenue and your gran gave my family scones?' Katrina said.

'I thought you were so cool in your cropped top and leopard-print leggings. I couldn't wait to meet you.'

'I was cool. But I was also scared. I did not know what new house would be like. You freaked me out at first because you smiled a lot. But the thing I remember most of all that evening was when my mama made tea, we ate those scones. And my mama said, I think we are going to like it here. We felt a warm welcome with every sugary bite. It is not only you who would like to make those scones. Maybe one day, I can give same welcome to a new neighbour, as your gran did for us. So, will you teach me?'

'Teach me too, please. I have so many happy memories of eating scones in your kitchen as a kid,' Stephanie said. 'We can have a bake-off! Have you watched *The Great British Baking Show* on Netflix? It's so good. I'm on season four and, when I grow up, I know who I want to be. Mary Berry!'

'That is not a name of person,' Katrina said.

'It is!' Stephanie dived into a Google search and pulled up a photo. 'See!'

Katrina shrugged in the way she did when she was surprised, happy, mad or sad. It was a universal shrug that only she could pull off. 'So we all bake scones when we get home. Maybe not next day, because of jet lag. But soon after. You don't need to worry about not continuing on your family legacy, Bea O'Connor, OK?'

'You are the best, best friends forever. Both of you. You know that?'

'We do. But it takes one to know one,' Katrina said.

We clinked our teacups to seal the deal and got back to eating.

Once we'd dropped our bags in our room, we decided to walk to Nellie's. It was only a short walk and as it was such a beautiful day, it was a shame to drive. I texted Lucy to let her know we were on the way and she responded with a happy-face emoji. Progress. When we got to the bar, Lucy and Mark were there waiting for us. And someone else too. I'd recognize her face anywhere: it was the third amigo, Michelle.

My heart hammered so loudly in my chest, it beat a song. Mark moved towards me. *He knew.* I could see it in the way he looked at me, taking in the bump in my nose, the slant of my eyes, my freckles. He was looking for traces of himself in that search. And I did the same with him. He was so like my father and grandfather, it was impossible not to see that. But he looked like me too.

'Head wreck, to be fair,' he said at last.

I used my hands to demonstrate my own head exploding. 'Do you have Spock ears?' I asked.

He pulled back his hair and showed me the pointy tips. 'I do!'

I think I jumped up a little, I was so delighted to see my ears on someone else. Not just someone. My brother. 'Are you upset? Silly question. You must be.'

'Not in the least. I'm happy. My dad has a name now. And even if he doesn't want to know me, I've got you. Which I think is a pretty damn fine deal.' He took a step closer to me. 'Could I have a hug? I've never hugged a sibling before.'

'Me neither,' I said, moving into his arms. And as we breathed in each other, I felt a recognition ripple through me. Recognition of my brother, someone I had only just met, but *knew* with every part of me. He was the missing piece of the puzzle. A puzzle I'd not planned on finishing, but now that I had, it was the most beautiful thing I'd ever made.

'Promise me you'll never leave me again, not now that I've found you,' he said.

'I won't leave you, unless I have absolutely no choice in the matter,' I promised.

We pulled apart and I turned to Lucy, who was crying. I could only imagine how emotional this moment must be for her.

'Are you OK?' I asked.

'Better than I've been for the longest time. I'm sorry, Bea. More than I can ever express to you.'

'You have nothing to apologize about,' I said, and I meant that. 'You did the best you could with the cards you were dealt. We all have our secrets that we keep because we feel we have no choice but to keep them. Families are complex, I've learnt that much over the years I've worked at the agency. You need to let go of any guilt you have. We've reconnected now. That's all that matters.'

'Talking about reconnecting, we've decided to go back to New York with you,' Mark said. 'If that's OK? I'd like to meet Ryan sooner rather than later. Or would you prefer we wait until you go home and talk to him yourself?'

'Let's not waste any more time. Dad will be really happy to meet you, Mark. So will Uncle Mike. I only wish Gran and Grandad were still alive.'

'I'd love to hear about them.'

'Well, that's good. Because I love to talk about them.'

Michelle moved towards me, 'Can I have a hug too? I've waited a very long time for one,' and as she held me, she said how much I was like Maeve. I told her that I'd found the note that she'd sent Mom all those years ago. 'I think she knew that you were right, Michelle. That she needed to make amends. That's why she held on to it.'

'I had planned to visit her, after you were born. But I

got married, then I got pregnant and time went by too quickly. I'll regret that I didn't get to her in time till the day I die.' She clasped both my hands and said, 'I've thought of you often. And I want you to know that Maeve was so loved. She had this way of lighting up a room. The happiest of times, we had in our Three Amigos apartment in Dublin. If my Tadgh knew the half of what I got up to . . . well, let's say, he'd lose what little hair he has left now!'

We all giggled and I told her that I was glad Mom had her in her corner. Then I felt light-headed, so I took a seat on one of the high bar stools. 'This is all very emotional.'

'Oh. My. God. I swore I'd never drink again, after the hangover I had in Cork. But I need a drink again. What is this country doing to me!' Stephanie said, wiping tears away.

'I think we could all do with a drink. But there's something I'd like us to do together first. I've asked a friend to take us on a short boat ride. I'd like to show you where we scattered your mom's ashes. A place that was very special to both of us growing up.'

Lucy held a hand out to me and Michelle held another. And decades later, I took my mom's place, between her two best friends. We walked to the quayside where a red-and-white boat called *Autumn Dream* waited for us. We all climbed in and the skipper Eamonn told us that the boats were chartered for deep sea angling and scuba diving, along with trips to the Saltee Islands.

Lucy turned to Mark, Stephanie and Katrina and made a request. 'I wonder if you three would mind if it was just us who take this boat trip? Michelle and I would like one last Three Amigo's moment with our darling Maeve's daughter. Is that OK?'

They all agreed at once. Mark hugged me goodbye and while it still felt surreal that this man was my brother, I had a feeling that we'd get to where we needed to be soon enough.

Stephanie stuck a pack of tissues into my pocket. I sat in between Lucy and Michelle. And as the boat bobbed its way out of the harbour, Lucy told us about her childhood. 'Dad used to have a boat. It's long gone, he sold it before we went to college in Dublin. But when we were kids, some of our happiest memories were spent in that boat. And one of our favourite outings was always the Saltee Islands. We'd play a game to see who was the first to spot the . . .' she paused, then smiled when I squealed.

'Oh my goodness. That's a dolphin! There, in the water, a dolphin! Look, I swear a dolphin just did a flip right beside us!'

Lucy laughed, 'I was about to say that Maeve was always the first to see the dolphins. I shouldn't be surprised that you did too. You *are* so like your mom.'

*So like my mom.*

Words I'd craved my entire life but never quite believed when they were spoken by Dad. But hearing them from Lucy, her sister, her almost twin, made me want to weep with gratitude. I wiped the tears away though, because I didn't want to miss a moment of this trip. And I knew that if I started to cry, I may not be able to stop.

The boat slowed down as we got closer to the island and then I saw half a dozen seals. Some playfully swam and others lay on rocks, rolling on their round tummies as they took in the beauty of the blue sky above.

'Maeve loved seals. When we were kids, her bedroom wall was covered with posters of them. They all had these big black soulful eyes. She said she could get lost in the secrets they held. When Maeve died . . .' Lucy couldn't finish. She began to sob. She wasn't alone, I could hear Michelle also giving into the high emotion that was impossible to avoid. But still I pushed the tears away and tried to comfort Lucy as best I could.

Michelle spoke through her tears. 'Seals are supposed to signify great imagination and creativity you know. I read that somewhere. I think that's why Maeve felt such a connection with them. Because there was nobody alive with a bigger imagination and bigger dreams than Maeve Mernagh.'

'The last time I saw her, I said some awful things,' Lucy said.

'You could never have known what was going to happen. And you had good cause. Let's not forget that,' Michelle said.

'But I wish . . . I wish I could have told her that I still loved her, even though I hated what she did.'

'I think she knew that,' I said. 'Don't ask me why or how I know that. But I feel it.'

'I kept my hurt bottled up inside of me for so long. But I could never switch off how much I missed her. How much I loved her. What I'd give for one more chance to tell her that.'

Michelle said, 'There's still time to do that, Lucy. This is where we scattered her ashes, isn't it?'

Lucy looked around her and confirmed. I tried to imagine them opening the lid on an urn and letting pieces of my mother float into the air and out to the sea.

Then two seals poked their heads up from the water. They watched us with their dark sorrowful knowing eyes as they bobbed in the water, side by side.

Mother and child or siblings. I wasn't sure which.

And as I looked at them, they became all of us.

Dad and Mark.

Lucy and Maeve.

Mark and me.

*Mom and me.*

One of the seals moved closer towards us and I searched its black soulful eyes. 'She's still here,' I whispered. 'But I think it's time for us to say our goodbyes now. To let her go.'

Lucy nodded. She locked eyes with the seal and then whispered to the wind, 'I never stopped loving you and I forgave you a long time ago. And I'm sorry too, for not being with you when you needed me. But most of all, Maeve, I want to thank you for every wonderful moment in my life that came from you.'

Michelle then spoke, 'I miss you, Maeve, my lovely amigo. Life has never been the same without you. But we'll see each other again on the other side, for another bottle of Blue Nun.'

I looked at them both, my mom's amigos. And I felt their love for each other mirrored in the love I felt for my own amigos. Stephanie and Katrina were part of every big and small moment of my life. I made myself speak with a strength I didn't feel, because I wanted to make sure I was heard by every living and dead thing around us. 'I hope you are happy here. You were loved, Mom. You are still loved by so many. Thank you for loving me. Until we see each other again . . .'

I took in every single ripple of water as the foam crashed into the island's shore. The sound of the gulls as they danced in the sky above. The smell of the salty air. And the feeling that here, I had finally found my mom.

# 43

## Lucy

February 2020

*Woodside, Brooklyn, Manhattan*

I'd thought about taking Mark to the place where his story began many times. But the time had never felt right. But now that I was back in Woodside, my son grown to be a man himself, I felt only excitement and happy nostalgia as I retraced the footpaths of my younger self.

'This is where the Woodside Steakhouse used to be. I was a waitress there. A singing one! Such a shame that it's burned down now. I loved working here. Do you remember when you were ten or eleven, someone came to visit from my New York days?'

Mark said, 'Yeah, I remember. Small fella, grey hair?'

'That's him. Mick was my manager in the steakhouse. He was a good man. He died a few years ago. His wife wrote to tell me. We kept in contact all this time.' I grabbed Mark's arm and pulled him towards the Stop Inn on the other side of the road. 'But I'm so happy this place is still here. Come on, I'll buy you a milkshake and the best burger you'll ever eat.'

It hadn't changed a bit. It was as if time had stood still in this small diner. As we took a seat in the same booth that Maeve and I sat in on our very first morning in Brooklyn, it was bittersweet. But I refused to allow myself to look back in sorrow any longer. I'd wasted so much of my life in regret and disappointment. No more. We ordered burgers and fries, fully loaded, with a vanilla milkshake, and I'm sure the waitress thought I was crazy, such was my giddiness when they arrived. They tasted as good today as they had done when I was a young woman.

I watched Mark eat his and it felt ridiculously important that he enjoy his burger. 'Well?'

'It's good. Really good,' he said, in between bites.

We'd earned this meal. We'd walked from Sunnyside to Woodside this morning, passing Maggie May's, the Butcher's Block, St Joseph's Church. Memories picked at me at every sidewalk on the corner of every street. Maeve and I together, giggling, wide-eyed, excited, at our new world we found ourselves living in. Ryan and I, kissing, head to head, so in love that we didn't notice the Budweiser truck that almost thundered its way over us.

'Do you ever wish you had stayed here?' Mark asked, pushing his now empty plate away.

'I've spent a lifetime with what-ifs and maybes. But now, sitting here with you, I wouldn't change a thing. We have a good life, don't we? At home in Kilmore Quay?'

Mark was quick to confirm this. He was a good boy, always had been. 'You gave me everything, Mam. Put me through university. I never wanted for a thing. And I love Nellie's. Always have done.'

I sighed in pleasure at his words. I'd always felt his happiness bubble around me. Other than wishing for a dad who wasn't on the scene at moments in his life where he needed a male figurehead, he'd been a happy, content boy, who grew into a happy, content man. He was the best of me and of Ryan. The same way that Bea was the best of Maeve and Ryan.

'Are you nervous about seeing him?' he asked.

I nodded. 'I won't lie. It's going to be weird for me. I loved him, Mark. He was my entire world and when he betrayed me with Maeve, I nearly didn't recover. But you saved me. So it will be OK. We'll make it OK.'

'And Bea hasn't told him about me? He's only expecting you?'

'Yep.' We'd checked into a hotel in Manhattan the previous day and slept off our jet lag. I wanted a clear head when I saw Ryan again. However I reacted, I didn't want to blame a long flight for my behaviour. I wanted to be of clear mind. Perhaps not of clear heart, no matter how hard I tried.

We left a big tip for the waitress. I remembered how important those 20 per cent tips were. Then we grabbed a cab to Prospect Avenue. We could have gone on the subway, but I wanted to be above ground, to see everything. And finally we stopped outside the beautiful brownstone that was as much a part of the O'Connor family as the people who lived in it.

'A bit different from home, Mam. If things had been different, I would have grown up here,' Mark said.

'True, but then Bea wouldn't have existed, and that

doesn't seem right. I suppose we can't put this off any longer. Are you ready?'

He nodded, so together we walked up the short drive and knocked on the door.

They must have been practically sitting on the other side of the door, because it opened after seconds.

'Lucy,' Ryan whispered.

'Ryan,' I whispered back.

'Can I hug you?'

I hadn't expected that. I wasn't ready for that. I shook my head.

Bea saved the moment, and invited us in. Ryan seemed to notice Mark for the first time. He looked at us in surprise. We walked into the sitting room that I'd spent so many happy moments in with Peggy and Joe, Mike and my love, my heart, my Ryan.

'The thinking chair is still there,' I said, pointing to the green lazy boy in the corner. I told Mark that Ryan always planned his novels from that chair. I ended feeling a little bit foolish. Who was I to say what he did any more?

'I still do. I don't think I could ever part with it. I reckon it's my good luck charm.' Ryan looked away from me to Mark, who stood beside me. I could see the confusion on his face as he looked at what could have been his younger self. There was no putting off this moment any further.

'Ryan, I'd like you to meet my son. Mark.'

The room was silent. I moved closer to Mark, ready to protect him from whatever reaction came his way.

Father and son looked each other up and down. Finding the words was harder than I thought it would be. But I reminded myself of something Bea had said in Ireland.

I did the best with the situation I found myself in. I had to live with that.

'After I went home to Ireland, I found out I was pregnant. I'd not been well and I put it down to . . . well, to being heartbroken. But . . .'

'Mark is my son,' Ryan said, his eyes never leaving Mark's.

'Yes.'

We went back to silence again.

'Why didn't you tell me?' Ryan said, every word an accusation.

Bea stepped closer to me and said, 'I don't think you are in any position to ask that, Dad. Not after what you did.'

Mark spoke then, speaking with the ease and confidence that I'd always been proud to witness, 'Nice to meet ya. Not sure what to call you though.'

Ryan said, 'You look just like my dad. And I suppose that means you look just like me too. It's good to meet you too.'

'Will we try a hug or something?' Mark asked.

'I'd like that.'

I watched them do the hug that men do, where they slap each other on the back as they embrace. It didn't linger and was over as quick as it began. But it was a start and they both grinned identical smiles when they parted.

'I'd no idea, I swear,' Ryan said to Mark.

'I know. Mam told me that. I only found out when Bea came to visit. She copped it when she saw me. Said I was the image of you.'

'You never told me,' Ryan said to Bea.

'Don't, Ryan!' I said, my voice rising. 'Don't you dare say a word to this lovely young woman. She said nothing because I asked her not to. It had to come from me.'

Ryan sat down in his ugly green chair that was so battered it should be on a rubbish tip somewhere. I gave him a beat to process everything.

Bea moved closer to her dad and said, 'Think about how difficult this has been for Aunty Lucy. This situation was thrust on her. She didn't choose it.'

He nodded, looking from Mark to me.

'Bea, I wonder if you'd take Mark down to see your studio apartment? I'd like to have a chat with Ryan on my own. I think we need to clear the air.'

The two kids left and, as crazy as this situation was, I was glad they had each other.

'If I'd known . . .' Ryan said again.

'Then what?'

'I don't know. Then *something*. Why didn't you tell me?'

'If I'd realized before I left New York, I would have. But it was months before I discovered I was pregnant. I was going to call after my first scan to tell you. Then I received Maeve's letter with your wedding invitation. It was deeply upsetting for me.'

'Oh Lucy.' His head dropped in sorrow and shame.

'Did you love her, Ryan?'

'I grew to love her, but not in the way I loved you. After you went, we leaned into each other for comfort. And we had the baby to think about. I proposed after Maeve's first scan. Mam thought it was a mistake. She said I'd regret marrying Maeve, baby or no baby. That it was you I loved.'

I felt a rush of gratitude for Peggy. She'd always had my back. 'Did Maeve love you?' I thought about all the guys she'd dated and how she'd never called it love with any of them. Was it possible that she found love with Ryan before she died? I realized to my surprise that I half hoped she had. Everyone deserved to find love at least once in their lives.

Ryan burst that bubble in an instant. 'I'm pretty certain that she only put up with me. I was never her type of man. And had she lived, we'd never have lasted. I irritated her, she thought I was boring, writing all the time, or with my head in a book. She wanted to be out partying. Maeve would have left me eventually.'

I saw the truth of his words. They had been like chalk and cheese. Always had been.

'If I'd known about you and Mark, I'd never have married her.'

'And what? You'd have come to Ireland and married me instead?' The arrogance astounded me. 'Well, surprise, I would never have married you!'

'I'm sorry. I didn't mean it like that. I only meant . . . fuck . . . I don't know what I meant.'

'I came here once.' I told him about my secret trip to New York all those years ago. 'I realized how stupid I was to think that we could ever move backwards. My life was and always will be in Ireland. Mark's too. We're happy there.'

'You must hate me so much,' Ryan whispered.

'For a long time I did. But I don't any more. I hate what you did. Not you. There's a difference. Bea did something incredible for me by visiting. She gave me back my sister. Through her, I've managed to let go of all the anger I'd held onto. And over the past few days, I've been able to remember the Maeve that I loved with all my heart, without any of the pain.'

'Her last two words she uttered, right before she died, were your names – Lucy and Bea. You asked did she love me? The truth was that you both were the great loves of her life.'

That was nearly the undoing of me.

'She would have done anything to make things right with you. If she'd known you had a child too . . .'

'We can't waste another moment on a what-if, Ryan. You have a son and I'm sorry that it's taken me this long to tell you. But I can't beat myself up about that either. What's done is done. He's an incredible young man. Clever, funny, kind. And he makes me proud every day. You'll like him. I know you will.'

'I already do. I made a right old mess of things, didn't I?'

There wasn't an answer to that.

'There's something else I need to say. If it wasn't for you, I'm not sure I would be writing now. You gave me the confidence to walk away from the police academy and to pursue my dreams. I've never forgotten that. So thank you, Lucy.'

It surprised me how much I needed to hear him acknowledge this. I had been important to him, to his life. Over the years, it's easy to doubt memories.

'Can we be friends now, do you think?' Ryan asked.

I had been worried that when I saw him all the old feelings would come flooding back. But whatever love I'd felt for him was long gone. Taking this walk down memory lane had allowed me to run into ghosts of my past, both the living and the dead. And I'd survived the experience.

For the first time in almost thirty years, I'd let go of my lost love. Maybe in its place, I could welcome a new friendship, with the father of my son. Maybe. I gave him my answer. 'I'll take that hug now.'

# 44

*Bea*

February 2020

*Innisfree, Prospect Avenue, Brooklyn*

Lucy and Mark stayed on in New York for a week. Dad had become their official guide, taking them to all the sights. I promised to meet them at the Rockefeller Center that evening, to take in the view from the top of the tower. We'd formed a new WhatsApp group that Lucy had named the 'Jerry Springer Crew'. Funny lady.

I was back in work and picked up the phone to call Olive, to check in on her. I wouldn't normally do after-care for clients, but somehow Olive's journey to find Ted was all mixed up in my journey to find my mom. But as she answered the phone, I lost my ability to speak. You know that saying, on the tip of your tongue? Well, it was true. I could feel the words dancing on the tip of my tongue, but they refused to sashay their way out of my mouth. It wasn't the first time this had happened either and it terrified me.

Katrina walked in. Her timing could not have been worse. 'What is wrong? Bea?'

I looked in my handbag and grabbed a pen and a receipt from our lunch earlier. I scribbled on the back of the receipt, *I can't speak.*

'You've lost your voice?' Katrina asked, reaching up to feel my forehead. 'You are not warm. No fever.'

I shook my head and tried again to make the words cooperate. But the only thing that came out was gobble-degook that sounded like, 'Inbhalosthaoume.'

The fear I felt hearing this gibberish was echoed in my friend's face.

'We're going to the emergency room,' she said, and for once I didn't try to stop her. I needed help. We grabbed a cab and made our way to Lenox Hill Hospital.

'Maybe you should call your dad,' Katrina said.

I looked at her and pointed to my mouth, then gave her a look that I hoped screamed 'Seriously?'

She giggled then said, 'You can't be that sick, smart Alec. I'll call him.'

I shook my head. Then scribbled an instruction down. 'Under no circumstances call anyone.' He'd only worry and for what? He was having fun getting to know his son. I was not going to mess that up for them. By the time Katrina checked me in with the hospital reception, my voice returned. I felt like a fraud. But the attending physician insisted on checking me over all the same. 'Aphasia – losing your speech – warrants some investigation into what caused it.'

'Like what?' Katrina asked her.

'It could be caused by a neurological disorder. But let's not jump ahead of ourselves. I'm going to run some tests and we'll take it from there. Right, let's take a look at your eyes. Look at my right ear.' She shone a light in my eye, making me blink. 'Now the left ear. Good. Any other symptoms other than the loss of speech?'

'No,' I replied, as Katrina shouted out, 'Yes.'

I threw a look of annoyance at my friend. 'Nothing else worth mentioning,' I said pointedly.

'Let me be the judge of that,' the doctor said, waiting for me to continue. When I didn't oblige, she looked at Katrina. The bloody traitor sung like a canary.

'To start with, she has been more forgetful than normal.'

'Aren't we all?' I said, forcing joviality into my voice. 'Work has been busy this year. That's all.'

'You have been getting headaches too.'

That was true, I couldn't deny it. 'From the jet lag, that's all. I'm not long back from a trip to Ireland.'

'You had headaches before Ireland. And you're tired all the time.'

The doctor scribbled notes as Katrina and I argued about my symptoms.

'Any nausea or vomiting?' the doctor asked.

I shook my head and closed my mind to the mornings I'd been ill in the bathroom.

'Tell the doctor about the letter,' Katrina said.

Now I really wanted to hit her. There was no way I wanted to repeat that.

'What letter?' the doc asked.

'Bea thinks she is getting messages from her younger self through a magical letter.'

That hurt. Where did the 'think' come from? I thought she believed me.

'I'd rather not discuss this,' I hissed.

'I'd like to hear about it,' the doctor said, smiling. Then she pulled up a stool and sat down, like we were two girlfriends about to have a gossip.

'I don't see how my childhood letter is relevant to this,' I said.

But the doctor and Katrina just looked at me, waiting for me to continue.

'You're going to think I'm crazy. And I'm not. I'm perfectly sane.'

Katrina at least backed me up on this fact. 'She is sane. I can verify that. Not one to fantasize about things. In fact, the opposite. She's one of the most logical people I know, which is why she is such a good investigator.'

I felt mollified by this. Slightly. But I was still reluctant to share this secret I'd carried with me for weeks now.

'I've heard all sorts in ER, Bea. Nothing you can say will shock me. I need you to tell me everything, in case it has relevance to your aphasia. OK?'

I nodded and suddenly felt afraid. But I also felt trapped and couldn't think of a reason not to confess.

'I used to smoke,' I said. 'But then a few weeks ago, I woke up and was no longer a smoker.'

'You quit overnight. Impressive,' the doctor said.

I shook my head. 'No, it wasn't like that. I woke up and no longer felt the need to smoke.' I took a deep breath and continued. 'And I couldn't find my cigarettes anywhere. In fact all evidence that I'd ever been a smoker was gone. I was convinced my dad had staged an intervention to make me quit.'

'Had he?' she asked, looking a bit sceptical.

I shook my head.

Katrina jumped in, determined to get the whole story in. 'I've known Bea since we were ten years old. And to my knowledge, she has never been a smoker.'

Now the doctor looked confused. I felt sorry for her. I knew that feeling well. 'You imagined that you were a smoker.'

I didn't like it when she said it out loud.

'There's more,' Katrina said.

'The night before I became a non-smoker, I received a letter I'd written when I was ten years old, to my future self. It had been placed in a time capsule. Well, I scribbled a message to my younger self, on the letter. I said that smoking didn't make me look cool and would be a pain to quit. I advised myself not to start smoking. And the next morning . . .' I trailed off. I found myself unable to complete the sentence.

'So you think . . . ?' the doctor also was unable to finish the thought.

'She thinks her time-capsule letter is some sort of time-travel portal. That she can give messages to her younger self and effect change. That's what she thinks,' Katrina blurted out.

I felt tears sting my eyes again. I wanted to get out of this room, away from the doctor's prying eyes and Katrina's interference, no matter how good a place it was coming from.

The doctor leaned over and patted my hand. 'I think I'd like to have a letter like that. The things I'd tell my younger self. A dodgy perm when I was sixteen – meant to emulate Christina Aguilera, but actually made me look

like a prize poodle – springs to mind. Not a good look.'
She shuddered to emphasize the point.

The tears halted.

'And have there been any other messages?'

I nodded. 'I've had about half a dozen. And they've all
meant something. They led me to Ireland and I found my
half-brother.'

'Her dad got two sisters pregnant at the same time,'
Katrina said, delighted to share this juicy part of the story.

The doctor's expression at this revelation was quite
funny. I knew Katrina and I would giggle about that look
for a long time to come. But to her credit, she continued,
'The things you've described, from the headaches to
forgetfulness and tiredness, to the delusions about your
letters, they could be neurocognitive issues. I'm going to
send you for a CT scan.'

'I'm supposed to be meeting my dad, my aunt and my
brother this evening.'

She shook her head. 'Let's get the results of the scan,
then we can work on getting you home.'

Have you ever had a moment in life when you realized
that the game was up? I'd spent months lying to myself,
to my family and friends, but here in Lenox, I knew that
it was time to come clean. And to be honest, I was bone-
tired from juggling everything on my own.

'Erm . . . there's something you should know. I've
already a scan.'

That admission was the beginning of the end.

And I could no longer ignore or hide that fateful day,
a few days before Christmas, when I was in this very
hospital discussing CT scans. Only that time, Dan was
by my side.

# 45

## *Bea*

December 2019

*Lenox Hill Hospital, New York*

I woke up, disorientated and thirsty. I felt the pinch of plaster on my hand and saw a drip had been attached to my arm. I cried out, relief flooding my body when Dan leaned in, whispering love and support into my hair.

'Where am I?'

'Remember, you had a seizure last night, love. You're in Lenox,' Dan said. 'You frightened the shit out of me, Bea. One minute we were drinking tea at my place, the next you were on the ground. You've been asleep for hours.'

His words were a bit like re-watching a movie you'd seen when you were drunk. You kind of remember the overall story, but the details are hazy. 'You didn't tell anyone?'

'No, I respected your wishes. Making me promise that while you were in an ambulance was unfair. This is too big to keep from Ryan. And Katrina will kill me if she finds out you're in hospital and nobody told her.'

I smiled because he was right. But I was still adamant that I didn't want anyone to know, not until I *knew* what was going on. Dad was working around the clock to meet a deadline on his latest novel. Uncle Mike was on nights, so would be asleep right now. It was better to keep it to ourselves, at least until we knew what was wrong. I'd had an MRI and a CT scan yesterday. Results were due today and I was bloody terrified. For the past few weeks, things hadn't been right. I'd become forgetful to the point that I had to keep writing things down. I had what I called brain freezes. My mind went blank and I forgot words for everyday objects. Then two nights ago, I forgot how to speak. I know that sounds so strange, but there's no other way to describe it. Dizzy spells came and went along with headaches. Now, none of this was constant, just every now and then. But I could no longer pretend that I was hungover or overworked. I knew there was something wrong.

The door opened and Dan and I both jumped at the sound. Dr Talis came in and I knew that, whatever she had to share with me, it wasn't good news. I'd never been a pessimist in my life – the opposite in fact – but I could see it in her eyes. 'How are you feeling, Beatrice?'

'Call me Bea. Nobody calls me Beatrice. And I feel great now.'

'I'm glad to hear that . . . Bea. As you know, we've run some tests and I need to talk to you about the results. Would you like your boyfriend to stay?'

Dan answered for me, 'I'm not going anywhere.'

'You have a tumour.'

Four words to turn a world upside down.

'A glioblastoma.'

'That's a mouthful,' I said.

'Yes. I prefer to call it a GBM. Easier to get our teeth around, right? Well, each tumour is graded. One to two is low grade. Three to four is high grade.'

'I've never been a high-grade type of gal,' I said. I waited for the laughs but none came. 'Am I right in assuming that this is the one occasion where I don't want to get high grades?'

The doctor smiled as she nodded. 'Yes. That's right. I'm afraid yours is a four.'

I heard a strangled sob and I wasn't sure if it was me or Dan who had made it.

I looked at Dan and he said, 'You picked a fine time to become an over-achiever.'

I tried to smile, which I knew was the right thing to do, but instead I felt tears sting my eyes. Leftover mascara from the day before leaked and stung.

'The mass swelling is in the cerebral hemisphere of your brain. And between that and the fluid surrounding it, there's been quite a lot of pressure. That's why you've been experiencing some changes. Forgetfulness. Headaches. All common from GBM. As are neurocognitive issues. And in some cases, seizures, as you had yesterday.'

'What are the options for treatment?' I asked. Dan moved closer to me. One more inch and he'd be in bed with me. 'Can you cut the tumour out?'

My mind filled with terror at the thought of anyone putting a knife to my skull. They'd have to shave my head. Shelley's *Frankenstein* popped into my head. When I was in kindergarten that had been one of my childhood Halloween costumes, complete with pencilled in staples on my forehead. I couldn't speak again. I wasn't sure if this was shock or another of my losing-speech episodes. One thing was for sure, my imagination was still firing on all cylinders.

'Surgery is not an option for you in this case, Bea. Your GBM has finger-like tentacles and they've infiltrated your brain. And we simply can't reach them.'

'Chemo?' Dan asked. 'My mam had chemo, when she had breast cancer.'

'That is one of the options that we need to explore to slow down the GBM's growth. I know this is a lot for you to take in. Have you any questions for me?'

'How long do I have?'

'For fuck's sake, Bea! That's no question to ask.' Dan jumped up and I thought he was going to punch the wall, he was so annoyed with me.

'I'm sorry,' I whispered. I wasn't sure what I was apologizing for. Me being sick, or for asking a difficult question that he wasn't ready to hear the answer to. But I needed to know.

Dr Talis moved a step forward and we locked eyes.

'I'd like to know. Please.'

'It's hard to say. We'll do more tests, but in my best judgement, we're looking at twelve months at most . . .'

This couldn't be it. I'd not really had a chance to live. There was so much I needed to still do. I looked at Dan. He stood in the corner of our room, a few feet from me. His face was distorted in pain, his two hands held to his face. I'd made my kind, loving, funny man a Munch painting and I felt a wave of unbelievable sadness overwhelm me.

For Dan.

For my family and friends.

*And me.*

# 46

## *Bea*

December 2019

*Innisfree, Prospect Avenue, Brooklyn*

We left the hospital and went home to Innisfree. Dan held my hand the whole way and I watched tears run down his face. As fast as he brushed them away, more came. I couldn't breathe, my whole body feeling pain at being the one to cause Dan so much heartache. Dad was at the library writing, and Mike was at work, so I settled into my studio without seeing anyone. And all the time I watched Dan, I knew what I had to do. It was crystal-clear to me.

'I can't bear it,' Dan said for the third time.

Another four words that cut me. 'I know you can't,' I whispered. Dan was still broken from watching his mother die of cancer. How could he ever go through that all over again? I loved this man more than life itself.

*He was my everything.* I'd thought he was going to be my future, but one that was very different to what had been given to me now.

'Sit down, Dan. We need to talk.'

# 47

## *Bea*

### February 2020

*Lenox Hill Hospital, New York*

My admission about the previous CT scan caused chaos.
Katrina cursed. Dr Talis was paged and arrived clutching
my files. A second scan was scheduled. Then, when the
room cleared, Katrina said, 'Tell me everything.'

So I did. She moved closer to me. All the while I
spoke, she remained silent. As still as a statue. All those
small things that hadn't added up – the headaches, the
lost days, the forgetfulness, the tiredness, the speech
issues – were all caused by a mass growing inside my
head.

'Sorry,' I whispered. It seemed to be the done thing to
do, to seek forgiveness for the illness.

'And now we know for sure that you've been writing
the messages on your letters yourself.'

'Looks that way.' It hurt to admit this out loud. 'There was no chicken pecking after all.'

Katrina winced. 'Dan knows about this and that's why you are not together.'

I nodded.

'You broke it off with him, trying to be a martyr.'

'I had no choice. His mother died of cancer and he couldn't...'

She cut me off. 'You always have choice.'

'You're cross with me. That's not allowed – I'm dying.' I chanced a joke.

'Too soon, Bea.'

'What? Me dying, or me playing the dying card?'

A tear escaped and I watched it fall down my best friend's cheek.

'Dan told me to watch you,' Katrina said. 'He rang me at Christmas and we went for a drink. He never broke your confidence, but he told me that you were hiding something. And that I had to be extra vigilant.'

So many of us keeping secrets. Look what I'd started.

'He messages me every single day for an update on how you are.'

'Has he messaged you today yet?' I asked.

'Yes. He's on his way here now. I care not one fucking jot what you think about that, Bea O'Connor.'

And as she said the words, Dan walked in. Unshaven, tired, desperate. It was evident that me pushing him away had not given him the peace that I hoped it would.

'Hey blue-eyes.'

'Hey,' I whispered.

'It is time to put an end to this idea you have that you have to face this on your own. I am here and I am going nowhere,' Dan said. 'I love you, Bea. You know that. And it's cruel, pushing me away as you have done.'

'I didn't know what else to do.'

He moved closer. 'Of course you didn't. You'd just received the shock of your life. But that's not good enough any more. We've wasted months with this staying apart nonsense.'

'Be careful, she will use the dying card on you,' Katrina said. She reached over and brushed a lock of my hair from my forehead in a gesture that was so gentle, it made us both sob.

I held my hands out to both of them. 'I need you both. And Dad, Stephanie, Lucy and Mark too. I know that now.'

'Who's Mark? Dan asked, panic flashing across his face.

'My brother. There's a lot I've got to fill you in on,' I said. 'But first, I need to do this.' I pulled him towards me and I kissed him. Katrina let go of my hand and I heard the door close softly behind her as she left us alone.

'I missed you. I'm not very good on my own without you,' Dan said.

'Me either,' I admitted. 'Give me my purse; I want to show you something.' I opened it up and pulled out my wallet, where a small photograph sat behind a plastic window. It was a snap of my grandparents on their wedding day. Gran wore a long, fitted lace dress, with a tiara nestled into her bright red curls. Her blue eyes crinkled and she was smiling that big beautiful smile of hers that was evident in every photograph I have of her. Standing beside her was my grandad, in a sharp grey suit with black shiny shoes. But Grandad wasn't looking at the camera; he was looking at his bride.

'They were a good-looking couple,' he said. 'I wish I could have known them.'

'Me too. You know, Gran always said to me that I needed to find someone to love me who looked at me the way grandad looked at her in this photo. You look at me like that. I thought I could save you from pain by pushing you away. But that was wrong, because this is it for us both, isn't it? Tumour or no tumour, it's got to be us, together.'

'Yes. There is no other way.'

'It's going to be hard.'

'I've no doubt that it will break us both many times.'

'Are you sure, Dan? Things might get a little crazy with me. In fact, things have been pretty whack for the past month. There are some things I need to tell you.'

'All the best people are crazy,' he countered.

And it was in that moment that I accepted that I didn't have to face this on my own. The relief was staggering. 'Will you stay with me while I tell everyone else?'

'Of course. You can count on it – I'm not leaving your side again,' Dan promised, and my big giant of a man climbed in beside me in the small hospital bed.

# 48

## *Bea*

March 2020

*Innisfree, Prospect Avenue, Brooklyn*

The garden in Innisfree looked beautiful. Bunting in every colour of the rainbow hung on the wooden panels of the fence. Paper lanterns hung from the trees and the small courtyard had a large table running from one end to the other, borrowed from Farrell's.

Uncle Mike and Dad set up a beer keg in the corner. Katrina and Stephanie clocked up their ten thousand steps by bringing out platters of food. Earlier today, the three of us made scones together, something we'd done a few times since that day in Kilmore Quay. I heard Mario's voice, shouting orders to everyone in the kitchen, with the exception of my cousin, Nancy, who took orders from nobody. Mario was in charge of catering and his meatloaf and mashed potato was on the menu, for dad and me.

Mark and Lucy's week-long vacation had been extended to a month as a result of the fallout of my illness coming to light. In two days' time, they would leave. None of us were ready to say goodbye, but life moves on and responsibilities must be met.

The past few weeks had been both the hardest and best of my life. As I struggled to come to terms with my new normal, so did my loved ones. So many changes in such a short space of time, it demanded payback. Every now and then one of us would pull too tight and snap. Yesterday it had been Dad's turn, when he had a massive meltdown over a lukewarm review in a regional newspaper, something that normally would just bounce off him. He'd been incredible since that day of reckoning in hospital. He'd arrived with Lucy and Mark, who stood outside for a moment, unsure of their place in our family. I called them in and found out that they'd been on the Staten Island Ferry, taking snaps in front of the Statue of Liberty, when Katrina called to say I was in hospital. Mark told me afterwards that Dad had freaked out and wanted to jump into the water to swim back to shore. Uncle Mike and Stephanie came moments later and I was grateful for their timing, because that way I got to break all of their hearts in one swoop, rather than in instalments, which would have been too hard.

Their shock was hard to witness. And more than once my voice faltered and Dan had to take over. He took control and calmly answered everyone's questions to the best of his knowledge. Any doubts I had disappeared. I needed him, but he needed me too, and if that meant dealing with my tumour, so be it.

Stephanie and Katrina became my guardian angels. I

touched the necklace that Katrina had given me earlier this year. I'd added Stephanie's initials to Katrina and mine, my two BFF's. They were with me every day, in some way. Their daily WhatsApp videos, along with visits to hospital, gave me life.

At first, there was a lot of *doing*. Tests. Treatment plans. Drugs. Oh, the drugs. Handing my open missing person cases to Katrina. Moving Lucy and Mark from their hotel to our spare rooms in Innisfree. More tests. After all the doing, there was then time to digest and think. Thinking led to worry. Worry led to stress and breaking points, like the one Dad had yesterday.

I'd experienced a few breakdown moments myself too. As news spread to our wider circle of friends and family, cards and flowers began to arrive. At one point, Innisfree began to look like a Hallmark shop. And reading the notes became its own kind of torture. Some were hopeful, sending me good karma vibes. Others were fatalistic and spoke of the sad, grave situation. Most asked what they could do to help. And that was the hardest part. Because there was nothing anyone could do. I remembered bumping into a school friend a few years back. She was pregnant and her bump was a sight to behold. She'd told me something that resonated with me now: 'As soon as I told everyone I was pregnant, it was as if my body let loose and my belly exploded!' The same happened for me. Once my diagnosis was out in the open, my symptoms got worse. The speech apraxia continued in spurts. I slurred words – I'm sure everyone thought I was having sneaky drinks. And my vision deteriorated. And then my legs gave up working, which in turn meant my independence went too. I now am the proud owner of a wheelchair. Top of the range and motorized, because Dad insisted he spend every cent of a recent royalty cheque on me. Little things have become big things for me. Even having a shower needs forethought. Physically, I am no longer the Bea O'Connor I used to be. But inside, I'm still me.

Dr Talis had explained that, while rare, some brain tumours present themselves through neurobehavioral or psychiatric symptoms. I accepted that I had never smoked. My younger self had not written notes to me via my time-capsule letter. All of it had been done by me. But I would always be grateful for those 'magical' messages. Because, like Katrina's grandmother's chicken when it found her husband's pipe, my letter had uncovered so many hidden truths.

Ultimately it had led me to Lucy and Mark.

The letter had one last beautifully penned note for me though that I found a week ago.

*Bea, you should throw a party and celebrate you, me, us! x*

I loved that idea. As soon as I broached the idea to my family, they grabbed it with both hands. It *was* time to come out in the sunshine and party. So here we were, in Innisfree's beautiful courtyard, for one last blowout.

'I'll get it,' Dan called out as he went to answer the door. Nikki followed him back into the garden, along with two men who looked familiar. It took me a second to work out who they were. The bartenders from Cassidy's bar! They were carrying the karaoke machine that we'd belted out numbers on for years.

'The takings in the pub have been down by about 50 per cent since you stopped coming every Friday night, Bea,' one of them joked. 'Not to mention the fact that we've missed your singing skills!'

I laughed out loud in delight. 'If I'd known that all I had to do to get your karaoke machine in my back garden was get sick . . .' It was good to see them.

A rush of friends arrived at once. The Gallahues, Kehoes, Howlins, Murphys and Longs, followed by a group of women my own age who carried boxes of beer and wine with them. To my horror, I couldn't remember their names. I could see they knew me, but I couldn't remember how. It was only when Stephanie ran over squealing and hugging them all, saving me by saying their names loudly that I realized they were my old school friends. The tumour was beginning to win more battles. But I had a secret weapon – good friends who always had my back, ready to step in and help me when I had a forgetful moment like now.

'Nice wheels,' Tiffany said.

I touched the controls to make my wheelchair spin – a trick I'd been working on for days – and was gratified by their reaction. I had a few battles left in me, I decided.

'You look good,' Tiffany said, and I took the compliment, because I felt good. Katrina and Stephanie had given me a full pamper session before the party, followed by a makeover. Katrina had wielded her tweezers with no mercy, plucking stray hairs from my upper lip and eyebrows. I made her promise that if the time came that I was no longer with it, she'd always take care of my errant hairs. As she'd promised, both my friends wept. While they were strong most of the time, they had moments where it became too hard. But still they remained by my side. *My constants.*

Olive and her son Teddy arrived next. She had a large lasagne in her arms. 'I wasn't sure if you needed food. It's just out of the oven. And Teddy has a tray of cannelloni.'

'Hey, Uncle Mike, look what Olive has made. It's his favourite, he'll inhale that in seconds!'

He walked over and leaned down to breathe in the creamy tomato aroma. 'That smells wonderful, Olive.' Then he looked her in the eyes, in a way that made her blush. I wonder, could the two of them be right for each other? Now wouldn't that be something?

Corinne came shortly afterwards. She'd been to see me several times over the past few weeks. Her gentle support became a godsend as I dealt with my new normal. And any awkwardness from seeing Dad again had already been dealt with. She looked good and moved easily from group to group in the garden, mingling with grace. And when she and Lucy started to chat, they hit it off immediately.

'Regrets?' I asked Dad as he watched them together.

'A lifetime's worth. Two good women there. It takes a special kind of eejit to blow it with both.'

'Do you still love her?'

'Who do you mean?' he asked, the hint of a smile dancing on his lips.

'Either. Both. I'm not sure who I mean really.'

'I will always care for Corinne. We'd some great times together. But our time has gone. If Lucy would have me, that would be a different conversation. She was the great love of my life.'

'There's something I've been curious about. But with everything going on, I've not had a chance to ask you this. When I was a kid, you'd talk about your great love story with Mom. But you were talking about you and Lucy, weren't you?'

'I'm sorry.' His apology was an admission of truth.

'It hurts, Dad. The lies you told me. And it makes me so sad that Mom lost her sister, because of that one night of infidelity. But I reckon you've paid a high price for that. For what it's worth, I think you should tell Lucy that you still love her.'

'I should never have slept with your mom. It was an unforgivable thing to do. A one-off that we both regretted instantly. But at the same, had I not done that, I wouldn't have you. And the single best thing I've ever accomplished in this life is *you*. And, because of you, I now have Mark too. Had you not gone on your journey to Ireland, I wouldn't even know he existed.'

I watched my brother chatting to Tiffany and her friends and knew he would help Dad when I was gone. But for now, I had to leave those thoughts aside. I'd made everyone promise that there would be no maudlin good-byes allowed at today's party. No what-ifs or maybes. No sad reflections or angry recants.

We had one job to do and that was to have fun.

'Well, if you want to thank me for all of that, Dad, you need to get up there and start singing "Whiskey in the Jar"! Let's get this party started.'

And party hard we did, until late into the night. We sang, danced, laughed and told stories. Then Uncle Mike called for quiet, 'Will you sing it for me, love?'

He didn't need to say which song, I knew. And so, as

the moon shone into our courtyard, I sang 'The Isle of Innisfree' one last time. Not just for him, but for all of my loved ones, here with me and those that were waiting for me on the other side.

And this dreamer knew she was home.

# 49

December 2020
Innisfree, Prospect Avenue, Brooklyn

Dear Katrina and Stephanie

If you're reading this letter, then it means I've gone. Now there's a delicious line full of Agatha Christie drama. You'll forgive me enjoying this, just a little bit. I know it's time for me to go. I can feel it. But before then, I have one last letter to write. This time it's not to myself, either past, present or future. This one is to you both.

My hearts, my best friends forever.

Dan is asleep beside me. He's exhausted, because he's trying to stay awake twenty-four seven. He keeps telling me that he doesn't want to miss a thing. At midnight, I'm going to wake him up so we can ring in one last year together. We made a mess of things last year, didn't we? Oh OK, I made a mess of things. I'll kiss him until I have no breath and I'll tell him that he's my everything. I need you to keep an eye on Dan for me. And when the time is right, make sure he knows that it's OK to move on, to fall in love again. But, if either of you go there, I'll haunt you. Haha! <u>No, honestly, you'll never sleep again!</u>

I've been reflecting about my time-capsule letter a lot. Even though I know it was a tumour that caused me to unknowingly write those messages, I can't help but think that there was more to it than that. Every single message led me to a beautiful moment in my life.

Corinne

Lucy

Mark

Mom

And they brought us three back together too, didn't they?

That has to mean something. I need you to both promise to always be there for each other. I know you hate the sappy stuff, Katrina, but Stephanie likes it. I thought you could meet somewhere in the middle. I've bought you each a necklace with three discs on it, and the discs have been engraved with our initials. I figure, this way, we'll always be linking arms with each other. Dan has them and will give them to you, if he hasn't already. When the Macarena comes on, it is now BFF by-law that you have to get up and join in.

I don't care if you are in church, you both have to swivel your hips like we did that night in the Clongibbon House Hotel.

I'm afraid that Dad will fall to pieces. He's lost too many people in his life, so he'll need looking after. And while Uncle Mike will step up, he's got his own life now with Olive and Teddy. I'm so happy that fate put them in each other's lives. They work, don't they? I hope they've both finally found their forever after. Once again, I'm calling on you, my sisters in every way but blood, to keep an eye on Dad for me. I think he should go to Ireland, to spend time with Mark. It will help both of them to cope with their grief. He won't discuss it with me now, but I feel it will be the best thing for him, in the long run. I have an idea how to get him to go. I'll come to that in a minute.

I saw my grandparents last night. I woke up and they were standing at the foot of my bed smiling. Gran said to me, 'I was forever telling you that you'd be late for your own funeral. And the one time we want you to be late, you decide to be early. We don't want you to join us yet, love, but we can see you are so tired. Please know that when the time comes, we'll be here waiting for you.'

I am trying my best to hold on. But I just want to close my eyes and go. I need to talk to Dan about this tomorrow, make him understand that it's time for me to let go.

I want you all to bring my ashes to the Saltee Islands. Scatter me by the seals, so I can find my mom again. Afterwards, go back to the harbour wall in Kilmore and eat fish and chips out of paper. Finish the night in Nellie's pub. Sing, dance, drink, be all kinds of merry. And think of me.

Tell Dad that he must stay in Kilmore Quay. He can rent a cottage and write a great novel there. It's my dying wish, so he can't say no. Even though Lucy says there is no chance for them, I can't help think that in time she might change her mind. They truly did have a beautiful love story once upon another time. Grandad used to say that we need to be kind to everyone, especially those that seem the least deserving. Because kindness gets the best out of even the worst of us. I've tried to remember this in my life, I hope I got it right the odd time. Will you tell Lucy this for me?

Speaking of love, Stephanie, I have a plan for you too. You need to go get your man. Katrina will drive you to Cork. Sing Whitney and Celine, all the way down the M7. You've spent months messaging Donal. If it hadn't been for Covid, you'd have visited each other by now. It's time to work out if what you have is worth fighting for. I think it is. Wouldn't it be wonderful if your future was to be a farmer's wife?

I know you are both so sad right now. But

if it helps, know that I'm at peace. I'm pissed off, don't get me wrong. I mean, I'm way too young to die. But them's the breaks, right? What I can tell you is something happened to me when I found out that I was dying. I had an awakening of sorts. I suppose finding out that your time is limited on earth brings a clarity. I've taken stock. And I think I've done OK in the bigger scheme of things. OK, I never managed to save a president from the dastardly clutches of the Russian mafia, but I did find a long-lost brother. I'm loved and I love, which is the biggest and best achievement of all. As I leave this world, that's what I'll cling on to.

I've got to say goodbye now. But you know that I'm not really gone, don't you? When you hear Beyoncé singing about all the single ladies, know that's me saying hello. When you see three friends linking arms, heads bent low as they laugh and scheme great adventures, that's me too. Katrina and Stephanie, my BFFs, my amigos, my magicians who have turned my tears to laughter for decades.

I love you both,

Bea x

It's time to

## Curl up with Carmel

Read on for an Author's Note,
an exclusive Q&A with Carmel,
and news about her next novel.

**Dear Reader,**

I've always wanted to write a story with immigration at its heart. In particular, I have always been interested in the lives of first- and second-generation immigrants. You see, I was born in London, to an Irish father, who left Wexford for a better life when he was sixteen. Daddy made firm friends in the Irish centres, which helped him overcome his homesickness. He played hurling for the Fr Murphy's and met my mother, a pretty north-west Londoner, over the garden fence at a friend's house.

My early childhood in London was happy and like most children who are born to Irish parents outside of Ireland, I always felt Irish, no matter where we lived. Identity and culture is dictated by those who raise you, I suppose. As a kid, I learnt to Irish dance and attended a predominantly Irish Catholic school. Once a year, our family holidayed in Wexford. Ghosts of my father's early life were never far away. When he spoke about his home town, a look would steal over his face and his eyes would glisten with memories of a different world. He *longed* for home. And luckily for him, my mother agreed to take her turn as an emigrant and the decision was made to move back home to Ireland when I was nine years old. I thank all the stars for that, because I could not imagine living anywhere else but Wexford.

In 2014, I was invited to march in the New York Saint Patrick's Day Parade, with the *Wexford Association of New York*. Wearing my purple and gold sash, I helped carry the flag up front and it was such a fun and memorable thing to do. I met dozens of the Wexford diaspora who called New York home and as we chatted and laughed, I recognized something in their faces when they spoke about Ireland. The same look I'd always seen on my dad's face as a young child. I knew that one day I wanted to write a story about the Irish who left and the ones who were left behind. And finally, with *The Moon Over Kilmore Quay*, I realized that ambition.

As part of my research for Bea and Lucy's story, I visited New York early in 2020, before the world came to a standstill. During that trip, I spent most of my time walking through Queens and Brooklyn and with every step, I thought about the thousands of Irish people whose footprints were invisible on the sidewalk below me. I interviewed Irish immigrants who kindly shared their own stories. It was particularly wonderful to bear witness to how close-knit the Irish community is in New York. They look out for each other and paying it forward is the norm, not the exception.

I worked hard to research all aspects of the characters' lives, but my story is fiction, so once or twice a truth may seem manipulated slightly, to make it work. Please forgive me if any inaccuracies jar.

I hope you enjoy *The Moon Over Kilmore Quay* as much as I loved writing it. It was one of those books that came together beautifully, with most stages of the process a joy.

Much love to all,
Carmel

# AUTHOR Q&A

**The settings in *The Moon Over Kilmore Quay* are written in great detail. Did you do a lot of research into places?**

Yes I did! The story takes place in Ireland and USA. Both locations are as much characters in the book really, as the people are. Kilmore Quay is a beautiful fishing village in my home county of Wexford. It's one of my favourite places to visit. Eating fish and chips from the paper, sitting on the quayside, watching the kids collect stones with the backdrop of the Saltee Islands behind them, is a good day out for us H's. The locations I used in Kilmore Quay are all real, with the exception of Nellie's Pub, which I created from my imagination. As for New York, I've been visiting that gorgeous city ever since I was twenty years old. And I try to get there at least once every couple of years. My last visit, which was purely for research, was spent in the Irish communities of Brooklyn and Queens, as opposed to the usual touristy spots. That was invaluable in creating Bea and Lucy's worlds. In many ways, writing this book was a love letter to both locations.

**What does the writing process look like for you, and has the way that you write changed throughout your career?**

I start with an idea, perhaps a theme I want to explore, or a character that intrigues me. For *The Moon Over Kilmore Quay*, it began with an idea to explore the consequences of receiving a time-capsule letter. But as I began to write the first draft, I realized that the story was so much more and really at its heart, it was about immigration and the pull between two homes. My writing process is to write a first draft quickly, usually in three months, then I'll spend nine months on edits. I write every day when I'm deep into the story, so that I can carry the characters with me at all times.

**Have you always wanted to be a writer?**

Yes! My earliest memories involve placing my teddy bears in a semi-circle around me, as I regaled them with stories from my imagination. I always had a pretty notebook as a child, and I loved to fill that with thoughts. I had a pony when I was a kid too and everyday as I exercised Mr Bojangles, I'd tell him stories too. As I got older, I began to dream that one day I could expand my readership from my cuddly bear collection and pony to real people! I still pinch myself that I've realized that life-long dream.

**You write about a lot of different kinds of relationships – romantic, familial and friendships. Which is your favourite to write about and why?**

I'm not sure I could choose between them. I love to write about love in all its formats. I think it depends on the story really, which kind of love is most prominent. But there will always be love, that's a guarantee.

**If you had to describe *The Moon Over Kilmore Quay* in three words, what would they be?**

Ooh, I know three words I'd love to use – International Award-winning Bestseller! You've got to dream, right? Here's three words that came up a lot from my editorial team, that I hope readers will agree with: life-affirming, warm, romantic.

**What are your three favourite novels that you've read recently, and why?**

I think the definition of a great book is one that stays with you, long after you get to the end. Three recent reads that fit into that category are *Where the Crawdads Sing* by Delia Owens, *The Midnight Library* by Matt Haig, and *The Next Person You Meet in Heaven* by Mitch Albom.

**Are there any books or authors that inspire you either in your career or writing style?**

I'm inspired by every book I've read or listened to, from childhood to now. But an early influence, one that's stayed with me, is Maeve Binchy. She was the first author that bridged the gap between my childhood and adult reads. I have an almost full set of her hardback editions, that sits on a book shelf directly in my eyeline when I write. Something that Maeve said about writing has stayed with me too, 'always write as if you are talking to someone. It works. Don't put on any fancy phrases or accents or things you wouldn't say in real life.' She's right, it *does* work. And if a reader feels the same glow from the warmth and wisdom that I've felt whenever I read a Binchy novel, with one of my books, then I'm happy.

**What do you like to do when you're not writing?**

Most of my spare time is taken up with my family and dog! But a new hobby that I adore is playing the piano. During lockdown in April 2020, I downloaded an app so that my daughter could learn how to play on a keyboard she was gifted for her birthday. I decided to learn alongside her. And I pretty soon realized that when I played the piano, I stopped thinking about everything else. Within a few weeks, I outgrew the small keyboard, so my lovely friend Caroline gave me her Casio keyboard. Then for our anniversary in October, my husband surprised me by buying me my own baby grand digital piano. It sits in my writing room now, in front of my library wall.

# READING GROUP QUESTIONS

- Discuss the meaning of the title *The Moon Over Kilmore Quay.*

- How did the setting of Kilmore Quay and New York impact the story? Would you like to visit any of the locations Carmel described?

- Which character did you relate to the most and what was it about them that you connected with?

- Carmel has said that while she is known for her emotional reads, she works hard to ensure that humour is weaved throughout her novels too. As she often says, to get a rainbow you need both rain and sunshine. What parts of the novel made you laugh or cry?

- If you were to write a letter to your future self, what would you say?

- Did any particular passages strike you as insightful, or was there a moment in *The Moon Over Kilmore Quay* that made you see things differently?

- The friendships of Bea, Katrina and Stephanie, and Lucy, Maeve and Michelle play an important role in the story. Discuss.

- There are some big romantic scenes for Bea and Lucy in *The Moon Over Kilmore Quay*. Were you happy with how things ended up for them with Dan and Ryan?

- During her research, the author interviewed many Irish immigrants who have made their home in New York. Have you ever lived overseas? Did she capture the immigrant's emotions?

- What surprised you the most when you read this story? Did you pick up on the hints for the plot twists? And how did you feel about the ending, was it what you were expecting?

Curl up with Carmel's new book...

# A Mother's Heart

### Hawkes Bay, New Zealand

While Rachel Butler likes her life in a pretty Dublin coastal village, her heart lies in Hawkes Bay, where she grew up. Visiting for the first time since tragedy tore her family apart, she and her stepchildren fall for its beauty and outdoor lifestyle.

### Malahide, Ireland

As Rachel picks up the threads of her life as a single parent, she can't shake off the memories of her loving family in New Zealand – and her dream house, the villa on the bay. But it's time to move forwards with their life in Ireland, close to the children's grandparents, amid the familiar surroundings they all know well.

Until the children's grandmother, still grieving, starts to interfere, questioning Rachel's position as stepmother.

Until Rachel's attempts to strengthen the family she loves so dearly backfires, pitting everyone against each other.

And until her late husband's parents mend the rift that has existed as long as she's been married – bringing with them an explosive secret . . .

**Out summer 2022**

# ACKNOWLEDGEMENTS

It takes a village to raise a child, it's said. Well, if that's the case, it takes a whole county to raise a book! There are so many people who play a part in an author's life, some in the background unseen, others up front. But without them all playing their part, well, there'd be no new Carmel Harrington book each year!

*So, I would like to pay special tribute to*:

Rowan Lawton, my UK literary agent and friend – she is a wonder and I would be lost without her and the entire team at Soho Literary Agency. Team Carmel has grown a little over the past year actually, with Abigail Koons, my US Literary Agent, and Rich Green, my US TV/Movie agent, both representing me stateside. I'm lucky to have each of these in my corner.

My publishers at HarperCollins work so hard on my behalf – Lynne Drew, Charlotte Ledger, Kimberley Young, Charlie Redmayne, Kate Elton, Lara Stevenson, Emma

Pickard, Elizabeth Dawson, Jaime Frost, Patricia McVeigh, Tony Purdue, Jacq Murphy, Lucy Vanderbilt and so many more who work tirelessly behind the scenes. I'm forever grateful.

Making sure my book doesn't languish in a dusty corner when it is published are the many cheerleaders from the book industry. Book retailers, media, bloggers, reviewers, libraries, book clubs, festivals – all working tirelessly to find new ways to get books into the laps of readers. Your job has never been as important or difficult as it has been over the past year. Know that your passionate love of all things literary helps authors like me every day, and I appreciate it so much.

Hazel Gaynor and Catherine Ryan Howard, to whom the book is dedicated. There are a trio of friends in the 'now and then' of this book, and I thought of you both often as I wrote their stories. And how you are both friendship magicians too, with the power to turn tears to laughter and frustration to hope. French 75' zoom chat, anyone?

The writing community both inspires me and supports me every day. Okay, the odd time, it confounds me. But never these crew, who are just lovely! Claudia Carroll, Caroline Grace Cassidy, Alex Browne, Debbie Johnson, Cecelia Ahern, Marian Keyes, Cathy Kelly, Sheila O'Flanagan, Susan Lewis, Cathy Bramley, Milly Johnson, Katie Fforde, Vanessa O'Loughlin, Shane Dunphy, Sheila Forsey, Caroline Busher, Fionnuala Kearney, Liz Nugent, Mary Clerkin and the entire staff at Tyrone Guthrie.

I will forever be grateful to the generous, warm, open and important testimonies I received from Irish immigrants living in New York. They helped add so much warmth and colour to this story – Martin Kehoe (I'm still thinking about your first few days in New York! What a story) and his two charming daughters, Allison and Laura, I think we could have stayed chatting for hours more. Elizabeth Long – your map was a godsend throughout the writing process, I used it every day I wrote the New York scenes. The Gallahue family – Patricia, Helena and Tom – any resemblance *Inisfree* has to your family home is 100% deliberate! When we visited your home, I could hear the echoes of your family, partying with the Irish community on holidays, and I had to borrow a version of it for my own fictional family. I managed to sneak in your wonderful story about moving your dad's cars on street-cleaning days, Patricia and Helena; it makes me smile whenever I think of that. While in New York I stayed at the Fitzpatrick Hotel and they took such good care of Roger and me. Much thanks to manager, Shane Cookman. And it's official Shane, you do make the best tea in New York! Stacey Howlin, thank you for sharing that story about how your parents met. It was so just so romantic and fateful, a fictionalised version was used for Bea's grandparents.

To all at Virgin Media One on the *Elaine* show, but in particular Elaine Crowley, Ruth Scott, Sinead Dalton and Kelly Rufus, thank you for letting me be part of your gang.

To Valerie Whitford, Genevieve Sheehan and Rachel Mahon, my admin team in *Carmel Harrington's Reading Room* on Facebook. This group with monthly reading challenges and bookish chat is so much fun to be a part of. New members are always welcome, so come find us!

To my dearest friends for the giggles, love and general

cheerleading you all do, to help me reach the end of each book, I thank you all – Ann & John, Margaret & Lisa, Caroline & Shay, Sarah & John, Fiona & Philip, Davnet & Kevin, Gillian & Ken, Siobhan & Paul, Liz, Siobhan and Maria.

The O'Grady and Harrington gang, all that matters is family, right? We knew it before but 2020 punctuated that every day. I love you all – Tina & Mike O'Grady, Fiona, Michael, Amy & Louis Gainfort, John, Fiona & Matilda O'Grady, Michelle & Anthony Mernagh, and Sheryl O'Grady, Ann & Nigel Payne, Evelyn Harrington, Adrienne Harrington & George Whyte, Evelyn, Seamus & Patrick Moher, Leah Harrington, and my beautiful, clever step-daughter, Eva Corrigan. Special thanks to my fabulous mam Tina, who is my first reader and also the calmer of my nerves before I submit each new book to my agent.

And now the final thanks goes to my H's, the one constant in life, no matter what chaos and madness surrounds me. Let's be honest, 2020 was a doozy! George Bailey, our rescue cockerpoo keeps my feet warm as I write. And no matter how late I write, he never leaves my side. And the love and kindness I get from Amelia, Nate and Roger, Mr H, is my everything.